Margaret Yorke lives in Buckinghamshire. She is a past chairman of the Crime Writers' Association and her outstanding contribution to the genre has been recognised by the award of the 1999 CWA Cartier Diamond Dagger.

EVIDENCE TO DESTROY
and
THE SMOOTH FACE OF EVIL

—— **OMNIBUS** ——

Two Novels in One Volume

Margaret Yorke

timewarner
paperbacks

A *Time Warner* Paperback

First published in this omnibus edition in 2002 by Warner Books

Evidence to Destroy and The Smooth Face of Evil Omnibus
Copyright © 2002 by Margaret Yorke
Evidence to Destroy Copyright © 1987 by Margaret Yorke
The Smooth Face of Evil Copyright © 1984 by Margaret Yorke

A CIP catalogue record for this book
is available from the British Library.

ISBN 0 7515 3305 X

Printed and bound in Great Britain by
Clays Ltd, St Ives plc

Time Warner Paperbacks
An imprint of
Time Warner Books UK
Brettenham House
Lancaster Place
London WC2E 7EN

www.TimeWarnerBooks.co.uk

EVIDENCE TO DESTROY

1

She carried the moss in an old, stained strawberry chip, walking along the narrow path that curved between rose beds and past the vegetable patch to the boundary. The day had been overcast, though mild, and now the young moon was obscured by cloud, but Lydia Cunningham could have found her way down the garden blindfold.

She stood by the fence and took aim. A handful of moss – it was thick, dank stuff which had formed on the roof of the garage – soared silently through the night air towards the huge expanse of bright orange tiles that roofed the new chalet bungalow which blocked her view beyond the Manor to the distant hills.

The bungalow had been named *Mauden* in a blend of its owners' names, Maureen and Roger Dennis. Lydia hurled more moss in the direction of the offending tiles. If it took root, it would spread and mask some of that hideous terra cotta. Much of what she threw simply rolled down to the gutter, but she hoped that some would lodge between the tiles. Would lichen attach itself, too? She could try it; there used to be plenty growing round the church porch. She never went there now except, for form's sake, to lay a holly wreath on Henry's grave at Christmas.

Her ammunition spent, Lydia walked back to the small house which had once been the gatekeeper's lodge at the Manor. Boris, an elderly basset hound, snuffled along beside her, his bandy legs splayed out beneath his lowslung, heavy body.

Gerald, Lydia's son, had been forced to sell the Manor after he and Iris had separated in order to meet her claim for a large settlement. Lydia thought he should have resisted her excessive demands, for it was she who had walked out of the marriage, but, as always, he was generous. The Manor House and its land had been bought by a property development company. The house itself was a listed building and so protected from demolition; its new owners had sold it, with enough acres to ensure seclusion, to a small hotel group which ran several similar establishments in what had once been large country houses. Because, in the perception of the local authority, it constituted in-filling, planning consent was given for an estate of bungalows and houses on the remainder of the land, and work had only recently been finished on the last of them.

The weather this year had been dismal; cafés and tourist shops by the coast, five miles away, had had a disappointing season, though maritime activities had gone on as usual; the estuary was full of boats. Now, in mid-September, the roads were coming back to normal; life was quietening down as holiday-makers departed from the district.

Lydia's fate had been determined by Henry's extraordinary will, in which he had left everything to their son Gerald 'in the confident knowledge that he will provide adequately for his mother'. A trust had been set up for Thelma, funded by an insurance policy in her favour, but there was no provision for the widow beyond the expressed wish that she should live in the lodge. When the estate was sold, one of the clauses in the agreement was that she should be permitted to rent the house at a peppercorn rate for her lifetime.

2

Lydia had endured more than two years of din from cement mixers and earth-shifters; now she had lost her view and had acquired noisy neighbours.

She could have contested the will; dourly, the solicitor who had drawn it up had so advised her, knowing, as Henry had done, that she would never stoop to such an action.

She had always known that if Henry were to die before her, she must leave the Manor. It was only right that Gerald and Iris should live there, but she had hoped to turn part of the stable block into a small house for herself; thus, she would keep in touch with him and his family and retain her position in the village. However, the development of the new estate had transformed not only her life but had altered the whole character of Milton St Gabriel, and the lodge was not hers to sell in order to move away. Besides, where would she go? She had lived in the village nearly all her life.

Gerald had explained that it had all been done to save capital transfer tax. The house, with the land that still remained in the estate, was extremely valuable, though Henry had left little else except some heavy debts. Gerald now paid Lydia's small rent and provided the allowance that supplemented her state pension.

When Henry Cunningham died, Gerald and Iris were living in Surrey, from where he commuted to London and his city office. Elegant in black, her hair a froth of russet curls around her pale, pointed face, Iris had attended the funeral and assessed her future. After less than a year of living at the Manor, she had left Gerald, and within weeks of their divorce being made final she had married a former neighbour from the Surrey area where they had spent so many years. Iris and her new husband, who had himself left a wife and three young children, had opened a business dealing in art materials and stationery and, according to Gerald's son and daughter, they were prospering. People seemed to think nothing of chopping and changing partners these days; things had been very different in Lydia's youth.

She entered the lodge through the back door and set her chip down in the lobby. Some things in life must be endured but others could be altered; she was tied to the lodge, but she could attempt to improve the outlook.

Her bungalow neighbours were not the first newcomers to Milton St Gabriel. It had once been an agricultural village with farm workers living in the cottages that clustered near the church and by the pond. For several generations the Cunninghams had owned them and most of the surrounding land, but during the thirties all the farms except one were sold. Later, the old cottages were bought by retired colonial servants and ex-service officers who restored and renovated them, darkening their sturdy beams and displaying ivories and Benares wear. Then, weekenders who stripped and bleached the ancient oak and excavated ingle-nooks arrived, and a few new houses were built in former paddocks or over-large gardens. The recent arrivals were not pleased when the Manor was sold and a new estate was proposed within its former grounds, but when it became clear that the expansion would be separated from the original village area and that it would include two shops and, eventually, a modern health centre serving several neighbouring villages, objections dwindled. One couple had even moved from a beetle-browed thatched cottage to an airy modern bungalow. The old village hall had been refurbished and was used more frequently; there were folk evenings and bingo, and even an occasional disco.

Formerly, Lydia and Henry had entertained the retired tea planters and colonels, the old admiral and his

4

wife, even some former civil servants at the Manor, and were invited back, but since Henry's death she had seen little of the survivors – some of them had also died – of this village nucleus. Few had money to spare and after suitable condolences had been expressed, both sides were relieved to let the socializing lapse. In Henry's life-time, Lydia had conscientiously tried to undertake the role expected of her; she had led committees, run the Guides, arranged the flowers in church. Now, a new élite managed such affairs.

Several of the newcomers were retired people lured south by the prospect of a mild climate. The fitter ones played golf; some played bridge. Lydia knew a few of them by sight. The Dennises at the bottom of the garden were younger and they both went out to work; she did not know what their occupations were. To the west of the lodge, away from the Manor entrance, a row of six small terraced houses had been built. One day the lodge itself would be pulled down and more bungalows or some other new construction would fill up the space. Lydia drew some satisfaction from denying the developers this expansion for the present.

Her immediate neighbours in the terraced block were a long-distance lorry driver and his wife, the Whites. Their daughter Karen liked pop music and she played it loudly. Tonight, as Lydia closed the back door, a pulsating burst of sound came from next door. If it continued after midnight, she would telephone to complain. It wouldn't be the first time, and she was wearily aware that neither would it be the last.

She glanced round the kitchen. Everything was orderly, the tea towel hanging on its rail, the draining-board wiped down and gleaming, nothing out of place.

'Goodnight, Boris,' she said, and was answered by the thumping of his tail against the side of his basket.

Before she went to bed, Lydia returned to the sitting

room where, on a card table, was a nearly completed jigsaw puzzle depicting tigers in the jungle. She stared at it for a moment, then inserted three pieces into position; if you returned after an interval, you could often see where something fitted. Finally, she slowly climbed the stairs, a thin, tall woman in a much-washed Marks and Spencer's sweater and an old grey flannel skirt.

Her preparations for retiring were a ritual: swift undressing, followed by the washing of underwear and tights which she hung on a rail above the bath to dry. She put her skirt away in her wardrobe on a hanger. Her sweater was neatly folded on a chair and covered with a lace-edged piece of silk which her mother had always used for this purpose. Latterly, the thought of sudden death had become a spectre in Lydia's mind. If she were to die in her sleep, whoever found her must discover no confusion, even in the last extremity.

Gerald Cunningham was an ugly man. He was short and solid, looking almost stout although he was, in fact, merely well-muscled. All his life he had striven to overcome his physical disadvantages where there was any chance of success, and even where there was not, and with his failed marriage behind him, he had quickly looked for sexual comfort.

His present partner was preparing for the night as Gerald lay in bed and watched her. He saw the bright face, the blusher and the vivid eye-shadow, disappear, replaced by pallor and a tiny pimple on a cheek, and sighed. Without her paint, her thick mascara, she was just a very average woman and no longer young, but he had felt good at being seen with her in the restaurant where they had dined. In an expensive dress. her hair-do sleek, bracelets on her arm and earrings dangling, she had seemed to be a symbol of success, evidence of conquest.

But he knew that it was his money that had attracted her. Iris had made it plain not long after they were married that no woman could be drawn to him for any other reason.

Gerald had learned that he was ugly when he was four years old. Another little boy had come to play. The visitor was blond and fresh-faced, with large blue eyes. When he fell over in the garden and grazed his knee, Gerald's mother had comforted him and had even kissed him. She had bathed the knee and taken the casualty on her lap to read him a story till the pain had eased.

Gerald had later deliberately cast himself upon the same paved path and wounded himself more severely than the guest.

'Duffer, aren't you?' Lydia had said. 'Be brave, Gerald.'

His ruse had failed. She ignored his quivering lip and, as usual, Gerald blinked his tears away. He did not flinch when his wound was cleansed with TCP, which stung.

'You're ugly,' said the visitor when they were again playing in the garden. Seated in Gerald's pedal car, the other child was intent on running down his host in every way. Quoting the ultimate authority, he added, 'My mummy said so.'

'What's ugly?' Gerald asked Betty, the girl who at that time, during the war, helped his mother in the house.

Betty was busy washing behind his ears.

'Not nice to look at,' she replied, concentrating on the task in hand. She'd missed some honest grime before and Mrs Cunningham had been cross.

'Is Thelma ugly?' Gerald inquired.

'Course not, silly,' said Betty, who had no idea what lay behind this interrogation. 'Your sister is a lovely little girl.'

'She's fat,' said Gerald.

'It's only puppy fat. She'll lose it,' said Betty, who was still waiting for her own to disappear.

After that, Gerald would now and then inspect himself in a mirror, facing up to what was so repellent. He had thick, straight brows above brown eyes and his hair fell naturally in a heavy fringe, refusing to lie back in the manner decreed by his stern father who occasionally appeared on leave during those years.

If you were good, and rather small, you could hide in corners. If you kept quiet, people often didn't notice you. Gerald had learned this before he was six. He had also learned to read, taught first by Betty, who thought the sturdy child a manly little fellow, and then by a retired schoolmistress who gave lessons to several children in the village. At that time his mother was working as a nurse at the Manor, which had become a convalescent home; wounded men, in rough blue suits, with bandages and crutches, walked about the grounds and sat beneath the trees. Gerald's grandparents had moved into one of the cottages, and his mother, with the children, was living in the lodge.

After the war, when the house was returned to the family, Gerald's grandparents decided to remain in the small, convenient cottage, and, on a dwindling income, his parents moved into the Manor when Henry was demobilized from the army. Soon, the old man died and Gerald's grandmother moved to a flat in London. Henry, with a manager, ran the farm and became a JP. Gerald, at the age of eight, had been sent away to school. There, he found there were other boys whose appearance caused comment. One, with red hair and freckles, was called 'Carrots' but he did not seem to mind; he won popularity by telling ghost stories in the dormitory after lights-out.

Gerald never shone at anything at school, but he held his own at work and on the playing-field. At fourteen, he ran a book on any event which caught the fancy of his peers – the Derby, the Boat Race, inter-house matches – and so earned their respect as well as making quite a little profit.

After university, determined to escape the genteel poverty in which his parents strove to maintain appearances – by this time the last farm had been sold – Gerald became a merchant banker. He met Iris at a dance, one among many she attended in pursuit of a husband with money and, with any luck, position. Even when Gerald understood her reasons for accepting him, the marriage had superficially worked. Iris's material wishes were granted; they had a son and daughter and, eventually, a small house in a Surrey suburb from which they later moved to a large one in a green-belt area, complete with swimming pool. Though Iris had liked the grandeur of the Manor, it was in such a state of disrepair, so cold and draughty, and so inconvenient, that when she went to live there she soon grew to hate it, and she missed her friends. It was too far for Gerald to travel every day; he had a one-roomed flat in London and, with the children both away at boarding schools, perhaps her defection was inevitable.

Gerald stared at the woman as she brushed her copper-coloured hair, one white arm moving slowly to and fro, her brush strokes languid. He had met her at a conference; she was personal assistant to a business manager. Now he sensed reluctance in her unhurried actions and realized that she too was bored.

'Were you ever ugly?' he inquired as at last she came towards him.

'Hideous,' she answered cheerfully. 'I was fat and spotty and had braces on my teeth.'

But she'd got over that and now she could paint on a mask to face the day, Gerald thought, preparing to embrace her.

What if she should plan to marry him? The idea was appalling. It wouldn't do, and he must end it.

Money always helped at such a moment. A cheque to take her to Bermuda or Marrakesh would soften any disappointment. Meanwhile, there was a ritual to be performed, and he had learned to do it skilfully.

2

Thelma Hallows, Gerald's sister, had noticed the young man when he boarded the late train. He wore jeans and a bomber jacket, and he carried a small canvas bag. He was narrow-hipped, with long, thin legs, and his short brown hair was curly.

He took a seat at the rear of the same coach and she was able to watch him over the magazine she pretended to read. He was perhaps twenty-two, or less – a student, maybe. He sat very still, staring out of the window at the dark night through which they passed, his own reflection gazing back at him. Soon he grew aware of Thelma's interest and began to play the game of gradual response. By the time the train reached Swindon they were the only two left in the coach, and he moved up to sit facing her.

She was quite a looker – older, he now saw, than he had thought her from a distance, but with clear, fresh skin and deep blue eyes, her blonde hair styled in near-Afro fashion. Her suede jacket was the real thing; the high-heeled sandals on her bare feet with their scarlet-painted nails not cheap. It was a long time since he'd had social contact with a woman, and talking to her would pass the time.

He had told the probation officer that he was going to stay with his sister after his release, but Julie didn't know that he was on his way. He hadn't warned her,

11

afraid that she would tell him not to come, though she must know he was due out soon. If he turned up in the small hours of the morning, she would have to take him in, he reasoned. There'd be a corner for him somewhere.

She hadn't been to see him since she took this job, though she'd gone on writing regularly. Throughout his life, she had always stuck by him, and she had visited him at first, after his arrest and then his sentence.

He was frightened that he'd gone too far this time, that she had run away and left him. Without her, he had nothing.

Lydia was dreaming the dream when the telephone woke her.

In her dream, workmen were decorating the house into which she was to move. Cans of paint in colours she did not like – reds and browns and violent purples – stood about, and she moved around the unfamiliar rooms with dread, unable to halt their actions. All the while heavy beat music assaulted her ears, and a nurse with a hypodermic syringe in her hand steadily followed her, needle upraised.

She had telephoned the Whites' house next door at ten minutes past midnight and asked them to tone down their so-called music.

A male voice had answered the telephone and called out, 'Hey, Karen, some old bag's complaining. Tell her to get ear-plugs if she doesn't like it.'

Then Karen White had come to the telephone. She had once seemed a nice girl, yet now she wore her hair spiked out like the spines of a hedgehog, often dyed in strange colours or with blue or red tufts at the front like a cock's comb. She would come up the road after school with several schoolboys, giggling and indulging in horseplay. What were her parents thinking of to allow such behaviour? But they were seldom at home: the

12

mother worked as a barmaid in Heronsmouth, and the father was often away. Karen was obviously having a party tonight. Surely the mother was back by this time?

Girls asked for trouble, these days, but if they fell into it, they could climb out. Years ago, there had been no such chance.

Well, once again she had survived the first hours of sleep without dying, she thought, reaching out for the telephone extension beside her bed. Who could be calling her at this hour? A wrong number, probably, or perhaps Karen's friends wanting to taunt her.

She hadn't expected it to be Thelma.

'But you're in Los Angeles,' she said.

'No, mother. I'm at Cheverton station,' said Thelma. 'It didn't work out with Lucian, so I've left him. Will you collect me, please?'

Lydia fetched clean undergarments and tights. She put on a warm sweater and her grey skirt. Then she did her hair, taking trouble to arrange the long grey strands with care, securing them under a snood of velvet ribbon so that they concealed the bald expanse of skull above her forehead. She had lost her hair soon after Thelma's birth and it had never grown again.

'You're not going to get your mum to come out and fetch you at this time of night – or morning – are you?' Edward Fletcher had protested when together they left the train. 'Won't you take a taxi?' In which he'd cadge a lift, since they had discovered that they were both going to Milton St Gabriel.

'I've no money,' said Thelma. She'd got a few dollars left, but no sterling, and anyway, why pay good money for something her mother could provide at no cost? That was what mothers were for.

'Oh!' That was a surprise to Edward, who had been intrigued by what seemed to him her worldly air and her poise.

13

They got better acquainted while they waited for Lydia's arrival. She would be forty minutes or more by the time she had dressed and got the car out, Thelma informed him, leading him into the deserted waiting-room. When the small dark blue Metro arrived, it seemed to be agreed that Edward would go with Thelma to her mother's house, for, she told him, it was far too late to disturb his sister.

Lydia's rapid heartbeat and her raised blood pressure had settled somewhat as she drove to fetch her daughter. Mist hung between the high banks that bordered the narrow lanes before she reached the main road, and she went slowly. No useful purpose would be served by having an accident now. As she neared the roundabout where one road led to Heronsmouth and the other to Cheverton, her headlights picked up a hedgehog waddling across the tarmac. Lydia steered to avoid it, her wheels passing either side of its rotund body; it would probably be run over before the night was done, but she need not be its executioner.

It was typical of Thelma to arrive at an anti-social hour, and with no warning. In the past, Lydia had met her at airports and stations after various phases of her life had ended either in failure or disaster. This last was only the latest of several romantic escapades.

On the strength of two walk-on parts when she was nineteen and a brief stage-managing spell when she was also an understudy and appeared as Nina in *The Seagull* for four performances, Thelma described herself as an actress, but she had had no paid dramatic role since those early years. Lucian, whom she had gone to America to visit with a view to remaining there, was an actor she had once known. They had exchanged some letters after his marriage ended and Thelma had been certain that when they met again, all would be roses.

14

'He's begged me to come,' Thelma had told her mother.

Lydia had remained unconvinced by this assurance. Thelma tended to arrange versions of events to suit the scripts she structured in her imagination. She had been away only three weeks, having sub-let her flat in Clapham for two years.

As Lydia drove into the station yard, two figures stepped out of the shadows.

'This is Edward,' introduced Thelma, without greeting her mother at all.

'Hi,' said Edward, who had not been told the old woman's name. As Lydia struggled to open the car door, preparatory to getting out, he added, 'Please don't move. I'll see to the bags.'

Thelma had a lot of luggage. He managed to stack it all in the small car, putting what would not fit in the rear compartment on the back seat; then he got in beside it, fitting his skinny legs around a duty-free carrier bag and a soft holdall. However had she managed to get on to the train with all this load? Maybe someone helped her; most blokes would want to help a bird like her.

Thelma sat in front beside her mother and they set off in silence which, to Edward, soon grew oppressive. Had they nothing to say to each other after their separation?

'How far is it to Milton St Gabriel?' he asked at last, and was answered at once by seeing a signpost which announced a distance of eight miles.

The old lady drove well and smoothly, at a steady forty miles an hour or so until they reached the lanes, where she dropped her speed. Steep banks on each side of the car reminded Edward of high walls. He felt hemmed in and nervous.

'What happens if you meet a car?' he asked.

'There are passing places,' said the old lady.

He couldn't see them in the misty darkness, but they met no other traffic.

'Did you have a good journey?' Lydia eventually inquired.

Edward had not had much of a look at her so far; she was wearing one of those khaki-coloured padded anoraks you saw on real battle axes of the female sex, and perhaps she was one, but at least she hadn't got a superior-sounding penetrating voice.

Thelma was describing her long flight and her landing earlier in the day.

'Why didn't you come straight down?' her mother asked.

'I had people to see,' Thelma answered curtly.

She had spent the day ringing round old friends. The last of her sterling had gone on drinks at a pub frequented by resting actors and actresses. No one had offered her a bed, with or without strings attached. She hadn't rung Gerald, who might have been expected to take his sister in for the night. He would only have preached to her about using prudence in her life and not sponging on their mother.

They ran out of the mist as they entered the village, passing quiet, darkened cottages and the two original shops, one housing a sub-post office, and came to wide entrance gates with a discreet sign which advertised *The Manor Hotel*. Beyond them, Lydia drew up at the lodge.

As Boris lumbered out to greet them, wagging his tail, the young man carried in Thelma's bags. Meanwhile, Lydia went into the kitchen and put the kettle on. She would not sleep without a hot drink to settle her.

'The beds are made up,' she said. She kept them ready and aired, used to Thelma's sudden arrivals and ever hopeful that Gerald or a grandchild might turn up unexpectedly, but they never came without warning and then not often enough for her.

'Show your friend the way to the yellow room,' Lydia told her daughter. This was more tactful than describing it as the small bedroom.

They'd take no notice; she knew that, but at least she was not openly condoning their liaison. This man looked young enough to be Thelma's son. Where had she found him? She'd lost no time in replacing the rejected Lucian. How long would this one last?

'Would you like something to eat?' she offered. 'Some sandwiches?'

'Oh, thanks,' said Thelma. 'Got any Scotch?'

Silently, Lydia went to a cupboard and took out a half-empty bottle of Dewar's. Then she built a pile of sandwiches with what was left of the bread, some cheddar cheese and the last of the butter. She had not been expecting guests and supplies were low.

'I'm going back to bed now,' she told the pair when this was done. She would have liked to ask Thelma what had gone wrong in America, and what her plans, if any, were, but such things could not be discussed in front of a stranger. Besides, she was too tired. Explanations must wait.

Thelma and Edward finished the whisky before they went to bed, and both were rather disappointed with what followed.

Edward woke early the next morning. He stretched out in the bed; it was soft, and his head rested on a down pillow. This was better than the nick. He lay savouring the sybaritic bliss of physical ease until a faint sound came from the other bed. Then he remembered. During the night he had found himself perched on its edge, with Thelma, curled into a ball like a hibernating

17

dormouse, occupying the middle. He had moved out to the second bed.

She hadn't woken. He had heard faint, snorting little snores.

They had not talked much. She had no settled job and did not know how long she would be staying with her mother.

'Till something else turns up,' she had said.

If she was thinking of making him the something else, he'd have to make sure what he was in for, Edward reflected.

He swung himself out of bed and dressed quickly, then let himself quietly out of the bedroom. His trainers made no sound as he padded down the stairs. When he opened the kitchen door, the fat old dog waddled over to him, wagging his heavy tail and making small sounds of welcome in his throat.

'I suppose you want to go out, boy,' said Edward, and opened the back door.

Boris sauntered into the garden, and Edward followed him down the path. The air smelled fresh and damp; he inhaled greedily. Beyond the fence he saw a bright orange roof rearing up almost like a wall; there were similar high-vaulted roofs on either side. Last night, when he arrived, Milton St Gabriel had seemed to be a picture postcard village with its stone cottages, thatched roofs and the pond that he had noticed, driving through. Here was total contrast.

Boris blundered up to him and sniffed at the ends of his jeans. Edward bent and patted him, then walked back towards the house, followed by the dog. He shut the animal in, then set off down the road. He meant to look for Julie now.

Lydia had slept very little when at last she had returned to bed. She heard Edward's quiet movements in the house, and she watched him from the window as he studied the outlook. He seemed pleasant enough, and he was well-mannered, but he would need a lot of food, if he was staying.

She sighed. Your children were supposed to be off your hands when they were adult, but Thelma had never stayed away for long. Lydia hoped she was always pleased to see her daughter, but it was a pleasure seldom untinged with dismay as she waited to learn the nature of the latest crisis that had brought her home. She had always been a creature of sudden enthusiasms, swayed by whims, and when she chose the stage as a career she had selected a life of insecurity. The wonder was that Henry hadn't put his foot down and forbidden it, but then she had always been able to twist him round her little finger.

She must be still asleep.

Lydia went downstairs and made herself a cup of tea which she took back to bed with her. She needed time to prepare herself to meet the day and all its new demands, and until Mrs Dodds's shop, up the road, was open, there was no bread for breakfast.

Edward walked past the row of terraced houses next to the lodge and turned down the road beyond them. This led through the estate which backed on to the garden of the lodge. The new bungalows all seemed steeped in sleep, the curtains drawn across their picture windows. The mist had gone and thin sunlight filtered between the young shrubs and sapling trees in their freshly landscaped gardens.

He came to a sturdy fence, strong chain-linked wire which stretched between solid posts where the new road turned to the right past another row of bungalows. On the farther side were tall trees and well-established shrubs. Edward, no gardener, could not identify any of them. He walked along until he saw a strong bough within his reach, grasped it and swung himself over the fence, landing on the leafy ground. He must have worked his way round towards the hotel by now; this fence had to be its boundary. Staying within the cover provided by the undergrowth, Edward went on, his trainer shoes by this time sopping wet.

He came to the house quite soon. It was a large, square-fronted building made of the local granite, dark grey and with a darker roof of slates. It had been built in the days when merchants and ship-owners prospered by shipping goods in and out of the estuaries along the coast. A glossy virginia creeper covered one wall of the house. Some cars were parked outside.

Edward retreated into the shelter of the bushes so that he could circle the place and approach it from the rear. The guests would still be sleeping, but the staff must be about, preparing breakfast and cleaning the public rooms. Moving quietly, Edward eventually reached a rear drive just as two scooters puttered by bringing staff in for the day's work.

He followed them, walking confidently now. He had every right to come and see his sister.

There was a row of outbuildings, once stabling, behind the house. Edward passed an open door and saw two enormous washing machines and a tumble drier. There was a mechanized ironer like one he had used in the prison laundry where he had worked during part of his sentence. Maybe they could use a temporary laundryman here, though really he didn't fancy being cooped up in that damp, steamy atmosphere again; he'd rather be out of doors. A few weeks in the country, while he got used to his freedom and before winter set in, was what he wanted, if he could find some work. Edward never stayed long in any job, though he worked well enough until the feeling grew that someone was gunning for him, picking on him, finding needless fault. Then he'd leave, but he hadn't always managed to do this before the compulsion to light a fire overwhelmed him. He'd told the doctors at the prison about it; he wanted to punish someone, they'd explained, and it all went back to the fact that his mother had abandoned him when he was only six. This had made him want to get back at the world. He had done a great deal of damage by yielding to the urge.

Through the kitchen window he could see the breakfast cook and her assistant hard at work. Julie wouldn't be among the white-coated people here; she worked on the domestic side.

Edward slipped in through the unlocked back door and walked silently along the corridor into which it opened. A flight of stairs led off to the left, and he ran swiftly up them, finding himself in a long passage with doors punctuating either side. It would be easy to do this place; there'd be plenty of casual pickings. He padded on and at the end of the passage saw another door, half open. From within came chinking sounds, and as he approached, out came Julie with a laden early-morning tea tray.

She gave a single shriek and dropped it when she saw him, sending scalding tea over her legs and smashing most of the china. Edward grabbed her before she could yell again and pulled her back into the housemaid's pantry where she prepared the trays.

'Eddie, what are you doing here?' she gasped, when her first shock had abated. Her words came mingled with little wails as she dabbed at her legs with a damp tea towel.

'Well, I'm out, aren't I, so I came to see you,' he said reasonably. He bent down and began to pick up the broken crockery. Most of the damage was on the landing. 'Oh, the carpet,' he tutted, like an anxious housewife. A soggy section of patterned Axminster confronted them, with two teabags marooned in the midst of the swamp.

'It'll wipe off,' said Julie. 'There's a floorcloth in the cupboard under the sink. You just get on with it, Eddie. Use plenty of hot water.'

This was how she had always talked to him, his elder sister behaving like a mother. After their own mother had gone, Julie had done her best to look after him and their father, although she was only twelve. Then Dad had remarried and had another family, and he and Julie became outsiders.

'I wish you wouldn't call me Eddie,' he grumbled.

'I always have, and I shan't stop now,' said Julie. 'You haven't escaped, have you?'

'Of course not. I've served my time,' he said. 'I'll take that tray for you. Where's it got to go?'

'What? And terrify the guests out of their lives?' she said. 'Look at you! Not shaved and with your jeans sopping wet. Do you want to get me the sack?' Then she began to laugh. He had always had the trick of making her feel happy, even though he never seemed able to stay out of trouble.

'How're the legs?' he asked.

'Better,' she said, though they still stung. She poured boiling water into a fresh teapot. 'I won't have enough crocks now,' she added. 'Mrs Thomson will have something to say about that.'

'What do you need? I'll go down and nick them from the pantry,' Edward said. 'Let those folk down there do the explaining.' He studied the tray. 'What's missing?'

'You'll do no such thing,' she said. 'Stay here till I get back.'

She went off with another loaded tray and Edward made himself a cup of tea while she was gone. There were Osborne biscuits in a tin and he ate six of them.

'You can't stay here,' she said when she returned,

having tried to think constructively while she drew the curtains in the room where a retired doctor and his wife were staying for a restful week.

'There's no need,' said Edward, taking another biscuit from the tin. 'I've got friends in Milton St Gabriel.'

'You can't have, Eddie. That's impossible,' said Julie.

'I have, too. And what's more they used to live in this house,' said Edward. Thelma had told him some of her family history. 'I'm staying with Mrs Cunningham.'

'I don't believe it!' Julie stared at him, amazed.

'Well, it's her daughter I know really,' Edward said. 'She's just back from Los Angeles.'

'How could you have got to know her? When did you get out?' asked Julie suspiciously.

'I got out yesterday, and I met Thelma on the train. She invited me to stay,' he said. He was on the point of boasting about his conquest, then thought better of it; Julie would be sure to disapprove.

'How long are you going to be there?' she asked, while the familiar cloud of anxiety about her brother descended on her once again.

'Oh, I've no definite plans,' said Edward.

'You've got to stay out of trouble,' said Julie.

'I mean to, don't you worry,' Edward told her. 'I understand my motivation now.'

Julie was not reassured, but she felt guilty herself because she had travelled all this way to escape responsibility for him. She had let him down. Until his prison sentence, she had always managed to protect him from the consequences of his actions, pleading for him with the headmaster when he put lighted matches in the waste-paper basket at school, and keeping it a secret when she later learned that he had set fire to some rubbish in a disused warehouse. He had confessed to that offence when he was arrested for firing a car. It had

23

gone off like a bomb and he had been sent to prison for two years.

'Well, for God's sake keep on like that,' she told him. 'Now, I must finish my trays or they'll be screaming. Number seven will have finished hers; I'll fetch that to make up for what you smashed. Stay here while I'm gone.'

Julie knew he meant what he had said, but was he strong enough to stick to it? He'd always said he was sorry when caught out in any minor misdemeanour as a child and he didn't like upsetting people. But he loved the sparkle and the glitter of the fires he made. He stood and watched them burn and that was how he had been caught. A man who could do a thing like that, the judge had said, had shown a total disregard for human life.

3

Thelma woke with a headache and a sour taste in her mouth. She'd overdone the whisky, but she had hoped that it would help her through the inevitable ending to the evening. Nothing ever did, however; she should know that by now.

He wasn't still in her bed: that was something to be thankful for, and perhaps he had even left the house. She peered around her, blinking in the pale light which filtered through the printed chintz curtains. Then she saw the holdall that had been his sole piece of luggage standing in a corner of the room.

She had done none of her own unpacking yet; her cases stood where Edward had left them in what she regarded as, in perpetuity, her bedroom. Some of her possessions remained here wherever she herself might be and now she found an old blue quilted dressing gown in the cupboard. She put it on and, barefoot, went downstairs in search of coffee.

Her mother was standing by the table in the sitting-room where her current jigsaw was set out, a jagged fragment in her hand. She turned as her daughter entered the room. Thelma's hair stood out in an aureole around her pale face; her eyes looked haggard. Once, she had been a predictable if sometimes sulky little girl, and was always pretty, but her mother had found it hard to love her and for that reason was perpetually consumed with guilt and self-reproach, aggravated by Thelma's failure to build herself a happy life.

Lydia had put the percolator on, using the last coffee beans; normally, she drank instant coffee, which Thelma scorned.

'Good morning, Thelma,' she said, and did not ask her daughter if she had slept well; least said about the night's activities the better. 'There isn't any bread,' she added. 'But Mrs Dodds will have opened up by now, though she won't have had a fresh delivery yet. Still, there may be a loaf left over from yesterday.'

'I don't know why you don't keep some in the freezer, Mother,' Thelma said.

'I do, often,' said Lydia. 'I've run out. That's all.' With Thelma in America, it hadn't seemed necessary to be equipped against a sudden siege.

Lydia put the jigsaw segment into her skirt pocket and accompanied her daughter to the kitchen, where she poured her out a cup of coffee. Boris, half asleep, opened one eye and regarded both of them benevolently from his basket.

'That dog's getting old,' said Thelma.

Lydia ignored the comment.

'Your friend's gone out,' she said. 'Will he be staying long?'

'I've no idea,' said Thelma carelessly. 'I only met him yesterday. In the train, as a matter of fact. We'll have to wait and see.'

Lydia would not give Thelma the satisfaction of registering shock, but her hand shook as she put down the percolator. She always sought excuses for her daughter's waywardness: poor Thelma had been married less than six years when her first husband, Charles Hallows, was killed in a motor accident. No other car was involved; he had run off the road and hit a tree one Tuesday afternoon. He had left the office early, suffering from flu, but the spot where the crash had occurred was not on his route home. No explanation was forthcoming; the post-mortem showed no evidence of alcohol, or of heart attack or other seizure; it had all been very difficult to understand and accept. Within a few months Thelma had married again, but her husband had left her after only three weeks. She had reverted to her earlier married name and, as soon as it was possible, had obtained a divorce. Her father had bought her a flat in London where she had lived on and off ever since, reappearing in Milton St Gabriel at frequent intervals when pressed for cash or emotionally suffering. She had taken various temporary, often insubstantial jobs, sometimes as a demonstrator at trade exhibitions or in stores, always hoping to get into the theatre again. There was much talk of Equity; Lydia was uncertain whether Thelma had qualified for the essential card or for want of it failed to secure any parts, or whether there was some other cause for her lack of professional success.

Thelma finished her coffee. She was longing for a cigarette but had smoked her last; her mother did not smoke and did not care for others to do so in her presence or in her house.

'There's some Ry-Vita,' said Lydia.

'I don't want anything to eat,' said Thelma. 'I've got a stinking headache.'

Lydia had seen the empty whisky bottle.

'Have you, dear? I'm sorry. There are aspirins in the bathroom,' she said.

She left the room to avoid losing patience with Thelma. That must never be allowed to happen. Boris levered himself out of his basket and trundled after her into the garden. She was standing under an apple tree turning the jigsaw piece round in her pocket when she heard a cheery whistling, and the young man, Thelma's latest acquisition, came towards her. Boris waddled towards him, tail wagging; he, at least, approved.

Edward, coming up behind her, had whistled to announce his presence for she had been standing so still, her back towards him, lost in thought, that he did not want to startle her by suddenly appearing. He wondered how old she was; nearer seventy than sixty, that was certain. Her soft, fine hair was nearly white. She wore it in an odd, old-fashioned style with that band around her brow.

'I've been to see my sister,' he volunteered. 'Did Thelma tell you she lives here? She was ever so glad I didn't turn up in the middle of the night. She hasn't got a bed for me just now.' Julie would find a corner for him later, he was blithely certain; in a place that size there must be some odd spot where he could sleep unnoticed. Meanwhile, he'd hope to stay here. 'It's really nice of you to put me up,' he added. 'What can I do to help? Shall I cut the grass?'

He'd had a smashing breakfast at the hotel: fried egg and bacon, sausage and tomato. The going rate for that, if you were a guest and came in casually, was four pounds ninety-five, but for residents it was included in the bedroom price: thirty-five pounds at least, depending on the room. The staff seemed a friendly crowd: he'd met Victor and Mavis, both friends of Julie's who worked in the dining-room, and a nice old man, Ferdy, the barman, who had some sort of foreign accent. Edward foresaw no problem about getting the odd meal up there. Now, with his first fears lulled, he was full of goodwill towards the world and in particular his hostess.

'That would be very kind,' said Lydia. 'It's still growing fast; all the rain has meant it's needed cutting more often than usual this summer.'

'What sort of mower have you got?' asked Edward.

'It's one that doesn't mind damp grass, if that's what you were thinking of,' said Lydia, and her face softened slightly; she did not smile, however. Did she ever, Edward wondered, and wondered more at having such a strange thought himself.

He ran his hand over his chin and realized that he had not shaved yet; an old girl like this one wouldn't like that.

'I'll have a wash and shave first, if that's all right,' he said. 'Sorry if I look untidy but I got up rather early and didn't want to wake anyone up.'

'There's petrol in a can in the garage, if the mower needs refilling,' Lydia said.

A fragile amity between them, Lydia and Edward returned to the house.

Thelma had gone back to bed. She would be the problem, Edward decided, not her mother. Still, not to worry; he'd sort something out to keep them both happy.

Thelma wanted something from him now, he discovered when he went into the bedroom to collect his razor.

'Not while your mum's about,' he told her sternly, but he gave her one of his most winning smiles as he left the room.

Thelma pouted sulkily, rolling over in the bed, but she was really quite relieved; it was just a way to pass the time and meant you didn't have to talk.

That evening, Gerald telephoned to invite himself down the following weekend.

'Thelma's here,' said Lydia.

'What? Oh, no! What's happened now?' Gerald was taken too much by surprise at the news to hide his dismay.

'It didn't work out.' Lydia repeated her daughter's explanation.

29

Gerald could imagine his mother sitting by the telephone, lips pursed as she finished speaking, perhaps
fiddling with a pencil, or fragment of jigsaw, or other
small object which she would suddenly set aside as she
disciplined herself not to fidget.

'Oh dear!'

'She's got a friend with her,' said Lydia.

'Male?' As if he needed to ask: Thelma had no female
friends.

'Yes.'

'Hm. You're not being very forthcoming, Mother.
Can't you talk freely?'

'No.' The telephone was in the hall and while they
were talking, Thelma was watching television in the
sitting-room while Edward was doing Lydia's jigsaw.
He had an eye for it.

'What's the matter with this one? Is he another lame
duck?' asked Gerald.

'I don't know,' said Lydia.

Sometimes they were; there had been two alcoholics,
an unemployed steel-worker, a monk who had returned
to the world and whom she'd met when she'd spent
some weeks in a commune in a remote Cotswold
village.

'You aren't happy about it,' Gerald stated. 'It's as well
that I'm coming down.' He swiftly reshaped his
thinking; he had intended the weekend as a chance to
get away from things, or rather, from himself, for he was
not proud of the manner in which he had ended his
recent liaison. Now he must accept the new problems
posed by his sister. The first one that came to mind was
purely domestic; no doubt she and this man, whoever
he was, were occupying the double spare room in the
lodge and this would leave the small room free for him,
but it might not be safe to assume overt arrangements
which his mother would certainly not approve, even

30

though it would not be the first time she had had to accept such a situation. Whatever the circumstances, there was only one bathroom and Thelma would be unlikely to consider the wishes of himself or even their mother in the demands she made upon it. He would be much more comfortable at the hotel, and his absence would remove some strain from his mother as she juggled with her sense of duty towards them both. 'I'll stay at the Manor,' he told her. 'If they're full, I'll go to the Swan in Heronsmouth. We'll all have dinner at the Manor on Saturday. How does that appeal to you?'

'Very much,' she answered. 'Thank you.'

Gerald sat staring at the telephone after he had replaced the handset. Her voice was never warm or enthusiastic. When she was young, had she been eager and ardent? He found it impossible to imagine intimacy between her and his father, a stern man forced by the death of his elder brother in the war to settle for farming the land and running the estate he would inherit. He'd wanted to make the army his career but had told Gerald that there wasn't money enough for him to join the sort of regiment he would have chosen, where a private income was essential. He had read law before the war, and was a territorial soldier.

Henry Cunningham had failed to run the farm with profit and had let the estate decline, but he had seen Gerald prove his own business acumen and died hoping that he would rescue the family fortunes.

He had not foreseen Iris's defection.

As it was, Gerald had invested in the hotel group so that at least he kept in touch with what went on there. Once his decision to sell was made, Gerald had quite enjoyed imagining his father's disapproval. The old man had been so strict: Gerald had never won praise for any achievement and had soon learned to conceal his small sins which were usually of omission. All Henry's warmth was reserved for Thelma; he had adored the pretty little fair-haired girl with her big blue eyes and had indulged her every whim. He had found excuses for her scholastic failures and had revelled in her sporting prowess, for Thelma was good at all games and she loved riding. Gerald still remembered the birthday when their father had given her Rondo, a liver chestnut pony which had subsequently helped her secure many a rosette at local gymkhanas and hunter trials. Thelma was a good horsewoman, and fearless; Gerald acknowledged that, while admitting that he was, himself, a poor performer, except at golf where the ball was attacked while stationary.

After Charles was killed, Thelma had come home. She had ridden about the place on an old cob which was the only mount her father was then able to provide for her, and had got herself involved with the stockman. Even Henry had had to pay some attention when the stockman's wife had come to the Manor in tears to protest; he had interviewed Thelma who had then been sent to London to do an advanced cookery course. While there, she had met and married her second husband, and Gerald had been made to feel that he was at fault for not keeping more of an eye on her during that time.

It was no good dwelling on past old jealousies and resentments. Gerald determined to rise above prejudice when he went down to Milton St Gabriel, and to deal with the present while he was in it. He telephoned his daughter Fiona, who lived in a mixed flat in Shepherd's Bush and was, at the moment, unemployed. She was pleased to accept his invitation to lunch.

They met at a French restaurant in the City. Fiona arrived wearing what seemed to Gerald to be a romper suit in pale pink cotton, rather crumpled, and an enormous baggy sweater which she unpeeled when they sat down. Her long dark hair was secured in a thick plait, and she wore a lot of eye make-up. She looked striking, attracting notice from others in the restaurant as she entered, and causing the waiters to hover round her in a covey.

'Hullo, Daddy!' She kissed him warmly. 'This is fun.'

'I want to be sure you get an occasional square meal,' he told her, trying not to show too much delight at being in her company.

'Oh, I don't do too badly,' said Fiona airily. 'I get given my dinner most nights.'

Looking at her more attentively, he saw that beyond the first impression of general health and energy, there were faint shadows under the large brown eyes, and that the colour on her cheeks came from blusher sparingly applied.

'Who gave it to you last night?' he asked.

'Oh, just a man I know,' said Fiona carelessly. 'Can I have steak, please? Any kind, but large and rare.'

She looked as if she could do with a month in the country. If he still owned the Manor, she would automatically go to Milton St Gabriel when no more attractive prospect offered and, as her Aunt Thelma still contrived, be nourished and refreshed. Well, he couldn't put the clock back. Nor could he turn her once again into the little girl who loved her pony to distraction and was going to be a show jumper when she grew up. About the age of fourteen that artless child had disappeared, to be replaced by a young female stranger keen on pop music and who wore wild, freaky clothing when she could get away with it.

Had he spoiled her, over-indulged her, as his own father had Thelma? Was she destined to follow her aunt's feckless example, and if so, would it be his fault?

Such thoughts made Gerald uncomfortable.

'She'll marry well,' Iris had declared. 'She must have

her chance in London. She'll meet young men with prospects there.'

But Gerald wanted her to marry a man who loved her and would want to make her happy.

'As you met me,' he had attacked, and Iris had smiled.

'Of course,' she said. 'And I did my bit – you can't deny that.'

It was true. She had run the house efficiently, and she was decorative. She had played her part in the circle of similar couples among whom they had lived for most of their married life, giving tasteful dinner parties and getting the children's teeth dealt with by a leading orthodontist. She had known that one day the Manor at Milton St Gabriel would come to him and had pictured herself as a potential leader of county society; what she had not expected was that the house would be so badly run down, so much in need of restoration; and she had not known about sea mists which clung damply round the hills, the pervading chill, and the winter gales. Very soon, she gave in to boredom. She enjoyed exciting admiration; men were attracted to her, and she had had several discreet affairs with wandering neighbours before she made her bid for freedom.

Fiona, eating pheasant pâté before her steak arrived, revealed, under her father's gentle questioning, that she rose late most mornings and idled away the day, sometimes shopping, sometimes pottering into a museum or a gallery, going occasionally to see a film, all the while waiting for the evening. It seemed to him a pointless way of life. He gave her an allowance which was enough to cover her share of the flat's rent; there could be little over. Was she drawing the dole? He dreaded to hear that, in her parasite existence, she was entitled to it, so he did not ask. What if he docked her monthly cheque? Would she then be forced to find a proper job or would it drive her into something worse?

'These men –' he hesitated. There had been mention of Gavin, Robert, Peter. 'Any of them special?' he essayed.

'Not really, Daddy,' she declared, smiling sunnily.

'I wish you knew what you really wanted to do,' he told her.

'I'm having a good time,' she said. 'Isn't that enough, at my age? It's OK by Mummy. She says it's only what girls of Granny's generation did, waiting to get married.'

'Some of them,' said Gerald grimly. 'Your grandmother helped in the parish – looked after her parents. Then, in the war, she was a nurse.'

'I didn't mean Granny C. I meant Granny,' said Fiona patiently, referring to her maternal grandmother who had done the season properly and been presented, wearing ostrich feathers. She had married an impoverished younger son of a baronet after her third circuit.

'Girls can do anything, these days,' said Gerald. Various able young women were steadily rising at the bank; only if they succumbed to family demands would they fail to maintain a continuing ascent. 'You could be Prime Minister,' he added.

'Don't be silly, Daddy dear,' said Fiona. 'Of course I'll get married in the end and be a mother all my days.' She sighed. 'But twenty years is a long time.'

'Is twenty years all you give your marriage?' Gerald asked her.

'It's a long time to live with one person,' said Fiona. 'Must get boring, doesn't it?'

'Your mother thought so,' Gerald said. 'But Granny – Granny C. and Grandfather were together for over forty years.'

'Yes, and it was hell, I bet,' said Fiona. 'At least

nowadays, if things go wrong, you can get out of it without a lot of hassle.'

'I'm sure Granny C. and Grandfather never contemplated such a thing,' said Gerald, truly shocked.

'I don't suppose they did,' said Fiona. 'Granny C. is much too proper. Do you suppose Grandfather had affairs?'

'Of course not. What gave you that idea?' asked Gerald.

'I don't know. He was a lusty sort of man, wasn't he? Vigorous? And Granny C. is rather decidulated.'

'There's no such word,' said Gerald. 'What do you mean?' But he knew, and she was right.

'Her leaves have kind of dropped off, right?' said Fiona.

'She wasn't always old,' said Gerald sadly.

'Oh, I know, and she was always nice to me, showed me lots of things, like birds' nests and how to knit,' said Fiona. 'But even now I'm afraid of blotting my copybook with her, and you are, too, Daddy. Don't deny it.'

'Thelma's come back.' Gerald flung the information into their conversation, where he was rapidly getting out of his depth. 'I'm going down to Milton St Gabriel on Friday – staying at the hotel to leave room at the lodge.' He wouldn't mention Thelma's boyfriend in case that provoked more uncomfortable remarks from Fiona.

'Oh dear. I thought she'd gone to America for keeps,' said Fiona.

'Your aunt never goes anywhere for keeps,' said Gerald.

'She got tired of Lucian, I suppose. Didn't fancy twenty years of his tickly beard and yellow teeth,' said Fiona.

'I didn't know you'd met him,' Gerald said.

'Oh yes. She had a party once, and in a fit of auntly

36

duty, asked me along. She had a thing going with someone else then. A painter, I think it was.' And Lucian had fancied Fiona and she had let him kiss her in order to try out the beard. She hadn't liked it much.

'Why don't you come with me?' Gerald said, on impulse. He looked across the table at her pretty, bright face. How lovely it would be to drive down with her, hear more talk, have a chance to deal better with her opinions, mend bridges between her and her grandmother. 'I'm sure the hotel will have another room,' he urged her.

'Sorry, Daddy. I've got people to see and things to do this weekend,' said Fiona. 'Thanks, though.'

What was she going to do? Whom would she see? Gavin? Robert? Peter?

'Another time, then,' Gerald said.

'Mm. Rather.' Fiona looked at her watch, a tiny gold one he had given her for her eighteenth birthday. 'Wow, it's late. I must dash. Thanks for lunch, Daddy.'

Where was she rushing to? She had no typewriter waiting for her, no tutor, no essay to write, no angry supervisor or executive with dictation to impart.

'I'll ring you in the week,' was all he said as she kissed him on the top of his head and left, with three waiters supervising her departure from the premises.

4

Edward had put more petrol into Lydia's old mower. He had found the mixture wrongly adjusted and had corrected it, then oiled the machine thoroughly. He cleaned it well when the job was done before putting it away in the garden shed. There was a big tin of paraffin there, under the shelf; she used it for bonfires, he supposed.

Edward liked putting things right and had a feeling for engines; as a schoolboy he had sometimes done odd hours on the pumps at a garage where he had learned what went on under a bonnet. He had thought of becoming apprenticed there, but the owner had found out about his escapades with fire and had turned him down. Edward had got off, then, with being put on probation, but in the end, as the magistrate had said, he had had to be properly punished. Now he was an ex-con and would receive no mercy if he offended again. He was running scared: the sensible thing would have been to go into the approved lodgings suggested by his probation officer, let her help him towards a job. But who would take him on when there were plenty of other young men without records also looking for work? He had fled to Julie, as usual relying on her help, but when he saw her dismay that morning he had suddenly understood what a burden he had become.

Mrs Cunningham was nice, in her odd, stiff way. She

wouldn't turn him out at once, not if he gave no trouble and helped about the place; there were plenty of little jobs that needed doing. He'd sign on at the nearest DHSS and perhaps he could get some work in the village to supplement his social security. It wasn't Edward's way to look too far ahead: the next week was enough. He'd postpone the problem of Thelma, too; he'd been stupid to play her game but it had seemed the only thing to do at the time.

The old lady had gone off shopping now, in her Metro, which needed a wash. He'd do that when she came back, and check its oil and water and tyre pressures. She might be careless about things of that sort. Edward had finished the jigsaw she was doing, all but one piece which was missing, too late for her to take it with her to Cheverton. She'd taken a pile of others, some with battered boxes, to return to a charity shop. It seemed that when people donated them, they had to be sorted out and assembled as pieces got mixed. If any were incomplete, that had to be stated on the outside, and Edward wrote carefully, in ballpoint on the lid, that one piece of the jungle scene was missing. Then, reluctant to face Thelma when she decided to get up, he went off to the new estate through which he had walked that morning and began knocking on doors in search of odd jobs. He told potential employers that he was staying with Mrs Cunningham for a while and needed work while he looked for a permanent post. Thus he established credentials; everyone knew who Mrs Cunningham was, even if they had never met her, and that first day he got several offers. It was not easy to find casual help in the village because the hotel employed so many local people; only a nucleus of staff lived in.

Edward was well pleased with his morning's canvass, although he found no one at home at some of the bungalows. He was shocked to see half-lights open at windows and other invitations to prowlers. Just because the place seemed so quiet and peaceful didn't mean it was immune to visits from villains. After all, he was an ex-con himself.

There were fire hazards, too; piles of rubbish in garages and weedkiller in bags in garden sheds. A puff of flame was all it would take.

After she had delivered six jigsaw puzzles to the charity shop and collected several more, Lydia did some shopping in Sainsbury's. There was no comparable supermarket in Heronsmouth, where she went for what could not be obtained in Milton St Gabriel. When she was alone she needed so little, but now that Thelma and Edward were staying, she must stock up. And there would be Gerald at the weekend. Lydia wrote a cheque in Sainsbury's, shuddering inwardly at the amount. Then she went to the bank and cashed another cheque for money she was certain to need for day-to-day expenses. Even the milk bill would be double; she used only two pints a week but Edward would probably pour half a pint on his cereal, if he was anything like her grandson, Christopher. A young person needed good food, and plenty of it.

Her tasks done, Lydia was reluctant to return home, where she would have to face the problem of Thelma. She decided to have lunch in Cheverton's big department store; it needn't cost much if she chose her meal with care, and it would be a small treat. Now and then she allowed herself this, or a bar snack at the Manor. It was nice to eat something she hadn't prepared herself and need not wash up.

She took Boris for a run, then left him in the car in a parking lot near the store. While she was sitting at a small table in the no-smoking area of the self-service restaurant, eating an egg salad attractively garnished with pineapple slices and cress, she saw a small girl wandering between the aisles on her own. The child could not be more than two years old. Lydia looked about for the mother. It wasn't easy to collect a tray and keep an eye on a child at the same time, but surely one so young could be attached to a harness?

As the child's lower jaw dropped and her mouth opened to cry, Lydia got up and approached her.

'Now, dear,' she said, bending down. 'Where's your mummy? We'll soon find her, don't worry.' She took the child's hand and peered round.

The child was comforted by the firm grasp but she did not know this person who had stooped down to her level and was now asking her name. She let out a loud yell and at that moment there was a flurry of movement beside Lydia as the little girl's hand was snatched from hers.

'What do you mean by getting away from me?' demanded the mother, yanking at the child. She glared at Lydia. 'And what do you think you're doing?' she demanded. 'Poking your nose in where it's not wanted?'

Before Lydia could reply, the mother had swept the child, now bawling, away to a table in a far corner.

Lydia returned to her own place, her heart thumping fast in anger. The incident had sent her appetite away and spoiled her fragmentary pleasure in what she was doing, but she forced herself to eat the food she had paid for and to drink her coffee, which was now cool. It was so tiresome having to collect everything all at once; coffee never stayed hot while you ate your main course. She was unaware of any reaction to the small episode, and indeed few people had paid any attention.

Later, Lydia went to the store's hosiery department where she bought herself a pair of warm navy wool tights for the winter. As she paid for her purchase, she saw the same mother walking through the department, dragging the child by the arm. The small girl was still crying; sobs of grief, not of temper, rent the air.

Lydia glared at the mother, and the mother glared back.

Thelma knew that she was alone in the house. She had heard the mower outside and had seen Edward's busy activity; then there was silence. Her mother had gone off in the Metro and after that, apart from an occasional car passing in the lane, there was no noise.

Then the radio next door came on. Beat music throbbed through Karen White's window, opened because she had been doing her hair and had filled the room with spray. Thelma liked pop music; it drove away thought. She welcomed the noise.

She had a bath, put on trousers and sweater, then filled the washing machine with the clothes she had travelled in from America and switched it on. Her hangover had abated and she felt hungry, but when she looked in the fridge there seemed to be nothing to eat. Surely her mother could have gone along to Mrs Dodds's shop by now and stocked up, before going out?

Thelma decided to go to the Manor for a drink and some food.

She still found it strange to walk down the drive of what had been her home, with the colony of bright new dwellings away to the right behind the rhododendrons. The place was so familiar, yet so changed. Here, she had ridden her pony around the grounds. Here, on the somewhat uneven grass court, she had learned to play tennis, hitting the ball across the frayed, mended net to her father. They had never been able to afford a hard court, but now there was one, and a swimming pool. In his study, now the bar, her father had pretended to be cross when her school reports were poor, but his disapproval had never lasted long.

'You'll soon get married,' he'd say. 'You won't have to worry about a career.'

He hadn't taken her wish to go on the stage very seriously but when she was turned down by various recognized drama schools, he paid for her to go to one more obscure. Marrying Charles Hallows, the son of the local doctor, rescued her from the failure of her early career but supplied her with fresh problems. Charles, who had failed to get into medical school and was anyway not keen to follow his father's profession, was working as an estate agent, learning the business from the bottom up, with exams to be passed as he progressed. He was serious about his work, studying at home in the evenings, and was reluctant to take Thelma out dancing or even to the cinema. She was lonely and bored, but she enjoyed her married status and being able to refer to 'my husband'. Occasionally they gave dinner parties, returning the hospitality of other young couples encountered mainly through Charles's work, and Thelma enjoyed these. She took cooking lessons at a local college but gave up after less than a term; the course was not geared towards entertaining and she found it dull. Her mother had taught her the essentials and it was more amusing to try out recipes from books and magazines. She enjoyed dabbling about in the kitchen in an unstructured way.

She and Charles were both disappointed in their marriage. He had always admired Thelma. When they were children she had been a tomboy – first up the highest tree, able to swim faster and further than either he or Gerald could manage. When Charles saw her performance as Nina, he had felt a sudden love for her, but she only agreed to their marriage when no more parts came her way. Charles had expected things to

43

work out easily after the wedding; after all, they had known each other so long and all girls wanted to settle down, or so he had thought. But it didn't happen like that; Thelma was bored at home and didn't want children, and she didn't enjoy Charles as a lover.

He flung himself more and more into his work; she haunted the local pubs and went frequently up to London in quest of theatrical work.

He did not know what would follow if she were to win a part in a London production, but it didn't happen. Then he was killed. He never knew what sometimes went on when she was supposed to be at an audition; nor did he know that within two years of their marriage she had had an abortion. She took care not to need another.

Thelma was truly shocked by Charles's tragic death, but now she attracted pity and she enjoyed her role as a young widow. After the episode with her father's stockman, several men attempted to console her and as she missed being one of a conventional pair, she tried marriage again.

Since then she had lost count of how many lovers she had had, but she had never found whatever it was that she sought. Her pleasure came from knowing that she could enchant; she swiftly grew bored and moved on. But it was to have been different with Lucian. After he left for America, he had written her several amusing letters. She'd read, *You should come over*, and had taken this as a serious proposition when he had meant it as merely an idle suggestion. After she arrived, at first he had made the best of things; but because they had been incompatible both in and out of bed, he had brought the affair to an end.

The arrival into her life of Edward had restored Thelma's confidence, and now she stepped optimistically across the Manor threshold. She'd nearly ceased to expect her father to appear and greet her with a cool kiss on her cheek. She had liked the feel of his scratchy tweed jacket, the scent of the special stuff he used on his hair.

'Well, poppet, and what have you been up to?' he would say. He was gentler with her than with anyone, but now he had gone.

She went into the bar, where Ferdy was behind the counter polishing glasses. He was an elderly Pole who had served in the Army during the war and had lived in England ever since. He seldom went off duty, serving tea in the afternoon and morning coffee as well. He lived in a council flat in Heronsmouth, where he had worked at the Swan until they retired him because of his age. Gerald had been instrumental in getting him the job at the Manor where his experience was useful. Most of the staff were young, and guests found Ferdy's presence reassuring.

'Well, Ferdy,' she greeted him. 'How're you?'

'Splendid, splendid, Miss Thelma,' said Ferdy, who had known her since the days when her father used to treat her to lunch at the Swan. He smiled at her. The sight of a pretty woman still cheered him up.

Thelma ordered a double gin and tonic.

'I haven't brought any money,' she said. 'Chalk it up, will you, Ferdy? And have one yourself.'

'Thank you,' said Ferdy, but he frowned. Miss Thelma never had any money when she came in alone and he didn't like asking her mother to pay, which was what had to happen. Miss Thelma seemed to forget that her father wasn't around any more to pick up the tab. He did not take up her invitation to himself.

'Busy?' asked Thelma, gazing round.

'We're half full,' answered Ferdy. 'It's been a bad season. There have been a lot of cancellations because of the weather. It's not been a summer to sit by the pool and sunbathe.'

'No.'

Thelma picked up her drink and looked round. Two middle-aged couples were sitting at a table in a corner; otherwise, the bar was empty. She sighed. Well, something – or someone – might yet turn up: it was still early. She'd order some lunch and see how things went.

The bar filled up while Thelma was eating a prawn salad. She was suffering from jet-lag and the scene around her had a touch of unreality about it; she could almost imagine that this was some party her parents were throwing. Everyone seemed to be paired; she saw no one alone.

When she had finished her meal, she went upstairs for a prowl. She often did this on her visits home. No one challenged her. She tried the door of what had been her father's bedroom but it was locked. In the renovation process, bathrooms had been added to all the main bedrooms and an efficient heating system installed. No guest would get chilblains now, as she had done as a child. Along here had been her room. It was one of the nicest, with a view towards the distant sea. Her mother had let her choose material for new curtains when the room was done up just before her sixteenth birthday. No one else's had been refurbished at all; Gerald's had stayed just the same as it was in her grandparents' time. Some of the furniture had been valuable, and what hadn't been bought in by the hotel had been auctioned by a branch of the firm in which Charles, if he had lived, would by now have been a partner.

Why had he gone and got killed like that, hurtling her into widowhood while she was still a girl? It wasn't her fault that he'd come home early that day and found that she wasn't alone. He'd rushed off and given her no chance to explain that the man had been no one important; it was only because she was bored.

She still sometimes wondered if he had driven into

that tree on purpose or if it was really an accident. But it didn't matter now. Only the other man knew that Charles had come home first, and he wouldn't tell for he had been married. Thelma couldn't even remember his name.

She wandered about the upper floors of the Manor for quite some time. Luckily Mrs Thomson did not emerge from her flat; Thelma always felt that the manageress did not approve of her visits, though why shouldn't she return to her former home? She tried several doors and found one or two, in the staff quarters, unlocked. There were posters on walls, make-up on dressing-tables, made beds, unmade beds; signs of alien life. Why had it all had to go?

When her thoughts turned this way, Thelma felt desperate; movement helped, and she hurried downstairs again, coming into the bar once more.

'Coffee. Miss Thelma?' asked Ferdy.

'Yes, please.'

Thelma sat at a table drumming her fingers until it arrived. What was she going to do? If she stayed with her mother, the sparks would fly. Thelma had always wanted to shock her, beginning when she was quite young and had climbed all over the roof of the Manor, with Gerald so frightened that he had fetched their parents. She had come down fairly easily, the way she had ascended, over the parapet above the gallery and in through a window, and her father had secretly been delighted although he had made her vow never to do it again. As for Gerald, he was beaten for tale-bearing.

Thelma scarcely noticed an elderly man sitting in a wing chair near the hearth, but he saw her.

When she had finished her coffee, she went out into the garden and down to the pool. Some wet towels hung over lounger chairs at its side, but no one was swimming. Only the hardy would bathe today.

Thelma peeled off her clothes. She loved swimming naked and there was no one about. Even if there had been, she didn't much care. She dived in and swam up and down until she was out of breath.

The elderly man from the bar came up to the pool while she was in the water. Her back was turned to him as she climbed out of the pool, shook back her wet hair and grabbed a towel from a nearby chair. He thought he was dreaming.

5

Edward went out after dinner that evening.

It had been an excellent meal. Walking home from the Manor, Thelma had decided to give her mother a treat by cooking her something delicious. She had persuaded the new butcher in the village to bone her some lamb, and had stuffed the fillet thus obtained with herbs and small mushrooms. They had zabaglione for pudding.

Lydia knew that the various items would all have been charged up to her. In fact, she no longer ran an account anywhere in the village; her wants were few when she was alone, so it wasn't worth while, and she liked to pay as she went along. She was, however, such a respected resident that Thelma would have encountered no problems about shopping, like royalty, without money. After her visits, Lydia always went round paying whatever was owed.

But Edward knew nothing of this. He revised some of his harsher thoughts about Thelma in the light of what seemed to him to be generous conduct.

He'd discovered, however, that there was a disco in the village hall that night, and he had decided to go. After his time inside it would be a real thrill, and he might meet some girl who'd be more his style than Thelma.

He helped clear the table and wash up – he had

always helped at home, Julie had seen to that – and slipped out while Thelma was making the coffee.

She put the television on when she brought in the tray. Any sound was better than silence.

'Where's Edward?' she asked, when she had poured out three cups and he had not appeared in the sitting room.

'I've no idea,' said Lydia.

Thelma went to the foot of the stairs and called him. She tried the cloakroom door, then went into the garden and called again, in vain.

'He's not here,' she said.

'How odd to go out without saying where he was going,' said Lydia, but she spoke placidly. She had enjoyed her dinner; Thelma was certainly a very good cook. There was quite a lot of the lamb left; it would do for two more meals at least.

'He's probably gone down to the Bell,' said Thelma. 'I'll go along later and see.'

But he wasn't at the pub. Thelma knew some of the people who were there, however, including the Dennises from the bungalow beyond her mother's garden. She ended up playing darts and didn't come home until closing time.

Her mother was still up, putting pieces in a jigsaw; she seemed never to weary of this occupation. She had let Boris out for a final run in the garden and had washed up the coffee things.

'Edward is not back,' she told her daughter, who was flushed and animated, but at least had returned alone. 'Will you be sure to lock up when he does return?'

'I will. Don't worry,' said Thelma. 'I'm not going to bed yet myself – my metabolism is still running on American time.'

Lydia left her watching the late film.

She was very tired, herself, and fell asleep over her book, a biography of Florence Nightingale.

Edward left the disco when it finished soon after midnight. The swirling lights and loud music had excited him, and he had revelled in the movement and contact provided by the entertainment. Young people from neighbouring villages had come in cars and on motorbikes. Julie and her friends from the hotel came in when the restaurant closed; Edward left with them and a girl he had met who lived near the lodge.

'I'll walk you home,' he told her. 'I'm going your way. You shouldn't go home on your own.'

'Why ever not?' asked Karen White. 'Nothing ever happens in Milton St Gabriel.'

'You can't be sure it won't, one day,' said Edward. 'A stranger may come to the village and turn the place over.'

'One like you, you mean,' said Karen.

'Exactly,' said Edward, grinning in the harsh light from the street lamp outside the hall. There were now eight strategically placed street lights in the village; one faction on the parish council said more were needed but another declared that the old-world charm of the original area would be spoiled by this modern intrusion.

'You must be joking,' said Karen. 'You're Julie's brother.'

'That's my passport, is it?' asked Edward, laughing. He took Karen's arm. 'Well, you're safe enough with me, but it doesn't do to be too trusting of blokes you've just met, you know.' He'd come across some very unpleasant customers when he was inside.

'I've got some wine in my room,' said Victor. 'Let's keep the party going.'

'Why not?' agreed Edward.

They went back with him to his room in the stable block, where Victor produced cans of beer and a bottle of rough red wine. He put on a tape of Duran Duran and they all sat round enjoying their drinks. The music removed any need to talk, but it was too loud for Julie who worriedly told Victor to turn it down. Sound travelled across the yard to the hotel, she explained, and the guests might complain. It had happened before and she did not want Mrs Thomson to come storming across. Julie was reluctant to account for Eddie's presence among them.

Karen thought this was really living. Here she was, in the early hours of the morning, drinking wine from a plastic mug and smoking, though it was nothing more daring than ordinary tobacco.

Not much happened, however. There was no kissing or cuddling. Perhaps that would come later, on the way home. Boys always wanted it. She swallowed her wine, which was rather nasty, and held out her mug for some more.

It was Julie who broke up the evening, sending Edward and Karen off into the darkness and reminding Victor that she and Mavis had to get up early, in her case to attend to the tea trays, and in Mavis's, to serve breakfast.

Edward and Karen walked hand in hand down the dark drive. There was no moon, and the air was mild, as if it was still summer. They kept wandering from the tarred track on to the grass, giggling as they stumbled along. Soon Edward's arm was around Karen's waist and they stopped now and then to kiss.

They had both had a good deal to drink, and one thing led to another, so that they took some time to reach Karen's house, next to the lodge.

'How convenient,' said Edward.

She giggled, then put a finger to her lips and said, 'Ssh.'

'How are you going to get in?' he asked. 'Have you got a key?'

She had, and opened the door quietly. Her mother was probably back from Heronsmouth by now, but she never cut up rough if Karen was late; it was her father who wanted to know chapter and verse.

'Can I come in too?' Edward whispered. 'Just for a minute?'

She had sobered up enough not to let him. Edward didn't insist; they arranged to meet the following evening instead, at the Bell. The landlord knew she was under age and he wouldn't let her in if he recognized her, but Karen decided to think about that tomorrow.

The door at the lodge was unlatched. He let himself in and crept quietly up to the small single room at the top of the stairs, where he fell happily asleep and did not wake until he heard Mrs Cunningham go to the bathroom at seven o'clock the next morning.

Betty, who during the war had helped Lydia to look after the children and thus freed her to work at the hospital which the Manor had become, came from Heronsmouth once a week to clean. She did not need the work but she liked to keep an eye on Lydia, for whom she felt a sort of affection.

During the intervening years, Betty had married, raised a family and been widowed herself. She had never lived far from Milton St Gabriel, and now occupied a bungalow in the outskirts of Heronsmouth. Lydia drove her each way because the buses were few and inconvenient; she did shopping errands after she took Betty back. Betty's husband, a chief petty officer in the Royal Navy, had opened a newsagent's shop when he retired. Their son, an accountant, was now with a multi-national firm, and their daughter, a teacher, had married a lecturer at the University of Durham. Betty had never lost touch with the Cunninghams, and often during her husband's tours at sea had helped out at the Manor.

She was waiting at the corner of Malplaquet Drive when Lydia drove up, as she was every Thursday morning at a quarter past nine, a small, dumpy woman with neatly waved grey hair and today wearing a smart pale green raincoat. She carried a holdall in which were her apron and the slippers she wore at the lodge.

'Good morning, Mrs Cunningham,' she said brightly, getting into the Metro. Long ago, when she had just left school and used to bath Thelma and Gerald and read them stories, she had addressed Lydia as 'Madam'. This had ceased when her husband was no longer a mere naval rating.

'Good morning, Betty.' Lydia engaged the gears as Betty buckled her seat belt.

'Wretched thing, I'll never get used to it,' she grumbled, as she did every week, and Lydia felt comforted. One thing which never altered in the changing world was Betty and her reactions.

'How are Brian and Pat?' Lydia inquired, in her own ritual.

A report on the lives of Betty's children followed. Over the years, Lydia had followed their progress through measles, mumps, examinations and courtship to parenthood and their present satisfactory positions in life. Today's chapter contained no startling news: Brian and his wife were off to a villa in Corfu for a late holiday; Pat and her family had earlier rented a gîte in the Dordogne.

As she talked, subconsciously Betty noticed how thin and veined were Lydia's hands on the steering wheel, how bony the wrists that protruded from her carefully washed blue cardigan. Did she eat enough? Betty hated taking money from her, aware that her own income probably equalled or even surpassed that of her employer. It had not been possible to conceal the terms of Henry Cunningham's will: the *Cheverton Gazette* had given its details and Betty had been shocked, but she was sure Gerald took good care of his mother. He'd done well, but then that Iris had cost him a packet. Betty had never taken to her and she'd been proved right in the end. She, Betty, had been lucky. She'd had a good life with her Bill, a cheerful, kindly man, whereas what she had seen of Mrs Cunningham's marriage depressed her. There didn't seem to be any laughter. Mrs Cunningham, always quiet during the war years when he was away, had later grown quieter still; she had had no glow about her. Betty and Bill had laughed a lot and there wasn't a tiff or a disagreement that hadn't been resolved with a smile from one or the other. Some years before the old man died, Mrs Cunningham had moved out of the main bedroom at the Manor to quite a small one in another wing. She had given no explanation and Betty had not commented on the change, but she felt sad. She had spent many a lonely night when Bill was at sea, and all the more precious had been those last years together, curled up in their cosy bed like spoons; she missed him still in every way.

Now, Betty could tell that something was wrong. Mrs Cunningham was tensing herself up to raise some distasteful subject. Was she to be given the sack in an economy drive? Betty resolved not to take it, if so. She settled her holdall more firmly on her lap and waited for the disclosure.

At last, as they entered the village, Lydia found the words.

'Thelma's home,' she said.

'She's never! I thought she was gone for good, this time,' said Betty, who had been to the States herself, three times, to visit her sister, a GI bride who had stayed the course. 'What happened?' she asked.

'It didn't work.' Lydia repeated Thelma's explanation.

'Why ever not?'

'I don't know. She hasn't told me,' said Lydia.

No, and I bet you didn't ask, thought Betty.

'And there's someone else here,' Lydia managed to add. 'A young man whom Thelma has invited to stay for a while – he has relatives in the village and they haven't a spare bed at the moment. I think they let rooms.'

This was a long speech for Lydia, and a lot of information for her to give at one time. Clam wasn't the name for her; safe deposit, more likely.

'I see,' said Betty.

'He's pleasant enough,' said Lydia. 'He cut the grass and adjusted the mower so that it works better.'

'Good,' said Betty.

When they arrived at the lodge, Edward was to be seen up a ladder cleaning the windows.

'There he is,' said Lydia.

'Well, now!' Betty was pleased. A window cleaner occasionally came to Milton St Gabriel, but he sometimes forgot to call at the lodge. The bungalow windows were easier to clean if he was pressed for time. 'I'll soon find him a little list of jobs that want doing,' she promised, getting out of the car.

Edward had decided to carry out one useful task for Mrs Cunningham every day. In that way, she would feel awkward about asking him to move on, and besides, it was only right that he should do something for her in return for his bed and board. He'd noticed how smeary the windows were after the rain. The job

56

wouldn't take long and he polished away with a will, whistling.

Thelma was in the kitchen finishing a late breakfast when the two older women entered.

'Well, Betty, you see the bad penny's turned up again,' she said.

'You're lucky to have your mother to take you in,' said Betty, taking off her Dannimac and hanging it on the back of the kitchen door. 'Now, what's the trouble this time?' After knowing Thelma all her life, she had no inhibitions about questioning her.

'Oh – men,' said Thelma largely.

'You liked him enough to go all that way, didn't you?' Betty said, putting on her house slippers. She tied her apron round her generous waist.

'You can't tell till you live with someone,' said Thelma.

'Well, I know that's the modern way, more's the pity,' said Betty. 'But at your age you should act more respectable.'

'Come off it, Betty,' said Thelma. 'Life begins at forty. Didn't you know?' She got up as Betty began to clear the table.

'Time you settled down,' said Betty, but she spoke in a tolerant tone. Thelma hadn't been lucky; she'd married that second husband on the rebound, for sure, after Charles's death. Her father had been anxious about it right from the start, but even he hadn't been able to prevent her from going ahead. It was all very sad and just showed you could never tell how things would work out. Thelma had been such a pretty child, with appealing ways; she'd twisted her father round her little finger and even her mother let her get away with blue murder, though they were both always picking on Gerald, who was such a good little boy. Betty hadn't seen much of him after his marriage; she'd

57

thought that Iris a stuck-up sort of girl but the two children, Fiona and Christopher, were nice enough. Really poor Mrs Cunningham didn't get much joy from her family, Betty thought, getting the vacuum cleaner out of the cupboard.

She plugged the machine into a socket in the sitting room, then, before switching it on, began moving the furniture away from the walls. Perhaps that young man would look at the cleaner; it hadn't been working very well lately. If it needed a part, Mrs C. could collect it that afternoon when she took Betty home.

But Thelma decided that she would do that.

'It'll save you the trouble, Mother,' she said.

She'd scream if she spent another whole day in the village. Besides, she wanted to get her hair done and buy a few things. She'd got her bank card which she could use to save paying now; the next instalment of her income would reach her account on the first of the month.

'Where'd you find that young man, then?' Betty asked as Thelma drove her, much too fast, down the lane. Various signs, as she tidied up Thelma's room and made her bed, had revealed to her the nature of their relationship which they seemed to be having the tact to conceal from Mrs C., poor blind soul.

'In London,' said Thelma airily. It wasn't a lie; the train had begun its journey at Paddington.

'Hm.'

'Oh, Betty, you and your "hms",' said Thelma, and laughed. 'Where's your sense of adventure? You only live once.'

'Yes, and you only die once, too,' said Betty. 'And then you've got to account for it all.'

'Do you still believe that?' Thelma asked, changing gear roughly. Her mother was a far better driver, Betty reflected, glad now of the support of the seat belt as

Thelma hurled the car round corners. She had to jam on the brakes hard when they met a delivery van head on with no room to pass. The van driver reversed to a passing place and Thelma gave him a cheery wave as they drove by, so that he smiled.

'Of course, and so should you,' said Betty, a staunch Baptist. 'I'm sure your mother always brought you up to do so.'

'Well, she's given it up now,' said Thelma. 'She never goes to church.'

'How can you say that? Of course she does!' exclaimed Betty. Regular as clockwork, off they'd gone every Sunday, and Mr C. had been a churchwarden right up to his death, reading the lesson each week.

'You're wrong, Betty. She gave it up after Daddy died. I don't think she's been since the funeral.'

The church had been full then; local dignitaries, the Lord Lieutenant, the Chief Constable and representatives from the council had turned out that day, as well as most of the village, and Thelma had wept throughout the service while her mother had remained dry-eyed and stony-faced, exhibiting the stiff upper lip for which women of her and earlier generations were renowned. Thelma had not seen her shed a single tear.

'I didn't know,' said Betty. 'Are you sure?'

'The vicar spoke to Gerald about it,' said Thelma. 'Typical of the church – always wanting someone else to do its dirty work. Why couldn't he ask Mother direct?'

'Did Gerald?'

'No, and quite right too. She still supports the good causes – goes to the fête – all that sort of thing,' said Thelma.

Perhaps she thought the Lord had deserted her, Betty reflected. Poor soul, denying herself such a source of comfort. Betty didn't know where she would be without the support her religion gave her. Still, that was the way of it, these days. All the same, she was surprised that Mrs C. was to be numbered among the heathen.

6

Thelma swirled the Metro into Malplaquet Drive and dropped Betty outside her bungalow.

'See you next week,' she called, thus answering Betty's unspoken query as to whether she planned to stay on in Milton St Gabriel.

She drove towards the town and left the car in a side road before sauntering into the main street. The day was grey: clouds lowered over the estuary where the boats lapped at their moorings. Thelma felt chilly in her cotton boiler suit. She saw an end-of-season sale on at Liza's, a fashion shop, and went inside, where she bought a voluminous sweater knitted in heathery shades of mohair, and not reduced. She paid for it with her bank card and put it on, feeling warmer straight away. The climate here compared unfavourably with that of California. Her departure from the States had left no time for general maintenance and her hair needed a fresh brightening rinse; she went along to see if The Copper Nob could fit her in this afternoon. Her mother never went to the hairdresser; she trimmed her own hair, pulling it over her shoulder and clipping the ends. Thelma had once caught her doing it, had seen the bald dome of her mother's head and been shocked by its ugliness. Lydia had put her hands to her skull to hide it and shouted to her to go away, quite frightening Thelma.

Her luck was in. The hairdresser had a cancellation and soon Thelma was leaning back over a basin being shampooed.

The atmosphere soothed her; while she waited for Luigi to attend to her, she listened to the talk around her and heard another customer, who was being dyed, talking to the girl daubing her hair about a new drama group which was going to put on *The Seagull* in November. They were casting now, and she hoped to secure the role of Arkadina.

Immediately, Thelma knew what she must do. That part shall be mine, she decided; and everything else went out of her head as she listened hard, hoping to learn who the producer was, or any other relevant details. She was unsuccessful; the salon was busy and most of the clients were chatty, their voices drowning the one she wanted to hear. The other woman was still being worked over when Thelma left, her own hair now standing out in a gleaming mass of golden spirals.

She walked down the road wondering how to find out more. In the Public Library, perhaps?

Her attention was caught by a billboard outside the newsagent's, once owned by Betty's husband. RATE RISE FORECAST, she read, and wandered in. She wanted to order *The Stage*, and it occurred to her that the shopkeeper might know about the dramatic society.

He did. There was a feature about it in the latest *Cheverton Gazette*. The new group replaced one that had withered away some years ago, prone as it was to putting on Brecht and other difficult works of limited appeal. The newsagent thought *The Seagull* sounded good; he supposed it to have a maritime theme of local interest.

Thelma did not disabuse him. She bought the paper and took it away to study. There were details of a meeting that evening at the producer's house in Willow

Close; some parts would be cast then, and if necessary there would be readings. Thelma went to the bookshop, and rather to her surprise, found that they had a paperback volume of Chekov's plays, which she bought, again using her card. By now the bank was shut and it was too late to get any money. She walked on up the hill to the Swan Hotel, where years ago she had so often been with her father. A treat had been lunch in the restaurant, or tea in the panelled lounge – toasted tea cakes sopping with butter in winter, by the fire; clotted cream and jam with scones in summer.

The lounge was unaltered. It contained comfortable chairs, and Thelma sat there reading the play, thinking herself into the part of the vain and beautiful actress as she refreshed her memory.

She had just enough cash to pay for her tea. When she went back to collect her mother's car, there was a parking ticket under the wiper blade. Thelma tore it up and drove off to Willow Close. A number of other cars were drawn up outside, and she saw the woman from the hairdresser's walking ahead of her up the path.

Thelma displayed confidence; she mentioned that she had been a professional actress before her marriage, and when several scenes were read, she performed with attack. The dark woman, who had failed to prepare the part, was cast as Masha, and Thelma secured the role of Arkadina.

Edward had spent the afternoon with Julie. She usually had the afternoon off because she came on duty so early, but she sometimes had to turn beds down at night and be ready to help out elsewhere.

They'd got a lift down to Worton Bay with Victor, who had a girlfriend there. Her parents ran a café lying back a short way from the beach in the huddle of tourist shops and fishermen's cottages which clustered in a fold of the hills. Because of the poor weather, they had had a bad season, and the place was empty when the trio from the hotel arrived. After they had all had tea, Julie and Edward went for a walk on the beach.

The tide was coming in. Edward picked up a stone and flung it as far as he could towards the horizon. A ship in the distance moved slowly along, a dark smudge against heavy clouds.

'Bit miserable, isn't it, when it's not sunny,' he said. 'Still, it's nice to get out.'

'Mind you stay out,' said Julie.

'Oh, I will,' said Edward. 'I'm going to light a bonfire for Mrs Cunningham tonight, or maybe tomorrow. She's got a pile of stuff waiting to be burnt. That'll do me.' He was looking forward to it, had planned how he would lay paper and the drier stems and stalks at the base, touch it off with maybe a little paraffin to obtain a blaze, then stoke it and allow it to smoulder.

'See that it does,' said Julie. She had never been able to understand his compulsion which came on when things weren't going too well for him. He had fired the car after a girlfriend he'd been going out with for several months threw him over. At school, when exams loomed or when he found work difficult, he had started blazes in waste-paper baskets and once in the boiler room. He'd gone to a psychologist then, and had been suitably penitent, but it hadn't lasted. It would be dreadful if something went wrong at the lodge. Suppose he annoyed the old lady in some way, and she got cross? He might want to kick back at her. There was something fishy about his being a guest of the daughter: Julie had never seen Thelma, but she had heard about her; she didn't sound like a do-gooder or prisoner's friend.

'How long are you planning to stay here?' she asked.

'I don't know. I'll see how it goes,' said Edward. 'I've got myself a few little jobs, mowing lawns and painting, things like that. Some of the folk in the new bungalows are wanting help in the garden. They'll pay me well.'

'Has Mrs Cunningham said you can stay on?'

It seemed that putting him up at the hotel had not crossed Julie's mind.

'We've not discussed it,' he replied. 'I'm doing jobs for her, too. She needs someone to help her along.'

'Be careful,' Julie warned.

'Why wouldn't I be? She's a nice old bat and Thelma doesn't treat her any too well,' said Edward. 'She went off in the car taking the cleaning lady home, and she wasn't home when I left just now. Mrs Cunningham's meant to be going to supper with some friend in Wilcombe. I hope Thelma comes back in time.'

'Oh, she will, surely?' said Julie. She hesitated, then had to ask. 'What about you and Thelma?'

'Oh, that's nothing,' said Edward. 'Bit of a turn-off, as a matter of fact.'

'Oh, Eddie, you don't mean to say you and she—?' Julie's heart sank. What had he got himself into? 'Why, she must be years older than you.'

'I can't help it if she fancies me,' said Edward smugly. 'But if you ask me, she doesn't like it all that much. I had to go along with it, didn't I? It'd have been rude not to.'

'Just fancying isn't enough,' said Julie curtly. 'You've got to like the bloke.'

'Oh, is that right?' Edward was put out at the thought that Thelma had found him wanting. 'I'd say it won't happen again,' he added, promising nothing.

Julie was only partly mollified.

'Watch it,' she repeated.

'What's her brother like?' Edward thought it was time to change the subject.

'I don't know. I haven't seen him,' said Julie.

'Well, he's coming for the weekend. Staying up at your place, it seems,' said Edward.

'You just watch your step, then,' Julie warned. 'You may have got round the old lady and her daughter but he'll know what's what. He'll have you out in minutes if he takes against what's going on.'

'Nothing's going on,' said Edward. 'And you don't have to worry. I don't want another stretch, believe me.'

'But you said you couldn't help yourself, before. You could get like that again.'

'No way. I just flipped,' said Edward.

But that hadn't been the first time and he might flip again. Julie watched worriedly as he suddenly ran away from her down the beach, arms waving like a small boy pretending to be an aeroplane. He let out chortles of pure joy at his physical freedom, swooping and swerving and leaping into the air, thin legs in faded jeans twinkling as he pounded over the band of seaweed at the tideline and across the foreshore towards the café where they had left Victor.

Julie followed more slowly. He had inveigled his way into Mrs Cunningham's house, whatever he might say about having been invited. What if she found out about him? Challenged him? Turned him out? For she wouldn't knowingly house an ex-con.

Julie shook herself. If she wouldn't believe in him, who would? She had a duty to him, like it or not, and she'd run away from it during his sentence. What if he were to get a regular job here, in the district? Would he settle to it or would he become bored in the winter, when there was so little to do? Thelma Hallows was only slumming, taking up with him; wouldn't she throw him away as a dog might an old bone?

Filled with foreboding, Julie followed her brother across the road, passing the souvenir shop with its racks of fading postcards but no customers, to the deserted café.

7

Gerald Cunningham's emotions as he turned into the Manor drive on Friday evening differed from Thelma's, but he too regretted that this was no longer his home.

If things had been different, he could have contrived to stay on, striking a deal over selling off some of the land to provide funds for putting the house to rights, as in fact had eventually happened. But on paper the place was worth a great deal and the smart divorce lawyer Iris had hired had pressed her entitlement to a very big settlement, so that now she and her new husband occupied quite a large house and had been able to open their business. Gerald hoped that, since he had subsidized this, the other family – Iris's step-children and their mother – were suitably supported too. It was all a sad pity.

It pleased him to find the Manor restored and fully used, and with his investment he still had a stake in its future. He took his bag into the hall, registered at the desk and was allotted his room, following the porter up the wide front staircase and along the passage to number eleven. This had been a spare bedroom, seldom used. Part of it had been sectioned off and turned into a bathroom. A television set was supplied for the guest, and brochures advertised places of local interest; there were potteries and gardens, museums and a few stately homes all within a moderate radius. Gerald glanced idly through the leaflets; he hadn't known about half these places.

He wasted no more time in nostalgic reflection. All his life he had got on with the next task as soon as the last one was finished, and now he washed, shaved quickly – his beard was so dark that he looked unkempt by evening – put on a clean shirt and then walked down the drive to the lodge. It was good to stretch his legs after spending so long in the car, and he gratefully inhaled the warm night air. In spite of the appalling summer, autumn was delaying its arrival. All the extra rain must have persuaded the leaves to cling longer to the trees, he thought.

As he approached his mother's house, he reminded himself of some facts. I am a successful banker earning a high salary and attempts have been made to head-hunt me to other concerns where I would earn still more. My advice is asked for and listened to with respect by eminent persons. Therefore it is foolish to feel now as though I were ten years old, returning from school and longing for an affectionate, approving welcome from my mother. I didn't receive it then, and I won't now. I'll never please her, he decided, but at least I can do a little to help her, unlike Thelma, who turns up whenever the fancy takes her and expects a welcome like that given to the prodigal son – and gets it. That story had always seemed to him an example of grave injustice.

Squaring his shoulders, Gerald approached the house, where lights showed behind the curtains. The garage doors were open, the light above them on, and the car was out. It was irrational to expect his mother to be at home waiting as eagerly to greet him as he was to see her. He had said he would stop for a meal on the way down and might be late arriving. Why shouldn't she be out? Though she rarely was, unless she went to see Dorothy Butler, her one real friend, a retired schoolmistress who lived some thirty miles away.

His spirits had already slumped as he moved to the front door. It was Thelma whom he must now prepare to meet. He nearly turned back, putting it off till the morning, but Gerald was one who always saw things through.

The door was on the latch. Gerald opened it and went into the small hall. Boris at once came to welcome him. Friend and foe alike, Boris would greet any visitor with joy.

'Well, boy.' Gerald stooped to pat the dog. The sitting-room door was ajar, and he went into the room, followed by Boris still wagging his tail.

His mother was seated in front of the table before an incomplete jigsaw puzzle. The outline was filled in, and she held a piece in her hand as she turned to him. Sitting close to her was a young man in jeans and a red sweater. Gerald immediately sensed the accord between the two. It did not cross his mind as he advanced, his features arranged in a warm smile, that this was Thelma's friend, and his head was full of questions.

'Ah, Gerald. There you are,' Lydia said. She stood up, moving easily, with no sign of arthritis or rheumatism. They did not kiss; she was taller than he was, and it would have looked ridiculous. 'I never heard the car,' she added, and he detected reproof in her tone.

'I went straight up to the house – I needed a wash,' he said.

'There is a bathroom here,' Lydia observed.

Two put-downs in less than a minute: that must be a record.

'Well, I'm here now,' said Gerald firmly, and looked towards the stranger, who had risen to his feet. He was thin and rather pale, with short brown curly hair.

'This is Edward Fletcher,' Lydia introduced. 'My son Gerald.'

'Pleased to meet you,' said Edward. He beamed at Gerald, anxious to create a favourable impression.

'Thelma's friend,' Lydia supplied in level tones.

'Where is Thelma?' Gerald asked.

'She went out,' said Lydia.

'She's acting in a play, in Heronsmouth,' said Edward eagerly. 'She's the star.'

'What, already?' Gerald's thick, dark eyebrows rose.

'It's a rehearsal tonight,' Edward explained. 'It's all about a seagull. By some Russian.'

Gerald looked at his mother, who nodded.

'She's Arkadina,' she told him.

'So she'll be staying here a while,' said Gerald, with misgiving.

'Where else is she to go? She's let her flat,' said Lydia.

'And how long are you staying?' Gerald turned to Edward, smiling pleasantly to take any hint of challenge from the question.

'I'm not sure,' Edward answered. He hesitated, then took a gamble. 'Do you want me to go?' he asked Lydia.

'Only when you're ready,' said Lydia equivocally.

'You're on holiday, I suppose?' said Gerald, who supposed nothing of the sort. The young man's much-washed sweater and his faded jeans were no real guide to status, but his wrists were gaunt; he looked – what? Unloved was the word that came into Gerald's mind as he surveyed the visitor.

'No. I'm unemployed,' said Edward. 'I've a sister in the village and Mrs Cunningham is very kindly letting me stay so I can see her. I'm hoping something in the work line will turn up.'

'Edward has done a lot of useful jobs since he arrived,' said Lydia. 'Cut the grass, mended the mower, cleaned the windows, repaired the vacuum cleaner, unblocked the sink –' she paused to think of another achievement to add to the catalogue.

'Splendid.' Gerald admired the interloper's frankness. The length of his sojourn depended, no doubt, upon Thelma's whim. What was their relationship? 'Are you performing in the play too?' he asked.

'Oh no,' said Edward hastily, and to avoid further questions he offered to take Boris out for a final run, leaving mother and son alone.

The whisky, brandy and sherry that Gerald had brought for his mother were in the boot of his car. He did not suggest they had a drink as Thelma might well have used up all his mother's supplies. Here was his chance, though, to have a proper talk with her, find out what was in Thelma's mind, but he could not take it; instead, he asked about the jigsaw and, tentatively, tried to put a piece in position.

Now that she was a member of the drama group, Thelma was more cheerful. After she had secured the part, she had gone with her new associates to the King's Arms, where some of them, Thelma included, made it a prolonged session. She was unaware of the fact that her mother had wanted the car to go to Wilcombe for supper with Dorothy Butler.

Thelma had held court in the pub. She had told amusing tales of life in Los Angeles, repeating stories she had heard from others, mimicking them and using their success to achieve her own. Her blue eyes sparkled, her cheeks grew flushed, and the man cast as Trigorin, a dentist with a practice in Cheverton, thought himself lucky to be playing opposite someone so full of life and charm.

Left at home, Lydia had eventually telephoned Dorothy, who was Thelma's godmother.

'I didn't make it clear to her that I needed the car,' she

71

excused, when Dorothy made tutting sounds on the line.

She had rustled up omelettes for herself and Edward. He went out after they had eaten, not telling her that he was meeting Karen White from next door lest she might think him faithless.

In the morning, Lydia did point out to Thelma that she – and what was worse, Dorothy – had been inconvenienced.

'You should have said you wanted the car,' Thelma answered sulkily.

'It never occurred to me that you wouldn't come home fairly soon,' said Lydia. 'Never mind. Let's just make sure we don't misunderstand one another again.'

'I'd like the car tonight, then,' Thelma said. 'And I don't know what time I'll be back.' On the excuse of reading through the play in preparation for the first rehearsal, some of the company had planned to meet again.

'Gerald's coming down,' her had mother pointed out.

'Well, I'll see him in the morning,' Thelma said.

For different reasons, Lydia and Edward were both relieved to be spared her presence and were content to spend the evening together. Karen's father had come home and she was staying in; there was nowhere else to go, except to the pub or the hotel. Edward washed up, whistling; then he made coffee for Lydia, sending her into the sitting-room while he did so.

Interrupting their concentration on the jigsaw only to watch the television news at nine, they had spent a harmonious evening until, at last, Gerald arrived.

'That's Thelma's latest, is it?' Gerald said, after he had failed to fit any pieces in the jigsaw.

'I think she's lost interest already,' Lydia said. 'It was just a passing fancy.'

'Well, he is a bit young for her, isn't he?' said Gerald

lightly. It was better not to make too much of it. 'I expect she was upset at that American thing not working out.'

'She's so unlucky,' Lydia sighed.

Oh, of course, thought Gerald. There's always an excuse for her.

'Don't let her take advantage of you, Mother,' he had said aloud. 'She'll wear you out, if you give her half a chance.'

'This is Thelma's home,' Lydia said. 'She is welcome here.'

It had happened again. The atmosphere between them had become strained within minutes of their meeting. Gerald stood up, turning away from her as Edward returned.

'I'll go now,' he said. 'It's late and I'm sure you're tired.' It would not occur to him to plead fatigue himself after his day in the City and the long drive, although he suddenly felt totally exhausted.

'Nice guy, your son,' Edward observed when Gerald had gone. 'Successful, too, isn't he?'

'Yes,' said Lydia. 'I suppose he is, in a way.'

But he had not been able to keep his wife, and he had lost the family home which had meant everything to his father.

As Gerald was walking away from the lodge, Thelma returned. She braked, with a scurry of gravel, her headlights picking up the short, stocky form of her brother, his hands in his pockets, trudging towards the entrance to the Manor. Thelma pipped the horn, making a lot of noise.

'Hullo, Gerald,' she called.

He walked back to meet her, his resentment giving way to rueful affection as he focused on her, blonde hair in alluring disorder, a light coat worn over her pale tracksuit. She was a pretty woman.

73

'So it didn't work,' he said bluntly.

'No. Lucian isn't good husband material,' said Thelma.

'Good thing you found out in time, then.'

'Yes, well, I'd rather live in England, anyway,' said Thelma, who had just thought of this idea.

'I hear you've landed a fat part,' Gerald said.

'Mm – only amateurs, but still, it'll be fun, and I'll add strength to the company, with my experience,' she said.

It was years since Thelma had performed, even with amateurs; still, Gerald answered kindly.

'It'll help you get back into the swing, I expect,' he said.

'Like a lift up the drive?' she offered, in her turn making an attempt to bridge the divide between them.

'No, thanks. The walk will do me good,' he replied.

'Suit yourself,' said Thelma.

Gerald walked away from her full of anger at himself. This was not how he had intended things to be, with discord between his mother and himself and now a surge of hostile feelings towards his sister. Trying to capture a more positive mood, he walked past the house across the garden to the swimming pool. A pale blue bubbled plastic sheet covered it now, retaining warmth until the morning. They wouldn't keep it going for much longer, with this dark, dank weather. Behind the wall that sheltered it, well-tended beds produced vegetables for the hotel guests. He turned to look back at the building, where lights showed at several bedroom windows and were still on in the public rooms. Inside was comfort, if not company, and he slowly walked towards it.

The receptionist was listening to someone on the telephone, and before she saw Gerald, he heard a burst of laughter from her. The sound was such an unusual one to Gerald, in his present life, that it startled him.

She put the telephone down and came towards him, smiling still.

'Yes sir?' she asked, an ordinary girl of twenty-five or so, with unremarkable features and brown hair, but a person who was happy.

'I've got my key,' said Gerald. 'Room eleven. I didn't hand it in.'

'Oh, that's all right, Mr Cunningham,' she answered. 'Would you like tea in the morning, or a paper?'

'I'd like *The Times*, please,' said Gerald. 'No tea, though, thank you.' Then he hesitated. He always woke so early. Why not have a cup of tea and a lie-in, for a change? His mother wouldn't want to see him very early.

He asked for it at seven-thirty, and the cheerful receptionist wrote it down.

8

Next morning, Gerald's tea was brought by a pale girl in a grey dress. Her dark hair was tied in a ponytail and she had sandals on her bare feet.

Julie knew who he was, of course. She glanced curiously at the dark man who, when she entered, was already sitting up in bed with his glasses on, reading a very thick book. He wore pale cream pyjamas piped with crimson, and a forest of dark hair was exposed at the neck.

Would he find out about Eddie's past and send him packing?

She worried about it all the morning, and in her agitation she broke a saucer, which meant that she had yet another breakage that week to confess to the housekeeper.

Gerald went for a swim before breakfast. He had to uncover the pool first, rolling the plastic back, a task better done by two people. He must mention it to Mrs Thomson, discover tactfully if energetic guests were catered for when the weather was better; they should not have to do this themselves. It was quite useful to stay in the hotel, find out its merits and flaws for himself.

The water was pleasantly chill, refreshing him. He swam a great many lengths, not enjoying it much but aware that it must be doing him good. By the time he had showered, shaved, and had breakfast, he was feeling more relaxed than for several weeks. The same cheerful receptionist was on duty. He wondered what shifts they did; it was something like hospital doctors, he thought: long spells on and then a good break.

'I shall have some guests for dinner tonight,' he told her. 'I should have mentioned it in the dining-room but the head waiter wasn't on duty.'

'No. He doesn't do breakfast,' said the girl. 'I'll see to it for you, Mr Cunningham. How many will you be?'

'Oh – four, I think,' said Gerald. 'Yes.' That was right, with Thelma's young man. 'About eight?' His mother did not like eating late.

'I'll pass it on to the dining-room right away,' she said.

Gerald walked briskly down the drive in a much lighter mood than that of the previous evening, but when he reached the lodge, no one seemed to have time for him. Edward was out in the garden trimming the tufted grass beneath the trees which the mower could not reach, his mother was arranging some late roses in a bowl in the sitting-room, and Thelma was in the kitchen, ironing. His mother went on with her flower arranging after her usual cool greeting, and even Boris barely looked up.

Gerald went into the kitchen to talk to his sister.

'Want to tell me what happened in America?' he asked.

'It's none of your business. I told you as much as you need to know last night,' said Thelma.

Gerald counted to five in his head before he replied.

'I'm not just being curious,' he said, successfully keeping impatience out of his tone. 'I thought you might need some brotherly sympathy, that's all.'

'I'm not asking for any,' said Thelma, thumping the iron down hard on the sleeve of a shirt.

'I don't like to see you unhappy,' said Gerald.

'I'm not unhappy,'said Thelma. 'Not at all. Unlucky, yes, but then we're an unlucky family.'

'Why do you say that?'

'Well, Daddy dying and losing our money,' she said.

'Father was getting on for seventy. He'd had a full life,' said Gerald. 'And he didn't lose money. He never had a lot of it.'

'He should have married a woman who had some, then,' said Thelma, now tackling a green cotton skirt. She poked the iron into a fold by the zip. 'Not a penni- less vicar's daughter.'

'What a dreadful thing to say!' Gerald was outraged.

'I don't know why you're so shocked,' said Thelma. 'People have always done that.'

'You know perfectly well that theirs was a wartime romance,' said Gerald.

'It wasn't like that at all,' said Thelma. 'Daddy was never in love with mother. He married to carry on the line. He was afraid he'd be killed, like his brother, before he had an heir.'

'Good God!' Gerald exploded. 'You talk as if he was a duke or something. His family had a manor house and some land. That was all.'

'It was very important,' said Thelma. 'But it didn't mean a thing to you or you'd have never let it go.' Then she smiled, a sly, smug grin. 'Anyway, he made sure she could have children before he married her,' she said. 'Got her pregnant first. He told me he was very disap- pointed because I was a girl but as soon as he saw me he forgot about that, and you arrived ten months later, so it was all right in the end.'

Gerald stared at her. She was saying that it had been a shotgun marriage. Surely that couldn't be true! Not his parents! He realized that he had never known the actual date of their wedding, only the year. They had never celebrated their anniversaries, and even their birthdays had passed without the exchange of gifts and greetings, though the children's were suitably marked. As he grew old enough to realize how swiftly his own birth had followed that of his sister, Gerald had decided that he had been premature and that this was why he was so short, a notion he had held for many years until Iris laughed it to scorn. She had been shocked when she discovered that Gerald was vague about his parents' birthdays and she had found out the dates and seen that they were greeted thereafter. Their silver wedding had already passed by the time she and Gerald were married.

Thelma was pleased with the effect of her words.

'Daddy told me. It's the truth,' she said, ironing on.

His mother seduced, misled: Gerald couldn't take it in.

'Well, he didn't get killed,' he said, and abruptly turned the conversation. 'How long are you staying?'

'I haven't decided,' said Thelma. 'I'm doing this play in November.'

November! There was the rest of September and all October to get through first! Gerald looked round the kitchen. Thelma's clothes lay about on every surface, some ironed, some awaiting attention.

'Doesn't Mother want to get into the kitchen?' he asked. 'Couldn't you do your ironing in your room?'

'I shan't be long,' said Thelma.

'I think you should let Mother know your plans,' he said.

'It makes no difference to her,' said Thelma. 'I'm sure she's glad of my company. Besides, this is my home.'

This was just what their mother had said. Gerald's patience snapped.

'We've left the nest, Thelma,' he said. 'We've both been married, for heaven's sake. If you are going to stay, you should make some contribution towards your keep. Maybe Betty could come more often. It's a lot for Mother, having two extra. She's getting on, you know, and she's used to a quiet life.'

'She's as fit as a flea,' said Thelma. 'She walks miles with Boris. It'll do her good to be dug out of her rut. Besides, I'll do most of the cooking. I'm a much better cook than she is.'

'Well, as long as you do,' said Gerald. 'Don't just let things drift. Couldn't you get a job?'

'Doing what?'

'Well – cooking,' said Gerald. 'You could be a country cousin, or whatever they're called. Go as a temporary live-in cook and be paid very well, and all found.' What an inspiration, he thought, pleased with it.

'I wouldn't be able to go to rehearsals then,' said Thelma. 'Besides, I'd be just a skivvy.'

'You wouldn't. You'd run the house,' said Gerald.

'What – for someone like Mother? Some senile old woman who can't manage her own affairs?' Thelma set the iron down hard and glared at him.

Gerald felt his blood pressure rising.

'Mother is anything but senile, as you very well know,' he said. 'And she could perfectly well manage her own affairs if Father had left her any to handle. If you can't stand working for a woman, find yourself some old man to look after, a rich widower. That might be just what you need.'

So saying, he angrily left the room. Thelma was distracted from replying only by the smell of singeing as she scorched her skirt.

'You bloody man!' she yelled after him as Edward came into the kitchen through the back door.

'Not quarrelling with your brother, are you?' he asked. 'Dear, dear, that won't do.'

'He's a pompous, interfering ass,' seethed Thelma.

'Thinks he's so bloody marvellous because he sits in a damned bank all day deciding who can and who can't buy companies. Well, he can't tell me how to run my life, that's for sure.'

'He seems all right to me,' said Edward, and then, 'Oh look, you've scorched your skirt.'

Thelma picked up the dish cloth and flung it at him.

'Don't you start,' she shrieked, but Edward had already retreated.

Lydia had heard the sounds of her children's raised voices as she finished arranging the roses. She gathered up the paper containing the stripped-off thorns and snipped leaves and stems and went through the french window into the garden. Would they never learn to agree? Their hostility had been limited in their adolescence because they had spent most of their time apart at separate schools, and in the holidays pursued different activities. Gerald had preferred riding his bike to ponies; he had liked watching birds, and helping the men on the farm.

Edward had intercepted Lydia as she set off down the garden to put her rubbish on the bonfire pile.

'I'll take that for you,' he offered. 'I'll burn up what's there, too, before it rains and gets soaked.'

'Make sure it won't blow across any of the neighbours,' said Lydia.

'There's no wind,' Edward pointed out. Then he laughed. 'My word, you wouldn't think Thelma had such a temper, would you? What are they fighting about?'

Lydia thought it might very well be him and his unsuitability as a partner for Thelma.

'I don't know,' she said. 'Gerald isn't always very clever with Thelma.'

'Nor are you, are you?' asked Edward, holding the

bundle of clippings to his chest and regarding her quizzically.

'What do you mean?' Lydia's invisible hackles rose, and the tone of her voice ascended in response to this impertinence.

'Let her walk all over you, don't you?' said Edward. 'She takes your car without so much as a word – turns your place over – even moves me in without a by-your-leave. It's not right.' He backed off towards the bonfire spot as he spoke. He might have gone too far.

But Lydia followed.

'She's my daughter,' she said. 'She has a right to be here and to borrow my car. This is her home.'

'Well, you've got rights too, haven't you?' Edward said.

Sometimes this very thought had occurred to Lydia, when Thelma returned in tatters at the end of one of her sorry adventures, but she had always banished it; a mother's obligation to a child was the greater.

'She's been unlucky,' she said. 'Have you matches?' She nodded towards the rubbish dump.

'Oh yes,' said Edward. He wasn't comfortable unless he had a small pack or a lighter, though he didn't smoke at all.

Lydia returned to the house, disturbed. It had been wrong to discuss Thelma behind her back, and she never permitted adverse criticism of her daughter.

Gerald had been cooling down in the garage, where he checked the Metro which shone after Edward's ministrations. Oil and water were in order. When he could prolong this activity no more, he walked the length of the garden to where Edward had started the bonfire. Gerald watched him for a while without speaking. He was rapt, absorbed.

'You're quite the boy scout, aren't you?' Gerald said at last.

'What? Oh!' Edward rubbed a grimy hand across his forehead and laughed. 'Sorry – I didn't realize you were there,' he said.

'It's all so damp, I'm surprised it burns,' said Gerald. 'I'd never have got that to go without paraffin, I'm sure.'

Edward did not reveal that he had used some, pouring it liberally over the kindling base, watching it flare up high before piling on refuse.

'It's got a good bottom,' he said. 'That's the secret.' Oddly, a memory came to him of helping his old grandfather with a fire at the end of the long, narrow garden in the part of Birmingham where his grandparents had lived. He'd forgotten about that until now.

He heaved a forkful of rubbish over part of the blaze; it was a pity to douse it like that, but still, the fire had a purpose. Smoke rose in a plume as he stacked on more rubbish.

'You're a useful guest,' said Gerald.

'It's ever so good of Mrs Cunningham to put me up,' said Edward, and went on quickly, 'I've fixed myself up with some gardening and decorating jobs in the village. It'd be just temporary, for the next week or two. I was going to suggest that I might be a proper lodger – pay for my room and that – if you don't think she'd be offended?'

'Hm.' Under such an arrangement, would Lydia be able to turn him out if she tired of his presence? Present-day laws favoured tenants over landlords and criminals over their victims. But a couple of weeks shouldn't be enough to establish squatter's rights.

Edward had sensed his hesitation.

'If she wants me to go, she's only to say,' he assured Gerald. 'My sister will be able to put me up later. She can't at the moment.'

'Where does she live?' asked Gerald.

'Over there.' Edward pointed vaguely in the general direction of the Manor.

He was saved from having to give more details by Lydia, who came out to say that the Dennises had rung up to ask if the bonfire would be alight long. They were having a barbecue that evening, and would prefer it to be extinguished by then.

'Funny, that. They'd be within rights to complain because we'd lit it before six o'clock,' said Edward. 'Or it may be six-thirty. I'm not quite sure.'

'What do you mean?' asked Lydia.

'He's right,' said Gerald, chuckling. 'In built-up areas, you're not meant to light bonfires until the evening. On the principle, I suppose, that people will have gone indoors by then.'

'We don't worry about things like that in Milton St Gabriel,' said Lydia regally. 'But now I suppose we're to put up with the smell of fried onions wafting across the fence.'

'Well, that won't bother you. You'll be tucking into a good dinner down at the Manor,' said Gerald. 'You and Thelma are coming too, of course,' he told Edward. 'Would you like to invite your sister and her husband?'

What a thought! Julie, a chambermaid at the hotel, to be included in the evening! As it was, it would be quite a turn-up for him to be there, himself.

'That's kind, but she's busy this evening,' said Edward. He couldn't begin to explain.

'Some other time, then,' said Gerald.

'Right,' agreed Edward.

'You're not going to be able to get into the kitchen, Mother,' Gerald told Lydia. 'Thelma's got half her wardrobe draped all over it. Why don't we take Boris for a walk on the shore and leave these two to it? We could have something to eat at the Crab and Winkle.'

'Oh, that would be nice, Gerald. Thank you,' said Lydia. 'Boris will enjoy that.'

'And so will you, Mrs Cunningham, won't you?'

Edward prompted her. 'Get you away from her for a bit.' He nodded his head towards the house. 'She'll soon cool down. Leave her to me.'

He always felt powerful when in control of a fire.

Perhaps some attention from her latest conquest would soothe Thelma's ruffled feelings, Gerald thought; he was amused at the young man's masterful advice and happy to take it as he drove off with his mother.

'Do you know Edward's sister?' he asked as he edged his BMW carefully down the main street past the mail van, parked while the postman made deliveries. A couple from the hotel, in strong shoes and raincoats, tweed hats on their heads, trudged along for the good of their health, and old Admiral Hughes tottered towards them on his way to Mrs Dodds's shop, a basket over his arm. As a young man the admiral, then a lieutenant, had been responsible for the destruction of at least two German submarines in the Mediterranean.

'I know very few of these new younger people,' said Lydia.

'He wants to stay on with you until she's got space for him – as a paying lodger, I mean,' Gerald told her.

'Oh! He's said nothing about it to me,' said Lydia.

'No. He thought you might be offended,' Gerald explained.

'I don't think anyone's offended at being offered money these days,' said Lydia, who for some years had acted as custodian at a stately home not because she enjoyed mounting guard over the treasures, but because she was paid a small sum for attending. This year, for no given reason, she had been told that there were enough guardians and it would be unnecessary for her to put herself out to take on the duty.

Lydia had bitten back protest: what was the use? Their minds were made up to exclude her from the clique that had developed among the group of women and the few men who annually acted as guides and supervisors.

'I can hardly take money from one of Thelma's friends,' she said.

Gerald thought that she could, and from Thelma, too, if she planned to stay long.

'I think he means this independently of her,' he said. 'It wouldn't be for more than a week or two, I gather.'

'Well, we'll see,' said Lydia.

Gerald parked the car on the cliff above Worton Bay and hurried round to open the door for her. Boris tumbled out of the back, and they set off down a narrow track to the beach. Gerald was reminded sharply of past expeditions to this spot laden with beach towels and picnic baskets, himself always overburdened in his perpetual endeavour to exhibit masculine strength while Thelma skipped ahead empty-handed, her fair hair bouncing about on her shoulders. She swam better than he. He sighed at the recollection.

'Are you lonely, Gerald?' Lydia asked suddenly, as they walked along on the shore.

Gerald was startled. He could not remember her asking him anything so personal before.

'I've plenty of company during the day, at the bank,' he replied.

'You know that's not what I meant,' said his mother. 'You must miss – er – being married?' Her voice rose at the end of the sentence, demonstrating that she expected an answer.

She meant sex, of course.

'Well, now and then, perhaps,' he said carefully. 'But I have friends, mother.'

Women friends were implied: Lydia did not wish to pry.

'You might marry again,' she said, and added

quickly, 'Your private affairs are your own business. I'm sure you're discreet.'

He didn't think that he was, particularly.

'There's no one special,' he said.

'It's all so different, these days,' Lydia said, with unusual feeling in her voice. 'People – er – taking up with one another and then moving on.'

'Like Thelma, you mean?' he dared to say.

'And most of the population, from schoolgirls upwards,' said Lydia tartly. 'If one can believe what one hears. It makes for a very unstable society.'

'People have always had affairs,' he said gently, not wanting to snub her but anxious to turn her observations into a discussion, and prompted, too, by Thelma's earlier remarks into feeling tentatively curious.

'But with much more serious consequences than today,' she replied. 'Girls took risks. They didn't have the opportunities that they've got now. Not that it makes for happiness, all this freedom. There's no sense of duty.' As she spoke, she walked faster, head poking forward studying the ground ahead. 'Ttch – look at that rubbish.' A plastic detergent bottle, some carrier bags, an old tin and other detritus adorned the band of seaweed rimming the beach.

Gerald was more interested in watching the sand dry out around his feet under the pressure of his weight, a phenomenon that had always fascinated him. He thought of his daughter, whose way of life worried him.

'I don't think people today work at their marriages much,' he said. 'That's a generalization, of course. But I'm sure Iris and I didn't. I just took it for granted that she was content, but she wasn't.'

'People demand such a lot,' said Lydia. 'In my day, girls adopted the position in life their husband provided. Some bettered themselves, others didn't, but each knew her duty.' And if you didn't marry, you were reckoned to be on the shelf at twenty-two, a doomed old maid. 'You were provided for,' she continued aloud, 'and you vowed to be faithful and obedient.' She paused. 'It meant total submission. For better or worse, and if worse you just knuckled under and didn't complain.'

'No young girl makes that sort of promise today,' he said. Then, cautiously, he asked, 'Was father a hard taskmaster to you, like he was to me? When you were young, I mean?'

'Oh yes!' Lydia addressed her reply to her sensibly shod feet in their K Skips.

The admission could cover so much. Gerald waited before adding a gentle prompt.

'I suppose as a child I wouldn't have noticed,' he ventured at last. 'I mean, if Father and you quarrelled.'

'We didn't,' said Lydia. 'I had promised to obey, you see. Soon, as a person, I ceased to exist. I'm what he made me – a robot, you could say.'

'Oh Mother, no!' Gerald was appalled, yet even as he protested, he realized that what she said was true. When had he ever heard her, until this moment, express her own views?

Now that she had at last started to speak, Lydia's words began to flow, somewhat jerkily, like a stream breaking past a dam.

'I'm probably shocking you, Gerald, but your generation needs reminding what life was like for mine. How things were between your father and me wasn't untypical. And one carried on, you see. Divorce was a scandalous thing and took place for one reason, adultery.' The word spilled harshly into the damp, salty air between them. Two seagulls spiralled nearby, raucously calling.

Gerald remembered the easy dissolution he and Iris had obtained two years after they parted; there had been no contumacious argument, very little rancour. Of course, he had surrendered without a struggle.

'Girls have it too easy today,' Lydia pronounced. 'Things were too hard in my time – if you left a marriage, you got no support and what could a young mother do? It's quite the thing to be a single parent these days, it seems – even without ever having been married. A whole generation of lost, unanchored children will be roaming the world.'

Gerald sometimes shared this view, when he woke in the night depressed about Fiona.

'Any infidelity is serious,' Lydia went on. 'It's a symptom. It happened in the war because people couldn't stand the loneliness. That's a reason, not an excuse. People took risks and marriages broke up later over things that were only a matter of consolation.' She walked on, head down, marshalling her thoughts. 'Girls married – or sometimes they – er – anticipated marriage because the man might be killed the next week. Often they'd only met a few times and then they had to try to build a whole life together. Like Betty's GI bride sister.'

'But you and father had known each other for years,' Gerald said, unable to relate any of this to his parents, even after what Thelma had told him.

'We were acquainted,' Lydia said. 'The age gap between us would have kept us apart anyway as children, but later I was thought suitable to be asked to tennis. Then we coincided once on leave. I was doing my nursing training then. I never finished it.'

'You were good at tennis,' said Gerald. 'I never managed to beat you.'

'No. You weren't much good at games,' his mother said dismissively.

To his horror, Gerald felt his male middle-aged eyes prickle with sudden unbidden tears at the familiar disparagement.

'Thelma was,' he said with an effort. 'Is, I mean. Perhaps she'll take it up again. Tennis.'

His mother sensed the strain in his voice and knew that she had made a mistake. She too withdrew, changing the subject to ask about Fiona.

'Isn't it time she found something worthwhile to do?' she said. 'She should train for a career.'

'I agree,' said Gerald. 'But Iris has other ideas. She wants her to make a good marriage. In a material sense, that is. So you see, it still goes on.'

'Well, she won't get pregnant, will she?' said Lydia. 'However she occupies her time. She won't have to marry in order to save herself and her family from shame and disgrace.'

Was that why she had married his father? Soon afterwards, her father had moved to another living some distance away. Gerald did not remember his maternal grandparents at all. Had they failed to treat their daughter with Christian charity?

There were so many questions he wanted to ask, but he did not dare; his mother's mood had broken.

Surely, whatever the truth of the later years, there must once have been passion between his parents? Why else had he been conceived so soon after Thelma's birth?

The passion, of course, had died, as passion tended to do.

9

Perhaps the insurance company would pay for her scorched skirt, Thelma thought, banging the iron down hard on a pair of slacks. She was annoyed because her mother and Gerald had gone off in his car without saying where they were going, but Edward seemed to know when he returned to the house.

'He's taken your mum off for some peace,' he told her. 'And she needs it, poor soul, with you two at each other like that. Can't you get along?' It seemed sad to him; his own sister had been his best friend until he went to prison, and her failure to visit him latterly had been part of his punishment.

'I don't know why he had to come down here, poking his nose into what isn't his business,' Thelma grumbled.

'He probably wanted to make sure I wasn't going to rob you both, or murder you in your beds, or something,' said Edward cheerfully.

'Why ever should he think you might?' Thelma briefly emerged from her self-absorption to marvel at such an idea.

'Well, you haven't known me long, have you?' said Edward. 'For all you know, I'm an escaped murderer.' He pulled a face at her, gibbering.

'If you were, it would be on TV,' said Thelma flatly. 'Don't be silly.' She hung her slacks over the back of a chair and asked, 'Have you any washing?'

'Gee, thanks, I thought you'd never ask,' drawled Edward in what he thought was a Hollywood accent.

'I'm not offering to do it. I'm suggesting you should put it in the machine while Mother's out,' Thelma snapped.

'You're too kind.' Edward swept her an exaggerated bow. 'But I've already taken it to my sister. She's only too pleased to do it for me, knowing how helpless I am.'

Julie had grudgingly accepted a bundle he'd put in one of the hotel polythene bags supplied to guests for their laundry, and agreed to pass it into the system.

'Oh,' said Thelma. 'That's good.'

Edward bowed again, and this time, in spite of herself, Thelma's scowl was replaced by a wintry smile.

'You look pretty good when you smile,' he told her. 'Let's see you do it again.' He went towards her, set a hand on either arm, and kissed her nose.

Thelma laughed and melted against him. She felt no desire herself, but was always consoled if she aroused it in others, and they were alone in the house.

Edward had not meant things to go so far, but he had nothing better to do at the moment, and lighting that bonfire had made him feel rather good. Besides, he owed her something.

Thelma was rather ashamed of her conduct and wanted to drive the memory of it out of her mind. Her mother always adopted such a placatory, patient manner towards her, as if she must be humoured at all costs. It was almost as if she were afraid of her own daughter, but that couldn't be so; after all, what had Thelma ever done that had harmed her? The only person who ever got hurt was Thelma herself.

This thought, which came to Thelma as she tried to enjoy Edward's bony embrace, was not welcome. She pushed it from her mind, concentrating on her present activity, but once again she found no pleasure in it.

'Why do you bother?' asked Edward at last, sitting up in bed when their transports were concluded. 'I don't turn you on, do I?' He spoke sadly, regarding the failure as his.

'No,' she admitted, and then, with sudden candour, added, 'It's not just you, it's everyone. That is, everyone I've tried until now.'

Edward stared at her.

'Even your husbands?' He knew now that there had been two.

'Mm.'

'You've not got the knack.' he told her, after a pause for reflection. 'It's a gift, you know.'

'I suppose it is. Either you have it or you don't,' she said. 'Though why shouldn't I? I can do most things.'

'I didn't mean that,' said Edward. 'It's the gift of yourself.'

'Well, I did give you myself,' Thelma pointed out, swinging her legs over the side of the bed.

She still had a lovely body, her ribs tapering to a narrow waist and then swelling out into the soft curve of her hips. She might be too plump for some tastes, but Edward admired her generous charms and they had led him to expect a nature to match.

'We're not going on together, you and me,' he told her. 'Like this, I mean.' He gestured at the crumpled sheets. 'Not in your mother's house. It isn't right – she wouldn't approve, not a lady like her, at her age. She's one that'd have old-fashioned ideas about things and I don't want to upset her.'

'What about upsetting me?' Thelma demanded. 'Don't you care about that?'

'Not as much as her,' said Edward. 'Anyway, you do plenty of caring about yourself, so no more is needed.'

93

As he finished speaking, he snatched up his clothes and, holding them against his nakedness, left the room.

Thelma's instant pique turned to anger. They were all against her, every one of them trying to put her in the wrong, dumping her for their own selfish reasons, no one caring what became of her. Even her mother's welcome had been lukewarm and she hadn't asked how badly Thelma had been hurt by Lucian. For all her mother knew, he might have damaged her physically, instead of merely wanting her to leave. For some minutes she shed tears of fury; then – for there was no witness, no one to offer sympathy and her eyes would get all red – she began to simmer down. She blew her nose hard, went into the bathroom, turned on the taps and ran a deep bath. There was no bath oil, which annoyed her; her mother indulged no hedonistic weaknesses and used only Imperial Leather soap and Pond's cold cream, with a little compressed powder to mask the worst of the shine on her face. Funny, that; when Daddy was alive, she used a little lipstick. She'd always worn her hair in that curious Edwardian style; perhaps it was better than some ill-fitting, badly chosen wig.

She scrubbed herself hard, wanting to remove every trace of Edward from her body; then she dressed in clean clothes and made up her face carefully, outlining her eyes and applying deep pink shadow to the lids. Downstairs, the Metro's keys hung on a peg on the dresser: her mother, out with Gerald in his swanky BMW, could not possibly require it. Thelma drove off in search of diversion from yet another disappointment.

There was no sign of Edward. By the time she had left the village she had successfully forgotten him.

Never one to dawdle, Thelma pushed the little car along the twisting lane. Going round a bend too fast on the wrong side of the road, she narrowly missed an oncoming car whose driver stood on his brakes before reversing to let her pass.

'Silly fool,' she said, aloud.

She drove on, not showing any caution until, when she reached Heronsmouth, increased traffic forced her to slow down and begin to concentrate.

Where now? Why, to the Swan, of course, where Daddy had so often taken her for their little treats together. It was past one o'clock and she was hungry.

Thelma turned into the hotel yard, which bordered the estuary, and parked the car. Gulls cawed and some pecked in the mud below the tideline as she walked towards the hotel's side entrance, so convenient for access from the water. She went into the saloon bar, ordered a crab salad and a glass of lager, and sat down at a window table to enjoy them. Food was a great solace, and if it were not for the fact that she often felt compelled to take violent physical exercise, Thelma would have had a serious weight problem. Now, she felt a warm glow deep within her as she drank down half the glass of beer. Then she looked around her, waiting for her salad to arrive.

Thelma was used to going into bars on her own, and she had often, in her restless search for company, found adventure there.

She hated to be alone. For an honest instant, she admitted that to herself as she sat in the respectable panelled and leather surroundings of the Swan's bar. When you were by yourself, thoughts crowded in, many of them unwelcome and upsetting. In company, you could forget everything except the moment; there was always the chance that just around the corner was the cure to misery. It was like acting, when even if the character you portrayed was wretched and despairing, you knew that all her troubles were imaginary and would go at curtain fall.

Sitting there, Thelma told herself that she was a great actress, as talented as Peggy Ashcroft but as beautiful as Gladys Cooper in her youth. She had stayed beautiful all her life, Thelma remembered, and had not both these great ladies of the theatre been married more than once? All she need do was wait for the present clouds to pass and her life would blossom: some famous director would, by chance, be staying in the district when *The Seagull* was performed and would see her, deciding she was just the person he was seeking for his next production, and another man would come along to love her and take care of her, and turn her once again into one of a pair.

Her salad arrived while she sailed on this pleasant sea of fantasy; the comfort of the food and drink and her own invention wrought a transformation in Thelma's appearance as her low mood was dispersed. Her face filled with colour, and her body, which had drooped with dejection as she entered the hotel, grew tense and taut. Her pulse speeded up and she looked about her in a subtle way, avoiding any eyes which might be turned towards her, as some celebrity, aware of being stared at but evasive in her modesty, might do.

In fact, several people had looked up when Thelma took her seat. Most of them were middle-aged or elderly couples enjoying a Saturday drink, local residents pleased to have their town and their hotel returned to them as the season ended, and a few late tourists. One man, however, had seen Thelma before, and he remembered that occasion clearly for she had been wearing not a stitch. It was the elderly man who had witnessed her swim in the pool at Milton St Gabriel.

Thelma saw two women sitting together at one table; at another were three more; over in a corner, a quartet of what looked to her like aged crones talked animatedly about a golf foursome they had played the day before.

The thought that she might continue through her life unpartnered, ending up like them, frightened Thelma badly. She reminded herself that she still had the power to attract and thrust away the knowledge that what came next was what she lacked.

Arthur Morrison had noticed Thelma's quick, assessing glance about the room. Nowadays, you couldn't tell just by looking at her whether a woman was available or not, but he already knew that this one was unhampered by inhibition. He watched her covertly as she ate her salad. She had a second glass of lager, and as she fetched it from the counter, she saw him looking at her. Each held the other's gaze for just a moment, and Arthur smiled. He looked a nice old boy, thought Thelma, smiling back. It was encouraging to see a man alone, even though he was quite old.

Arthur had finished his veal and ham pie. He toyed with the dregs of his pint of bitter as she ate up her salad and slowly drank her beer. She left the bar first and he followed her. She returned to the car park, but she did not get into her car; he saw her leaning over the wall looking at the water where the moored boats moved gently on the incoming tide. A customs launch puttered down towards the sea, and some people in a dinghy rowed out to a tall-masted yacht, their oilskins yellow against the blurred greys and browns of the dull day. Further up the river, the ferry chuntered across to the other side where small houses rose in stepped layers among the yellowing trees to the skyline.

Arthur Morrison moved to a spot by the wall away to her right. He did not speak to her for several minutes, for it was many years since he had attempted this manoeuvre.

10

Arthur Morrison was a widower. Soon after they had moved to Heronsmouth, when he retired, his wife had fallen ill and within three months was dead. They had come to the West Country to be near their son, but within a year Nicholas was moved by his firm to Leeds. This was promotion which he could not turn down. Arthur decided to remain in the solid, comfortable house above the estuary; there was no guarantee that Nicholas would not be moved again, and the notion of retirement spent in Leeds was less appealing than life here, where the pace and the climate were gentler. He had made some friends, mainly through the bridge club he had joined. Most of the members were elderly widows but there were some couples, a few of whom were also new to the area.

Arthur enjoyed the company of women and sadly missed his wife, whom he had loved with faithfulness for more than forty years, but he sometimes grew depressed by the white heads and arthritis common to the members of the bridge club.

This girl in the boiler suit, with her mass of springy golden curls was not conventional. If he spoke to her, she was unlikely to be shocked, Arthur thought, composing and discarding various opening sentences in his mind. Foolish old man, he told himself: of course you want to pick her up, to talk to her, because you're intrigued by her and because you're bored. She's alone. She may be bored, too. You can drop her, sharpish, if you've miscalculated, and she won't scream and cry rape if you simply speak about the weather. At the worst, she'll walk away.

But she wouldn't; he knew that; not after that smile.

Aloud, Arthur regretted the grey skies and damp air.

'Yes.' Thelma said, and added, tritely, 'Winter won't be long.' She turned on him the radiant look which had captivated more sophisticated men than he. 'But it's lovely to be back in England. Everything's so green. Oh – not here –' she waved at the grey water and the leaden skies, '– but in the countryside.'

'Oh – have you been away?' For she was a native Briton, that was certain from her voice.

'I've just got back from Los Angeles,' Thelma said.

'And what were you doing there?'

For some reason that she couldn't understand, Thelma immediately told him the truth.

'Shall we go for a walk?' Arthur suggested. 'I often stroll along here by the water.'

'All right,' agreed Thelma, who now felt embarrassed by her frankness.

But Arthur had seen, as her bleak words fell quietly between them, that her spirit was bruised, and he knew that it was often easier to confide in a stranger than someone closer.

'You were well out of it,' he told her.

'Yes, but what am I going to do now?' Thelma appealed to him.

'Have you made no plans?' Poor dear, how sad she looked with her beguiling blue eyes brimming full of tears and her pretty fair curls misted with damp from the moist air around them.

'Not really,' said Thelma. 'Only the play.'

She told him about it, forgetting her self-pity in her enthusiasm.

'But that's good,' he enthused. 'I used to like acting.' Long ago, he and his wife had been members of a dramatic society.

'Why don't you join us?' she suggested.

'I'm too old,' he said.

'No, you're not,' she said. 'But Shamrayev's been cast. What a pity. Do you know the play?'

He did, and was sorry she had not seen him as the doctor rather than the wheelchair-bound old soldier.

'I'll come to the performance,' he promised.

'Do you live in Heronsmouth?' she asked.

'Yes. Up there.' He pointed in the direction they were going, up the hill out of the town. 'You can't see the house from here. It's beyond the headland, before you reach the Cliff Hotel. It's called The Shieling.' He paused to glance sideways at her, not averse to being seen out in the town with so attractive a woman. He liked her pretty, petulant face, her provocative walk, the sudden flashing smile which turned her into a beauty. 'A most inappropriate name,' he added.

'Why?'

'A shieling's a hut. Mine's a comfortable Edwardian villa,' he told her.

'You could change the name.'

'There's a superstition that it's unlucky if you do,' he said.

'Oh, is there? I didn't know that,' said Thelma.

'What are you going to do now?' he asked. 'After our stroll, I mean? Go back to your mother's house?' She had told him that her mother lived in a village some six miles away. Did she make a habit of going round the local hotels for her lunch?

'I don't know,' she replied.

'I'd love to ask you to tea,' he said. 'But at four

100

o'clock I'm due to play bridge with three charming elderly ladies.' He laughed as he spoke. 'I'd much rather play truant, but there we are, I'd spoil the four.'

'My mother doesn't really want me at home,' Thelma said, and now she sounded like a sulky schoolgirl.

'I'm sure you're wrong,' said Arthur. 'Were you very attached to this man in Los Angeles, or did he just answer your problem about what to do next?'

'I thought I was,' said Thelma. 'But I was wrong.'

'You don't often admit that, do you?' he asked her.

How did he know?

'I suppose not,' she said grudgingly. 'You're a mind reader,' she added.

'Not really,' he said. 'I've just been about longer than you have and I know how stubborn one can be.'

'I'm not exactly young,' said Thelma. 'And I've been married twice.'

'You seem young to me,' he said. 'What happened?'

'My first husband was killed in an accident,' she said. 'And I split from the second.' That was a better way to put it than to say he had left her.

'I'm sorry about that,' he said. They had reached the end of the harbour walk, where the path now became a track approaching the headland. 'Look, you can see my house now,' he added and lifted his walking stick to point it out to her. 'There – the white one with the gables. The window frames are blue, but you can't see that from here.'

Thelma looked across at the row of solidly built houses, once the homes of tradesmen, Merchant Navy officers and other worthy citizens of Heronsmouth, most now converted into holiday flats or boarding houses.

'Isn't it rather big for you, on your own?' she asked. He must be unpartnered, like her, or perhaps his wife was away.

'My wife died after we'd moved here when I retired,' he said. 'I like the house and I don't want to move again.'

'I see.'

He did not want her to go, but the afternoon was passing and soon he must prepare for his bridge.

'Have you a car?' he asked.

She nodded.

'Yes – in the Swan yard.'

'I'll walk back with you, then,' he said.

'Won't that make you late?' Thelma glanced at her watch.

'I think there's just time,' he said.

She wondered what was wrong with his leg; he had quite a pronounced limp although he could walk quite fast. She did not like to ask, but when they returned to her car, she offered to drive him up the hill to his house.

'Otherwise you may be too tired for your game,' she said, smiling.

He accepted, inserting himself into the Metro's seat, then pulling his stiff leg in after him.

'How nice of you,' said Arthur. Then he plunged. 'Will you have lunch with me on Monday? Perhaps you'll have made some plans by then. You'll be staying in the area, won't you, because of the play?' He wondered how she was placed financially. Nowadays, appearances told you nothing. He was unsure if young widows received pensions; anyway, the remarriage would have cancelled that out. She obviously had means enough to run a car and take herself out to lunch, and to fly the Atlantic, but perhaps the American suitor had financed her trip.

'I'd like that. Thanks,' she said.

Both of them were pleased to have something to look forward to.

'Shall we make it the Swan?' he said. 'Quarter to one?'

It was agreed. She dropped him at his door, turning in the driveway, and he stood and waved her off.

Thelma drove down the hill again, past the narrow pavements where shops and houses leaned against one another, huddling into the lee of the hill. At the bottom, as she turned inland, there was a new block of holiday flats on the site of a former hotel. There had been an outcry because it had been totally gutted, but it had not been pulled down and the so-called renovation fell within planning regulations. There were To Let signs in a window, she noticed as she stopped at a pedestrian crossing nearby.

She could rent one.

She was elated when she returned to the lodge.

What had she been up to? Lydia's heart sank as she saw her daughter's shining eyes and heightened colour; she had learned that these were signs that Thelma had found a new interest which very often turned out to be masculine, and had embarked on a fresh path to disaster. Thus had she looked when she married Charles, radiant in cream satin to match the family Honiton lace; thus had she looked at her second wedding, in a register office, when she wore a white wool dress with a flower in her hair. Thus had she been before setting off for the States, and on countless occasions in between. Still, at least her sunny mood would probably last through the evening, and that was something.

They dressed for dinner according to their resources. For Thelma, this meant a white crepe off-the-shoulder dress with loose billowing sleeves which began at her upper arms, a gold necklace, bracelet and drop earrings to match, and a lot of eye make-up. Edward whistled when she appeared in this garb five minutes after they were due to meet Gerald in the bar at the Manor.

103

'We'd better take you in the car, Princess,' he said. 'It's damp out. What do you say, Mrs Cunningham?'

'That won't be necessary,' said Lydia. 'We've all got the use of our legs and the distance is only a few hundred yards.' But though her words and her tone were wintry, she was almost smiling.

'You're very smart, if I may say so,' Edward told her, deciding not to call Mrs Cunningham Duchess, which had occurred to him. He felt excited, stimulated by the prospect of dining in such style. His lifestyle had certainly undergone a fundamental change within a week.

'You may,' Lydia allowed, graciously. Tonight, her hair was secured by a purple velvet band, and she wore a plainly cut dress in shades of purple and maroon. It offset her high colouring and in it she looked almost handsome. The dress was one she had had for years and it had originally been expensive; it was too short, though: Edward noticed that as the two women put on their coats. Styles had changed. It displayed, however, Mrs Cunningham's thin and still shapely legs; on her long, narrow feet she wore black leather court shoes with a medium heel.

Edward had bought himself a pair of white cotton trousers for this engagement, deeming jeans in the evening unsuitable. Karen White from next door, hearing where he was going, had lent him one of her father's ties and a blue and white striped shirt with a white attached collar which was much too big but which looked good with the trousers. Edward was sorry that Karen could not be included in the party and had promised to take her to the Blue Dragon in Cheverton if he could borrow Mrs Cunningham's car some night.

They caused quite a stir as they entered the bar. Gerald had to admit that Thelma looked stunning, her bright hair set off by the costume jewellery, her fair skin emphasized by the white of her dress, her blue eyes shining. His face creased into a welcoming smile as he settled them round a table near the log fire which, on this chilly evening, was burning in the hearth. Edward hovered, at first ill at ease but soon reassured by Gerald's friendly greeting.

'Now – what will everyone have? Mother?' Gerald rested his hand on the back of his mother's chair, standing beside her, catching the eye of Ferdy who immediately came round from behind the bar to take the order.

Thelma, who wanted a Bloody Mary, might have been drinking already, thought her brother: the flush on her cheeks could very well have been caused by alcohol. She seemed to be in a good mood, whatever the reason.

Edward would have liked a beer but was not sure if that would be in order here. Mrs Cunningham had chosen sherry, so he did the same. When it came, it was so pale and dry that it made him wince. He sipped carefully, copying her.

Gerald ordered another double gin and tonic for himself. Somehow he felt a long evening lay ahead, and he had so far done nothing to solve the problem of Thelma's future. Perhaps her improved humour would endure until the next day and they might be able to have a constructive talk. This evening should be devoted to having a good time – not always easy in any family, and especially this one.

But one person was enjoying himself without any doubt. Edward, once the sherry took effect – which it did quite quickly – relaxed. If his companions of only a week ago could see him now, he thought, sitting back in the deep leather-upholstered armchair. Here he was, living it up like a lord, accepted simply because Thelma had introduced him into the family.

If they knew the truth, they'd all have shown him the door.

He thrust the thought away and spoke to Gerald.

'Must have been nice when you lived here,' he said. 'Don't you wish you still did?' He wasn't quite clear why Gerald hadn't been able to keep the place on; he wasn't short of a bob or two, after all. Something to do with his marriage breaking up, Thelma had said, and she felt bitter about it.

'It was lovely when we were children,' Gerald side-stepped the question. 'Wasn't it, Thelma? We had space – which we took for granted, of course – room to play, trees to climb.'

'Ponies and that?' Edward suggested.

'Thelma did. I never took to riding,' said Gerald. He grinned, not choosing to recall being forced to ride a small bad-tempered pony called Brownie with a mouth like iron and a perverse nature. Only after Gerald had broken his collar-bone and an ankle after his umpteenth fall from the animal had he been reprieved. It was a waste to keep a pony no one was using, his father had said, and Brownie had gone. Gerald never asked where; he didn't mind if the little brute had been turned into meat. 'I preferred my bike,' he told Edward. 'Where do you come from?'

'Birmingham,' Edward said. 'My dad worked in a car factory – still does.' He'd had spells out of work and spells on strike, but there had been prosperous periods too. He and Julie had always had plenty to eat and good clothes to wear.

Before Gerald could ask him any more questions, the head waiter arrived to take their order. Thelma took a long time to make her choice. She changed her mind several times, drawn variously to venison, roast duck, or veal in an elaborate wine sauce, finally settling for the venison. Edward chose it, too; he'd never eaten it and might not get another chance. Mrs Cunningham chose veal.

'Think of all those poor little calves,' said Thelma. 'How could you?'

'They're dead anyway. Not eating them won't resurrect them,' said Gerald, who had chosen duck.

He had suggested that everyone should select their main dish first, then a starter that would go with it. Edward longed to ask for smoked salmon, but saw that it cost extra.

'It's dear, isn't it?' he murmured to Lydia, who had decided on chilled cucumber soup.

'Thelma will choose it,' Lydia answered softly. 'You'll see.'

She was right. After deciding against crab mousse because she'd had crab for lunch, Thelma did so.

'Wouldn't you like that, too, Edward?' asked Gerald, who had caught his mother's eye and for once not misread its message.

'Yes, please,' Edward replied, eagerly.

Gerald was reminded of taking Fiona and Christopher out to meals, and their undisguised greed. Gluttony, although allegedly a deadly sin, was not as damaging to others as some of the remaining six, he thought: or not as practised at this level.

During the meal, Thelma began to talk about *The Seagull* and how she would interpret her role. Edward had no idea what the play was about, and so the story was related, everyone chipping in to make sure he missed none of the points.

'I was in it before,' Thelma told him. 'I was Nina, the young girl, then.'

No one mentioned that she had only been the understudy, called on because of the illness of the principal.

'She has a hard time, doesn't she? This old writer guy leading her up the garden, I mean,' said Edward.

'He's not so old,' said Thelma. 'But he and Arkadina had been together for years.'

'I've always disliked that woman,' said Lydia, setting down her glass. The waiter had topped it up three times without her noticing.

'Who?'

'Arkadina, of course. A very vain creature,' said Lydia firmly.

Gerald hid a smile. He was pleased to hear his mother speak so positively, and he resisted the temptation to say that Thelma had been perfectly cast.

'It's a classic role,' Thelma told Edward, ignoring her mother's remark.

'It's a classic play,' said Gerald. 'We must all go to see it. You must get us tickets, Thelma.'

'All right,' said Thelma. 'It'll cost you, though. It isn't free to members of the cast.'

'Relax. I'll pay,' said Gerald.

'Dorothy went to Russia in June,' said Lydia, breaking in. Thelma could be very tiresome.

'Dorothy is your friend you were going to have supper with when Thelma kept the car?' said Edward, wanting to make sure he'd got it sorted out.

'Yes,' said Lydia.

Gerald managed to bite back a comment on this revelation of his sister's behaviour.

'Tell us about Dorothy's trip,' he said quickly.

'You'll have to ask her yourself, really,' said Lydia. 'It seems to have been most interesting. Of course, she'd read it all up, as you'd expect, and knew what she was seeing. They were filming in Red Square, she said – Boris Godunov, it was – horses and actors everywhere. She went to Leningrad as well as Moscow. A land of contrasts – that was what she said. Magnificent palaces full of gilt and colour, and the people looking drab.' Lydia had grown quite animated, telling them about it.

'You should have gone with her,' Gerald said.

Lydia did not answer. Her friend had gone with an upmarket cultural group and Lydia could not have found the money, even if Dorothy had been prepared for her to join the tour.

Gerald resolved to sound Dorothy out about her future plans; he would gladly pay for his mother to join her on another trip. It was time she made up for all those years immured at the Manor with his father, going nowhere; it was not too late for her to see the world.

At this moment Lydia's cucumber soup arrived and Thelma decided to tell them all how it should be made. The head waiter, overhearing, said the chef had prepared it just as she described but with the addition of a secret ingredient.

'It's excellent, I'm sure,' said Lydia.

'You can't argue about smoked salmon, anyway,' said Gerald. 'It either is, or it isn't. How's yours, Edward?'

'Very tasty,' said Edward, who in fact found it rather disappointing. Still, you couldn't know unless you tried a thing.

He enjoyed the venison, though, savouring every morsel of the rich dish, shovelling it into his mouth as though he feared his plate might be snatched away before he had finished. Across the table, Gerald noticed this, and Lydia too, but Edward was not aware of their critical observation. He sensed interest from another area, however, and glanced up. A waitress standing beside the sweet trolley nearby was staring at him, and he saw that it was Julie, all tricked out in a black dress and frilly apron.

She was a chambermaid. What was she doing in the restaurant?

At this moment she was frowning at him severely

and gesturing as if using a knife and fork, and he realized she was commenting on his table manners.

He glanced round and saw that the others had rested their knives and forks on their plates whilst they were speaking. Lydia, anxious to mask his uncouth lapse, had begun a discussion with Gerald about Christopher, his son, who was working with a wine producer in Bordeaux, learning both the French language and the trade. Gerald said he seemed to be enjoying himself, though all he had received were several postcards. Lydia had had one too.

Thelma, not remotely interested in her nephew's career prospects, interrupted.

'I wonder how well the Heronsmouth Players will dress their production,' she said. 'I want some good costumes.'

'I'm sure you'll get them, Thelma,' said Lydia, unwilling to let this become a problem so far ahead of time.

'I suppose they'll hire them,' said the star.

'Maybe they've got a clever little woman who'll run them up out of old curtains, like Scarlett O'Hara,' said Gerald, who had been much taken with Vivien Leigh's striking appearance in her green velvet outfit.

'I don't like wearing things other people have used,' said Thelma, wrinkling her nose.

'I'm sure you won't have to do that, Thelma,' said Gerald. 'You very rarely do anything you don't want to, do you?' He leaned across the table to pour more wine for his mother, and Edward decided to draw the flak away by offering an excuse for his poor manners.

'I got rather hungry today,' he said. 'Sorry if I was eating too fast.' His plate was nearly empty.

'What were you doing, to give yourself such an appetite?' Lydia asked, looking kindly at him.

I was in bed with your daughter, trying to make the

earth move for her, Edward thought of saying, but instead informed her that he had taken out the row of runner beans that was over – another row was still cropping – and had burned them since he had the bonfire going so well.

'It has died down now, hasn't it?' Lydia asked anxiously.

'Yes. I made sure it was out,' said Edward. 'It hadn't all burnt up, but I can always light it again.' He liked that thought.

When Julie wheeled the sweet trolley to their table, she looked very demure, her mouth primly arranged in a straight line, happier now that Eddie seemed to have remembered where he was. They all chose raspberries and cream, with Thelma wanting meringue as well.

'And you, sir?' she asked Edward. 'Would you like trifle with yours?' She knew that he loved it.

'Yes, please,' said Edward, trying not to giggle as Julie served him generously, the cream washing dangerously close to the lip of his plate as she set it before him.

'She's taken a fancy to you,' remarked Thelma.

'I'm sure I can't think why,' said Edward, who was on the brink of dissolving into hysterical laughter.

The head waiter had noticed a certain amateur approach on the part of Julie Fletcher, the stand-in waitress. Victor had bribed one of the regular waitresses to feign toothache so that, as a dare, Julie could take her place and enjoy the spectacle of Edward dining in style.

Julie had been in two minds about accepting the challenge; she was so uneasy about Edward's presence, a cuckoo in the Cunningham nest, that part of her would prefer to ignore the whole thing; the other, less anxious part, thought it might all be rather fun, and she was reassured by seeing how easy the quartet seemed together; the Cunninghams could be a good influence on Eddie if only he didn't step out of line. As she finished serving the table, the head waiter swam up to Gerald.

'Everything all right, sir?' he inquired. 'Madam?' He inclined his head towards Lydia. He had spent a year at a big hotel in Lucerne and aspired to higher things than his present position; here, it was all too informal.

'Yes – excellent, thank you,' said Gerald.

'Very nice indeed,' affirmed Lydia. 'The raspberries are delicious. Are they from the garden?' In the old days, hers were long over by now but there were some new late-fruiting strains.

'They come from Scotland, madam,' said the head waiter, and he moved away in response to a call from another table.

Here was Edward's chance to introduce Julie, acknowledge his sister's identity and at the same time pay her out for her trick.

But Gerald was looking at her intently.

'Are you one of twins?' he asked. 'I could have sworn you brought me my tea this morning.'

'I did, sir,' said Julie. 'One of the proper waitresses is ill and I'm standing in for her.'

'I see,' said Gerald. 'You've worked a long day, then.'

Edward knew it was all a set-up; the illness was faked so that Julie could keep an eye on him. Gerald would take the deception in good part, he was sure, but the old girl and Thelma were different; there was no knowing how they would react.

He kept quiet.

11

Gerald walked back with them down the drive after they had all had coffee and liqueurs. Even Lydia had accepted a Cointreau.

'Just to settle the meal,' she excused her indulgence.

Why could she never enjoy something for its own sake, wondered her son.

'Are you coming in?' she asked him, when they reached the lodge.

What for, he wondered bleakly. There had already been longueurs in the conversation while they drank their coffee and sipped their drinks. If he went into the lodge with them now, what would follow? Would he and Thelma embark on another spat? He longed for his mother to press him, but she merely stood by the door waiting neutrally for his response.

'I'm sure you're tired, Mother,' he said. 'Goodnight. I'll come down again in the morning.'

'Goodnight, Gerald. Thank you for an excellent evening,' said Lydia.

'Yes – thanks – er.' Edward felt inhibited about calling Gerald by his first name. The word 'sir' kept springing to the tip of his tongue. Gerald was definitely one of 'them'. 'It was great,' he added.

Thelma had entered the house without a word. Gerald turned back feeling as forlorn as when he was a small boy returning to school. Well, on Monday he would be safely in the bank again, with the hum of computers and the ordered bustle of high finance to protect him from family life.

Back in the hotel, he ordered a brandy. An elderly couple touring the district began telling him how they had spent the day and he passed a pleasant half-hour with them.

Was this his future? Anxious visits to his mother, always tinged with guilt because his father had made her dependent upon him, interspersed with sexual encounters that were often furtive and too fleeting to merit any better description? Was there never to be more?

He went for a stroll in the grounds before going to bed, passing the stable block where his mother had hoped to live. Part of it had been converted into accommodation for resident male staff; the women workers were housed in the attics where Mrs Thomson had her flat. Several windows showed lights, and Gerald, glancing up from the shadows, saw a girl reach out to draw a curtain. He had time to recognize the maid who had brought his tea that morning and who had waited on them at dinner. A man stood beside her, and Gerald saw that it was Edward.

Well, he had not wasted much time, Gerald thought, and smiled to himself. How would Thelma react to this, if she discovered the dereliction?

He had not seen Victor, who had just handed Julie the ten pounds she had won by deputizing for Mavis and who was also in the room. The four stayed together for some time, listening to music and innocently drinking coffee.

Lydia had let Boris out for a final run. She walked down the garden behind him, inhaling the damp night air. People had been smoking in the hotel; not many, it was true, but enough to remind her of how the smell of Henry's tobacco had clung to the curtains and lingered about the place.

Boris, who rarely barked, lolloped up to the boundary fence uttering restrained yaps. From beyond came the strains of pop music as the Dennises' barbecue party continued. Lydia admonished Boris, wondering how long the noise would go on, and whether anyone besides herself would find it irksome. If she opened her bedroom window, she would hear it. Why must they play it so loudly? The Dennises, surely, both embarked on a second marriage, were too old for such juvenile conduct and lack of consideration for other people.

But people of any age jostled against you on pavements, pushed into you in shops, thrust you aside if you got in their way. She collected up Boris and returned to the house where Thelma was sitting looking at television.

'That party's still going on at the Dennises,' Lydia said.

'I know. I can hear it,' said Thelma. 'It's early yet. It'll last a lot longer, I expect.'

'Where's Edward?' asked Lydia.

'Gone to see his sister,' said Thelma.

'Isn't it rather late for that?'

'Not really. We don't all go to bed at ten,' said Thelma.

'It's almost eleven,' Lydia pointed out. 'And I'm going up. Goodnight, dear.'

She glanced round the room, plumped up a cushion, paused at the jigsaw but, without her glasses, saw no likely piece to insert, and went out of the room. Thelma heard her moving about in the kitchen settling Boris and no doubt finicking about with her obsessional tidying. At last she went upstairs.

Thelma lit a cigarette and puffed smoke defiantly

round the room. She rarely smoked, believing it to be unhealthy but as a girl she had done it to annoy her mother and demonstrate rebellion; it was in the same spirit that she now inhaled deeply, but almost at once she began to cough so she stubbed out the cigarette, leaving it in an ashtray where her mother would find it and take the point.

It was too early to go to bed. If she went down into the village she might meet Edward returning from his visit, except that she did not know where his sister lived.

She went out of the house, leaving the door unlatched, and took off her high-heeled sandals so that she could run lightly on her bare feet down the road and round the corner to the new estate from whence came the sounds of the Dennises' party. When the tarmac hurt her soles, she moved on to the grass verge, which was damp and springy with autumn growth. A street light on the corner showed her the way, and as she went on the clouds divided to allow a sliver of moon to lighten the scene.

The gate of Mauden, the Dennises' bungalow, was open. Thelma drifted through it and up the path.

A man stood in the front porch smoking a cigar, whose strong scent came wafting towards her as she briefly paused.

'Hail unto thee, fair sprite,' he addressed her. 'What fortunate wind blows you to these shores?'

'Oh, I was just drifting,' said Thelma airily, waving one pale arm on which her gold bracelets jangled. 'Sounds like fun here.'

'Float this way, lovely wanderer,' said the man, moving towards her. He was tall, brown-haired, with a little beard. 'Come and join us.'

'Why not?' Thelma said, shoes in hand, stepping on.

116

Lydia sat propped up in her high old bed, spectacles on, trying to concentrate on Florence Nightingale. She read no fiction, choosing to immerse herself in dense biographies of the long-dead who had been achievers, as an escape from what seemed to her the ugliness and licence of contemporary life.

This year she had desperately needed diversion from the continuing celebrations of the ending, forty years ago, of the Second World War, an event that had been cataclysmic to her generation. For what better world had so much been sacrificed? Every day there was news of violent disorder of one kind or another; men still killed; children starved. Lydia was weary of seeing films of old soldiers parading at the sites of their victories. What were their thoughts and hidden griefs? It was right that succeeding generations should be made aware of the past, especially when patriotism seemed to be out of fashion, but she could no longer bear to remember those bright youthful hopes and illusions which had been cast into ruin. At least, though, she could turn off the television and ignore the papers. Henry, if he were alive, would have missed none of it; out would have come his medals and off they'd have gone to Caen or some other place where his regiment had covered themselves with glory. VE day had come and gone, but VJ day still lay ahead and no doubt would receive the same treatment.

Resolutely, Lydia read about Florence Nightingale's busy correspondence from her chaise longue, but she was unable to absorb it. At last she snapped the book shut, took off her glasses, turned out the light and tried to compose herself for sleep, but the stresses of the evening combined with the rich meal and alcohol had over-stimulated her and she could not relax. Images chased one another in her mind: Henry back from the war for good, presiding over guests at their dinner table, port circulating; herself gathering up the dull wives, trying hard to make conversation but aware all the while that later there would be reprimand from Henry for the slightest fault or imperfection in either the meal or her conduct – and there were always some he could find. She had learned, in time, to discuss gardens, schools, and lack of help in the house as if nothing else was important. Now she need do it no longer; now, if things went wrong, she had only herself to please. Henry was not waiting to pounce on her slightest mistake.

It had been a very long punishment.

Unable to settle, Lydia got out of bed and went to the window. She could hear the sound of the Dennises' stereo. Surely it was too cold by now to be outside in the garden, and if they were in the house, wasn't the noise too loud to permit conversation?

She put on her dressing gown and stepped out of her room on to the landing. The house was still and silent; she knew she was alone in it before she glanced at the other bedroom doors, both ajar. It was odd how different it felt from when she was really alone; there was a tension now, a sense of something about to happen as the house waited for its occupants to return.

How fanciful she was! Lydia reproved herself for allowing her mind to stray in so foolish a manner. Slowly she went downstairs, unlocked the french window and walked across the garden. How could the Dennises endure such a noise so late? They must be both in their forties. Sometimes the teenage children from their previous marriages were at the bungalow and perhaps the party in progress was for them. Shadowy in the darkness, the mass of the bungalow roof rose up against the lighter night sky. She couldn't throw moss at it now, though to do so would relieve her feelings.

Suddenly she heard a woman's high, excited laugh. It

was Thelma's laugh; unmistakable to her mother. Well, that answered the puzzle of where she had gone, since she was not with Edward. Why had she not said she was going on to their party? Lydia was not aware that she knew them well enough to be invited.

Shivering now, partly with annoyance, Lydia went back to the house and turned on the electric fire in the sitting-room. She was still there, doing her jigsaw, when Edward came in half an hour later.

'What, still up?' he said. He had seen the light as he walked down the drive from the Manor and had come in expecting to see Thelma waiting for him in either an angry or a voracious mood: maybe both. Instead, he saw the thin figure of his hostess, in a blue wool dressing-gown, sitting intent at her puzzle.

'I couldn't sleep,' Lydia told him. 'Too much excitement, I suppose. I don't often eat such a meal, especially at night, unless Gerald takes me out.'

'He's a nice guy,' Edward said, pulling up a chair so that he could sit beside her and look at the puzzle. He picked up a piece, held it poised for an instant, then fitted it in.

'Yes,' said Lydia. 'He was always a good boy. He never gave any trouble.'

'Not like Thelma, eh? I bet she's kept you on the hop,' Edward said. 'I expect you miss him, now he doesn't live up at the big house any more.'

'Yes,' said Lydia.

'Sad, that, folk splitting up,' said Edward. 'My mum walked out on my dad when I was a kid. Funny, I thought it was my fault.'

'What gave you that idea?'

'Well, I was quite naughty. Used to be cheeky and that, and I kept tearing my clothes and getting told off at school for not paying attention,' said Edward. 'But I know now that wasn't why she left.'

'What was the reason?'

'Fancied another bloke more than my dad,' said Edward. He put in another piece. 'I never saw her again. Don't know where she is now.'

'How dreadful,' said Lydia.

Edward shrugged.

'It was OK until my dad married again,' he said. 'We got on well, the three of us. Julie, my sister, was like a little mother to me. Then Dad remarried.'

'And you didn't get on with your step-mother?'

'She didn't like me. Said I was just like my mum,' said Edward. 'I am, to look at. Julie looks like dad.'

'She was jealous,' said Lydia.

'Maybe. Anyway, it didn't work out and I left home as soon as I could,' said Edward. 'Stayed with an uncle for a bit, until I left school.'

'Don't you see your father?'

'No. We kind of lost touch. Julie sees him, though, sometimes.'

'What a pity,' said Lydia.

'Doesn't bother me,' Edward declared.

'You must find a new job,' Lydia told him. 'A proper one – not just bits of gardening and so on. Can't the Job Centre in Cheverton help?'

'I guess it's mostly seasonal down here, with the tourist trade and that,' Edward said. He had heard the staff at the hotel talking about it.

'You must take the car on Monday,' Lydia said. 'Haven't you got to sign on?' He'd be eligible for the dole, even if he was doing odd jobs in the village; moon-lighting, wasn't it?

'Oh thanks,' Edward said. 'I'll do that.' He reached into his pocket and pulled out the ten-pound note Julie had given him; with typical generosity she had passed on the proceeds of her wager. 'Here's something towards my keep in the meantime,' he said. 'I'll give you some more as soon as I draw my social security.'

Lydia hesitated. She did not want to take money from a young man in straits, but on the other hand he must be allowed to retain his self-respect. Charity was not beneficial when it sapped initiative.

'Thank you,' she said, accepting the note.

They stayed up until they had finished the puzzle. Then Edward made some tea and Lydia took her cup up to bed where she soon fell asleep.

Neither of them mentioned that Thelma had not come home, but Lydia left the front door on the latch.

Thelma and her new companions had been sitting under a tree, once part of her father's estate and spared by the bulldozers, in the small garden of Mauden. They were drinking a potent wine cup.

The assembled guests were several assorted couples, some married, others paired one way or another, all celebrating Roger Dennis's birthday. By the time Thelma arrived, surface inhibitions had gone and undercurrents of different emotions had risen with various effects. Maureen Dennis was in the kitchen, in earnest conversation with the boyfriend of one of her colleagues at work. Other minglings had caused new pairs to coalesce. Giggles and shrieks came from one shadowed corner of the patio; a couple had gone into a bedroom. Thelma's arrival produced a diversion and a chance for those who had so far drawn unlucky to regroup.

She felt at home at once. This was what she enjoyed – light, meaningless chatter, superficial flirting; and she was always full of confidence at such a time. She told the man who had greeted her that her name was Guinevere and that she had emerged from the lake on the marshes beyond the golf course. He promptly said that she must call him Lancelot.

121

After a while they moved indoors because it was getting chilly outside, and she sat with him on a sofa in the large living-room with its dining recess at one side. They talked frivolously, he pretending to be off to the jousts wearing her favour on his helmet. Something was wrong somewhere in this, Thelma thought: surely Lancelot didn't go jousting? But quite soon, sitting there, she began to wheeze and her eyes started to run.

'Oh damn,' she cursed, moving away from his encircling arm, pushing aside the hand that was resting on her thigh. She sat up, gasping for breath.

'What's wrong?' he asked. This wasn't a normal brush-off.

'There's a cat here. There must be,' she said.

'I've not seen one,' said Lancelot.

'There is a cat in this house,' Thelma insisted. She tried to breathe evenly, forcing the air out of her lungs so that they would reflate by reflex, trying to use her diaphragm and stomach muscles as she had been taught, but already she was panting.

'Roger – got a cat anywhere? The lady doesn't like them,' said Lancelot.

'We've got two,' Roger answered. 'But they're nowhere about. Off looking for fieldmice, most probably.'

'They don't have to be in the room.' Thelma's voice was already a croak. 'Their hair or their dust – it's enough to set me off. I'll have to go.'

She didn't look fit to depart the way she had come, mysteriously out of the air.

'Let me take you for a drive in the car,' suggested Lancelot. 'There's no cat in my Porsche.'

'All right.' She would probably get over her asthma attack quite quickly if she left the source of the trouble. Thelma went with him out of the room and he handed

122

her into the low black car which was parked outside in the road.

'My shoes!' she remembered.

He went back for them and had quite a job to find them. They were out in the garden beside the goldfish pool. She was still wheezing when he returned. The noise was mildly irritating so he hoped that she would soon recover.

'Can't you take something for it?' he asked.

'I've got an inhaler, but I came out without it,' she said.

'Shall we pick it up?' She was really in distress, he could see. 'Where do you live?'

'No – don't worry. I'll be all right in a few minutes,' Thelma said. But she should have washed her hands. Cat dust transferred easily from upholstery to hands and that was probably how the attack had started. She kept her hands locked in her lap, and eventually the spasms decreased, but they did not cease, and she knew she was in for a prolonged attack that might last for hours unless she used her medication.

Lancelot was sympathetic and forgiving when she refused his overtures, made after he parked in a gateway in a quiet lane not far from the village. Her gasps were rather a turn-off.

Thelma began to feel better as he drove her back to Milton St Gabriel and dropped her, as she had asked, at the entrance to the Manor Hotel. He supposed that she worked there; she might be a receptionist; Roger had seemed to know her and had called her Thelma.

Letting him go, Thelma told herself that such was her luck, he was the one who might have made all the difference.

12

Gerald was again called by Julie in the morning. She brought him the *Sunday Times* with his early tea.

'Oh good,' he said. 'I didn't expect it to arrive until later.' An irritation during weekends in Milton St Gabriel was the late delivery of the papers.

'One of the staff brings them from Heronsmouth,' Julie said. 'On his way in to work, I mean.'

'Oh.' Gerald had laid down his book and he looked at her over his glasses. 'Do you like working here?'

'Yes,' said Julie. 'It's nice being in the country and there's a friendly crowd here. We all help each other out.'

'Like you did last night,' he observed.

'Yes,' agreed Julie, turning quickly away so that he should not see her guilty blush. She hurried off, with, he supposed, other trays to deliver. Certainly, as a guest, he had no complaints about how the hotel was run; rather the reverse; and as an investor, this pleased him.

When he walked down to the lodge later on, the dull clouds were lifting and a hint of sunlight to come lightened the distant hills. His mother was already out in the garden snipping dead blooms from the rose bushes.

'Ah – there you are, Gerald,' she said.

Hypersensitive to her tone, he inferred that she had expected him sooner.

'Did you sleep well?' he asked her.

'Yes – after the noise from the Dennises' stopped,' she said.

'Their party went on a bit, did it?' He suffered from this in his block of flats, where one set of neighbours tended to live by night and sleep by day, and others overhead tramped about in what sounded like seven-leagued boots.

'They don't do it very often,' she allowed.

She wondered whether to tell him that Thelma had gone to the Dennises' party, then decided not to; his disapproval might fuel the friction between brother and sister. It did not occur to her that he might see no reason why Thelma should not be the Dennises' guest.

'I wish we could put the financial skids under Thelma,' he said, as if he had tuned in to the subject of her thoughts. 'If she was forced to earn her living, she might knuckle down to something specific instead of flitting from thing to thing.' And man to man, he silently added.

'The same could be said of your daughter, Gerald,' Lydia told him, her voice grim. 'You must remember that Thelma was widowed so young. If Charles hadn't died, things would have been entirely different.'

Gerald decided to ignore the bull's eye about Fiona.

'Yes, and she'd still have been bored,' he said. 'She was bored then. Mother, we can't go on making excuses for Thelma because of that tragedy. Plenty of women have been left alone in far worse circumstances and made good lives.'

While he was speaking, he made a snap decision: it was useless to stay and provoke more hostility. He rushed on before she could spring to Thelma's defence.

'I'm going to start back to London before lunch, if you don't mind. I want to call on some friends on the way. I haven't got anything positive out of Thelma about her plans and perhaps it's too soon to expect her to have any,' he said.

'Oh – very well, Gerald.' His mother's back stiffened. She must not let him see she was disappointed because he was leaving so soon; she had hoped he might suggest they should go for another walk; they might even have talked properly again. But she would not plead with him to linger; he had his own life to live and it was her strict rule never to make demands. She had planned to discuss Edward's position with him; now she must make her own decision about that. She told him what it was. 'I'll let Edward stay for a while,' she said. 'As long as it fits in with Thelma's plans and doesn't make anything awkward for her.'

'I think he may have other fish to fry,' Gerald said.

Lydia ignored this.

'He's quite a help,' she said. 'A thoughtful boy, and he seems to have no settled home, so it may do him good to stay here for a week or two while he looks for work, and until he can move to his sister's. He's already given me some money towards his keep.'

'Oh, has he?' So the young man had meant what he said. 'Well, keep him to that,' Gerald advised. 'Don't soften him up with acts of charity.' He hesitated, as unhappy about leaving as she was to see him go. 'I'll be off now, Mother, and let you get on.'

With what, she thought sadly.

'Well, goodbye,' he said.

He would have been amazed if he could have seen his mother, after he had gone, walking down the garden to the bonfire spot with her pile of dead roses, her face contorted with tears. It took her several minutes to compose herself enough to return to the house.

No one else, however, was up yet. Discipline directed Lydia's next actions: the meat must be prepared for the oven; potatoes must be scrubbed; there were runner beans and courgettes in the garden.

Why bother? Why spend the morning cooking the

meal for Thelma and Edward? Why wasn't Thelma up now, undertaking this task herself? Daughters were often compelled to look after their elderly mothers. Lydia supposed that she was, by now, elderly, although she felt she had changed very little in recent years.

She was not obliged to cook lunch for Thelma and Edward.

Lydia took a sheet of paper and wrote a note, which she put on the kitchen table. *Gone out. Back tonight. Meat in larder, vegetables in garden.*

Then she went upstairs, washed her hands and powdered her nose, checked that her hair was securely latched under her snood and slipped on a jacket. She left the house very quietly, not wanting to be detected in the act of playing truant. Boris followed her out to the car and hopped into it more alertly than usual, as if catching her own excitement at running away.

'Damn it, she's taken the car!'

Thelma had come downstairs and found her mother's message. Edward, who had already seen it, was sitting at the kitchen table eating toast thickly spread with butter and marmalade. In his new freedom, he still appreciated hot toast soaked with melting butter.

'Why shouldn't she?' he asked. 'It's hers, after all.'

Thelma tossed the note aside.

'Make me some coffee, Edward, there's a dear,' she said. She slumped on to a chair, her hands to her head. 'I've got a cracking hangover.'

'Where'd you go last night, then?' He had not heard her come in.

'To the Dennises.' Thelma waved towards the garden.

Edward had switched on the kettle. He heaped two large teaspoonsful of instant coffee into a mug and waited for the water to boil.

127

'Good, was it?' he asked her.

'All right, but I got an asthma attack,' said Thelma. 'They've got cats there. They affect me.'

'Oh. That's rough.' There had been a man in prison with Edward who had suffered from asthma; it was alarming to see him in the throes of an attack.

'It's a nuisance,' Thelma said. 'It's funny, horses don't bring it on, and they're very dusty.'

'Julie can't eat cheese,' Edward volunteered.

'Julie?'

'My sister.'

'What happens to her if she does?'

'She gets terrible headaches.. Chocolate, too. Makes her ever so sick and rotten,' said Edward.

'Poor thing,' said Thelma. She took the mug Edward gave here. It was too hot to drink straight away. 'Fancy mother going off like that without a word,' she marvelled.

'There is a word. She left a note,' Edward pointed out.

'But not to mention it yesterday,' Thelma insisted. 'That's unlike her.'

'You didn't mention where you were going last night, did you?' Edward said.

'That's different.'

'Why? Your mum's entitled to make her own arrangements. She doesn't have to consult you just because you've turned up – unexpectedly, as I remember.'

'It's not the same,' said Thelma sulkily, sipping her coffee. 'I want to know where she is. She never goes anywhere, apart from to Dorothy's.'

'More's the pity, then,' said Edward. 'You'd think she'd have lots of friends here.' Edward had noticed plenty of grey heads among the residents; he counted on them as his prospective employers.

'She thinks herself too grand to mix with the new people,' Thelma said dismissively. 'Because she was the lady of the manor, I mean,' she added, as Edward looked uncomprehending.

'Is that right?' She hadn't seemed the least bit toffee-nosed towards him. 'What was your dad like?' Edward asked, spreading more toast. 'A proper blimp, I bet.'

'In your terms, perhaps,' Thelma said. Out of deference to her father's views, she had not obeyed her impulse to demonstrate at Greenham Common. Now that he was no longer about to be upset by her actions, she might join the Peace Movement. 'He had high standards,' she told Edward. 'And he set a good example.'

'Like your mum does.'

Thelma was silent. She had never seen her mother's conduct in this light.

'She might have said where she was going,' she repeated. 'And what about Gerald? Where's he, I'd like to know?'

'He was here,' Edward said. 'I saw him talking to your mum in the garden. He went away.' Edward himself had gone back to bed after seeing them out of the bathroom window.

'I suppose he's got bored and gone back to London,' said Thelma, 'He'd done his bit, after all. Squared his conscience.'

'You are a cow,' Edward told her. 'He's really nice, your brother. Cost him a pretty penny last night, I'll bet. He didn't have to include me, and he even asked if I'd like to bring Julie.'

'Oh, Gerald always does the right thing,' Thelma said.

Edward was afraid that perhaps he had gone too far. To improve things, he said, 'Your mother's left us a lovely piece of meat. A whole leg of lamb – too much for just us two.'

With no other ally to hand, Thelma was not inclined to quarrel with Edward. She decided to overlook his insult.

'We could have a party,' she said. The coffee was beginning to take effect and the pulse in her head was easing.

'I suppose we could. Who shall we ask?' Edward had been wondering how he could avoid being alone with Thelma. Who knew what would happen once she got over her hangover?

'Why not your sister?' Thelma suggested. 'Could she get away? And I could ask the Dennises.' Then she would be able to find out who Lancelot was, and where he lived.

'Julie might be able to come,' Edward said. It was a daring idea.

'She lets rooms, doesn't she?' Thelma said carelessly. 'I wondered if she had to give lunch to her lodgers.'

'Not exactly,' Edward said. He ought to tell her, now, about Julie; still, it would be rather fun to surprise her. Thelma was recovering as he watched her; her pallor had gone and the pretty colour was returning to her cheeks. 'You certainly do snap back fast,' he said.

'I've had plenty of practice,' said Thelma.

She sent him off to issue the invitations in person while she set to work to roast the lamb and prepare the rest of the meal. He was gone so long that she had to pick the beans herself, a task she had planned to give him. She set him to slice them; they were so young that they barely needed stringing.

'They're all coming, I suppose,' Thelma said.

'Not Julie.' He had had second thoughts about inviting her; shades of Daddy might cause Thelma to issue a snub and he would not expose Julie to such a risk. Instead, he'd asked Karen. The girl was alone; her father had left to pick up a new load and her mother was working. She was delighted.

Thelma had quite recovered. She was at her best when entertaining, knowing that she did it well. Karen was the first to arrive, having spiked her short hair into a jagged halo that made her look like Puck, Thelma thought: there was a muted rose streak across the front and a hint of blue, and Thelma thought it attractive. She said so, and Karen, used to complaints from her father, beamed with pleasure.

The Dennises were late; they had had a tough morning clearing up after their party.

Now Thelma sparkled. She had made a chilled tomato soup to start the meal and had sent Edward to the Bell as soon as it opened to buy two bottles of wine, since her mother had no two alike and only three altogether. Everyone seemed to have plenty to say and even Karen relaxed. The Dennises had only agreed to come when they learned that Mrs Cuningham would be absent. They found her formidable.

They soon told Thelma that Lancelot, whose name was really Jim, was sales director at a big garage in Cheverton.

After lunch Thelma found some brandy, and as the sun had come out they all strolled, glass in hand, round the garden.

'Our roof looks pretty dreadful from here,' Roger Dennis said. 'I hadn't realized how it cut off your mother's view. She must mind about it.'

'She's used to it now,' said Thelma.

Edward and Karen, both so much younger than all the others, soon grew bored, and although they both drank some, neither appreciated brandy at that time of day. He went with her back to her house to listen to her new tapes, and soon the voice of Michael Jackson floating towards them showed the Dennises how noisy

131

a neighbour could be. But they and Thelma quite liked the choice of music now relayed across the space between the two houses.

Edward did not return to the lodge until after dark.

13

When she drove away that morning, Lydia had no goal in mind. Automatically, she took the Heronsmouth road, but as she approached the junction for Cheverton she slowed down. She knew no one in Heronsmouth now, apart from Betty. She must go further, stay out the whole day, give them all a breathing space.

Dorothy Butler was the only living person whom Lydia would contemplate visiting unannounced, though she could never remember doing so. The two had been at school together, before the war, and later, when Dorothy was in the WRNS and stationed in Dartmouth, she had spent some of her leaves at Milton St Gabriel. Dorothy, too, had made a swift wartime marriage; after her husband was killed, she had spent a short compassionate leave with Lydia at the lodge and there she had done her overt grieving. After that, she had continued her service, and when the war ended she trained as a teacher. The last years of her career were spent as headmistress of a girls' school in Kent. Now, she had taken up painting and foreign travel, sometimes combining the two. Some years ago, she had bought a holiday cottage in Wilcombe in preparation for retirement. In the winter, she attended various adult education classes and she had joined an association of local artists who exhibited their work and sold it to tourists. This kept her occupied and had brought her a new circle of friends, but she reserved space in her life for Lydia, kept in touch by telephone, and the two met at least once a month.

Dorothy had been annoyed when Lydia, at the last moment, cancelled their arrangement for supper because of Thelma's sudden homecoming. According to Lydia, she had not made it clear to her daughter that she needed the car. Dorothy saw the incident differently; it was another example of Lydia's failure to stake a claim to rights of her own. Thelma had been indulged by both parents throughout her childhood, and the pattern remained. Dorothy had been widowed at a younger age than Thelma; she was in the early stages of pregnancy, and had miscarried while at the lodge. Lydia's unemotional kindness and practical help had seen her through the worst days of her life, although now she found it difficult to remember Alan's features or the sound of his voice. Photographs showed a smooth, unformed face with a gentle expression. How would they have fared together if he had survived? She had never known if he had even received her letter containing the news of the forthcoming child.

As girls, she had been more academically minded than Lydia, who was good at games and had played both lacrosse and tennis for the school, where she had gone on a bursary available to the daughters of the clergy. Their friendship had continued because of the accident of geography and Dorothy's wartime presence nearby. Now, they were bound by the tie of the years.

As a teacher, Dorothy had encouraged her girls to pursue careers first and to think of marriage as a step for later, not as a means of escape. Many of her girls had built successful lives, but there were failures too, and sometimes unhappy young women sought her advice.

On that Sunday, as Lydia drove towards Wilcombe, Dorothy was meeting such a one.

Because she had been a frequent visitor to the Manor, Dorothy had seen beneath the surface of Lydia's marriage. Henry tolerated her because she was Thelma's godmother, and because he found her attitude towards him a challenge. Dorothy's views differed from his on almost every subject; she was more stimulating company than Lydia, who would never be goaded into argument. As the years passed, Dorothy had seen Lydia, who had always been shy and reserved, lose the small spark of irony that had once made her good company. Henry had killed some vital part of her nature, and in time Dorothy learned enough about him to make her pity Lydia.

In the end, his death had been sudden, although he had creaked along with a bad heart for some time, his condition not helped by his fondness for whisky and tobacco. Dorothy had hoped that Lydia would spring back into life herself, once she had had time to adjust to her new situation, but this had not happened. More than forty years of attrition had been too much for her.

Now, as Lydia drew up outside Honeysuckle Cottage, she could see there was no one at home. The small windows beneath the steep thatch were shut. She rang the bell, then peered into the garage, which was empty. Dorothy's garden was like a small jungle, untamed and lush; a rampant honeysuckle, no longer in bloom, smothered a rustic arch; clematis cascaded over the dead stump of a tree; vivid dahlias with huge faces formed bold blobs of colour in the beds. It made Lydia uncomfortable; she preferred her own plot with its barbered lawn and straight rows of vegetables marching in echelon across the red earth like soldiers on parade.

She returned to the car. What now? She couldn't go

home until at least three o'clock or her gesture would be useless.

Driving out of the village, she saw that there was not much petrol left in the car. It never occurred to Thelma to fill the tank. Keeping a vague lookout for a filling station, Lydia turned away from home. She'd stop somewhere and give Boris a good walk. After a while, beside a lay-by, she saw a fingerpost indicating a footpath and parked the car. She and the dog set off together, climbing a stile over a low stone wall, following the trail. They walked for several miles, the path taking them through woodland and across a stream. She lost all sense of time, as often happened when she walked like this. She had learned to make her mind a blank, noticing only plants and wild life as she passed. Eventually, because the weather was uncertain, she turned back.

When she reached the car, Boris displayed fatigue and Lydia, too, felt tired and hungry. She always carried a bowl and a bottle of water in the car, for such long expeditions were quite usual, and she gave him a drink before setting off again. When she was in no hurry, Lydia chose to drive along the lanes rather than on the busy main roads, but now she was aware of the need to pick up petrol, so she took the major road at the next opportunity. This brought her close to the motorway service station, and because she was now afraid of running out of petrol, Lydia followed the signs towards it. The needle was showing empty when she stopped at the pumps. She felt relieved, filling up the tank.

Since she was here, she might as well deal with the wants of nature for herself, and buy a sandwich.

She drove on into the parking area and locked Boris into the car, telling him she would not be many minutes. After so much exercise, he was feeling sleepy and merely blinked an eye at her.

136

Because it was Sunday, the place was very busy. Lydia, who had seldom used a motorway service area, felt confused by having to buy her sandwich from one counter and her coffee from another, then queue to pay at a third. She found a place to sit and eat her meal, swallowing it quickly. People milled about with trays. How young they all looked, Lydia thought, and so many of them were so overweight. She saw heavy, fleshy faces, beer bellies, broad chests straining against taut shirts, huge buttocks and round stomachs swelling out tight jeans or wobbling under baggy cotton pants.

She had just finished her coffee when the little girl came past her table. She was about two years old and she was wandering along with her face already puckered, ready to cry.

Lydia did not reason for an instant. She swooped upon the child, said in her ear, 'We'll soon find your mummy,' and led her out of the cafeteria. It was time someone learned a lesson.

The child was already bemused, stunned because among a forest of knees and thighs she saw no familiar face. The seizure of her hand and the swift movement deprived her, for a moment, of the ability to yell although she drew in a preparatory breath. Lydia picked her up and carried her out to the car. Held on high, hearing a friendly voice telling her what a nice little girl she was and that she was going to see a lovely dog, she still held back her tears. Lydia found her very heavy. She set her down before they reached the car and held her hand. The child trotted along beside her, to anyone who cared to notice them, apparently her grandchild. Lydia let Boris out to stretch his legs and they went for a stroll among the cars. There was a play area for children, but Lydia decided not to take her there because that action could be challenged if the parents came along before she was ready to return her.

As it was, a police car had just drawn up outside the main building when Lydia and her charge reached it again.

'This little girl's lost,' Lydia told the constable, coming up beside him before he could get out of his vehicle. 'I found her wandering about.'

The constable, despatched to the scene because a small girl had been reported missing, saw that this one matched the issued description, even to her red shoes. It was not often that a search ended before it had started.

'Ah,' he began, getting out of the car.

'It was lucky I found her. It could have been anyone,' said Lydia sternly. 'Her parents had let her stray.'

'Well, kids are little devils sometimes,' said the constable. 'Move like eels, they do. Give you the slip as soon as you let go their hands to pay.'

By this time Lydia had transferred the child's hand to the policeman's grasp. She left before the officer could ask her name.

A teenage couple, the girl with cropped purple hair, the boy with three earrings in one ear, both his arms tattooed, had come forward when, over the intercom in the refreshment area, the child had been reported missing. They had seen a little girl wearing the clothes described going off with an old lady. No one paid attention to their information. Old ladies did not abduct children and there were plenty of grandmothers legitimately about the place with their families. In vain did Sandra insist she had seen the old woman carry the child away. She'd not taken any notice at the time, not until she heard the broadcast, when she realized that there was something wrong.

When the child had been safely restored to her distraught parents, Sandra heard that an old lady had found her outside. She told the policeman about her doubts but he was not the least bit interested.

Sandra, however, didn't like it at all.

That evening, when Thelma had grown bored with watching television, she told her mother she wanted the car the next day.

'Is that all right?' She made an effort. 'Do you need it?'

'I told Edward he could have it,' Lydia said. 'He must go to the Job Centre.'

'And sign on,' said Edward practically.

'Where do you have to go for that?' asked Thelma.

'To Cheverton,' said Edward.

'Well, you can drop me in Heronsmouth on the way,' said Thelma. 'I'm meeting a friend for lunch but I don't mind going early. I've one or two things to do in the town.' Like go to an estate agent about a flat.

'Is it really all right if we take the car?' asked Edward. 'Don't you really need it, Mrs Cunningham?'

'No,' she answered.

'OK, then,' said Edward. 'I'll pick you up on the way back, Thelma.' He wouldn't mind whiling time away in Cheverton.

Lydia hugged to herself the knowledge that if they were out for most of the day, she would be peacefully alone.

They had been gone for only a very short time the following morning when the police arrived.

14

The sight of a uniformed woman police officer standing on the doorstep made Lydia's heart lurch. One of them had had an accident. Which was it? Thelma, on the way to Heronsmouth, or had something happened to Gerald?

While she braced herself to receive bad news, the young woman made certain that she was, in fact, Mrs Lydia Cunningham.

'Yes – yes. What is it? What's happened?' Lydia asked testily.

'May I come in?' requested WPC Cotton, who was a sturdy girl with fresh pink cheeks and straight brown hair cut short beneath her cap.

Lydia motioned her to enter, then led the way to the sitting-room.

'What's happened?' she repeated.

'Shall we sit down?' suggested WPC Cotton.

She's saying that in case I faint, thought Lydia, smoothing her skirt and sitting in her usual highbacked wing chair. WPC Cotton took another chair, pulled out her notebook and consulted it.

'Your car is a blue Metro, registration number—' and she quoted it.

'Yes,' Oh God! Thelma had driven too fast down the lane and killed herself and the boy.

Lydia took a deep breath and waited, her mind

already flying to mortuaries and funerals, the paraphernalia of death.

The policewoman asked her if she had stopped at the service station near the motorway the previous afternoon.

'Yes, I did.' What had this to do with Thelma? Oh, couldn't she get on – tell her the worst?

At least Mrs Cunningham had not denied the facts so far. WPC Cotton plodded routinely on. This old woman certainly did not look remotely like a kidnapper.

'A little girl, Melanie Smith, aged two, went missing,' WPC Cotton pursued.

'I found her straying,' Lydia said. Was that the reason for the visit? Colour began returning to her face and her heartbeat steadied as she realized that there had been no accident. 'I took her to a policeman.'

'You left before the constable could take your name,' said WPC Cotton.

'There was no need,' said Lydia. 'The child had come to no harm.'

'Where did you find her, Mrs Cunningham?' asked WPC Cotton.

'Wandering about,' said Lydia.

'You approached the police officer from outside – from the car park area,' said the girl.

'This is correct. I had hoped her parents would appear. Meanwhile, I amused her by showing her my dog. We gave him a little run – he'd been shut in the car,' said Lydia. She glanced across to Boris, lying nearby.

'Where was she wandering, Mrs Cunningham?' WPC Cotton persisted.

'Oh, just about,' said Lydia. 'She was frightened. It must be terrifying for a child to lose its parents in a crowd.'

'It's easily done,' said the policewoman. 'Children slip away.'

'Yes – and then they get run over, or worse,' said Lydia. 'Someone else might have come across that little girl. Some pervert.'

'Well – that can happen,' allowed the girl.

'The parents should have taken better care of her,' said Lydia.

'No one's perfect, Mrs Cunningham. A moment's inattention – that's all it takes,' said WPC Cotton.

'I don't understand why you're here. I want no thanks for stopping her from wandering away or going off with someone who might have hurt her,' Lydia said.

'Mrs Cunningham, it's been alleged that you abducted the child, then thought better of it,' said WPC Cotton. 'Two witnesses saw you take her out of the cafeteria and go outside with her. They thought at first that you must be her grandmother, but when she was reported missing over the loudspeaker system, they came forward. They recognized Melanie when the constable reunited her with her parents.'

Barry and Sandra, riding home on Barry's motorbike, had passed Lydia as she drove sedately home. Sandra, glancing back, had recognized her. They'd pulled into a lay-by, let her pass, checked again and noted down the number of her car. Then they had reported her.

'But that's ridiculous,' said Lydia. 'At least—' she floundered briefly, then pulled herself together. 'I did take her into the open, away from the crowds, to give her parents the opportunity to see her with me when they searched for her. They would not have easily seen her in the cafeteria, it was so busy.'

'It's very well staffed, Mrs Cunningham. An assistant would soon have noticed a lost child.'

'Well, they hadn't by the time I saw her,' said Lydia, truthfully enough. 'I hope you're not seriously accusing me of stealing her?'

'No, certainly not.' If she'd meant to abduct the child,

she'd have driven off with her. Obviously the informants had made a mistake, or for some reason had a grudge against Mrs Cunningham, who was of a type to rouse ire in certain kinds of people. You got all sorts at service stations. 'It was just to keep the record straight, to tidy up the files,' said WPC Cotton, now smiling. 'It had been reported, you see, entered in the book. We had to look into it.'

'Hm,' said Lydia.

'What would you have done if the police officer hadn't come along, Mrs Cunningham?' asked the girl, closing her notebook.

'Why – looked for someone in authority at the place and got them to telephone the police,' said Lydia. 'The child could have been abandoned, officer. It happens.'

'Yes, I know.'

'The parents ought to be more careful,' Lydia repeated. 'Careless parents don't deserve the blessing of a child.'

'Cruel parents don't. Careless ones should learn better ways,' said WPC Cotton. 'I'm sure Melanie's will take more care of her in future.'

'Good.'

Lydia stood up. The interview was over.

'I was afraid you had bad news for me,' she confessed, leading the way out to the hall. 'My daughter is out just now, in my car. I was afraid she might have had an accident.'

'Oh no. I'm sorry if you were alarmed,' said WPC Cotton.

'Well – no harm done,' Lydia said.

That was soon tidied up, thought WPC Cotton, driving off. The only odd thing about it was that the old woman had clearly taken the child outside instead of immediately trying to locate the parents through the administration of the building. Younger women, frustrated mothers, sometimes stole babies out of prams; was there a similar grandmother syndrome?

She'd make a full report, of course; that was routine; but Mrs Cunningham was no criminal.

The policewoman's visit had unsettled Lydia, not that she was in a calm state of mind in any case. It was horrible to think that someone had been spying on her, had described her to the police, perhaps noted down the number of her car, for that must be how they had traced her. Even Lydia had heard of the police computer. She shivered. Suddenly, she felt quite ill.

She sat down in her armchair to allow the dizzy, disoriented feeling to pass, then, with an effort, got up and called Boris. Exercise was a good antidote to worry so she would go for a nice long walk. She set out, forcing her mind away from her anxieties, concentrating on her surroundings, the bracken by the roadside with its curious, musty smell, the fuchsias in the gardens. Boris waddled along, keeping pace with her; sometimes he paused to investigate a seductive odour, sometimes he lolloped clumsily ahead, but he always kept close to the verge, an obedient dog who came to heel immediately when she called him, as she did each time a car went by. There were few today, but in high summer this lane was perilous with traffic.

There were large, dark storm clouds in the sky but the sun shafted down between them and there was a breeze. Lydia walked for over two hours and was so tired when she reached home again that, after drinking some fresh orange juice and changing from her walking shoes into low-heeled pumps, she sank down in her chair and found her eyelids closing.

She woke to hear a female voice.

'Lydia – are you asleep? Goodness, are you ill?'

Dorothy Butler had expected Lydia to be working in

the garden on this sunny afternoon and had walked round the back way, leaving the car outside the garage, which Edward had closed when he and Thelma left that morning. Lydia was nowhere to be seen, but the french window was open and Dorothy was startled by the unlikely sight of her friend's surrender to physical fatigue.

'What? Oh—!' Lydia sat up, blinking. She had been having that dream again, the one where she was forced to move to some other house. Dorothy's bulk obscured the light from the french window and it took Lydia a moment or two to recognize her visitor. 'Whatever is the time?' she said. 'I must have just dropped off.'

'It's nearly four o'clock,' said Dorothy.

Lydia had been asleep for over an hour.

'Oh dear!' She struggled to her feet, blinking. 'Goodness, I'd no idea it was so late,' she said.

'Well, you aren't going anywhere, are you?' Dorothy said mildly. 'I expect you needed forty winks. I'll go and put the kettle on. A cup of tea will wake you up, and I could use one too.'

That morning her neighbour had come hurrying round to tell her that someone had called while she was out the previous day.

'That friend of yours in the blue car who sometimes comes,' she'd said. 'She looked quite put out when she found you weren't at home. Didn't she leave a note?' The inquisitive neighbour hadn't seen Lydia writing one, but she had observed her air of indecision.

After this conversation, Dorothy had telephoned Lydia but had got no reply. She had tried again at lunchtime, then at intervals during the afternoon, still with no result. It was so much out of character for Lydia to come over unannounced that Dorothy had felt uneasy; Thelma was staying with her mother and Thelma spelled trouble. Unable to settle to the still-life on her easel which needed only final touches, Dorothy had decided to make a surprise call herself and if Lydia were still out, she would put a note through the door asking her to telephone when she returned.

Dorothy headed for the kitchen while Lydia went into the cloakroom, emerging after she had sponged her face and settled some straying wisps of hair under her snood. She still felt heavy and slow when she joined Dorothy, who meanwhile had laid a tray and found two cups and saucers and the china teapot. The silver one, by Henry's decree always used at the Manor, had vanished when Lydia moved; perhaps it had been sold in the hotch-potch of the estate, or maybe Iris had collared it among her spoils.

'There isn't any cake,' said Lydia. 'Would you like a biscuit?' There were some custard creams in a tin; she had discovered that Edward was very fond of them. Lydia put five on a plate and took the tray which Dorothy had prepared back to the sitting-room. She now seemed perfectly composed.

'I'm sorry I missed you yesterday,' said Dorothy. 'I went to see a former pupil who's in trouble.'

'How did you know I'd been over?' Lydia snapped the words at her, quite fiercely.

'A neighbour noticed – Madge Green from opposite. I think you've met her,' said Dorothy.

'People are much too keen on minding what's not their business,' Lydia muttered crossly.

'True, true, but I'm glad she mentioned it,' said Dorothy. Lydia was getting very difficult these days.

'I was just passing by and thought I'd drop in,' said Lydia, making an effort to speak more calmly. 'I should have telephoned first, as I usually do.'

'It's quite all right by me if you don't,' said Dorothy.

'You might have found me out this afternoon,' said Lydia, ungraciously. 'Or were you passing too?'

Dorothy decided to embroider the truth.

'I felt like going for a drive and so I came this way,' she said. Honours were even.

The tea had drawn. Lydia poured it out, two cups of pale clear fluid with a slice of lemon; one of her few luxuries was her Lapsang Souchong. She had never acquired a nurse's taste for strong dark tea.

'A biscuit?' she suggested.

Dorothy took one, then watched in surprise as Lydia ate her own up quickly and started on another.

'Didn't you have any lunch?' she asked, not really seriously; Lydia's strict timetable, structuring her life, was well known to her.

'No – now that you mention it, I forgot,' said Lydia. 'Boris and I went for a very long walk and I must have fallen asleep straight away when we got back.'

This was not like Lydia at all: even if she had no appetite, a bowl of soup, an apple, or some cheese would be consumed while listening to *The World at One*, especially when it was Sir Robin Day in charge.

Though she looked her normal self now, her hand shook slightly as she drank her tea.

'What's upset you?' Dorothy asked.

'Nothing – there's nothing wrong,' said Lydia brusquely.

Dorothy sighed. How easy it would be to walk away, accept this statement at its face value and go home. But she owed Lydia more than that.

'You don't deceive me,' she said gently. 'Come on. Out with it. Is it Thelma?'

'No, not really. Not more than usual,' said Lydia. 'It's something so ridiculous. The police came to question me this morning.'

'Oh Lydia! Whatever have you done?' For a wild moment the thought that Lydia might have started shoplifting ran through Dorothy's mind.

'Nothing. Nothing at all,' said Lydia. I let a man die once, she thought, but no one now will ever find that out.

'They must have had a reason. Did you witness an accident?'

'No. It was about a little girl – a toddler,' Lydia said. 'Her parents let her wander off at the big motorway service area yesterday. I called there for petrol and found her wandering about. I handed her over to a policeman who arrived in a car.'

What on earth had she been doing, driving all that way?

'I see,' Dorothy replied. 'Why should that upset you? Weren't they just tidying up their records?'

'They seemed to think I'd kidnapped her,' said Lydia.

'Oh, what nonsense! It was lucky you found her and not some suspicious character,' said Dorothy.

This robust reaction cheered Lydia.

'I told them that,' she said.

'Good for you. I don't know why you're fussing,' Dorothy declared. 'Anyway, as soon as the policeman saw you, he must have known it was rubbish.'

'It was a policewoman.'

'Well, she was satisfied, wasn't she?'

'I think so. Yes, she seemed to be,' said Lydia.

'I expect it was just a formality,' said Dorothy. 'Suppose you had been some sort of baby farmer and they hadn't checked, there'd have been an awful song and dance.'

'That's true,' said Lydia.

'Now tell me about Thelma,' Dorothy instructed. That was really the trouble, the reason for Lydia's unheralded visit, she was sure: this other thing, the alleged baby snatching, had happened after that abortive call. 'What state is she in this time?'

'She seems all right,' said Lydia carefully. 'It's as well

148

this American dream of hers didn't work out, I suppose.'

Dorothy didn't agree. She had hoped that Thelma would settle down far enough away to let her mother have some peace.

'Is she heartbroken again?' she asked.

'Not really. She's mended very quickly,' said Lydia. As she spoke, she heard a car draw up outside. 'Here she is,' she added, and went on quickly, 'There's someone else staying here. Edward Fletcher is his name.'

Thelma came in looking beautiful. She seemed pleased to see her godmother, greeting her warmly with a kiss. Her face was smooth and cool. Dorothy, when Edward was introduced, held out her hand as she had taught her girls, and, awkwardly, he shook it. His palm was slightly damp. Now, why should he be nervous?

'No need to ask you how you are,' Dorothy remarked to Thelma. 'You look marvellous.'

'She had a real good lunch with this old guy,' said Edward eagerly. 'And he's offered her a job. She's going to be his housekeeper. How about that?' This news had been a big relief to him.

Lydia would not allow herself to share that feeling. She needed to know more.

'Living in?' asked Dorothy practically.

'Not at first,' said Thelma. 'In case it doesn't work. We're both agreed on that. I'd already decided to rent a flat in Heronsmouth – there are plenty going, now the season's over, and I've got one down by the harbour below the Swan. It'll be handy for rehearsals.'

'And who is your employer?' Dorothy pursued.

'He's a widower who needs looking after. Gerald suggested I should get a job like that. Aren't you pleased?' She looked at the two women defiantly. Both

149

had seen her with that expression so many times before, beginning at the age of four or five; she had something to conceal.

'He's really nice,' said Edward. 'I met him when I picked Thelma up. We had tea with him. He wants a few things doing round the place and I said I'd help him out. Painting and that.'

'Are you moving out too?' asked Lydia faintly. Perhaps he planned to share the flat with Thelma.

'Not right away – unless you want me to,' said Edward.

How did he fit in here, wondered Dorothy.

'I'm glad you've got something satisfactory settled,' she told Thelma.

The whole atmosphere had lightened and Lydia looked quite different, her torpor gone.

'Will you stay to supper, Dorothy?' she asked. There should be plenty of cold meat left from yesterday.

Dorothy accepted, but Lydia had a shock when she went to take it from the fridge. Very little remained beneath the foil which Thelma had carefully wrapped round what was mostly bone. Lydia had to eke it out with a tin of ham.

They spent an animated evening, with Lydia controlling the conversation in the manner Dorothy had watched her painfully acquire over the years. She told Dorothy that Edward had a sister in the village who let rooms and that he was moving there when she had space. Thelma must have given her this idea, Edward supposed; he felt worried by their continuing wrong assumption but told himself that this was not the time to put it right. He was relieved when the talk turned towards *The Seagull*, then the state of the theatre in general, which interested Dorothy. Edward fed in questions to keep the conversation safe.

When Dorothy left, she realized that she had learned

nothing about the young man except that he had a sister in the village. Lydia must have taken him in from the kindness of her heart.

15

Things moved fast the next week. Thelma borrowed the car again to go over to Heronsmouth to take possession of the flat. Edward went with her to help with any tasks that had to be done. Thelma had filled the washing machine before they left. The girl was forever laundering her clothes; no wonder they soon wore out, Lydia thought, pegging them on the rotary line.

When the pair came home in the late afternoon they were in high spirits. They had cleaned up the flat and stocked the store cupboard in preparation for Thelma's removal.

'The old guy came down with some wine and stuff for lunch,' Edward said. 'He's taken a fancy to Thelma. I reckon she'll have to watch out. He's still got a twinkle in his eye, for all he's so old. What do you say, Thelma?'

She shrugged.

'Who can tell?' she replied, but she was laughing.

Edward found that this line of thought eased his guilt about Thelma.

'He's bald,' he said in a more critical tone.

'I like bald men,' said Thelma staunchly. 'Think of Yul Brynner.'

Edward couldn't remember him.

'What nonsense you both talk.' Lydia spoke tolerantly. Thelma might be bored again before long, but for now she had an aim.

'I need some linen – sheets and things,' Thelma said. 'They're not provided.'

'I'll find you some,' her mother said.

The following day, Edward helped Thelma move and he returned to the lodge alone.

'Well, she's settled,' he told Lydia. 'And I've made a start up at the old guy's house. He's having a second bathroom put in just for her – imagine! I'm to do that up, to madam's taste, when the plumber's finished. It'll be like a palace for her.'

'If she stays,' said Lydia.

'Why shouldn't she?' asked Edward. 'They get on a treat. She'll be OK now. I'm going over again tomorrow to start on the bedroom. I'll hitch a ride.'

'I'll drop you,' said Lydia. 'Thanks to you, all the jigsaws are done, so I'll take them back and see if there are more waiting for me. Maybe you could come back on the bus.'

'OK. Thanks,' said Edward. 'I might be late so don't wait your meal for me. I'll fix myself a sandwich if I'm hungry, if that's all right.' He might see what sort of night life Heronsmouth offered; not a lot, he thought. He took some money from his pocket and counted out twenty pounds. 'There. That's my next week's rent in advance,' he said. He was suddenly wildly happy. He had a place to live where he felt at home and work for the days ahead; what more did a fellow need?

'That's far too much,' said Lydia. 'You've already given me ten pounds.'

'That was for this week,' said Edward. 'And it's not enough. I should give you thirty pounds at least, as you give me so many meals.'

'I don't want to make a profit,' Lydia said.

'Why not? Everyone else does,' Edward said. 'And you give me the run of the house, and free baths and everything.'

'Well, of course,' Lydia said. Poor boy, where had he been living before he came here? 'I like having you around,' she said, the warmest remark she had made to a human soul for a very long time, although Edward was not to know that.

Lydia dropped him the next day at The Shieling. The house stood back from the road behind a small front garden; a short drive led up to the front door. It was a solid building with twin gables under a grey slate roof, the brickwork plastered over and painted white, the woodwork rather too blue. A prefabricated garage stood at one side.

'Ugly old place, isn't it, but it's nice inside,' said Edward. 'It's got big rooms and a garden running up behind. He grows lots of vegetables.'

Lydia read the name on the gateposts, which were freshly painted – Edward's work, she learned. Everything looked well kept. Lydia would have selected black for the paintwork, if the house were hers, but otherwise she could not fault it. Fuchsias leaned over the iron fencing, with among them tall, spiked dahlias, mainly yellow, not like Dorothy's multi-coloured display, and some old-fashioned blue Michaelmas daisies.

'See you later,' Edward said. 'Thanks.'

Lydia felt almost cheerful as she drove on. Edward's optimism was infectious. She carried out her errands at the charity shop, pointing out there was a piece missing from one of the puzzles; she always mentioned such details although it was written on the box. Then she went on to the car park, and had lunch in the department store again after giving Boris a short run. It was advisable to place oneself among other people occasionally, otherwise even speech became difficult and she had found that she sometimes felt quite unreal in crowds after days of isolation.

She had always been reserved but she had grown almost reclusive lately. It was like dreaming to look back at that summer so many years ago, when she had felt like bursting into song or laughter all the time. It had been so brief, just a few short weeks and then he was killed.

Lydia would not let herself think about it now. She selected a cheese salad and ate it quickly. No unattended children roamed the store today, and she went home without adventure.

Thelma's job wouldn't last; nothing did, with her; but it might take them past the performance of *The Seagull*.

Edward came in late. Lydia was in bed, but not asleep, when she heard him close the front door softly. Perhaps she should let him have a key; it wasn't a very good idea to leave the door on the latch, even in a peaceful place like this, if one took heed of what was in the papers. But things hadn't got to that pass in Milton St Gabriel: not yet.

When Betty came on Thursday, she was delighted to learn that Thelma had moved out and got a job.

'What's she doing, then?' she asked.

'She's housekeeper to some old man on Harbour Hill,' said Lydia. 'A widower. I don't know his name. He lives at The Shieling – the white house with the blue paint.'

'I know it,' Betty said. 'Used to belong to Phil Draper from the chemist, but the family moved after he died.' And the long established pharmacy had been bought by a multiple and lost its individuality. 'I heard a couple'd bought it and she died.'

'That would be right, then,' Lydia said.

'I don't know the new folk,' Betty said. 'Or rather him, as she's passed on.' That meant they were not members of Betty's chapel. 'The name's Anderson or

Harrison – something like that. In the old days I'd have known all about him. When we had the shop. He'd have a paper delivered, that's for sure. Well, it sounds all right and she's old enough to know what she's about,' she added. 'I'll give her room a good going-over and then it'll be ready for Gerald next time he comes down.'

While she did so, Lydia listened to the morning story on the radio and began one of the new jigsaws. The house was almost back to normal; Edward was no trouble at all.

Gerald telephoned that evening, and when he learned that Thelma had taken his advice and had even moved out already, he was very relieved. He'd come down soon, he said, but he was taking a late holiday and going to France to visit Christopher. He'd suggested that Fiona might like to go with him, but she'd refused; she'd got some big date coming up in Scotland, it appeared, some lairdling's coming-of-age she'd been invited to attend.

'Mother, would you—' Gerald began, then stopped. He had been on the point of asking her if she would like to go with him. How embarrassed she would be at having to find an excuse! Boris wouldn't do as one, with Edward there to see to him.

'Yes?'

'Oh – nothing. I've forgotten. It wasn't important,' Gerald said.

Two weeks passed tranquilly. Lydia saw little of Edward during the day as he was working either in the village or at The Shieling, where he was tiling Thelma's new bathroom. He hadn't done such work before but he was learning. No more was said about him moving to his sister's place; Lydia supposed she had late guests. Some

156

evenings he went out after the meal they had together, but often he sat helping with her jigsaw, one eye on television. Sometimes he spent the evening round at Karen's when she was alone, and he took her to the cinema in Lydia's car, a trip for which she gladly gave permission.

It was quite a shock when he told Lydia that he had been offered the post as boiler attendant and odd-job man at the hotel, taking over when the present man retired; he would eventually be given accommodation in staff quarters there. Meanwhile, he was spending time learning the ropes from his predecessor.

'Oh, that's splendid news,' said Lydia. He seemed happy working with his hands. 'I didn't know you'd applied for it.'

'I hadn't,' Edward answered. He hesitated. She still didn't know about Julie. 'I – er – I've got friends up there and I've done a few bits and pieces when they've been shorthanded. That's how it came up,' he said, which was more or less the truth.

He wasn't sure how long he'd stay. It might be too quiet in the winter, but now he'd be able to put down a deposit on a scooter and be independent. If a year went uneventfully by, with him keeping out of trouble, he'd trust himself enough to broaden out a bit. He'd been ready to tell Mrs Thomson about his past but it hadn't come up. She'd assumed he'd been made redundant by some normal process and had come to the village because of his sister. Julie was a good, reliable worker; no doubt her brother would be, too.

'I'll miss you,' Lydia said.

She smiled at him as she spoke. He'd noticed her smiling sometimes lately, a thing she hadn't done at all when he first arrived. It quite changed her face, wiping out the severe lines. She might have been pretty when she was a girl. Odd to think that she had once been young.

'I'd hoped I might get something a bit more up-market,' he admitted. 'Be a rep – something like that. I couldn't stand being stuck in an office all day.'

'You can regard it as experience,' Lydia said. 'You can always look for something else later. It's not like getting married, for better or for worse, until death.'

'No!' Edward was startled by this heavy comparison. 'Well, marriage isn't like that now, either, is it?' he said.

'I'm afraid not,' Lydia said. 'More's the pity.'

'Can I stay until my room's ready at the hotel?' Edward asked. 'It'll be a week or two yet.'

'Of course you may.' Lydia was delighted that his departure was to be delayed.

16

In some ways Edward was looking forward to having a place that was really his own, but he had never before lived anywhere with such a calm domestic atmosphere. Now that Thelma had moved out the place was as tranquil as a cloister.

'How do you like Thelma's flat?' he asked Lydia one day.

'I haven't seen it,' she replied.

'What? Haven't you been to visit her?' Edward was astonished.

'She hasn't asked me,' Lydia told him.

'But she's your daughter! Surely you don't need an invitation to drop in?' said Edward.

'I respect her privacy,' Lydia said.

'I bet she doesn't pay you the same compliment,' said Edward. 'If it suited her, she'd turn up at any time, even if you'd got the Queen coming to tea.'

That was perfectly true.

The next evening, Thelma rang up to invite her mother to dinner a week later. When Lydia accepted, Thelma said she would ask Dorothy as well. Lydia felt sure that the whole idea was Edward's and this took away some of her pleasure in receiving the invitation.

Soon afterwards, Dorothy telephoned to ask if she might stay at the lodge that night; it was quite a long way to go back to Wilcombe if the evening was a late one, and would mean, too, that a glass of sherry and perhaps a glass of wine would be all that she could safely drink in case a breathalysing constable was on the prowl. It only needed someone else to drive into her car, however blameless she was, for her to land in trouble, Dorothy declared.

When the evening came, she arrived in good time, ready changed, while Edward, who was going with them, was still in the bathroom. She had brought some cushions as a house-warming present for her god-daughter.

'Oh dear,' said Lydia. 'I never thought about a house-warming. She isn't going to be there long. It didn't cross my mind.'

'Take her a bottle of sherry,' Dorothy advised. 'Have you got one that hasn't been opened?'

Thanks to Gerald, Lydia had. She found some giftwrapping paper and put it round the bottle, feeling mortified. Why couldn't she think of these sort of gestures herself? And there was Dorothy looking so handsome in her lacy lilac knitted suit, with her abun-dant white hair smoothly set and rinsed a steely blue. Lydia, in the dress that she had worn to dine with Gerald at the Manor, felt inadequate and dowdy.

'Let's have a drink before we go,' she suggested, to Dorothy's surprise. She was always so abstemious.

She poured Dorothy a strong gin and tonic and a small glass of sherry for herself, and both were sitting comfortably in front of the electric fire when Edward made his entrance. He wore a pair of dark green slacks and a cream shirt with a dark green tie. He carried his bomber jacket.

'You do look smart,' said Lydia warmly.

'Yeah – well, I want to get a blazer but I'm still saving,' Edward said, obviously pleased by this reac-tion.

160

A blazer! How conventional! Lydia's reactionary influence was having its effect, thought Dorothy in amusement.

'Come along. We must go,' said Lydia, getting up.

He held their coats for them, faultlessly polite, and he drove the car. He must stand high in Lydia's favour, thought her friend.

They were able to park on the harbour front close to the block where Thelma lived.

She was ready for them, wearing a yellow dress which set off her gilded hair. Gold bracelets clattered on each wrist and gilt pendant earrings dangled from her ears.

Dorothy and Lydia handed over their presents which were received with apparent pleasure.

'This seems very comfortable,' said Lydia, glancing round the unremarkable sitting-room with its dull, serviceable furniture and its patterned carpet.

'It's convenient,' Thelma said. 'But my rooms at The Shieling will be really attractive. It's all being done up for me, you know,' she told Dorothy. 'Arthur's getting new curtains and things – I'm choosing everything myself.'

'Nothing's too good for her ladyship,' said Edward. 'Mr Morrison keeps finding me new jobs to do.' He laughed. 'I should worry.' Now that he was working regularly by day, he'd been up there in the evenings and at weekends carrying out the latest schemes. The old boy paid in cash, no questions asked.

'He was coming tonight,' said Thelma. 'But he's got a bit of a cold and he thought he'd keep it to himself, as he put it.'

'Oh dear! I hope it's nothing much,' said Dorothy, visualizing this ancient man succumbing to a fatal virus and thus relinquishing his role as Lydia's saviour.

'No – it's just a cold, but he has a weak chest,' Thelma said. 'Something to do with the war.'

161

'Was he wounded in it? His chest I mean?' asked Dorothy.

'I don't think so. No. In the legs – he walks quite stiffly, his left knee is fixed. He was lucky not to lose it,' Thelma said. 'He was shot down over Germany and taken prisoner. He said he was well looked after in hospital but he wasn't found for quite some time – he lay in a wood, unable to move, and got pneumonia. He nearly died.'

'Poor man,' said Dorothy.

'What did you say his name was?' Lydia asked. Betty had said it was Harrison, or Anderson, she wasn't sure. She hadn't heard his first name until now.

'Arthur Morrison,' said Thelma. Really, her mother was getting so forgetful; she must have heard his name a dozen times before. 'His wife was called Phyllis and he's got a son called Nicholas and several grandchildren. Anything more you want to know?'

'And he was in the Air Force?' Lydia said. Her head was spinning. She had once known an Arthur Morrison, common enough names, perhaps. The one she knew was dead. 'Was he a pilot?'

'I don't know,' said Thelma, who wasn't interested.

Lydia breathed deeply, trying to control the flutter in her chest. It was so silly to get upset after all this time. Her Arthur was long dead, and this other man who bore his name was just a stranger.

Dorothy had begun to circle round the room inspecting the pictures the landlord had thought fit to put upon the walls – prints of the district – and the row of tattered paperbacks on a shelf. She pulled out a Dick Francis, one she had not read, and told Thelma that she wished to borrow it.

'Doesn't it go with the flat?' Lydia tried to speak normally though she felt that she was choking.

'I expect these have all been left by different tenants,' Dorothy said. 'But I'll give it back.'

162

'I'm sure no one will ever notice,' Thelma said, giving her mother a pitying look. 'The books aren't listed on the inventory. Dinner's ready. Shall we eat?'

She had made the table look very attractive, with yellow miniature chrysanthemums in a low bowl and some of her mother's linen table napkins. There were tall yellow candles in silver candlesticks which she had borrowed from The Shieling. She had taken trouble and the meal was delicious – beef fillets in a rich wine sauce after a frothy shrimp mousse. There was fresh fruit salad to follow. Lydia drank very little; someone must be in a proper condition to drive home. The other three enjoyed their wine, talking cheerfully. Edward wanted to hear about Dorothy's visit to Russia and was more interested in Peter the Great's boat, the forerunner of the Russian Navy, now in the Maritime Museum in Leningrad, than the glories of the Hermitage and the restored great palaces.

'They're such nice people, what I saw of them,' said Dorothy, and explained how she had tried to describe, by song and mime, which ballet she had seen to a delighted hotel maid who wore knee socks and bursting canvas shoes. 'I think I'll learn some Russian and go back.'

Lydia let the conversation ebb and flow around her, trying to do justice to the meal because she did not want to seem rude to Thelma, but her mind was haunted by the past.

'How does he occupy his time, your Mr Morrison?' she asked abruptly, interrupting Dorothy's description of delicious blinis.

'What – oh, he's in with the bridge-playing crowd,' said Thelma. 'More deeply than he wants to be, I think. His wife was rather keen and I gather they scooped him up after she died. The dear ladies keep trying to fix up games with him.'

'Bridge is such a waste of time,' said Lydia.

'People who play it don't think so,' Dorothy said. 'They might find your passion for jigsaws equally useless.'

'Yes. I'm sorry,' said Lydia, crumpling immediately.

'Oh Lydia, I'm only teasing.' Dorothy was instantly contrite.

'We all waste time in ways, don't we?' said Edward. 'Like watching telly when we could be painting a picture or learning Russian.'

'I'm too intolerant,' Lydia said. Her voice was harsh.

That was true, but Dorothy did not like to see her friend upset.

'One man's relaxation is another man's hard work,' she said lightly.

After the meal she insisted on helping Thelma wash up.

'We can't leave you like Cinderella at the sink after we've gone,' she said, putting on an apron that hung in the kitchen and setting to work while Thelma sorted things out and Edward put the coffee on. There were jokes about smears on plates and shiny stainless steel.

Dorothy was so good at making an evening go, thought Lydia, drying a wine glass. Thank goodness she had been included in the invitation. What if she hadn't been, and that Arthur Morrison had come? She would have been so thrown by hearing his name that no matter how different he was from the young man she had known, she would have found the evening a far worse strain even than it was. Dorothy never had any trouble finding things to talk about and drawing other people out. Now she had Edward telling some tale about a battle with the laundry-room door at the Manor. It had jammed with the ironing lady inside and she had felt claustrophobic. In the end he had extracted her through the window so that he could free the door in peace.

Dorothy had always had a gift for putting people at their ease; it was one of the things that Henry had admired about her and when she came to stay they always entertained because then, he would say, he could be certain someone would see that things went properly.

'I hope we meet this old boy of yours before long,' Dorothy told Thelma as they left.

'He's not all that old,' Thelma said. 'No older than you are – not as old as Daddy would have been.'

Back at the lodge, when Edward had gone up to bed and she and Lydia were having a nightcap together – whisky for Dorothy and orange juice for Lydia – Dorothy uttered a thought that had come to her that evening.

'Do you think Thelma might want to marry this old man?' she asked. 'This Arthur, who isn't all that old? Be an old man's darling again?'

'What do you mean, again?'

'Well, she was the apple of her father's eye, wasn't she? She misses him,' said Dorothy. 'I expect this old chap makes a fuss of her too.'

'But she's working for him,' Lydia said.

'My dear, haven't you heard of housekeepers marrying their employers?' Dorothy inquired. 'What could be more likely? It would save him paying wages.'

'But she can't feel like that about him, at his age,' said Lydia. 'Or him either,' she added, ungrammatically.

'Lydia dear, age has nothing to do with it,' Dorothy said, and added, 'Would it be so very terrible, if he's nice? It might sort her out – steady her down – restore her confidence, if it lasted long enough. I think she misses being married – the status that it offers, I mean. She might learn to be content at last. Isn't that what you want for her?'

'Of course it is,' said Lydia slowly.

'I'll bet you,' Dorothy was saying. 'I'll give it a year but it's more likely to happen sooner. At his age, he won't want to waste precious time.'

17

To keep the ghosts at bay, Lydia took two sleeping pills. Some still remained from those the doctor had prescribed after Henry's death. Their effect wore off after only a few hours and she lay fretting restlessly until she could rise and take Dorothy a cup of tea. Her friend had slept soundly; she was anxious to return home promptly as she had some people coming to lunch, so she did not linger after breakfast.

In the morning light, Lydia suddenly looked every second of her age, which was, within three months, the same as Dorothy's. Old age did not begin until you let it encompass you, or physical deterioration restricted your life.

'You haven't had any more visits from the police, have you?' Dorothy asked.

'No. Why should I?' Lydia's answer came in her usual brusque tone.

'Why indeed.' Dorothy hesitated. 'Well, ring up if anything's bothering you,' she said. 'Take care.'

Lydia felt flat after she had gone. Edward had already left for work, and for once her precious solitude became oppressive. It was stupid to let herself be upset, she told herself. The coincidence of a name had brought back a rush of memories. That was understandable, and now she must forget it. But she had never been able to do that wholly; the past had marched along throughout her life beside the present, and she had harmed Henry just as much as he had hurt her. That was why she took the punishment. In the end, though, he had gone too far and she had let him die.

For Thelma was not Henry's child.

The pressure of her thoughts almost made Lydia forget that it was Thursday, Betty's day. She set off hastily to fetch her. All the scenery was grey and bleak today; odd to think that in spring the banks along the lanes would once again be starred with primroses. Winter, rarely severe down here, was even so a time of gales and penetrating damp.

Betty noticed that Lydia looked tired but put it down to the late night.

'Gave you a good dinner, did she? Thelma?' Betty asked.

'Yes, excellent. She is a first-class cook, you know,' said Lydia.

'Right enough. The gentleman she's working for – Morrison's the name,' said Betty. 'I meant to tell you. He's well thought of in the town. Credit good, all that. She's maybe fallen on her feet.'

'Nothing known against?' said Lydia, half smiling.

What a funny way to put it, but then Mrs Cunningham had always been unusual.

'That's right,' said Betty.

Lydia went into the garden while Betty was busy. She started digging up the vegetable bed, working hard, trying to think only of sending the spade in deep enough, leaving the soil level. Then, after she had taken Betty home, she drove into Heronsmouth, going up Harbour Hill to pass The Shieling in its quarter of an acre, a solid, safe house into which her daughter would be moving soon, a house owned by a man who had the same name as Thelma's natural father, and, like him, had been in the Royal Air Force.

Lydia drove on up the hill, past the Cliff Hotel, and turned at a fork in the road, then went back again. If she could just see the man, her fret would cease. Arthur, her Arthur, the lover of her youth, was dead, had died months before Thelma was born. This man was someone else. As she passed the house for the second time, no one came in or out; bald Mr Morrison was not to be seen. Thelma must be in there now; perhaps he was joking with her, planning her installation.

Why did she think he would be joking with her? Because Arthur – Lydia's Arthur – had always been so cheerful? He never admitted to the fear he must have felt as he went off on yet another bombing mission. He was shot down over Germany only a few hours after they had parted, leaving her pregnant. Such things happened to a lot of girls in those years.

On the way back, Lydia stopped to give Boris a walk, and once again trudged miles. Summer Time had ended the previous weekend, and dusk was falling when she reached home.

Lydia put the car away, closed the garage and went into the house, Boris shuffling ahead, her mind still full of Arthur Morrison, allowing herself to picture his fair wavy hair, his deep blue eyes, his smile. Thelma had his eyes and his fair, clear skin, but she had not inherited his happy temperament. Lydia put on the hall light, then went into the sitting-room and turned on a lamp.

Edward was sitting in a chair in the corner. He was crouched into a huddled ball, his arms hugging his knees.

'Why, Edward, what are you doing sitting here in the dark?' Lydia exclaimed. Then she realized that something was wrong, for he was making small keening sounds. Boris went up to him and began licking at him, trying to reach his hands with his pink rasping tongue. 'Whatever's happened?' she said, turning on another light.

He couldn't answer. At first she thought that he was ill, and then that he had lost his job, but he mumbled some negative response to both these theories.

'Edward, I can't help you unless you pull yourself together and tell me what's wrong,' she said. 'Now, let's have a cup of tea. Then you explain. Come along.'

He trailed after her into the kitchen in his socks. Whatever catastrophe had hit him had not prevented him from taking off his shoes before treading on the pale carpet.

Lydia brewed a pot of strong tea, let it stand, and then poured out two cups, ladling sugar into his.

'Drink it,' she instructed, and waited until he had swallowed quite a quantity before asking him again to explain.

'It's Karen,' he said at last.

'Karen? Why? Has something happened to her?'

'She's pregnant,' Edward said.

'Oh no! Oh, Edward, that is dreadful!' Lydia set her cup down. He'd seen a lot of Karen, come home from the Whites' quite late a good few times. He must have been responsible. Oh, the foolish pair! Then the full implication of what he had said struck her. 'Why, Edward, she's not sixteen yet, is she?'

'It wasn't me,' he said dully. 'I never went the whole way with her. Mind you, she would have.' He didn't know why he hadn't gone along with her and he certainly hadn't realized that she was only fifteen, though much good that would do him now. 'Her mum caught me on my way back from work. She's going to get the police and I'll be for it.'

'Not necessarily,' Lydia said. 'If it wasn't you, then it was someone else.'

'Karen told her mum it was me. She's annoyed because I've been seeing a bit of Cathy, up at the hotel,' said Edward.

'Edward, look at me,' Lydia commanded, sitting squarely facing him across the table.

He lifted his head and gazed back at her, his face blotched, eyes bloodshot.

'Do you promise that you didn't – that this child can't possibly be yours?' she asked.

'I do. It can't,' he answered, not evading her steady gaze. 'We necked, yes – but not the – the ultimate.'

'I believe you,' Lydia said. 'Now, let me think.' Life didn't change; the same old problems kept arising, only the solutions could be different. 'She'll have to have an abortion,' she said at last. 'There'll be no problem as she's under age.'

'She could marry the bloke. The real father,' Edward said.

'That's not the best way out, and anyway she can't till she's sixteen. Though she can't be far short of that.'

'Two weeks,' said Edward. 'That's enough to get me sent to prison.'

Lydia knew about the fever in the blood, though it took an effort to remember.

'It's the parents' fault,' she said. 'The mother out at night, the father away so much – what do they expect her to do but get into trouble? There's not enough to interest young people here – no youth club, no Guides.' Once, many years ago, she'd run the Guides. Eventually the scheme had died from want of recruits. She'd sometimes wondered if it was her fault.

'Guides!' The thought of Karen as a Guide made Edward, despite his predicament, give a feeble chuckle. Then he sat up straight and spoke firmly. 'I'm leaving,' he said. 'But I couldn't go without seeing you.'

'Don't be so silly, Edward,' Lydia said. 'That won't help. 'They'll soon find you if they mean to go ahead. Karen must be made to name the real father. He's the one to face the music. Have you seen her? Spoken to her about it?'

'No. Her mother's locked her in her room until her father comes back. He's due home sometime late tonight or else tomorrow,' Edward said. 'He'll certainly call the police, if he doesn't kill me first. Her mum's not going to work tonight. It's that bad.'

'Have another cup of tea,' said Lydia. She refilled both their cups. Some colour had returned to Edward's face.

'I was—' he began, then stopped. He had been going to confess about his prison sentence. And she still didn't know that Julie was a chambermaid.

'I suppose you haven't had time to tell your sister about this,' Lydia was saying, uncannily, in Edward's view, mirroring his own thoughts.

'No.'

'Hm.' Lydia finished her second cup of tea. 'When did you first meet Karen?'

'Just after I came here,' Edward said. He cast his mind back. 'I met her at a disco.'

'We can easily check the date,' said Lydia. 'You and Thelma arrived here on September the seventeenth. That's six weeks ago.' She rose and fetched a calendar depicting Scottish scenes on which she noted down her few engagements, then counted up. 'Yes – six weeks and two days.'

'What difference do the dates make?' Edward said. 'It's her word against mine. If she says it was me, they'll believe her.'

'Why shouldn't your word be as good as hers?' asked Lydia, busy calculating.

'Because I've been in prison,' he burst out. There! He'd told her! The deceit was over.

Lydia was silent for some time.

'What did you do?' she asked at last.

172

'Set fire to things,' said Edward. 'In the end I fired a car. No one was hurt,' he added quickly. 'It was in a parking lot, on a Sunday night. There was no one around and no other car nearby.' He stopped, remembering the blaze. He'd stood there gloating.

'Why did you do it?' Lydia asked.

'I like the brightness,' Edward said at once. 'The sparkle. But I wouldn't set another fire, Mrs Cunningham. Not if I can light a bonfire now and then.'

He might well be tempted to put a match to Karen, Lydia thought sourly.

'There's no reason for you to be blamed for something you haven't done,' she told him. 'I shall go and speak to Karen and her mother.' If they waited until the father came back, it might be too late; an angry man would not listen to what he would construe as the maunderings of an old woman. 'You must stay in Milton St Gabriel long enough for it to count when you want another job,' she added. 'You'd better come with me.' If she left him on his own while she did battle, his courage might not hold and he might flee – or go and start another fire. 'Go upstairs and change – have a good wash or bath and put on clean clothes and do your hair. I'll change too – I'm dusty after walking miles with Boris. But let's be quick.'

She didn't seem the least bit shocked by his confession. Like an obedient child, Edward went upstairs, and Lydia, left alone, felt the room start to sway around her. She gripped the back of a chair and breathed deeply, waiting till she steadied down. How did his crime weigh on the scales of justice, balanced against hers?

She must not faint. The only time she had ever done so was when a telephone call had come to the nurses' home where she was living while she did her training. It was one of Arthur's friends who had rung to tell her that he had not returned from a mission over Germany.

173

Later, the same friend told her he had been presumed killed. She had never heard another word. If he had survived, as people who were reported lost sometimes did, he would have sent a message to her. So the man in Heronsmouth was not his resurrected ghost; just his namesake. There was no need to be upset.

She went upstairs and took her ten-year-old good suit from her wardrobe. Then she waited for Edward to finish in the bathroom. She washed her face, made sure her nails were clean, did her hair carefully, blotted a little powder on to her nose and dabbed her lips with pallid lipstick. This was an occasion for putting on a mask.

To his wounded surprise, Boris found himself shut into the house when she and Edward set off for the Whites' house those few short yards away. Edward had shaved; his face shone and he smelled of Imperial Leather soap.

Strangely, no sound of pop music came to greet them as they walked up to the door. Even with the windows shut, the place thrummed and throbbed when Karen or her mother was at home; now the silence itself was ominous.

'Leave the talking to me,' Lydia instructed quietly. 'Don't get angry. Don't start arguing.' She put a hand on his arm. 'Attack is the best method of defence,' she told him. She wasn't too sure if this was true but there was comfort in a cliché. Then she gave a little chuckle, an odd sound coming from her. 'And don't be tempted to strike a match,' she added.

Standing on the doorstep, Lydia pressed the Whites' bell which sent a two-tone jangle through the house. The door was opened by Karen's mother, a woman of about forty, her hair rinsed a gleaming chestnut with a metallic sheen.

'Good evening, Mrs White,' said Lydia. 'I have something to discuss with you.' Her voice was firm, assured; she was once more in the role of Mrs Cunningham, the lady of the manor.

Their visit had clearly taken Mrs White by surprise. She stood staring from the one to the other.

'I don't think we should have this conversation on your doorstep, Mrs White,' Lydia went on. 'We could be overheard if someone walks past.' That was unlikely to happen at this hour, but Mrs White would not want to risk it.

'I'm not letting him across my doorstep,' she said, glaring at Edward in the light that fell from the hallway.

'I'm afraid you must, Mrs White,' said Lydia. 'I'm sure you have no wish to be sued for slander, have you? But I think we can avoid that if we sit down and talk the matter over.'

Slander! The word struck home to both her hearers and for the first time since the accusation had been made, Edward felt a flicker of hope. Mrs C. had something up her sleeve besides her arm.

Mrs White stood aside, and Edward followed Lydia into the house. Mrs White conducted them into her lounge, as she called the tiny sitting-room where a large electric fire filled the hearth and the carpet was heavily patterned with sprigs of flowers. More flowers danced over the curtains. The three-piece suite which took up most of the room was covered in gold Dralon and looked extremely comfortable. There was an enormous television set with a video recorder below it against one wall but no book or paper to be seen; indeed, there was no space for much else.

Lydia sat down in one of the armchairs.

'Will you fetch Karen, please?' she said, her tone turning the request into an order. 'Edward, sit down.' She nodded at the other chair.

Muttering, reluctant, but already at a disadvantage,

Mrs White left the room and went upstairs. Edward opened his mouth to speak but Lydia put a finger to her lips. She sat up very straight in her chair and made signs to him to do the same. It seemed an age before the woman returned, but she did at last. Behind her came Karen, whose face was red and blotched from recent tears. Her hands were clasped before her over the spot where the ill-begotten infant must repose, and she twisted them together. Lydia, who had put on her bi-focals, noticed two red marks across the back of one of them.

'Sit down, Mrs White and Karen,' she invited, as if she were in her own house. Because she and Edward were occupying the two chairs, Karen and her mother were forced into positions beside one another on the sofa so that they could not easily exchange glances if they were to face their interlocutor. Mrs White carefully smoothed her purple skirt beneath her buttocks and tucked her feet – she wore high-heeled sandals and sheer black patterned tights – close against the sofa. Karen sat as far away from her mother as she could.

'Now, Karen, will you tell me what you accuse Edward of having done?' Lydia asked in a cool, even voice.

'You know what it is,' interposed Mrs White. 'She's in trouble and he's the one responsible. She's under age, and that's a crime.'

'Her age is irrelevant to this discussion, since Edward is not the father of her child. Is he, Karen?' Lydia turned to address the girl.

'That's what I said,' muttered Karen, not looking at Lydia.

'Will you look at him and tell him to his face?' Lydia said.

'I've said he is,' reiterated Karen, still looking at her hands which she was twisting together in her lap.

Lydia turned to the girl's mother.

'Mrs White, did you suspect that Karen was pregnant or did she tell you?' she asked. She blanked down pity for the girl; this was no time for weakness.

'She's been being sick,' said Mrs White. 'And she's missed.'

'You always know when your daughter menstruates?' asked Lydia mildly.

The unfamiliar word threw Mrs White for a moment; then she caught on.

'Of course I do. Wants her Tampax, doesn't she?' she said, her careful accent wavering.

'She doesn't buy what she needs for herself?'

'I get it when I do the big monthly shop,' said Mrs White, who thought herself a caring mother.

'I see. When you get your own,' said Lydia, nodding.

'I've had a hysterectomy,' said Mrs White, speaking, as it seemed to Lydia, with some pride.

'Oh dear. Well, you buy your daughter's protection and she hasn't used it. Is that right? How did you know that?'

'She'd got two untouched packets in her drawer,' said Mrs White. 'There was one when I put the new one there. I thought it was a bit funny. Well, any mother would, wouldn't she?'

'Two untouched packets. I see. And she's been sick already. So you think she's missed two months? She's therefore seven weeks pregnant, maybe more,' said Lydia, and noticed Edward stir slightly in his chair. 'Is that right, Karen? Have you missed two months?'

A mumble came from Karen. Now she was pleating her cotton skirt through her fingers. Poor little girl, thought Lydia; she was too simple to see the trap ahead.

'I expect you've got a boyfriend at school, haven't you? Someone you're quite fond of?' Karen went on the school bus to Heronsmouth Comprehensive.

177

'I know lots of boys,' said Karen, with some defiance.

'I'm sure you do. You're a pretty girl, when you haven't spoiled yourself with silly make-up or with crying,' Lydia said. 'I expect plenty of boys like you. And you met Edward at a disco in the village, didn't you, the day after he arrived here, on September the eighteenth. I expect he danced with you because he liked the look of you. Is that so, Edward?' She nodded at him to show that she required an answer.

'That's right,' said Edward warily.

'But you were already late, weren't you?' asked Lydia smoothly.

The girl's miserable expression gave the answer, but Lydia would not let her get away with it.

'Well?' she asked.

'Right.' The word was barely audible.

Even the girl's mother had understood now.

'Why, you little liar,' she burst out and raised her hand. Karen had moved still further from her, edging close to the sofa arm.

'Mrs White, before you strike Karen again, hear what I have to say,' Lydia ordered. 'Karen, hold out your hands. No, palms down,' she corrected, as Karen slowly stretched them out towards her, palms uppermost.

The girl turned them over. In addition to the marks Lydia had already noticed, there were more on the other hand.

'Roll up your sleeves,' Lydia directed. Memories of Henry lashing out with his walking stick made her certain that she had correctly understood what had caused the weals.

As if mesmerized, Karen rolled up the sleeves of the white sweater she wore. Her already swollen breasts moved heavily beneath it. On the plump round arms were other lesions.

Lydia drew a deep breath. Her heart was thudding

and a pulse had begun to pound in her head, but it was nearly over.

'Your mother beat you, didn't she, Karen? When she found out that you were in trouble?'

As Karen nodded, Edward gasped.

'And now you're afraid she'll beat you again because you've lied,' said Lydia. She turned to the woman who had been sitting rigidly throughout this dialogue, her lip caught between her teeth, her chin thrust forward. 'If you do, Mrs White, I shall find out and I shall report you to the police and the social services,' she warned. 'I mean that. Don't doubt it. Now, it's obvious that the father of this baby is some schoolboy, some friend of Karen's whom she's been seeing while you leave her here alone. What do you expect to happen, letting a girl of her age have so much licence? You're seldom home yourself until after midnight. Karen is lonely and she wants affection.' Into her head came the wistful hope that Karen, with her schoolboy lover, might have known some tender joy and that this was why she had tried to protect him by sacrificing Edward. 'You like this boy, don't you Karen?' she asked, speaking gently now. 'You're very fond of him?'

Karen scuffed the carpet with her foot and muttered, 'Yes.'

'I don't want to know his name,' said Lydia. 'And my advice to you, Mrs White, is to take your daughter to the doctor and arrange an abortion for her. She's too young to ruin her life, and so is this boy, whoever he is – too young to be trapped into marriage – oh, you could probably force him into that, after her birthday. He's probably over sixteen himself. He'd think it better than being prosecuted, I'm sure, and it would take her off your hands.' She looked at Karen. 'You're lucky in a way, Karen. When I was young, most girls had to have their illegitimate babies and it brought shame and disgrace on them and their families. Nowadays, you have a choice. You're just a child yourself. You'll get over this. Grow up, and see about some birth control next time.' She paused, then continued. 'If you have any difficulty, Mrs White, I will be able to tell you how to arrange things.' Dorothy would know what to do; she had seen pupils through worse crises than this one, and if necessary Lydia would find the money for a private clinic. 'And I advise you to keep this business from your husband, Mrs White,' she went on. 'He might be rather angry and blame you for what has happened. So lose no time. The sooner this is seen to, the better. Now, before we go, you'll just sign this piece of paper, Karen,' she went on, and took it and a ballpoint from her bag. 'It testifies that you never had full sexual intercourse with Edward Fletcher and that he is not the father of your baby.'

The girl signed it, her hand with the red marks across the back shaking a little. The document might have no legal value, Lydia thought, but it had moral force.

'And I meant what I said about your treatment of Karen, Mrs White. In fact I may report you anyway. Those scars will take some time to go away. I shall have to think about it. Now, Edward, come along.'

She rose to leave, and he sprang ahead of her to open the door, then stood aside to let her leave the room first. Turning, Lydia saw him exchange a glance with Karen. On the girl's face was pure anguish.

'I'm sorry, Eddie,' she whispered.

'That's OK. It wasn't your fault,' he answered.

'She called you Eddie,' Lydia remarked as they walked away. 'Do many people use that nickname? Ted or Teddy is more usual, isn't it?'

'Julie – my sister – always calls me Eddie,' Edward told her. 'Karen's heard her.'

'I see.'

He ought to tell her the rest now; it was minor after what she knew already, but first he had to thank her.

'You were a blooming miracle,' he said. 'How can I make it up to you?'

'By keeping out of trouble in the future,' Lydia told him, promptly.

'Oh, I will,' he answered, and the moment for a full confession passed as she went on speaking.

'And you can make the supper,' she said. She unlocked the front door and they went into the house, Boris coming forward to wrap himself about their legs, tail thumping. 'I need a drink. We both do. Pour us each some brandy. I'll have mine neat but you might prefer to add some ginger ale to yours.'

He cooked sausages while she sat in the sitting-room, hands folded, staring at the hearth where Betty had laid the fire ready for the autumn nights ahead. Was it right to kill that foetus? Would Karen, later, wish that she had carried it to fruition? If, as was unlikely, she went on with her schoolboy lover, yes, she might. Lydia herself had not let Arthur's baby go because it was all that remained to her of him. Even as long ago as that, there were ways to manage things and, if she could have brought herself to ask for help, someone in the hospital would have known how to set about it.

But Karen couldn't hope to escape all punishment; this one was, after all, not a lot to bear.

18

Lydia found it difficult to drag herself out of bed the next morning at her usual time. She went slowly downstairs in her dressing gown. A cup of tea might pull her round.

Edward already had the kettle boiling. He took one look at her and said, 'You go back to bed. I'll bring you up some breakfast.'

She stared at him.

'You don't look very well,' he said gently. 'Have a little lie-in. It will do you good.'

Her face, usually florid because the fine skin was etched with threadlike broken veins, was a curious grey colour and her eyes had sunk back into her skull.

'I've got a headache,' she admitted.

'Off you go,' he said. 'Please.'

No one, nowadays, except occasionally Dorothy, ever told her what to do. She felt too weak to argue, so she did as she was bidden.

'Have you got something you can take?' asked Edward, when he brought her tray.

Lying still, excused from making any effort, Lydia was feeling marginally better.

'I've got two aspirins here. Look,' she showed him. 'I'll have them with my coffee. What a lovely tray.' He had found her best Coalport china to make it look attractive. 'You're spoiling me,' she added.

'About time someone did,' he answered. 'Besides, I owe you, Mrs Cunningham.'

'We'll forget that now,' she said. A creaky smile softened her face. He'd learned a lesson: so had Karen, who would bear the brunt of her folly's consequences. Lydia had almost forgotten that Edward had come here as her daughter's latest acquisition. Remembering, her heart gave an anxious flutter.

'Edward, sit down a minute, if you can spare the time,' she said. He was due at work soon.

'Course I can,' said Edward. He perched on the edge of her bed, crooking one leg across the other thigh and exposing a pale hairy ankle.

Lydia looked at his ingenuous face and remembered what she had learned about him. It hadn't seemed important at the time because of his immediate predicament, but here, sitting on her bed, was a convicted arsonist.

A lot of people had secrets, though: look at her own.

'Ask your sister to lunch on Sunday,' she told him. 'It's time we met. If she can't come then, arrange another day – supper one evening soon.'

'Right,' said Edward.

'And now tell me about – er – Arthur Morrison.' She stumbled over the name. 'You said you like him.'

'Yes, I do. But I don't know all that much about him. You'd better ask Thelma anything you want to know. He's pretty fond of her.'

'I wondered about that,' said Lydia carefully.

'You mean he might fancy her? He's too old for her.'

'She might not think so,' Lydia said. 'After all, you're much younger than she is and that didn't prevent – prevent—' she baulked at defining precisely what she meant.

'No.' Edward had the grace to blush.

'I don't blame you. I know my daughter.' Suddenly it

struck her that Thelma's true father might have been a womanizer. All those years ago, she had believed that he really loved her and that they would have married if he had not been killed. That conviction had sustained her ever since, but perhaps she had been too credulous: perhaps he had said all those things she still remembered just to get her to give in: as if she could have stopped herself, in the end.

Such a thought was treachery.

'He was a navigator in a bomber,' Edward volunteered, eager to move the conversation away from himself.

'A navigator?' Lydia stared at him.

'Yes – steering by the stars,' said Edward. 'I've got to go now, Mrs C. You'll be all right, won't you? Take it easy.'

Lydia barely noticed him leaving the room. She felt as if she were paralysed, unable to move a limb. She could scarcely breathe.

Her Arthur had been a navigator too.

It was coincidence, of course: he was dead, like countless other navigators who had been shot down and listed missing. There could have been ten or more with the same name. Lydia closed her eyes and lay beneath the bedclothes, brooding.

What if he hadn't died? What if he had been merely a philanderer and grown bored with her? Too much love could be a burden: had she stifled him? Could he have thought so little of her that he had ignored her feelings altogether? Wouldn't he have got in touch with her eventually, even if only to say that everything between them was over? He could have written to her at the hospital; mail would have been sent on.

Perhaps his letter had got lost, she thought for a wistful moment.

But she didn't want him to be alive: not now, not

living in Heronsmouth. He had died young and perfect, keeping their love immortal. He would never see her looking old and wrinkled.

She got out of bed and dressed, and when she had washed her breakfast things, she went into the garden. A few dead rose clippings and withered flowers discarded from the house lay on the ash pile at the bottom of the garden. Lydia glanced at them with sympathy for Edward's pyromania. If he had lived in the country, with space to let his anger out in some legitimate physical activity, he might never have started lighting fires. It would have relieved her to have lit a bonfire now, a really good one, the sort they used to have at the Manor where huge heaps of hedge trimmings and dead wood had been burnt up. But there wasn't enough today to make any sort of blaze.

She would have to meet this Arthur Morrison, or look at him, at least. It was the only way to regain her peace of mind. When she saw him for herself and realized how foolish she was being, the ghost would be laid.

She turned back towards the house, and as she entered it, the telephone began to ring.

Gerald had returned from France and wanted to come down tomorrow for the weekend. He'd arrive in time for dinner.

Lydia had to do the weekend shopping anyway. Ordinarily, she would have made the best of what was available in the village but with Gerald coming, things were different. She set off for Heronsmouth where, in the delicatessen, she would be able to buy ripe Brie or Camembert. She'd get some fish, too; he liked that. He mustn't take them out again so soon; it cost too much.

Since Edward had been in the house, she had been cooking more than when she was alone, trying things

185

she rarely prepared just for herself. He loved braised kidneys, liver and onions, shepherd's pie and kedgeree. No wonder he enjoyed home cooking if he'd only just come out of prison. She could see that he had put on weight in the past few weeks, and had more colour in his face. Did they ever get out, beyond walking in a courtyard? She must ask him; it might be good for him to talk about it.

On her way to the delicatessen, Lydia saw two people ahead of her going in the same direction. It was a second or two before she recognized the trousered figure of her daughter. She was talking animatedly to a man who walked beside her on the kerb edge of the pavement, slightly dragging one leg.

This was Arthur's namesake! Lydia's heart began to thump and her throat felt choked. She stopped abruptly, causing someone behind her to collide with her and drop the oranges she carried; the paper bag they were in burst and the fruit rolled into the gutter. Lydia, apologizing in a flustered manner, helped the woman pick them up, then walked on. Thelma and her companion had disappeared, but as she came up to the delicatessen, Lydia saw that they were inside, apparently discussing what to buy.

Lydia saw an old man wearing a tweed hat below which showed wisps of curly white hair. He had shaved in such a way as to leave pronounced sideboards on his pink cheeks, and his eyebrows were bushy. Young Arthur's hair had been cut so short that few curls were left, but they had been springy against her hand and lips. His brows had been strongly marked and in age might have thickened, but at this first glimpse, nothing about the man reminded Lydia of her lover. She was unaware of making a decision as her legs carried her into the shop and she heard herself speak.

'Thelma! What a lucky meeting! I was going to telephone to thank you for that delightful dinner the other evening.'

Thelma, startled, swung around.

'Hullo, Mother,' she said. 'What are you doing here today? I thought you only came to town on Thursdays.'

'Gerald's coming down tomorrow,' said Lydia. 'I need to buy some cheese.'

'You could get it in the village,' Thelma said.

'Not this selection,' Lydia explained. 'You know he loves ripe Brie, if they have some.' She peered at the counter lest she seem to be staring at the old man. He'd made a quick recovery from his chest infection, she thought inconsequentially.

'Oh yes, they have,' a male voice told her. 'We were just planning to buy some. And have you tried their home-made pâté?'

It was the voice. She knew the voice. That was the same warm tone, the slightly amused way of speaking. He had always been able to make her laugh. Lydia, who was wearing her bi-focal spectacles, slowly looked up. She saw the blue eyes, still merry though now a little faded, peering at her over half-glasses. She had only to look at Thelma to see them duplicated; surely the whole world could see the likeness? The face was fuller, lined and weatherbeaten like her own; he had put on several stone, and she would not have recognized him if she had not had what was to some extent a warning. But it was the voice that clinched it.

'Won't you introduce me, Thelma?' Again, that echo from the past.

'Mr Morrison – my mother, Mrs Cunningham,' said Thelma impatiently.

At least she'd done it formally, not in her normal casual manner using first names. Would hearing the name Lydia have sounded any knell with him?

'How do you do?' said Lydia faintly, gripping her bag and shopping basket tightly, not about to offer him her hand.

'We should have met on Wednesday,' he replied, and smiled.

'Yes. I hope you're better,' Lydia said conventionally, her own voice hoarse with shock.

'I've quite recovered,'he declared, and laughed. 'I'm sure I missed a splendid dinner. Thelma's such a tip-top cook. A great girl altogether.'

'Oh yes,' said Lydia, and inside her head was screaming, she's our daughter.

'Won't you come back with us now and have some lunch?' he was suggesting. 'We're just buying it – bread and cheese – you see the sort of thing.'

'No – no. I haven't time. I'm sorry. I must get home.' Lydia turned away to hide the fact that she was trembling. 'I'll go and get the fish now, and come back later when they're not so busy,' she said, and scuttled from the shop with Thelma staring after her in a pitying way. There was only one other customer waiting to be served.

'Mother's getting very stupid,' she said. 'I sometimes think she's going senile.'

'Oh, come now, Thelma,' Arthur said. 'Don't be naughty. You'll be old one day. She's just got too much to do, I expect.'

Thelma didn't mind the criticism.

'You don't know her,' was all she said, but in fact her mother had looked just as if she'd seen a ghost.

Lydia scurried to the fishmonger's and stood outside it gulping in deep breaths, trying to calm down enough to go in and buy some turbot. She had started on her way back to the car when she remembered the cheese for Gerald.

They'd be gone now. She walked cautiously towards the delicatessen but they were nowhere to be seen.

What if he asked Thelma about her parents? What if he wanted to know her mother's maiden name, found out that Thelma's grandfather had been a country parson? Or had he forgotten all about that young probationer nurse he'd met at a station dance to which she'd been persuaded to go by some bolder girls?

Lydia needed time to think about it. First, above all else, was her own sense of having been betrayed. A long time after that came the realization that another, dreadful danger threatened Thelma. For they had looked happy together; that had been obvious as she followed them along the road.

What if Dorothy's prophecy should come true and Arthur Morrison should seek to marry his own daughter?

Years ago, Henry had hinted that his relationship with Thelma was not entirely fatherly, taunting Lydia that there was no blood barrier between them. She had not known whether to believe what he was saying, for he lost no opportunity of hurting her and she never knew when he was lying. So, when her chance had come, she had taken it without any hesitation. She had planned nothing, but as Henry suddenly clutched his chest and grunted with pain, gasping for breath, she had made no attempt to help him. She had felt a sudden surge of power as she watched his agony, ignoring the appeal in his protuberant eyes. He had tried to struggle from his chair and she had not prevented him. Then he had lurched across the room and fallen to the gound where she had let him lie.

He had not died at once; they were alone in the house and she had simply left the room. When she returned, he was dead.

Now, Thelma was under threat of being party to a most horrible offence.

She must be saved.

But how?

19

In Heronsmouth, Arthur Morrison was now a happy man.

A few short weeks ago he was inured to loneliness, doing his best to enjoy playing bridge, working in the garden, visits to the library. Life would be like this for ever, till gradually he ailed and failed and even these diversions were curtailed. There was not a lot to look forward to apart from visits to his family and occasional holidays. He and Phyllis had often been to France, touring with the car – he drove an automatic which spared his stiff leg – but that would be no fun alone. Last year, he'd taken the coastal steamer and sailed from Bergen all along the coast of Norway to Kirkenes on the Russian border. They'd planned to take the trip together, and he had gone by himself as a sort of seal on their compact. To his surprise, he had thoroughly enjoyed the voyage, finding pleasant company among the other passengers in the tiny boat and awed by the majestic scenery. He hadn't even minded a Force-Eight gale one night during a passage in the open sea.

Thelma might go with him on some trip or other; perhaps to China? He'd like to see those terra-cotta warriors. Would she enjoy that? The future seemed suddenly to be filled with possibilities instead of being just a slow decline towards death. He didn't know quite how he expected their relationship to develop, nor had he analysed his feelings towards her. She was attractive, full of vitality, and being with her made him feel half his actual age. People would talk, inevitably, but he didn't mind gossip of such a flattering variety; and Thelma, with her chequered matrimonial career, would probably treat it as a joke.

She wasn't very keen on sex. She'd told him so; she'd said she'd always found it very disappointing. She'd hardly have said that if she foresaw any intimate involvement between the two of them, and she didn't know he'd seen her naked by the swimming pool. Arthur was content to let things drift. An old man with a gammy leg was hardly an alluring prospect to a woman in her prime. He knew she needed some stability in her life; her mother seemed a nervy sort of woman, poor old soul, dashing from the shop like that, but he hadn't cared for Thelma's attitude towards her. He must invite Mrs Cunningham to the house another time. It seemed a bit hard, though, that Thelma should be caught between two elderly people, her mother and himself, when she was young enough to enjoy a full personal life – and should have one. Maybe she'd meet some fellow in the drama group, and he, Arthur, would be torn with jealousy.

The idea amused him. He'd be pleased if she were happy. Meanwhile, as he had done throughout his life, he would make the best of what was good about the present.

Years and years ago there'd been a girl. She'd had soft, silky brown hair, so fine it seemed like gossamer blowing across his face in a summer breeze. He'd met her at some dance or other organized to entertain servicemen like himself. She had large, frightened eyes and had looked lost and timid; he'd rescued her, then become entranced with the shy ardour she so surprisingly revealed. He'd hoped that they would marry –

they'd talked about it, imprecisely, otherwise he was certain that she would not have contributed so willingly to her own seduction. They'd spent occasional nights at a pub near his station, signing in as Mr and Mrs Smith, giggling about it in the dipping double bed. Then he was shot down and badly wounded. By the time that he was well enough to write to her, he'd heard from someone in his squadron that she was married. So that was that. She hadn't even waited to find out his fate.

It had been a bitter blow to Arthur. In the prison camp his stiff leg excluded him from any chance of making a successful bid for freedom, so he decided to work towards some other goal. He had joined the Royal Air Force straight from school. As he had been good at figures, he embarked on an accountancy course. By the time he was released, he was nearly ready to take his final exams; his ultimate qualifications led him eventually to become company secretary in a light engineering firm. He had met Phyllis soon after he came home and they were married within a year. They had been very happy and he had almost forgotten Lydia. When he and Phyllis bought The Shieling, he remembered that she had come from somewhere in the West Country where her father was a parson. Lydia Newton was her name. She might be dead by now, for all he knew. He didn't know whom she had married, nor did he care; while he was in the camp, men were receiving Dear John letters all the time and his case was not at all unusual. He had made a monumental effort to put it all behind him and become, again, the cheerful person he had been before. He joined in amateur dramatics at the camp and found he had a talent for performing; in the end, through pretending that he was carefree, he became content. His good luck was to meet Phyllis so quickly and he made his mind up not to lose her.

Now, he missed her sadly but that was hidden from the world. People didn't want long faces round them; most had sorrows, aches and pains, and little tragedies.

On Saturday afternoon, Arthur was helping Thelma to go through her part as Arkadina in *The Seagull*. He was enjoying reading Trepliov's lines in Act Three when the doorbell rang, just as Arkadina said *'The doctor's late.'* He laughed at the interruption and said 'I'm not expecting him, are you?' to Thelma, who shook her head and giggled.

'I'll go,' she said, pushing him gently back into his chair. Some days his leg was very painful.

She was astonished to find her brother Gerald standing on the doorstep.

'What do you want?' she asked sourly.

'What a welcome!' He spoke mildly. 'I called at your flat and you were out, so I thought you'd be up here.'

'Well?' She was quite put out at seeing him.

'I just came to see you,' Gerald said. He was determined not to let her irritate him.

Meanwhile, in the background, Arthur had heard unfriendly noises and came to find out what was happening.

'It's my brother,' Thelma said, turning a cross face towards him.

'Well, ask him in,' said Arthur.

Gerald stepped across the threshold, forcing Thelma to move aside, and held out his hand.

'Gerald Cunningham,' he said. 'I hope I'm not interrupting anything?'

'You are, in fact. A rehearsal of *The Seagull*,' Arthur said. 'Billed as comedy, I notice, but I wouldn't really call it one, would you? I'm sure you know it well, as Thelma tells me she's already played Nina.'

'I don't think any of those Russians are really funny,' Gerald said.

'They're all forever setting off to Moscow,' Arthur said. 'They seem to have no other goal.'

He led the way into the square sitting-room where a bay window overlooked the estuary. A pair of field glasses lay on the windowsill; the old man probably spent hours watching what went on on the water, Gerald thought. The room was furnished in a pleasant, conventional way, rather like his mother's though it was much larger.

'I went to see Thelma at the flat and she was out.' Gerald repeated his explanation. 'I wondered if she'd already moved up here.' It occurred to him that he might have made a gaffe, and he added, 'She is moving, isn't she?'

'Yes,' said Thelma.

'It'll be better through the winter,'Arthur said. 'That haul up the hill can be quite a drag.'

She wouldn't be able to carry on with all and sundry under this nice old chap's roof; even Thelma would not do that, Gerald decided. Perhaps she'd settle for a spell of chastity.

'What a lovely view,' he said aloud.

'Isn't it?' Arthur moved to stand beside him at the window and they began discussing vessels in the estuary. Arthur knew who owned many of the boats which were still moored there, not yet hauled ashore for winter. Passing the field glasses to Gerald, he pointed out various interesting things to be observed and Thelma was forgotten by them both.

'I'll light the fire,' she said loudly.

Arthur had had a realistic gas fire installed after Phyllis died. It saved a lot of work and he derived enormous pleasure from its deceptive appearance.

'Do, do,' he said. 'Thank you, Thelma. And what about some tea? Shall we have some? You'd like a cup, I'm sure,' he said to Gerald.

195

'Yes, I would.' Gerald had not stopped, except for petrol, since he left London. 'But I mustn't stay too long. My mother's expecting me.'

'Telephone her,' Arthur said. 'Then she won't be watching for you at the window.'

As if she would, thought Gerald.

'The telephone's in the hall.' Arthur went on. 'Thelma will show you.'

'Mother was in Heronsmouth yesterday,' Thelma told Gerald as they went together to the hall, where a streamlined telephone rested on a table. 'She seemed quite dotty – came into the delicatessen and then dashed out again without buying anything. If you ask me, she's begun to lose her marbles.'

'She hasn't,' Gerald said. 'I expect she thought of something else she wanted.'

Thelma shrugged.

'Well, help yourself,' she said, and went into the kitchen.

Lydia answered the telephone promptly. Gerald told her where he was and said he would come on soon. Did she want anything from the town? He'd be on his way before the shops shut.

'No,' said Lydia; then she added, 'There is one thing you could do.'

'What's that?'

'Make sure he hasn't got a cat. That old man.' She would not speak his name. 'Because of Thelma's asthma,' she explained.

'I'll find out,' said Gerald.

He was smiling when he returned to the sitting-room where his host was admiring the leaping flames in the grate.

'Well, that's done,' he said. 'Thank you. My anxious mother asked me to find out if you have a cat. They give my sister asthma.'

'Do they? How strange,' said Arthur. 'I suffer from it too. It's got a little worse these last few years. Cats and boiler fumes and too much tobacco smoke are all hazardous for me. There are no cats here. You can reassure your mother.'

'I didn't think Thelma would take the job on if you had one,' Gerald said. 'It's beastly for her. And for you, of course.'

'It's a nuisance,' he admitted. 'I had injections once but they seem to have worn off now and I haven't bothered to be done again as I can usually avoid the cause of the trouble.'

At this point Thelma came in with a trolley bearing scones and home-made shortbread for tea.

'I'll put on too much weight with your sister's cooking,' Arthur said. He twinkled at them both. They were not at all alike, the one so fair, the other dark.

Gerald and his host found plenty to discuss since both had financial backgrounds, and Thelma soon began to fidget. When Arthur, quite aware that she was bored and jealous, changed the subject so that she could be included in the conversation, Gerald's own impatience with his sister's poor manners turned to admiring amusement. There were no flies on this old boy and he had a gift for cooling things; maybe a few weeks – or better, months – spent here would sort Thelma out.

'Thelma must bring you over to dinner some time when I'm down again,' he said, and added, 'At the hotel in the village where my mother lives, I mean. We go there now and then. The food is very good. It would be nice if she could meet you properly.'

'I'd like that,' Arthur said, and when he had gone, commented to Thelma, 'I like your brother.'

'You get on with everyone,' was Thelma's answer, given with a sulky frown. Then she softened the effect by smiling. This transformed her face and, as almost everyone had always done, he forgave her for her grace-lessness.

'He gets asthma too,' Gerald told his mother. 'Would you believe it? So no cats. Why, Mother, are you ill?' For she had gasped suddenly and closed her eyes.

Lydia rallied quickly.

'It's all right – I caught my breath,' she said. How the body could betray, and in so many ways! Doctors had expressed surprise that there was no allergic history in the family to account for Thelma's complaint. Lydia had blue eyes, which explained Thelma's. Gerald's were brown, following his father. If Henry's had been blue and Thelma's brown, then any informed individual would have been suspicious.

'They were reading the play together – *The Seagull*,' Gerald went on. 'He seems to know it well. When's the performance?'

'In about two weeks' time,' said Lydia. 'I thought she'd know her part backwards by now.'

'I expect she does. I think she just enjoys any audi-ence,' said Gerald. 'What'll she do afterwards? Be in a pantomime or something?'

'That would be a good idea,' said Lydia, taking him seriously. 'But there won't be much time to get one up, will there? When *The Seagull*'s over there'll be only a month or so till Christmas.'

'I was only joking, Mother,' Gerald said. 'I just thought she'd be lost without a part to play. Though she could be Wendy to this old boy's Peter Pan. I thought him a nice old chap and he seems to have her taped.' She'd gone off without a murmur to make the tea. 'I think they're somehow on the same wavelength. Let's hope it lasts.'

'Dorothy thinks that – er – that Mr Morrison –' Lydia

made herself enunciate the name '– that he might want to marry Thelma.

'Good heavens, does she?' Gerald found the idea most surprising. He gave it his attention. 'Well, she could do a lot worse,' he said. 'She might be wise to jump at it, if she gets a chance. Still, he's getting on a bit; I shouldn't think he'd bother. It struck me that his manner towards her was paternalistic. What did you think of him? I hear you met him yesterday.'

It never occurred to Lydia to confide in Gerald. A life-time's habit of concealment did not cease so easily.

'We barely spoke,' she said austerely. 'Thelma had to be reminded to introduce us.' And it was Arthur who had done the reminding, not her mother. The irony of this did not strike Lydia now any more than it had at the time.

But Gerald was registering the implicit criticism of Thelma and it amazed him.

'Well, you'll meet him properly soon enough,' he said. 'I'm going to invite them both to dinner at the Manor next time I'm down.' Then he had a thought. 'But why wait till then? We could all have lunch there tomorrow.'

'No, Gerald. It will have to wait,' said Lydia firmly. 'Edward's sister is visiting us tomorrow. One thing at a time.'

'Oh, very well. How is that young man?' asked Gerald.

'Working hard,' said Lydia. She would not tell even Gerald about Edward's narrow escape from litigation. 'He's a good boy, Gerald.'

'I'm sure he is.' Gerald was surprised at her insistence; he had already formed a favourable opinion of her guest.

Lydia had averted danger this time, but it would be impossible to avoid ultimately meeting Arthur, if

Thelma went on working for him. Sooner or later she would find herself face to face with him, and she would not be able to endure it. Her tortured thoughts scurried round inside her aching head. His had been a gross betrayal for which she had sacrificed her whole life, and now, as she neared the end of the long pilgrimage, the daughter whose protection had been her main aim could be on the brink of committing an offence too terrible to contemplate.

Of course, she wouldn't be at risk unless they married. Or something.

The 'or something' was what mattered. It could have happened already, if the pair had had a mind to it, but now Lydia allowed Gerald's comments to offer her a little consolation. Thelma was not yet living in the house and she was busy with rehearsals for the play. Later, when these circumstances had changed, the opportunity would be there. And the temptation.

20

'I can't do it,' Julie had said. 'I haven't the nerve.'

'You must,' Edward had told her. 'Now I'm staying in the village, you've got to meet her some day. There's nothing to be afraid of. She's not one of your stuck-up kind. Look how she's treated me. She'll be really offended if you don't turn up. And you're not on duty. You can make it.'

She gave in eventually, persuaded because it would be just the three of them. Edward did not learn that Gerald was coming down until after he had got her to agree, and then he wouldn't warn her for fear she would cry off. Once, she'd been game for anything; odd how cautious she'd become, he thought.

'Think of yourself as an insurance clerk,' he told her. 'You were one once.'

When she arrived at the lodge at a quarter to one on Sunday, as instructed, Gerald recognized her immediately, though he did a quick double-take. Here was the bringer of his early tea, the waitress who had served them at dinner just a few weeks before. Now, she wore a cherry-coloured wool skirt, full and sweeping with unpressed pleats, and a tailored shirt in checks that toned with it. Her dark, shoulder-length hair, previously unremarkably secured in a ponytail, was drawn back from a centre parting and curled softly upwards at the ends. When she saw Gerald, she raised her chin as if to counter a challenge. She had arching brows like crescent moons above her hazel eyes and her effect on him was instantly erotic.

'Hullo,' he said, and put a glass of champagne in her hand. 'How nice to see you again.'

'Oh, have you met before?' asked Lydia.

'Yes – and so have you, Mother. Don't you remember? Up at the hotel,' said Gerald. His mother had got the wrong end of the stick somehow; she'd thought Edward's sister let rooms in the village. And he'd leaped to the wrong conclusion when he saw the pair at the window after that evening at the hotel. In case his mother still hadn't caught on, he asked Julie, 'How long have you worked there?'

'Only this season,' she answered. 'I came in March.'

'So that's how Edward got his new job, is it?' Gerald asked. 'You knew it was coming up?'

'Something like that,' said Julie. She took a gulp from her glass and it braced her. 'Is it someone's birthday?'

'No,' said Lydia. 'Gerald does this sometimes. Brings champagne, I mean. It's a thing his grandfather used to do.'

'It's a natural tonic,' said Gerald, smiling. He, however, was celebrating the fact that Thelma had left their mother's house for a new phase in her troubled life. 'Will Edward like working at the hotel? Won't he find it rather quiet?' he asked her.

'Well – I don't know.' He had expressed Julie's own fear.

'Hey – I'm here. Let me answer for myself,' said Edward. 'I've got a scooter now – I can get around.'

'Are you staying on?' asked Gerald.

'I'll have to, won't I?' Julie said. 'Now Eddie's here, I'll have to keep an eye on him.' She spoke lightly, suddenly at ease. Gerald's friendly manner, or the champagne, or both, had dispelled her nervousness. 'Is your sister coming?' she added. How would Gerald feel about her involvement with Eddie?

'No. She's living in Heronsmouth now,' said Gerald.

'She's an actress, isn't she?' said Julie. 'Eddie told me.'

'Well – sort of. She's appearing in an amateur production of *The Seagull*.'

'It's a Russian play,' Edward told her, sure that she would not have heard of it. 'Full of people all in love with the wrong ones and miserable.'

'Well, that's just like life, then,' Julie said practically. 'You've only got to read the paper.'

'True,' said Gerald. Even *The Times* offered such examples to its readers. 'Come and sit down, Julie – may I call you Julie? And tell me what you were doing before you came down here.'

He manoeuvred her towards the sofa and, before he sat down beside her, refilled all their glasses.

'Gerald, this is really very nice,' said Lydia. 'You shouldn't, though. It's so extravagant. Sherry is quite adequate.'

Gerald decided not to take her remark as a reproof, he had seen his mother mellow after this medicine before. Just one glass was enough to do the trick.

'I think it's lovely,' Julie said. 'What else did your grandfather do?'

'Dabbled on the Stock Exchange, unfortunately,' said Gerald. 'But he was a nice old boy. I suppose he was a *bon viveur*. Would you say so, Mother? He knew how to get the utmost out of life.'

'You're like him in some ways,' said Lydia. Her father-in-law had given her bottles of Beaujolais from his cellar if he thought she looked a trifle pale during those war years when Henry was away. Now, Gerald brought her wine and spirits.

'I look like him,' said Gerald. 'He was short and dark

and—' he had been going to add 'ugly' but he bit back the word. 'He put on a lot of weight and got a drinker's nose. That hasn't happened to me so far.'

'You're very like him,' Lydia repeated. She stood up. 'Now, I'm going to dish up. Edward will help me. You two entertain each other.'

Julie turned amused eyes towards Gerald as the others left the room, as if to say, how shall we do that?

'Your brother's been good to my mother,' Gerald said. 'I don't mind admitting I was a bit doubtful about him staying on after Thelma left, but it's working well. She'll miss him when he moves into the hotel.'

'It's all over. Him and – and Thelma,' Julie said.

'I know,' said Gerald. 'I don't think it amounted to very much, do you?'

She shook her head. She'd made Eddie tell her the truth. He'd been lucky to get out of the entanglement so easily. The whole thing was an embarrassment to her. What had Eddie thought he was doing?

'One can drop into these things,' said Gerald. 'No harm done, anyway. Come and see the garden,' he suggested, and opened the french window. 'Will you be warm enough?' She had worn a showerproof jacket when she arrived.

'Yes, I'm fine,' said Julie. She walked ahead of him down the winding path between the rose bushes. 'It's a bit of a come-down for your mother, isn't it?' she asked. 'I mean, I think it's lovely, but after the Manor—?'

'In a way, but I don't think she was very happy there,' said Gerald.

'Wasn't she?'

'She and my father didn't get along too well,' he said. 'I don't think they'd have married but for the war.'

'You couldn't get divorced then, could you?'

'Well, you could, but it wasn't easy like it is today, and a lot of people found it rather scandalous, unless

204

you were a film star or a duchess,' Gerald said lightly. 'My sister was born very soon after they married. That would have stopped them from separating, even if they'd wanted to.'

'Still, they had space. They could get away from each other in a house that size,' she said, frowning.

What was her history? Had she been married? She was obviously several years older than her brother.

'I expect your mother's sorry you live so far away,' she was saying.

'Oh, I think she sees as much of me as she can take,' said Gerald. 'She's a lone bird. I don't descend on her too often.' He looked across to the Dennises' roof. 'She was upset when that huge expanse of ginger tiles rose up to block her view,' he added. 'Before that she could see across to the hills and know the sea was there beyond them.'

'I think it's lovely, even with the roof,' said Julie. 'I grew up in Birmingham.'

He'd picked up the hard G in her accent; she hadn't lost it altogether.

'What are you doing working as a chambermaid?' he asked her. 'You must have had other jobs before.'

'Better jobs, you mean? Status-wise?'

'I suppose I do.'

'I wanted to get away from – from everything,' she said. 'It was all found, and easy. A proper change.'

Some man, he thought, and he was right. Julie had had a long affair with a married man who, in the end, had elected to remain with his wife and she had cut and run away from him and from the perpetual problem of Eddie.

'Is there promotion? Could you change jobs?' he asked.

'Maybe, because it's small and we don't belong to unions,' she said. 'I hadn't really thought about it.'

He would, though. He'd talk to Paula Thomson about her, but not this weekend; it could wait.

Gerald had produced a bottle of claret to drink with the meal. Julie exhibited a hearty appetite which he found endearing.

'You are lucky, Eddie,' she declared. 'Living here, I mean, all this time. This is delicious.'

'The food's all right where you are too, isn't it?' asked Gerald with a smile. 'I expect the staff do quite well.' He hoped that was so.

'Oh yes, we do,' Julie hastened to assure him.

'Were you always such a good cook, Mother?' he inquired. 'Before you were married, I mean?'

'We ate plainly at the vicarage,' said Lydia. 'Milk puddings and mince.'

'Plain living and high thinking, eh?' said Gerald. 'It was different later. My father was a very particular man and if anything was not just as he thought it ought to be, he made a fearful fuss. If the meat was tough he always blamed mother, not the butcher.'

So he had noticed that, had he? Lydia was surprised.

'Tell us about life at the Manor,' Julie invited. 'Was it like *Upstairs, Downstairs*?'

'Gracious no,' said Lydia. 'Not in our time, anyway, though it may have been in the days of Gerald's great-grandfather. Most of the time we just had a woman from the village twice a week.' There'd been Betty sometimes, too. They'd shut up room after room; even so, Lydia had never seemed to cease cleaning and if she wasn't busy in the house, she was expected to labour in the garden where the help grew sketchier and sketchier as time went on.

'What was he like when he was little, Mrs Cunningham?' Julie asked. She looked at Gerald, not knowing what to call him. 'Your son, I mean,' she added, blushing slightly.

'Call me Gerald,' he instructed, and she blushed still more.

Lydia thought before she answered.

'Well, he was always very good,' she said. 'He worked hard at school and was hardly ever naughty.'

'I bet Thelma was naughty,' Edward said. 'She is still.'

'She doesn't change a lot,' Gerald agreed drily. 'Are you coming to the play, Edward? Julie, you must come with us.' He'd see her again if she joined them; he liked that prospect.

'It would be fun,' said Julie.

'Will you be free then?' Paula Thomson couldn't expect the girl to be always serving dinners as well as early-morning tea.

'That's no problem with some warning,' Julie said.

It was agreed that they would form a party for the Saturday performance, the last night of the run, and Gerald said that Arthur Morrison should be included in their group.

'He's bound to want to see it,' he said. 'We can't leave him out.'

'But—' Lydia began, then stopped. How could she object? Gerald's was a reasonable suggestion.

Julie was still curious about life in Milton St Gabriel before the war. and Lydia turned to talk to her, concentrating on her questions so that she was distracted from the anxiety that was becoming an obsession. She grew loquacious, describing tennis parties given by the Cunninghams, with lemonade to refresh the players and sponge cake for tea. Her manner became almost hectic; Gerald looked at her, perplexed by this most untypical behaviour.

'They still went on early in the war,' she said. It was after one of them that she had found it easy to trap Henry. 'When Gerald's father was on leave. And before he was killed, his uncle, too.'

Gerald was discomfited by his mother's suddenly shrill voice and almost manic stare.

'My uncle was another short, dark swarthy Cunningham,' he said.

'Are your children like you?' Julie's attention was successfully deflected. She had learned some of Gerald's history from Ferdy at the hotel.

'No. Luckily they take after their mother,' Gerald answered. 'I wouldn't wish my ugly mug on them.' He reached out with the wine bottle and refilled the glasses.

But Julie persisted.

'You aren't ugly,' she said. 'Whatever gave you that idea?'

'It's all right. I'm used to it after all this time,' he said cheerfully. 'Perhaps I'll look quite interesting when I'm old enough to be regarded as an ancient gargoyle.' He turned to his mother, whose expression during this exchange had become one of bewilderment. 'Mother, Christopher was in great shape when I saw him. His French is very good now.' He turned to the brother and sister. 'Christopher's my son. He's in France learning about wine.'

This diversion turned the talk into less personal channels. Gerald learned that Julie had once been on holiday to Spain, and on a day trip to Boulogne; that was the limit of her foreign travel. What fun it would be to take her to Paris – show her the Loire – the Dordogne. Images of a stone cottage in a grove of trees came to him; he pictured Julie barefoot, paddling in a stream, and laughing.

His mother had regained her normal control.

'Gerald, you're miles away,' she said. 'Come on, dear, and help me. We've got Queen of Puddings now.'

Gerald blinked himself back to the present. His mother, incredibly, had called him 'dear' and Julie had denied that he was ugly. Now he was being offered

208

one of his favourite puddings: it was better than a birthday.

He left for London after Edward had gone with Julie back to the hotel.

'You shouldn't spend too much time alone,' his mother told him as he put his bag into the car.

'I don't,' said Gerald. She'd talked like this before, that day when they walked on the beach. What was on her mind?

'You get out of the way of it,' said Lydia.

'Out of the way of what?' Something was bugging her, that was certain, but it couldn't be him and his affairs; her concern had always been reserved for Thelma.

'Of – of –' Lydia searched for words. 'Of sharing things, I suppose I mean. As I have done.'

She looked at him bleakly, a tall, thin woman, taller than himself, so that he still looked up to her as the apprehensive little boy had done. And like that same anxious little boy who feared a snub, he could not find an answer and he did not dare to hug her.

'Goodbye, Mother,' he said, and got into his car.

She stood and watched him drive away, not waving, simply standing in the road until the car had vanished round the bend.

209

21

How could she avoid meeting Arthur at the play performance? Lydia could fake flu, or a cold: but she must witness Thelma's little triumph, if she had one.

Edward would know when she planned to move into The Shieling, and thus closer to real risk. Lydia asked him about it, and he said that it would not be for a while, at least until the play was over. He did not tell her that one of the actors, who had some leading role, was now a constant visitor at Thelma's flat in the evenings, ostensibly running through their scenes together. Knowing Thelma, more than rehearsing was involved, but at least she wasn't carrying on under the old man's nose.

Lydia clung to the fragile comfort of knowing that Thelma was, to some extent, protected for the present. There was time to prevent calamity, but she did not know how to do it, and meanwhile she kept having dreams. Sometimes it was the recurring house removal that she dreamed of, but at other times she was haunted by the past. She had nightmares about her life with Henry, imagining that it was he who had not died but who was about to thrust himself upon her as she lay in bed, or to beat her with his stick. She would wake tense and sweating, her heart pounding as if it would burst its way past her rib-cage. Sitting up in bed, clutching her nightgown to her thin chest, she would gasp with relief at finding it was just a nightmare.

Sometimes, Arthur came to her in dreams, as he had failed to do throughout the years. Now, he floated towards her through fluffy white clouds as though arriving from heaven, dressed in his blue uniform and smiling, his fair hair crisp against the sky. Then his image dissolved and there was an old, red face above the uniform and it was Henry who scowled down at her.

She would get up in the night and pace about, go quietly downstairs and sit at her jigsaw. Once, Edward heard her and came down. He made her go back to bed and took her up a cup of tea and, because he saw that she was shivering, brought her a hot-water bottle.

She couldn't read. Even the newspaper demanded too much concentration. She had been like that before, in the first dreadful days after Arthur was reported missing and she had to face both grief and her own predicament.

Her father had questioned the wisdom of marrying Henry in such haste, though the couple had, of course, known each other for years.

Her answer was to say that Henry might be killed. They had to take their chance.

Her parents had made no comment on Thelma's so-called premature arrival when she so obviously was a full-term baby, but a year later they moved to another living two hundred miles away and thereafter had seen little of their daughter and grandchildren.

Lydia had very soon discovered that her assumption that Henry would evoke a natural response in her had been false, the first illusion of so many that were soon to be dispelled as her punishing marriage began. She had been wicked, tricking him to protect her lover's child, but she had subsequently done her duty, played the role demanded of her in the village and never turned away from him until those final years together when she had, at last, moved her possessions from their shared bedroom to another far along the corridor. Even there, he had pursued her.

Round and round went her tormented thoughts. If only she had known that Arthur was alive! Even with no prospect of his imminent return, she would never have trapped Henry into imagining he was the father of their child. Setting out to fabricate that possibility had been the darkest action of her life. Even now, she could remember the scent of mown grass about them as they went into the summerhouse where Henry shut the door and wedged it with a chair. The plank floor was hard and rough; she'd got a splinter in her hand; but Henry, red-faced, sweating after playing tennis, had been oblivious. Oddly, treacherously, she had liked that strong male smell which later she had grown to hate. It had been over very quickly. Naïvely, she had expected that in the future, in more comfortable surroundings, it would be better. But there had once been a wood with Arthur which she could remember: trees above their heads with glimpses of the sky between the leafy branches; she'd noticed no discordance then. Perhaps that was when Thelma had been conceived.

As soon as Henry heard that she was pregnant – which she told him in a letter little more than two weeks later – he at once agreed to marry her. At that time his regiment was stationed on Salisbury Plain and it was speedily arranged.

Lydia had no idea that he had given Thelma a different version of these events.

Henry, captivated by the fair, pretty baby, had not at first realized the extent of Lydia's subterfuge when Thelma, weighing eight pounds and very sturdy, was born five months after the wedding. When the child was three weeks old, his father, half in admiration, had quizzed him about how skilfully he and Lydia had concealed their romance.

'Those quiet ones are often the best,' he'd said.

Then Henry had understood.

Pride made him connive at the deception, but he had allowed Lydia no more time to recover from the birth before, in fury, violently impregnating her again. After this virtual rape her hair fell out. She felt sick and ill through her second pregnancy and was bewildered by the strong attachment she felt to the dark, squalling baby that resulted. To protect them both, she hid it, for if Henry saw where she was vulnerable, she would be handing him a weapon to be used against her. Instead, she aimed at toughening her son.

Now, past and present had caught up with her and further payment was demanded. Thelma must be prevented from the risk of forming an incestuous relationship with her true father.

But how?

She could not telephone. That was out of the question. He would think she was a madwoman.

What if she wrote a letter?

Dear Arthur, she recited in her mind. *You will think it strange that I should write to you after so long an interval, but I believed you to be dead. We had a daughter, Thelma, and you know her. Yours, Lydia.*

It would not do. She would have to go and see him.

She imagined herself going to The Shieling, parking in the narrow drive, ringing the doorbell.

Thelma might answer it. What then? What reason could she give for having called? Thelma would not take kindly to the notion that Lydia was paying a social call, and just suppose she did, how could she be dismissed while it was in progress, so that the true purpose of her visit could be revealed?

She could telephone while Thelma was rehearsing, ask him to meet her somewhere, say she had something important to discuss and beg him not to mention this request to Thelma. The idea terrified her. She could not do it.

She had made no decision by the time Edward moved down to the hotel. Lydia had grown so accustomed to his presence in the house that she had dreaded his departure, but now it released her from all need for concealment of her movements. She began going into Heronsmouth early in the morning. She would park in a side road above The Shieling and stand in the bus shelter which was almost opposite, dressed in her old gardening raincoat and a tweed hat bought at the charity shop. From this retreat she could watch the house unnoticed and she saw Thelma arrive on foot each day at half-past nine. Her hours were not demanding; Arthur clearly got his own breakfast.

Lydia could call on him before Thelma was due: she could go in and explain, and be gone again quite quickly. Once, she got as far as standing on the step, but she did not ring the bell. How could she face him, after what had been between them? How could she tell him what had happened? Most important of all, even if she managed that, how could she trust him to keep the secret she had guarded through the years?

She could not, even if he promised, and Thelma, who had idolized Henry, would be destroyed if she found out the truth.

She ran off quickly back to the car and drove away.

Most days Arthur and Thelma set out on expeditions of one sort or another. Arthur would get the Renault out and lean across to open the passenger door for Thelma, who would clamber in beside him. At that distance,

Lydia could not see their expressions, but she followed them several times, keeping well back so that Thelma would not recognize her car. They went for walks and had pub lunches, they visited museums and went shopping. At least, while occupied with these excursions, Thelma was not in moral danger.

Once, Lydia watched them through binoculars. Thelma took Arthur's arm and nestled up against him, looking happy. Lydia had not forgotten what joy there was in Arthur's touch; to think of sharing that with her daughter was horrifying. Lydia was not simply shocked, but jealous too.

After a number of journeys, Edward came to wash the Metro and check its oil and tyres, and he noticed her increased mileage.

'Well, you've been getting around,' he said. 'Been anywhere interesting?'

Lydia was missing him, but she snapped her answer back.

'Where I go is my business,' she retorted.

She had never spoken sharply to him before. Edward felt a chill wash over him.

'I'm sorry,' he said. 'Of course it is.'

Be like that, then, he thought bitterly, and did not linger. He did not come to see her again for several days and then they were very careful with each other, talking like two strangers.

Meanwhile, Arthur had suggested to Thelma that her mother should be invited to The Shieling, but Thelma made excuses.

'She's unsociable and odd,' she said.

'Perhaps she's lonely.'

'She's always been like it. That's how she prefers things,' Thelma insisted.

He let it pass. They would all meet at the performance of *The Seagull* and he would take it from there.

One day they went over to the Manor for a bar lunch.

'I've been there already,' he told her. 'But now I know you once lived there, I'd like to go again.' He thought of telling her that he had seen her swimming, then decided not to; she was a tricky, prickly girl and it was easy to upset her. He suspected that she had become involved with the man who was playing Trigorin and that things weren't going too smoothly there. Perhaps she wasn't so different from her mother; even that old lady had been young once and may have had a few adventures before she settled down in what had evidently been an unsuccessful marriage. Thelma had revealed that her father had complained to her about her mother many times, and that he derided her in front of the children.

'She just used to crumple,' Thelma said. 'He'd have respected her if she'd stood up to him. He liked a bit of guts. He told me so. I used to wonder if he'd made a play for Dorothy – that's my mother's friend, my godmother, quite a gutsy lady. But I never knew for sure.'

'People don't always play around, you know,' said Arthur. 'Some marriages last, and are happy. Mine was like that.'

'You were lucky,' Thelma said.

'Yes,' he agreed. 'I know it.'

'I'd like to be married again,' Thelma confessed, artlessly. 'It makes you feel respectable.'

'But you like your freedom, don't you?' he pointed out. 'Would you be faithful to another husband?'

'I don't know,' said Thelma honestly.

'You may be looking for something that doesn't exist,' he said. 'Some perfect fusion of two souls, like poets write about. It's very rare, and I question if it lasts.'

Long ago, when he was very young, he had felt lyrical about a girl, but she had soon forgotten him.

'I've never met anyone like you before,' Thelma said. 'You know I'm awful but you aren't shocked.' And you're not after me, she thought; I'm safe with you.

'I'm a father figure to you,' he declared, patting her hand. It was safer thus.

Ferdy served them in the Manor bar.

'How's Mrs Cunningham?' he asked. 'I haven't seen her lately.'

'She's all right,' said Thelma. 'How's Edward getting on?'

'Oh, very well. He's moved in here now. Very snug he is, in the stable block,' said Ferdy.

'So your mother's on her own again?' said Arthur as they ate their individual cottage pies.

'She was only helping out, letting him stay there,' Thelma answered.

'Let's call on her.' said Arthur. 'You can't be in the village and not look your mother up.'

But Lydia was out.

She had not gone to spy on them that day and had intended to go to the Manor, but when she walked up the drive she saw Arthur's Renault, whose number she now knew by heart, so she turned away and went over to inspect The Shieling itself; they would not return and catch her at it now.

Because she might be observed, she walked boldly up to the front door and rang the bell, as if on a genuine inquiry, and when no one came, went round to the back. The kitchen door was almost as solid as the front door; the windows were of the sash variety and there was double glazing. She didn't see how she could break in, and if she did, what then? She was no nearer a solution.

She couldn't trust him; not in any way. He'd never written to her; that was certain. A letter sent to the hospital would have found her, even months afterwards. He hadn't known her home address – luckily, as

217

it now turned out, for surely, even after all this time, some small memory would have stirred.

She could not trust Gerald's assessment of the situation either. Paternalistic, he had said; well, Henry had been officially Thelma's father, and was, eventually, old. She had never known the full extent of what passed between them, but he had taunted her for years about it, knowing that she had no remedy. He could have been responsible for Thelma's adult problems. It need not have been a great deal, after all – not the completed act, 'the ultimate', as Edward called it, just some build-up towards it. Not that that was Henry's way of doing things.

What could she do?

Lydia drove home by a different route so that she ran no risk of meeting Thelma and Arthur as they returned to Heronsmouth together.

She need take no action yet, but the deadline was the play, for then she would meet Arthur again. She knew he would not recognize her, but Dorothy had invited herself to join them, wanting to see her goddaughter's performance, and she would address Lydia by her first name. If he had not forgotten all about her, Arthur might say, 'I knew a Lydia once.'

Would that be the way to let it happen? Let the questions follow, his Lydia's surname be disclosed, amazement on all sides ensuing? Would he then realize the possibility that Thelma was his child?

At first, he wouldn't be able to realize that she, thin and scrawny, almost bald, was what had become of that happy, ardent girl. He would be shocked, incredulous: then hostile, surely, for his own emotions, long ago, were insincere.

She could not bear to see the horror in his eyes, and then the hatred that must follow.

Lydia telephoned Thelma and, awkwardly, because it was unusual for them to have such a conversation, asked how things were going. Thelma, who was expecting Trigorin to arrive at any minute, was anxious to get her mother off the line. She said that she had one becoming dress to wear and that the acting of the young woman playing Nina was pathetic.

'Have you many more rehearsals?' Lydia asked.

'Every night next week, then the dress rehearsal on Thursday,' Thelma answered. There were to be only two performances, on Friday and Saturday, and Arthur had wanted to take them all to dinner after the last one, but Thelma had said she would be at a party with the cast so that idea had perished.

Lydia went over to lunch with Dorothy on Sunday. She was very restless, walking round the garden looking for fallen apples in the grass – Dorothy's trees were prolific and she could not pick the highest branches – and refusing to settle with her coffee after the meal. They arranged that Dorothy, who was going to spend Saturday night at the lodge, after the play, should come over in plenty of time to set out with them for Heronsmouth. She was interested to learn that Edward's sister would be joining them.

'All her lodgers gone, then?' she asked.

'I don't know where we got that idea,' said Lydia. 'She works at the hotel.'

On Monday evening, when Thelma was rehearsing, Lydia drove again to Heronsmouth and once more parked in the side road near The Shieling. She walked to the bus shelter. Further up Harbour Hill, lights shone from the Cliff Hotel, and there was a faint glow showing behind the curtains at the bay window of The Shieling. One car went past but she saw no one out on foot. The people in the area were having their evening meal or watching television, and behind that bay window opposite was the man whose memory she had carried in her heart throughout her adult life, embellishing his image with careful touches, inventing what she did not know and rendering him more perfect than the truth could ever be. It was she, not Arthur, who had died all those years ago; her life since then had been one long charade. Oblivious of the cold and damp, Lydia stood there watching for an hour. He might come out, and she could follow him, though what she could do then, she didn't know.

The second night she took a torch, but once again her vigil brought no benefit. Behind his close-drawn curtains, Arthur Morrison occupied his evening unaware of the watcher in the road.

What was he doing in there? Reading? Watching television? Playing patience? She knew that he played bridge, but little else about his interests. He was a stranger.

Once again, she contemplated calling on him openly, ringing the bell and reintroducing herself as Thelma's mother, playing at small talk, then waiting for an opportunity. But for what? What did she mean to do? How could she silence him, the only person in the world who could reveal her secret – and might do so, less than three days hence.

On Wednesday, she approached the door, but as she raised her hand to press the bell, a car went past and she delayed, waiting till the sound of its engine faded in the distance. Then, shrill and distinct, she heard the telephone ring inside The Shieling. He'd be going to answer it, moving from whatever he was doing. Lydia scuttled off, back to the safety of her car.

Now time was running out if matters were to be resolved before the weekend. Lydia went to bed that night, but did not sleep. If she told Arthur the truth, the fear that he might react with joy and be pleased to acknowledge Thelma openly was almost as bad an alternative as the risk of incest, negating, as it would, the proud cover-up of over four decades. Lydia's own humiliation would be dreadful. There was no answer.

She got up and paced about the house. There was no Edward now to hear her, break the silence, send her back to bed and bring her up a cup of tea. Boris, in his basket, stared at her, unused to all these interruptions to his repose. She was still sitting in the kitchen when dawn rose, and that day, when she went for Betty, earned comments on her fatigued appearance.

'I'd have thought you'd be better now Thelma's moved out,' said Betty frankly. 'What you need's a holiday. Why not take yourself to Tenerife?'

She was missing that young lad: that was the trouble. It had done her good to have a bit of life about the place and someone who looked out for her, as he had done. Betty went home feeling quite concerned.

That evening, as Lydia walked slowly to the bus shelter along the grassy headland facing The Shieling, Arthur emerged. She grasped her torch more firmly as, illuminated by a light over the porch, he went to the garage, opened it, and drove his Renault out. Laboriously, he got out of the car again and closed the garage doors, the cold engine running fast, exhaust fumes fogging the atmosphere. She walked on as he turned the car and came down the drive into the road thrusting one gloved hand into her pocket, the other grasping the torch, head down, not wanting him to pick her up in his headlights. His tyres swished on the damp road, twin red tail lights gradually diminishing as he went towards the town.

Perhaps it was a bridge night. He hadn't played that when she knew him, or if he had, she hadn't known about it. There was a lot she hadn't known about him, she had learned. Perhaps he took it up in the prison camp, or perhaps his wife had played. Her mind closed up at the thought of this unknown woman.

She walked straight up the drive to his front door and looked quickly round. No one was in sight. Harbour Hill, she had discovered, was a lonely place at night.

Lydia reached up with the torch and knocked out the porch light.

The noise seemed to her to be deafening, and glass splinters spattered round her as she ducked out of the way. She stood trembling on the gravel driveway waiting for windows to open and shouts to ask what was happening, but there was no reaction. There was just the sound of the sea below and the pale light from the widely spaced street lamps in the road.

Lydia went round to the back of the house and crouched there trying to decide what she meant to do when Arthur came home. The night was cold and raw, and she began to shiver. He might be gone for hours, certainly would be if he had gone out to dinner or was playing bridge. Holding her fingers over the torch so that only just enough light filtered through them to let her see her way, she went round to the front again. She could enter the garage, lie in wait for him there. But what then? Could she stun him with her torch, then start the car and leave the engine running, shut him in, let time do the rest?

She thought about it, standing there, then tried the garage doors, but they were locked.

Anyway, he'd see her when he put the car away.

She was reprieved.

She walked back to the car and sat there, shivering, for some minutes as she tried to achieve some calm. Then she started the engine and put the heater on full. She was about to move off down the road when she remembered that there was only one more night before she must meet Arthur properly – unless she found some excuse to miss the play – and that even if she managed that, Thelma would be moving to The Shieling very soon.

The truth was bound to come out. Eventually he'd ask about her mother, find out who she was, learn that she had been a nurse in training, and where.

Silence was the only safety. She, as well as Thelma, needed that.

She let the engine run long enough to warm the car up. Then she sat and waited for Arthur to return.

She wouldn't see him, waiting here in a road above The Shieling. Lydia remained there for a while, then went back to the bus shelter. When a late bus came grinding up towards her, she walked off, letting it pass her near the Cliff Hotel, then turning back again. A few cars went by as she sat huddled there, but no one came that way on foot. Twice she returned to the car to warm up, hoping each time that Arthur would return during such an interval, and then she could postpone any decision once again. But she was in the shelter when, taking her by surprise, his Renault turned into the gateway of his house.

She was up the drive behind him and crouching round the side of the house as he closed the garage doors and walked towards the porch. He hesitated, and she heard him mutter something as he fumbled to fit his key into the lock. His feet scrunched on the broken glass on the tiled step as she came up behind him.

Lydia held the torch in her gloved right hand. She was nearly as tall as he was, and as she struck him down she was screaming in her head with hatred. Her thoughts, then, were not of Thelma but were for herself and her own pain. It was only as he fell that she remembered her daughter, and knew that she was safe.

223

Arthur Morrison fell inwards against the opening door and he gave a single grunt.

She could not leave him there. Lydia stepped over him into the narrow hall and put her torch down. Then she dragged him in by the shoulders until she could close the door. He was very heavy: dead weights were. But was he dead? She paused, panting, to look down at him. Light shone through the half-open door of a room on the right, and she could see his bald head gleaming above a little frill of silver curls. She picked up the torch to hit him again, but she could not do it. All her rage was spent. She set it down again and dragged him into the sitting-room. His shoes rasped against the carpet, setting her teeth on edge.

Was he dead?

She had bent to examine Henry without a qualm, but she could not touch this man again. Now he had become an object of horror.

Lydia looked round the room. A book lay on a table beside a big armchair; there were newspapers nearby. In the fireplace a fire was apparently laid, but without any kindling: fresh coals sat in the grate. Perhaps there was a gas poker. Living in the country without such refinements as mains gas, Lydia did not at first recognize the artificial device Arthur used with so much pleasure, but when she looked more closely and saw the gas tap, she understood. She tried to turn it and found you had to press it. Promptly she turned it off again; she had always been nervous of gas.

Now she felt a sudden calm. Perhaps this was what she had, without acknowledging it, planned all along. It was the only certain way, but she had to cover up her crime. Arthur's death must be made to seem an accident. Fire would destroy the evidence. She did not admit the conscious thought that if her victim were not already dead, it would complete what she had begun.

She looked about for matches and saw some in a bowl on the mantelpiece; there was a long wax taper in a pretty pot.

Lydia picked up the newspapers that lay to hand and separated some pages, crumpling them up; she laid them in a trail from the fireplace across the room to the linen-covered sofa and on towards the long plum velvet curtains which hung at the window. Then she lit the taper, turned on the gas tap and plunged the flame among the coals. Because she did not know precisely where to place it there was a tiny delay before it caught and quite a loud plop as the gas ignited. Lydia left the taper alight beside the already burning *Cheverton Gazette*.

She was at the door, on the point of leaving, when she remembered her torch which she had put down in the hall. She snatched it up. Arthur's keys were still in the lock as she shut the front door behind her and scurried down the drive to the road, where she slowed to a walk and went rapidly back to the car, just a lean, shadowy figure in the night, if anyone had seen her.

But no one did.

Lydia had no memory at all of driving home, but when she arrived she stripped off all her clothes and made a bonfire of everything she had worn except her old gardening raincoat and her shoes which, naked otherwise, she wore while she burned the rest. She felt soiled, corrupted. Fire would wipe out contamination. She did not think of the other fire which she had left in Heronsmouth.

Then she had a bath.

Boris watched all these activities with indifference; he had ceased to be surprised at her departure from routine.

From their bungalow, the Dennises saw the bonfire sparks ascending to the heavens.

'What an hour to light it,' Roger said.

'The old girl's dotty,' answered Maureen. 'I hope it's under control.'

'Can't reach us,' said Roger comfortably. 'The wind's the other way.'

'You're safe now, Thelma,' Lydia told herself as she stoked up the flames. She went on muttering it as she soaped herself in the bath and washed her silky, skimpy hair. She wanted to think she'd done this for her daughter, not herself: that alone was justification.

There were no clothes to put away neatly that night and no underclothes to wash, for everything had been destroyed.

22

A woman taking her dog out for a final run noticed a beacon glow at a downstairs window in The Shieling. At first she did not understand the reason for it; when she realized that the place was on fire, she rushed back to her own house further up the road and dialled 999.

By this time, Lydia had been gone more than twenty minutes; when the fire brigade arrived, the sitting-room was full of dense toxic fumes from the smouldering upholstery. Anyone trapped inside the room would die very quickly. And there was somebody there: the first fireman almost fell over Arthur Morrison as he lay on the floor.

In some unreasoned action, Lydia had closed the sitting-room door when she left the house, and this had helped to contain the blaze. There had been no explosion; the gas fire went on burning in the grate but the curtains, flaring, had been what the passer-by had noticed. Though the rest of the house was saturated with water from the firemen's hoses, it was not severely damaged and the wreckage was restricted to the main room.

Men trampled to and fro, first the firemen, then the men who took away the body in a coffin shell. Gas board engineers and electricians disconnected the mains supply. It was not until the next morning, when experts inspected the building in daylight, that the broken porch light was noticed. By that time the shattered glass had been trampled everywhere and there was nothing to show that it had been deliberately smashed. It could easily have happened during the fire-fighting operation.

Chief Inspector Drummond, from Heronsmouth police station, stood among the debris with the district head fire officer. It was obvious that the dead man had just entered the house for he was wearing his overcoat and his keys were still in the front door.

'He must have gone out leaving the fire on and papers nearby. Perhaps a sudden draught blew one of them across the fire, and when he returned he smelled smoke and hurried into the room, and was overcome by the fumes immediately,' hazarded Drummond.

The fire officer indicated a fire extinguisher attached to the wall in the hall.

'Why didn't he use that?' he asked.

'Perhaps he opened the door to investigate and a wave of smoke engulfed him,' Drummond said.

It was possible. The smoke would have billowed towards him.

'But the door was closed,' the fire expert said. 'Our men found it closed.'

'It might have banged to behind him.'

'Possibly, if it was the sort of door that did that.' Such a thing would be hard to prove now, with the solid door warped and charred.

The dead man's car had been in the garage. There were no signs of any break-in, nothing to hint at something more than a domestic accident.

Thelma, arriving at her normal time of half-past nine, found the men still there, poking about among the devastation. She had heard the fire engines roar past the previous evening after she had returned from the dress rehearsal which, like most dress rehearsals, had been fraught with small disasters. Now, as she approached the house, she saw several cars parked in the road outside and a police car in the drive. An acrid smell of smoke hung in the damp wintry morning air, and she broke into a run when she realized that The Shieling was the source.

'What's happened? Where's Arthur?' she cried.

They broke it to her gently, first finding out her name and why she was involved. Drummond took her round to the rear of the house where the kitchen was undamaged apart from being drenched with water which was still running down the walls.

'Oh no!' she wailed. 'Oh no! I won't believe it! He was out last night playing bridge at the Frobishers'. There must be some mistake.'

Drummond put forward the theory about the fire: that Mr Morrison had left it burning and been careless with some papers.

'But he wouldn't leave it on,' Thelma insisted. 'He always turned it off when he went out, for economy. The heating system was good. He liked the fire just for cosiness.' Saying this, she began to weep.

A constable had been despatched next door to see if the neighbour would provide sanctuary and a cup of tea for Thelma until she had calmed down enough to be questioned. She might know where to find the next of kin, and could provide information about the deceased's movements the night before. The neighbour was delighted to comply; she had been intrigued by Thelma's constant presence in the house. While Thelma drank her tea, watched over by a youthful constable, the neighbour, in another room, declared that Arthur Morrison had kept himself to himself since his wife died, but he had given them raspberries from his garden in the summer and was a good neighbour in that he was quiet. There were no rowdy parties nor irritating barking dogs.

In her turn, Thelma knew that Arthur's son lived in Leeds, and she knew where Arthur kept an address book which might provide more details.

'What am I to do?' she sobbed, when Drummond, having established her address so that she could be interviewed again if necessary, sent her back to her flat in the police car. 'Oh, why do these things always happen to me?'

The young policeman, quite distressed, brewed more tea and asked her if there was someone who could come and keep her company until she had recovered from the shock.

'I'll ring my mother,' she said. 'She lives not far away.'

'You do that,' said the constable, relieved.

When the telephone rang, Lydia was doing her jigsaw, singing to herself. She felt entirely calm.

Thelma was hysterical, but Lydia had heard her in this mood before, first when Charles was killed and later when her second husband had deserted her. And when Henry died.

'What is the matter, Thelma? Try to control yourself,' she directed. 'Take some deep breaths. I can't hear a word you're saying.'

'Arthur – dead – house on fire—' jumbled phrases came across the wire among the sobs.

Lydia felt her whole body flood with sudden warmth as blood pumped around it.

'What are you saying?' she asked.

'I want to come home,' Thelma cried. 'You must come and fetch me.'

'Pull yourself together, Thelma,' Lydia instructed. 'Tell me what is wrong exactly. Are you ill?' For she must feign unawareness, that was crucial; she already knew that it was very easy to deceive.

Still sobbing, but somehow managing to utter, Thelma described what she had found when she went to The Shieling.

Lydia had given no thought to who would discover the body or when the fire would be detected. Her mind had blanked about the aftermath.

'The police think a paper blew across the fire while he was out.' Thelma spoke in a wail.

'I expect they're right,' said Lydia. 'How dreadful.' The words seemed meaningless.

'I'm most upset,' said Thelma. 'And I must come home, Mother. Please fetch me now.'

'Nonsense, Thelma,' Lydia said robustly. 'Of course it's sad and you're distressed. That's natural. But get things in proportion. This man was only your employer. You must make some effort. You're performing in a play tonight. Had you forgotten that?'

'I can't possibly go on stage after what's happened,' Thelma said.

'Yes, you can. You're acting now,' her mother told her firmly. 'I'll come in and see you this afternoon and not a moment earlier. Now, blow your nose and wash your face and have a cup of tea.'

She replaced the receiver and returned to her jigsaw. Soon she was humming again, a tuneless dirge. She had never before, in the whole of Thelma's life, spoken so sharply to her. But now all debts were paid.

Thelma was dressed in a grey velour tracksuit; her eyes were red and she wore no lipstick when she opened the door to Lydia later that day.

Once again, she related what had happened, the water streaming down the walls of the damaged house, the men investigating, the smoky smell.

231

Thelma still insisted that she could not perform that evening.

'You must,' said Lydia. 'You'll let the others down, if you don't. The show must go on, you know. Goodness me, Thelma, I know it's very dreadful but you'd only met the man a little while ago.'

'He was good to me.' Thelma dabbed her eyes with a tissue. 'We were friends. It was easy with him. I felt safe.'

'What was easy?' Lydia snapped.

'Just being with him. He was fond of me, and I was very fond of him,' said Thelma, with a curious dignity which moved her mother. This was genuine grief, not just Thelma acting up.

'You'll get over it,' she said, more gently.

'What do you know about such things?' Thelma rounded on her suddenly. 'You hated Daddy. I know you weren't a bit sad when he died.'

'He was old and ill. He no longer got much pleasure out of life,' Lydia said. 'Now, I'm going, Thelma. I've got things to do, with Gerald and Dorothy coming tomorrow for the play.'

'This isn't stomach ache, you know,' said Thelma bitterly.

'Time heals,' said Lydia tritely. 'You know that. This is not comparable with when Charles died. Now, that was a tragedy.'

Thelma was outraged at her mother's callous attitude; she stormed about the flat when Lydia had gone, and, because she needed an audience, she rang Gerald at the bank.

She got a much more sympathetic response from him. He was truly shocked, said how much he had liked Arthur, and added, 'You don't have much luck, do you, old girl? But hang on in there and make a success of the play.'

'Arthur would want me to do that, I know,' Thelma decided. She sniffed, partly mollified as she contemplated rescripting her role.

'Of course he would. Look, I'll leave as early as I can tomorrow morning,' Gerald said. 'I'll come in on my way to Mother's and we'll have lunch together, shall we? There's no point in my coming down tonight because you've got the performance. You'll feel better when you get among your friends.'

She might. She'd rung Trigorin in his dental surgery, managing to get past his receptionist, and he had expressed appropriate regret over what had happened, but, as he had not been encouraged to think of Arthur as more than just a kind employer, her grief had seemed to him excessive.

Oh dear, thought Gerald, hanging up. Poor Thelma was a sort of Jonah; everything she touched went wrong. He'd have to try to help her sort out the consequences of this disaster or it would all rebound again towards their mother. She must be persuaded to keep on the flat until she had another long-term plan to prevent her from running back to Milton St Gabriel again.

By the time Gerald reached Heronsmouth the next day, Thelma had cheered up a lot. She saw herself now as the pale heroine of a tragedy which was the main talking point in the town. Arthur, though relatively a newcomer, had been a familiar figure walking down the hill and going round the shops, and people stood on corners discussing what had happened, posing theories. The play had gone well the night before and Thelma's own performance had won special plaudits. Stress had put an edge on how she faced her part; her rather light voice had deepened and she had developed real presence.

Later, sleep had eluded her; she was, on several counts, over-stimulated. Trigorin had left her at her door, muttering that he could not linger, and for once she was not sorry. Eventually, she took a sleeping pill and did not wake until eleven.

At twelve, Gerald rang her bell, taking a deep breath and resolving to count ten before replying if she riled him. He had brought her a bottle of brandy; she might need it.

She repeated what she had already told him on the telephone about her arrival at The Shieling the previous morning.

'They'd taken him off somewhere by then, of course,' she said.

Charles, dead on arrival at the hospital after his car smash, had been taken to the mortuary, and to spare Thelma, Gerald had formally identified him.

He remembered that now.

'You didn't have to identify him, did you?' he asked her.

'No. They sent for his son. I suppose he did it,' Thelma said.

'There will have to be an inquest, I imagine.'

'Yes. It's on Monday,' Thelma said.

Would she have to go to it, and if so, must he stay and lend her his support? Gerald sighed inwardly at the prospect, determining to escape if possible, for surely Thelma might reasonably be expected to support herself? He reproved himself for base, unworthy thinking, and told his sister it was time for lunch.

He took her to the Swan, where several people in the bar had seen the play the night before and came up to congratulate her. Thelma at once began to glow, and, briefly, Arthur was forgotten. When Gerald left her at her flat again, she said she was going to get some rest before the evening's performance.

'Good idea,' he said.

She'd get over it once everything was tidied up and settled but it was a wretched business. The old boy hadn't seemed the least bit casual; if the police really thought he'd let papers drift across the open fire, it sounded most untypical. Perhaps he'd felt ill, had a heart attack or something, or there'd been a gas fault of some kind. The police or the fire brigade would probably find out the truth in time; forensic science had developed many skills to aid them. He put his difficult sister and her problems out of his mind and thought instead of Julie Fletcher, whom he would see again this evening.

He played with the notion of taking her out somewhere, just the two of them, and seeing how they got along. Then he devised a scenario in which he stayed at the hotel once more and, when she brought his morning tea, persuaded her to join him in his bed. She might: the modern girl was seldom wholly chaste. She'd have other trays to take around, however; her time was not her own, he told himself, laughing at this fantasy. In theory, though, it might not be difficult to coax a hotel chambermaid into becoming his mistress, find a better job for her in London, set her up in a little flat. But he wanted none of that; Gerald was tired of meaningless encounters. He wanted love, and, in a rare moment of bitterness, he accepted that he had never known it in his life.

He found his mother looking rather better than the last time he was home and she seemed pleased to see him. He told her he had been to see Thelma who was bearing up quite well.

'I wonder what's the best way to help her now,' he said.

'She must stand on her own feet,' Lydia unexpectedly replied. 'She's independent. She has enough money to live on if she's not extravagant, and if she can't find a worthwhile job with a salary, she must look for some interest to occupy her time.'

Gerald could not believe what he was hearing. Always, in the past, excuses had been made for Thelma's failures and her failings.

'Had you anything in mind?' he asked.

'Aren't there training schemes she could go on? She could qualify for something,' Lydia said.

'Like what?'

'Oh, I don't know. Putting make-up on, something she's already good at,' Lydia said.

'Beauty counselling,' said Gerald, amazed that Lydia should suggest an occupation that in her view must seem worthless.

'Is that what it's called? How do you know?' Lydia asked.

'Some friend of Fiona's is doing it,' he answered. 'I wonder if she'd ever settle to it?' He could not see it happening. 'She likes being among people, of course. That's one of her difficulties. She can't bear being alone.'

'She picked Edward up on the train coming down here,' Lydia stated.

'Did she?' Gerald had not known that.

'She's so restless,' Lydia said. 'Always looking for something which she'll never find.'

'What sort of thing?'

'Some man. Some film star sort of man. A romantic falsity,' said Lydia.

'Or fantasy,' said Gerald.

'She's foolish about men, and she has no morals where they're concerned.'

'She's not a tart, Mother,' Gerald said gently.

'I don't suppose she asks for money,' Lydia said. 'That's not what she wants.'

'Maybe she's just a girl who can't say no.' Gerald

spoke lightly, afraid of saying the wrong thing. 'She might have settled down with Arthur Morrison. What's happened is a tragedy and it was a dreadful way to die.'

'Thelma will get over it.' Lydia spoke abruptly.

The spell had broken. Gerald made some excuse and went upstairs with his small bag. Things didn't really change. When he had unpacked, he took a stroll down the garden. A few late roses bloomed but most of the withered herbaceous plants had been cut down and burned. Nothing waited on the bonfire site, only a pile of ash. He saw a wisp of blue and bent to look at it. It was a scrap of fabric, some old rag, perhaps.

He marvelled at his mother's new, tougher attitude towards Thelma. Would it last? How ironic that Thelma had had some sort of passage of arms with Edward while he now entertained thoughts of the same thing with Julie. But she probably had a boyfriend, one close to her in age; in a way he hoped she had because then he could back off without chancing his luck. Of course, he could always try to marry her himself. If she consented, they might have some years of happiness before he bored her and she moved on to someone more exciting.

But when Julie and Edward arrived, he forgot such thoughts and set out simply to enjoy the evening. Dorothy, magnificent in a gold and purple dress made from a sari she had bought in India, had arrived earlier, and they all piled into Gerald's car. Dorothy and the two young people were wedged into the back and Lydia sat in front with him although she was much thinner than her friend. It would be inappropriate to suggest to her that she should sit cramped up into a corner but Dorothy was used to a certain lack of style.

Julie was in a sparkling mood. She wore a pink, full-skirted dress, and her hair was different, cut much shorter. Before the performance, they had dinner at a

237

restaurant in Heronsmouth which was noted for its lobster, and the subject of Arthur Morrison's death did not arise until they had begun their meal. Lydia had not mentioned it to Dorothy, and although hotel gossip had included news about a fatal fire in Heronsmouth, Edward and Julie were unaware of the connection.

Gerald raised the topic, saying that he had planned to invite Arthur Morrison to join them for the meal before the play.

'Why couldn't he come?' asked Edward.

As Gerald explained, Julie went quite white.

'When did it happen?' she asked.

'Some time on Thursday night,' said Gerald. 'He'd been out playing bridge, it seems. When he got home, he must have found the fire and been overcome by the smoke and fumes.'

'Oh!' Julie's colour slowly returned to her face. Last night, Eddie had been out late and she did not know where he'd gone. She'd wanted to find him to ask what time they were expected at the Cunninghams. On Thursday, though, they had been watching a film on Victor's video. But Eddie wouldn't set a fire like that; he liked the old man.

'Poor old geyser,' Edward said. 'How did it start?'

'Thelma says the police think a newspaper may have blown across the fire when he was out,' said Gerald.

'Would he have left it unguarded?' Dorothy asked.

'I expect he just forgot to turn it off,' said Lydia. 'People can be very careless.'

'Those coals don't fall out,' Gerald said. 'There's no need to use a spark guard.'

'Oh, it was a gas fire, was it?' Dorothy asked.

'Yes.'

They talked about the tragedy right through their first course – shrimps for Julie, who said she couldn't have too much shellfish, and the same for Edward, avocados for the others. When the lobster came, Gerald changed the subject; if they dwelt on the tragedy they would be in no mood to appreciate the evening's entertainment.

Edward had heard Thelma going through her part when he was working at The Shieling, but Julie did not know the story of the play. Dorothy outlined the plot, explaining how an older man had, for whim or simply vanity, destroyed a girl. Such things still happened, she declared.

'Or it could be the other way about,' said Julie. She looked across at Gerald as she spoke, and for a moment they held each other's gaze. She was the first to look away.

'It was so hot when I was in Moscow,' Dorothy was saying. 'There were specks of poplar dust dancing in the air like cotton buds. One could imagine the heat as they describe it in the play. You should get the feel of the humid, steamy atmosphere provoking tensions, ripe for festering jealousies. And of course none of them had enough to do and they were bored.'

When the play began, Julie sat forward on her upright chair in the school hall, peering round the head in front of her, entirely rapt. It was well done. Dorothy and Gerald, the two best qualified to judge, were both impressed by the quality of the acting and the production, and Thelma's performance was outstanding. Her face revealed unhappy passion, and when Trigorin started to encourage Nina, her anguish was made plain. Masha's drinking raised a laugh; the old man in his chair was appropriately irascible. The pace was slow enough to let the discontent seep through but with no longueurs.

There was great applause for Thelma at the end. They went round to see her before she left for a last-night party with the cast. She was elated, on another plane.

Edward and Julie walked up the Manor drive together after a final drink at the lodge. They parted at the side door of the hotel. There was an unfamiliar car in the yard outside the stable block, and when Edward reached his room, two plain-clothes police officers were waiting for him.

23

The post-mortem examination carried out earlier that day on Arthur Morrison had shown that death was due to suffocation from the fumes given out by the upholstery burning in the room. There was not a lot of actual fire damage to the body, and when it had been sluiced down and cleaned, a head wound was plainly visible. The skin across the scalp at the back of the bald head was lacerated and there was a depressed fracture of the skull. In the pathologist's opinion, the dead man had been struck from behind with some heavy object; because of the wound's position, and the fact that the body had been found centrally placed inside the room away from solid furniture, it was unlikely to have been sustained by accident, as in a fall.

Now the theory was that the deceased, returning from his evening's bridge, had surprised an intruder in the house. His assailant had then fired the house to avoid discovery. The police had looked for fingerprints and had found three distinct sets. Two were the dead man's and Thelma's; they had called to take hers after Gerald left on Saturday and because she was now mentally geared towards her dramatic performance in the evening, she had shown little interest in their reasons. 'For elimination,' they had said. The third set led them to Edward Fletcher, recently released from prison after serving a sentence for arson. Inquiries made during the day had enabled them to trace Fletcher's sister to the Manor Hotel in Milton St Gabriel, where they soon discovered that he had been taken on to the staff.

There was no charge of thieving recorded against him, but he would have fallen into bad company in custody and could have learned new skills and attitudes.

Detective Inspector Mobsby and his colleague, Detective Sergeant Young, were very pleased to have their case wrapped up so soon. Such serious crimes were rare on their patch.

The two policemen had had a talk with Mrs Thomson, the hotel manageress; then they had played it quietly, waiting in the suspect's room for his return.

Edward went with them meekly.

Gerald had arranged to meet Julie on Sunday afternoon.

He said goodbye to his mother and Dorothy, who had stayed to lunch, leaving them to assume he was going straight back to London. Instead, he and Julie planned to go for a walk or a drive, depending on the weather. Then they'd have tea in some quiet spot. Julie was on duty at six o'clock and so brief a meeting committed neither of them to proceeding further.

They had arranged to meet beyond the hotel where the back drive emerged on the coast road. Gerald was there five minutes before the appointed time.

She didn't come.

When she was just five minutes late, he expected her to turn up very shortly. After another five, he began to think that she had stood him up. Ten minutes later he was certain.

His impulse was to drive away at once, writing the experience off as another bitter lesson in rejection. But surely he couldn't be so wrong about her? Surely, if she had wanted to cry off, she'd have telephoned with some excusing lie? He decided he would hunt her down and find out what had made her change her mind. She might, of course, be ill – upset, maybe, by the shellfish she had eaten.

He walked up the drive, went in through the swing doors and found Ferdy serving early teas in the lounge. Gerald asked him if he had seen Julie that day and where she was just now.

'They took the brother off,' he answered. 'She's quite upset.'

'Who took him off?'

'The police, Mr Cunningham. I don't know any more.'

'Oh God!' What had the wretched fellow done? Hit someone with his scooter? 'Where can I find her, Ferdy? We were going for a walk and she hasn't turned up. I thought she'd given me the brush-off.'

'I don't think she'd do that,' said Ferdy.

'Nor do I,' said Gerald. 'Now, where is she?'

Ferdy cast a glance round the lounge. Two elderly couples were tucking in to scones and cream; a middle-aged woman was waiting for her tray. He vanished beyond a service door and came out with a girl.

'This is Mavis. She'll show you,' he said, and went off to finish preparing the tea tray Mavis had been getting ready.

Mavis led him up the back stairs, across a corridor, through several swing doors installed for fire safety, and up some more stairs to the attic floor.

'That's her door,' said Mavis, pointing. 'But I don't know if she's there. The police seem to think her brother had something to do with the fire in Heronsmouth on Thursday night. She's in an awful state about it.'

'But that's ridiculous,' said Gerald. Mavis must have got it wrong; the boy had probably simply landed himself in some silly scrape.

He tapped on Julie's door.

'Julie. Are you there? Can I come in? It's Gerald Cunningham,' he said.

Turning at the top of the stairs before returning to her duties, Mavis saw the door open and Julie stand there for a moment. Then Gerald went into the room.

She was distraught.

'I'll take you straight in to Heronsmouth,' he said. 'We'll soon sort it out.'

'He couldn't have started that fire,' Julie cried. 'He was here that evening. I know that, because he was with me. We were watching a video in one of the waiters' rooms. The police have been to see me and I told them so.'

'Of course he didn't do it,' Gerald said. 'Why ever should he? It's some stupid mistake.'

'It's because of his record, you see,' said Julie. 'That's why they'd pick him up.'

'His record?' Gerald tried to keep his voice level. In this context there could be only one sort of record and he knew he must tread warily, but in an odd way he was not surprised. It explained a lot.

'He's done time for arson,' Julie said. 'Your mother knows. Didn't you?'

Eddie had told her about Karen and how, in the aftermath, he had confessed to the old lady.

'No,' said Gerald.

'He wouldn't do it again. He'd no reason to,' said Julie.

Now Gerald remembered how white she had gone when she had heard about the fire and Arthur's death during dinner the previous evening and how she had asked particularly when the incident had happened.

'Fix your face, get your coat on, and we'll go,' he told her. 'You may not be back by six. You'd better let someone know – they'll have to let you go. This is serious.'

'Mavis will spell me,' Julie said.

He sat on her bed while she washed her face at the small basin in her room beneath the eaves. In his grand-parents' day, this had been one of the servants' rooms and now, ironically, it had been returned to its original purpose. The walls were painted white and there were pretty print curtains at the window. The narrow divan had a pink padded headboard; there were shelves and a wicker armchair fitted up with several cushions. There were posters illustrating country scenes attached to the wall.

He must not seem inquisitive. He looked at Julie instead and watched her brush her short hair with quick strokes. He had always found the sight of a woman brushing her hair erotic. Luckily Julie's was soon done. She dabbed on lipstick, blotted it and turned to face him, then attempted a smile.

'That's better.' Gerald laid his hands gently on her shoulders. She was much the same height as himself. 'Good girl,' he said, and kissed her lightly, his own warm mouth just brushing her soft lips, not lingering.

A few minutes later they were speeding towards Heronsmouth in his car. Mavis had undertaken to see that Julie's evening duties were covered.

'Now, tell me all about your brother,' Gerald instructed, and she did, covering their mother's aban-donment of the family, their father's second marriage, Edward's escapades at school and later the act which had ended in a prison sentence.

'But he'd no reason to want to harm Mr Morrison – why should he set a fire there?' she said.

'Not even if he thought the old boy had cut him out with Thelma?' asked Gerald.

'No. That was all over before he met Mr Morrison,'

Julie said. 'He drifted into it. Anyway, what would your sister want with him?'

She could have dropped him abruptly, hurtfully, Gerald thought; if the boy had been made to feel slighted, he might have felt he had a score to settle. Still, there was no point in upsetting Julie with this theory, and anyway, it seemed that there was an alibi.

'It doesn't add up,' he agreed, aloud.

'They'll have found his dabs in the house,' Julie said. 'He did all that painting for the old man. That's how they picked him up, of course.'

Her pat use of the slang expression made Gerald smile.

'Mrs Thomson was very angry because she didn't know about Eddie when she took him on,' Julie said. 'I don't blame her, really. But if we'd told her, she wouldn't have given him the job.'

Probably not: as a shareholder, Gerald himself was not eager to have arsonists on the payroll.

'Don't let's worry about that now,' he said. 'Now that they know where he was on Thursday night, they'll release him.'

'You don't know the police,' said Julie. 'They can wear you down, once they've made up their minds about something.'

Gerald, however, still believed in police fairmindedness.

'We'll get him out,' he assured her.

It was not nearly as easy as he had expected, but in the end, because Edward had been held for some time already, they let him go, warning him that he would be required to appear again for further questioning. Gerald, who had been prepared to stand bail if necessary, found the whole business alarming and instructive. It seemed that a much more serious case than straightforward arson was under investigation, for Arthur had been attacked by whoever had started the fire.

246

'You're not arresting him, are you?' Gerald asked Detective Inspector Mobsby, when at last he managed to see the man himself.

'Not yet,' Mobsby said, for an officer had questioned Victor, who had corroborated the sister's tale of watching the video, the group separating at eleven o'clock. The Frobishers had stated that Arthur Morrison had left their house at about twenty minutes to eleven. They lived the far side of Heronsmouth, beyond the customs office, and it would have taken him ten minutes, at most, to reach The Shieling at that time of night.

Gerald saw that the police had grounds for their suspicions. He feared that, without another candidate in line, they'd pick Edward up again. The boy must have a solicitor to protect his interests.

Mobsby did not let him leave with Gerald and Julie, until a police officer had been sent to bring in Victor Hudson for further questioning, before the two could meet. The sister had to be a doubtful witness; if Hudson were persuaded that he might have made a mistake about the time, the case was on: or if it could be found that the old man had stopped somewhere on his way home, however briefly, for a late-night stroll or any other reason. Inquiries might produce a witness who had seen his car.

The officer escorting Hudson timed the journey, estimating that a determined young man pushing his scooter to its limits could make the distance in ten minutes when there was little other traffic to consider.

Thelma was desolate.

In the aftermath of her dramatic triumph, all was anticlimax and the world, as so frequently before, seemed a sad and empty place. Others in the cast were relieved at being free to prepare for Christmas, but for Thelma there was now no happy future.

Trigorin, too, had ended their fleeting affair.

'It's been fun,' he said. 'But it was naughty. Thanks for everything, Thelma.' He hadn't even kissed her when he dropped her at her door after the final party, driving off at speed back to his wife. He wanted no scandal, nor did he wish to see his home life threatened by what had been, to him, a minor and disappointing diversion.

Now there was no play, no job, no Arthur to make her feel that someone really cared about her, and she was genuinely grief-stricken, moved as she had not been since her own father's death. Why should such a dreadful thing have happened to so kind and harmless a person?

When the police came to see her on Sunday, she welcomed the interruption. She had not been up long, and was dressed in her grey tracksuit, no make-up on her face, just duty-free Je Reviens dabbed liberally on her pulse points. She seemed very attractive to Detective Sergeant Young, who was delighted with his assignment as he prepared to ask her some questions designed to support the case against Edward Fletcher.

First, he expressed regret over the sad circumstances which had provoked his call. Then he asked how well Edward Fletcher had known the deceased. Thelma confirmed that Edward had done a great deal of work in the house, painting and papering and simple carpentry. They'd got on well, he and Mr Morrison; indeed, no one could dislike Mr Morrison. There was a pause here for a small weep, large tears coursing down Thelma's cheeks without making her face blotchy; she switched them off before that happened as Young asked her how Fletcher and Mr Morrison had met.

'Through me,' Thelma said, blinking the last tear away and opening her eyes widely.

'And how was that?' Young hid his surprise. 'Had you known Fletcher long?'

'No. I met him on the train to Cheverton one night in September,' said Thelma. 'I'm not exactly sure of the date but I can probably check it. About the seventeenth, I think. A Tuesday. I'd just returned from America.'

Fletcher had been released from custody on the seventeenth.

'You got talking on the train?' prompted Young.

'Yes. It was a long journey and we ended up alone in the coach,' said Thelma. 'He was going to Milton St Gabriel to look up his sister. My mother lives there, so we gave him a lift – she came to meet me at the station.'

'I see.' Young made an entry in his notebook.

'Why do you want to know?' asked Thelma, genuinely puzzled.

'Did Fletcher tell you he'd just come out of prison?' asked Young.

There was no doubt about Thelma's genuine shock at this revelation.

'No,' she said. 'What had he done?'

'Served a sentence for arson,' said Young.

Slowly, the implications of this sank in.

'But he didn't – he couldn't – he wouldn't have—' Thelma looked at the stocky, red-haired sergeant in dismay. 'Oh no,' she said.

'His prints were everywhere in the house,' said Young.

'Well yes – he'd worked there,' said Thelma. 'They would be.'

'And he'd maybe have been able to take a key and get another cut. He maybe knew that Mr Morrison went out to bridge regularly. He could enter then, poke about, do a bit of thieving undisturbed.'

'I suppose he could, if he had a mind to,' said Thelma. 'But why should he? He'd got a job – he seemed happy enough.'

'Simple greed, perhaps,' said Young. 'Then the old man came back and caught him at it,' he went on. 'So he clobbered him from behind and set the place alight to hide what he'd done.'

'You mean he was attacked? Mr Morrison was attacked? Is that what you're saying?' Thelma exclaimed. 'That it wasn't an accident?'

'The post-mortem showed a head wound,' said Young.

'He didn't just fall and bang his head?' Thelma tried.

'No. He'd quite definitely been struck from behind with some heavy object,' said Young.

'I can't believe it.' Thelma hid her face in her hands. Her shoulders heaved. Then she sat up. 'Edward got on well with my mother,' she said. 'She invited him to stay and he was there for several weeks, till he moved into the hotel. My God, he might have attacked her! It might have been her who was killed.' The idea horrified her. All the same, she found it hard to accept that Edward could have so dark a side to his nature. He had been so gentle with her, unlike some men she had known, and had given up with good grace and no angry accusations. Even Trigorin had mentioned that they hadn't exactly set the estuary alight together.

Alight. Fire. Agony.

'He may have just snapped,' said Young. 'There are some people who go along steadily without any trouble for long periods. Then something happens to upset them and they hit out. It may be a very trivial thing that sets them off – a quarrel with a girl, a tiff at work. They take it out on someone else.'

Young left at last, having learned nothing that particularly advanced the case against Fletcher. At present it rested on the circumstantial evidence from his prints in the house and anything else the forensic scientists might turn up. Some of Fletcher's clothes had been sent to the lab, and a search of traces at the scene was going on, but after all the trampling to and fro since the incident, the chances of a vital clue appearing there were slender. The weapon might be found; meanwhile, the hope was that the suspect would crumple during questioning and confess.

After Young had gone, Nicholas Morrison, Arthur's son, who had come down from Leeds and was staying with some friends, rang up. He had tried to contact Thelma the previous evening but in vain, because she was performing in the play.

He came round later, a shocked man, anxious to find the answers as to what had happened but eager, too, to return to his family as soon as possible.

Thelma told him what had passed between her and Detective Sergeant Young, and said she found it very hard to believe that Edward was responsible.

'They'll find out, I suppose,' said Nicholas. 'In a way it's a consolation to know Dad hadn't been simply careless. But it's dreadful. I can't take it in.'

'Nor can I,' said Thelma.

It was obvious to Nicholas that Thelma's grief was genuine. He was glad his father had found such an attractive woman to spend time with, whatever the true nature of their relationship. He asked her if she would keep an eye on things for him, a watching brief, during the police investigation.

'As a business arrangement, of course,' he added.

At the moment the house was under police guard while scientists sifted through the debris; it must be repaired as soon as that was permitted, and kept safe meanwhile against a further break-in.

Thelma was glad to agree.

'I don't want any money for it,' she said, and hesitated.

'Well?'

'Maybe, if the police agree, I could borrow the car. Just for a short time.'

'I'll see to it,' he told her. 'I'll have to make sure the insurance is in order first.'

Both were pleased with this arrangement. Thelma liked the freedom it would give her and Nicholas decided that if she had really been his father's mistress, as seemed possible, the least that could be done for her was, eventually, to make the car a gift. That should nicely solve the difficulty of what to do about her.

What a pity she couldn't use the car at once, thought Thelma. Then she could have driven straight over to Milton St Gabriel to find out what was going on. As it was, she could telephone her mother.

24

Lydia was sitting at the table with a large jigsaw that depicted the Tower of London spread before her. The edge had been completed but there was a big section in the middle waiting to be assembled. Outside, dusk was falling; the short winter afternoon had almost gone.

Over the weekend, Gerald had seemed in better spirits than for months; his holiday had done him good. He'd got on well with Julie who was a nice girl, but a serious attachment between the two would be most unsuitable; however, men had always been able to make discreet arrangements and she knew he could be trusted neither to take advantage of Julie nor to lose his head.

Thelma's telephone call was not a total surprise; some fresh appeal for sympathy was to be expected. But when Thelma told her that Edward was suspected of attacking Arthur and starting the fire to cover up his tracks, shock drove all vigour from her body. She felt icy cold and began to tremble.

'What are you saying?' she gasped.

Thelma described her interview with Detective Sergeant Young and the new police theory.

'Do you mean Edward's been arrested?' Lydia demanded.

'I suppose so,' Thelma said.

'But that's not possible,' said Lydia. 'Of course he didn't do it.'

'I know. I feel that, too,' said Thelma. For once they shared the same opinion. 'But the sergeant said that people can just snap. He'd been in prison, Mother. I didn't know that. If I had, I wouldn't have brought him home.'

Wouldn't you, her mother wondered: it was just the sort of challenge that would excite Thelma.

'I knew about it,' she said. 'He told me. But I'm certain he didn't do this. The police will find that out. He's only got to tell them where he was whenever it happened.'

'I hope you're right,' said Thelma. She went on to tell her mother that the inquest would be just a formality, to be completed later when the police had finished their investigation.

'That's how it was with Charles, if you remember,' Lydia reminded her. Though in his case no fresh evidence had emerged; no dose of drugs or alcohol explained that accident. 'I must go now, Thelma,' she said. She was shaking; surely Thelma must think her voice sounded strange? She needed time to pull herself together. She'd been so sure that the fire would obliterate all trace of the wound on Arthur's poor bald head. Now that he was dead, she could admit a little pity for him.

After Thelma had rung off, she poured herself a tot of brandy, then another, telling herself that the police would soon exonerate Edward. When Gerald returned, she was sitting before her jigsaw in the light of just one lamp, a trifle drunk.

'Gerald! But you've gone back to London!' she exclaimed, her words slurred.

'No, Mother. I've been at Heronsmouth police station,' Gerald said. 'You've heard about Edward?'

He had never seen her affected by drink before; indeed, he thought he had never seen her discomposed in any way.

'Thelma told me,' she said.

'The police have let him go,' said Gerald. 'For now, that is. I've found a solicitor for him – Roy Davis – you remember him.' Roy Davis was a junior partner in the firm that had helped Henry make his vengeful will. 'They won't give up, though – the police I mean – because of his record, although he was with Julie and one of the waiters on Thursday night at the time it must have happened.'

'Then he's all right,' Lydia said.

'No,' said Gerald. 'The police are trying to persuade them to admit that they broke up sooner. But don't distress yourself, Mother. I know you're fond of the boy and I'm sure he's innocent of this, but all the same I'm shocked to think you've been housing an ex-convict unawares.'

'I knew about it,' said Lydia.

'Yes, but not at first, did you?' Gerald said.

She had sobered up by the time he left. He had given Julie both his home and office telephone numbers, and had told her to get in touch immediately if there was further trouble. Edward was to do exactly as Roy Davis advised.

He'd ring her anyway, each evening. That was the silver lining in the present cloudy sky.

The police took Edward in once more after the inquest, which had gone along the lines foreseen. They questioned Victor again, as well, and Julie, but all three stood firm.

Julie said she had heard the church clock strike as she crossed the yard from the stable block, returning to her room.

Well, she would say that, Young reckoned, with her brother's liberty at stake.

At last Detective Inspector Mobsby let them all go;

there was not enough to charge Fletcher on: not yet, but the suspect was by now thoroughly scared. When the lab had finished tests upon his clothes, the police would have their evidence; they'd get a confession, after that.

He had decided to run for it. With his record and the police determined to fasten this one on him, Edward knew he did not stand a chance.

As soon as they let him go, late on Monday night, he packed his few things into several carriers and his original holdall and got his scooter out, leaving a note for Julie in his room.

As he puttered out of the Manor gates, he saw a light on in the sitting-room at the lodge.

Mrs Cunningham was still up.

Edward slowed down, then stopped. He would say goodbye to her – explain, and ask her to thank Gerald. She wouldn't give him away; look at what she'd done for him over Karen. She'd believe him, too: he knew that.

He wheeled his scooter into the yard beside the garage, then went up the path to the french window and gently tapped on the glass.

Inside the room Boris had lifted his head when he heard a movement outside in the night, so she had some warning.

'It's me, Mrs Cunningham. Eddie,' he called.

'Goodness!' Lydia had been startled by his tap at such an hour, but she did not fear muggers. As far as she knew, none had visited Milton St Gabriel yet. She got up and drew back the bolts to admit him. 'What are you doing, tiptoeing about at this time of night?' she asked. 'Come in, come in.'

She bustled him into the room and locked the door behind him. Boris welcomed him with wags of his tail and friendly snuffles.

'I'm leaving,' said Edward. 'I saw the light on and came to say goodbye.'

'Oh Edward, why? Have you been sacked because of the trouble?' she asked. 'Gerald told me about it. Surely all that's settled now?'

'It isn't,' Edward answered.

Mrs Thomson had already arranged for the retired man he had replaced to come back until someone else could be engaged. Edward could not really blame her; why should she believe him innocent?

'But why not?' Surely Roy Davis had attended to it all?

'The police think Victor and Julie are telling lies to save me,' Edward told her. 'We were all together, see, that night, until eleven. They've taken half my gear off for testing. They'll find plenty of proof that I've been in the house, because I have, more times than I can count. For sure I'll have picked up a hair or something, or some bit of thread. It needn't be a lot. There's nothing to say when it happened. It'll be my word against theirs.'

Listening to him, Lydia felt remote from the event: was it she who had found the strength to strike down an unsuspecting old man who had seemed like a stranger?

She pulled herself back to the present.

'You mustn't run away,' she said. 'That would be like admitting you were guilty.'

'It'll give me a chance,' he said. 'If I go now, I'll be a long way away by morning. Up in Birmingham.'

'They'll look for you there,' she said. 'You lived there once, didn't you?'

'Well, Wales then,' said Edward wildly. 'Anywhere but here.'

Shock was having its effect on him, and, as she had done on Sunday when she heard the news, he began to

257

tremble. Lydia got out the brandy and two glasses. She poured plenty into both and gave him one.

'Here, drink this,' she instructed.

Edward obeyed. Lydia's authoritative manner, when she chose to employ it, had that effect on most people.

'Now you can't go,' she said, when he had swallowed it all. 'You might have an accident and be breathalysed. You'll stay here, Edward. I'll hide you. Then it won't be like running away at all. You'll simply move back into your old room and just lie low for a day or two, until things blow over.'

It took her more than half an hour, during which she got Edward to drink more brandy, to persuade him to agree and then he gave in because she had worn him down.

'I'm going tomorrow night,' he said.

'We'll see,' was her response.

When he had gone upstairs, she wheeled his scooter into the garden shed where it would be safe from observation.

Edward found it pleasant to be back in his old room. Exhausted after hours of interrogation, he fell asleep before she came up to bed.

Lydia was sure the police would be looking for him the next morning. She made him stay upstairs, bringing him up some jigsaws and a tray on which to do them, and the radio from the kitchen which she said he might use with the volume turned down very low.

'Turn it off if anyone comes to the house,' she warned.

At eleven o'clock, someone did: the doorbell rang, and she found a young man with red hair on the step. Detective Sergeant Young showed her his warrant card and asked if she knew where Edward Fletcher was.

What a simple question! There was no need to answer with a lie.

'Isn't he at the hotel?' she asked. 'He lives there now.'

'He's done a flit,' said Young. 'When did you last see him?'

'Let me think.' Lydia pondered her reply. 'We all went to Heronsmouth on Saturday – Edward and his sister, my son and I, and a friend – to see an amateur performance of *The Seagull*. My daughter had the leading role.'

'Your daughter?'

'Mrs Hallows. Thelma Hallows,' Lydia told him.

Young had not made the connection between Thelma and this weatherbeaten woman. It was difficult to believe that one so beautiful could have sprung from such a source.

'You've not seen him since?'

Lydia shook her head.

Would they search the house? Didn't they need a warrant for that? She'd make them get one before she would allow them to do it; that would give her time to move Edward, hide him on the cliffs or somewhere till the danger had passed.

'Why do you want him?' she asked. 'Has he had some mishap with his scooter? Parked it in the wrong place or something?'

'No, it's nothing like that,' said Young. 'We want to question him about the fire at The Shieling in Heronsmouth last week.'

'Surely he's not connected with that in any way?' said Lydia.

'We just want to talk to him,' said Young. 'I'm sorry to have troubled you, Mrs Cunningham. He's probably far away by now.'

After Young had gone Lydia allowed Edward to move more freely about the place as long as he kept away from the windows and did not go into the garden.

'It's like being in the Resistance,' she said, almost smiling. 'Hiding a prisoner on the run.'

What did she mean? Was she talking about the war? Edward stared at her, not understanding.

When Julie discovered that Edward had fled, she telephoned Gerald.

'Oh dear – yes, it is the worst thing he could have done,' he agreed. 'It will look like an admission of guilt. But try to keep calm, Julie.' He thought that the police would probably find their quarry fairly rapidly. 'It'll all work out in the end,' he tried to reassure her.

Later, he telephoned his mother, who might not have heard the news.

'I know. The police came here to ask when I'd last seen him,' she reported. 'Silly boy.'

'There's no evidence against him,' Gerald said. 'They can't charge him without that. He should have sweated it out.'

It was easy to say that, Lydia thought, when you were not in Edward's shoes.

'They'll find traces of him in the house because he's worked there,' she said. 'How can he prove all that was legitimate?'

Gerald did not know.

'They'll soon find him,' he said. 'He can't hope to dodge them.'

That's where you're wrong, thought Lydia. Unless they looked in her shed and found the scooter, they'd be searching far away from the village.

That evening the regional television news showed film of Detective Superintendent Sawyer, from Cheverton, who told viewers that Edward Fletcher was wanted in connection with the death of Arthur Morrison in Heronsmouth on Thursday night. He appealed for help. A photograph of Edward – a prison mug shot – was displayed, and the registration number of his scooter was supplied.

The matter was extremely serious. That was evident.

25

Edward and Lydia had watched the programme. The curtains were drawn against the night and the fear of prying eyes; all the doors were locked and bolted and the windows tightly fastened.

'I'll have to move on,' he said. 'If they find me here, you'll be for it too. You'll be an accessory.'

'They aren't going to find you here,' said Lydia.

Thus it must have been in France and Belgium: young men concealed in barns and attics, smuggled on to safety. Had Arthur been concealed like that before his final capture?

She allowed Edward into the garden later, making him do exercises on the lawn in the darkness, running on the spot and press-ups.

'Otherwise you'll get flabby and unfit,' she declared.

He felt very silly carrying out her instructions, but he obeyed. When he returned to the house, she turned off the lights, so that no one could see him slip through the french window, not that anyone could look into her garden unless they were perched on the Dennises' angry orange tiles.

'You'd make a good conspirator,' he told her, almost laughing despite his predicament. Things had come right between them now; the faint, flaring hostility had vanished in his adversity.

That night, Lydia did not sleep at all. She spent hours

sitting by her bedroom window, the curtains drawn back, looking out over the quiet garden. A thin moon slid into view between the clouds and cast a hasp of light across the steep, monstrous roof which blocked out so much of the sky. Would the moss ever grow there?

She was downstairs very early, leaving Boris behind after giving him a quick run in the garden while she went to the shed and let the air out of the scooter's tyres. Then she took Edward's huge helmet and put it in the boot of her car. For him to ride off without it would be to invite instant arrest. She shut Boris back into the house and went quietly out again.

Less than half an hour later she was in Heronsmouth police station, asking to see the officer in charge of the investigation at The Shieling.

Neither Detective Inspector Mobsby nor Detective Sergeant Young had yet arrived. The desk sergeant invited Lydia to tell him whatever it was she wished to say.

'I want to see the officer in charge,' Lydia repeated.

'I'm afraid you'll have to wait, then, madam,' was the answer.

'Very well.' Lydia sat down on a bench across the small front office, folding her hands across her worn but once expensive leather handbag. After several minutes she looked up at him and said, 'I did it.'

'Excuse me, madam. What did you say?' asked the sergeant.

'I did it,' Lydia declared again.

The sergeant looked at the faded elderly woman with her neatly arranged grey hair firmly secured beneath its velvet band, her padded Husky jacket and her grey flannel skirt, and sighed. He put her in the interview room, ordered a cup of tea for her from a duty constable, and rang Young at his home.

'We've got a nutter here,' he said. 'Says she did The Shieling job. A nice old lady. Mrs Cunningham from Milton St Gabriel.'

'Mrs Cunningham, eh? You must have got it wrong,' said Young.

'That's what she says,' the sergeant told him.

'Probably remembered something about the suspect,' Young hazarded. 'I'll be over right away.'

When he arrived, Lydia recognized the red-headed man who had called at the lodge. This wasn't the officer who had been on television the night before, but he would have to do, otherwise she would be waiting all day and Edward might commit some further folly.

'Well, Mrs Cunningham,' Young said briskly. 'I hear you want to tell me something.'

'I did it, Mr Young.' Lydia's voice was firm. 'I waited for Mr Morrison to come home and then I hit him on the head. He fell dead. I lit the fire to hide what I had done.'

Poor old trout, thought Young.

'Why did you do this, Mrs Cunningham?' he asked.

She remembered what Edward had told her, and so her reply was, to the sergeant, inconsequential.

'I wanted to see the sparkle,' she said.

'What sparkle?'

'The fire, of course,' said Lydia.

'Why should you want to harm Mr Morrison?' asked Young.

'He got in the way,' said Lydia.

'The way of what?'

'My daughter's way,' said Lydia. 'Her pathway to the future.'

'Suppose you tell me about it.' He'd get rid of her faster if he listened to her maunderings, Young thought. 'Why should Mr Morrison be a threat to Mrs Hallows?'

'He would have tied her down. Curtailed her liberty,'

said Lydia. 'He was an old man. If he grew frail she might feel she could not leave him. She was his house-keeper, you know.'

'Yes,' said Young.

The motive she had supplied was a weak one, and Lydia hurried on to tell him what had happened. She told the truth, not mentioning how she had watched the house for several evenings first.

'The house was a little distance from its neighbours. I didn't think there would be a risk to them,' she said.

'I see,' said Young, when she had finished. 'Well, thank you for coming in. I'll bear in mind what you have said. Now, I'll get a car to run you home.'

'But aren't you going to arrest me?' Lydia asked.

'No,' he said gently. 'What you've said will have to be investigated.'

'I see,' said Lydia. 'I used my torch to hit him with,' she added.

'I'll note it down,' said Young.

Lydia rose to her feet.

'My car is in your yard,' she said. 'There's no need for you to take me home. You'll know where to find me when you want me.'

Was she all right to drive? He supposed so. Perhaps he'd better telephone her doctor. He asked her who that was and Lydia said that she was on Dr Garfield's list but had not consulted him for years.

'I'm quite well, I assure you,' she insisted.

As she left the station, a uniformed policewoman was walking through the front office. It was WPC Cotton, who had come to talk to her about little Melanie Smith's disappearance from the motorway service station.

She told Young about that incident when Lydia had gone.

*

Edward had come downstairs to find a note.

Have gone out. Stay inside until you hear. Don't answer phone. Look after Boris. L.C.

What a strange message. Until he heard what? Her return, presumably. She must have gone out shopping but she'd left extremely early. He made himself some breakfast and switched on the radio. The news had nothing about the fire. He turned to the local radio station and learned that a ship had been marooned on the rocks further west; that was the most important local item.

He could slip away now. By this time the police would expect him to have left the district. He quickly packed his few possessions and went to get his scooter from the shed, where he discovered what Lydia had done to stop him leaving. He had no means of pumping up his tyres. Lydia had a footpump, but that was in the Metro.

He couldn't hope to get away on foot. He'd have to wait for her.

She was a long time. Once, the telephone rang and Edward went to answer it, then remembered that he mustn't. The caller did not hang up until after fourteen rings; he counted them.

At last he heard the car.

She came in looking pale but seemed extremely calm. She brought no parcels with her.

'I've told them that I did it, Eddie,' she said, for the first time using his sister's name for him. 'I don't think they believed me but they'll check.'

'You did what?' He did not understand.

'I told the police that I hit Arthur Morrison on the head and lit the fire,' said Lydia.

Edward stared at her in horror.

'Oh Jesus! What a thing to do!' he cried.

'There were reasons,' Lydia said primly.

266

'But to go and tell the police such a story!' Edward said. 'I know you thought you'd be helping me, but you shouldn't do a thing like that.'

'But it's the truth, Eddie,' Lydia said. 'I couldn't have them arresting you for something you hadn't done. I never thought they'd accuse you. I imagined they'd think it was an accident.'

'I don't blame them for picking on me,' said Edward. 'It was bound to happen, given the evidence and my record.'

'But I did do it, Eddie,' Lydia said again.

'Of course you didn't. Why should you want to hurt him? You hadn't even met him,' Edward said.

'I met him and Thelma in a shop,' said Lydia. 'I thought he was too fond of her and she would be at risk. That was my reason. Thelma makes mistakes and I wanted to protect her from another.'

'You thought what?'

Lydia put the kettle on.

'I'd like a cup of coffee,' she declared.

'About Thelma,' he prompted. 'You wanted to protect her. Why?'

'He was much too old for her,' said Lydia. 'It wasn't suitable.'

'But he wasn't going to marry her, for Christ's sake! And even if he wanted to, what's wrong with that? He was a nice old guy – he'd be good to her. And she can't make it with younger men. She might have been all right with someone older.'

'What do you mean, she can't make it?' Lydia asked.

Edward stared down at the table top, tracing a pattern on it with his finger. Lydia resisted the urge to tell him to stop fidgeting and answer her.

'Sex,' he said. 'She doesn't like it. Never has, I think. There are girls like that.' He swept on. 'But an old man like Arthur mightn't want a lot.'

He was wrong, of course: Lydia knew that Thelma's trouble was her appetite.

'It wasn't suitable,' she reaffirmed.

Mrs Cunningham had gone and flipped her lid. The police had realized that and sent her home. People did make false confessions.

'How did you do it?' he asked. He'd soon shoot her story down.

'I waited till he went out. I'd been watching him – you said what a mileage I'd been doing with the car,' she told him. 'I wanted to surprise him, otherwise he'd be too strong for me.'

At her mention of the car, bile rose in Edward's throat. This was what had caused the little rift between them. Could she be telling the truth?

'When he came back on Thursday night, I hit him as he opened the front door. I'd already smashed the porch light and I came up the drive behind him. He fell down and I was able to drag him into the sitting-room. I thought a fire would hide what I had done.' She paused. 'He was very heavy. Bodies are,' she stated. Then she continued. 'I thought the fire was real at first, but it wasn't laid with sticks or paper. Then I realized it was gas. It made a popping noise when I lit it. I scattered papers round the room so that they would catch and make it look as if it was an accident. Then I left.'

'And he was lying there, perhaps not dead. You left him there to burn to death?' asked Edward, still only half believing her.

'He was unconscious,' Lydia said.

Edward had heard men in prison speaking callously about their victims, but Lydia's three words made him shudder. Why was she talking like this? Then he remembered their discussion in the restaurant on Saturday: they had wondered how Arthur had been careless enough to cause an accidental fire.

'I expect he forgot to turn it off,' Lydia had said.

She had known that there was a gas fire in The Shieling before they had mentioned it in the conversation.

She might have heard someone talk about it: he or Thelma might have done so, even Gerald. But Mrs Cunningham had shown no interest in the house or in its owner, and she'd just told him, now, how she had found out about the fire.

Oh God! It was the truth.

Edward felt quite sick. Without another word he left the room and ran upstairs.

Left alone, Lydia hummed to herself as she made some coffee and cut herself some sandwiches. There was plenty of cheddar cheese and she felt hungry.

It was natural that Edward should be upset by what she had told him. He would soon come to terms with his new knowledge when he realized that now he was safe. She made some sandwiches for him and put them on a plate which she covered with foil. He'd eat them later. Then, because there was nothing else to do but wait, she went to fit more pieces into her jigsaw.

She was still sitting there when Detective Sergeant Young arrived, this time with an older man who had a small moustache and said he was Detective Inspector Mobsby. Mobsby had talked by telephone to the pathologist who had carried out the post-mortem on Arthur Morrison; the wound could have been caused by a heavy torch, the doctor said, and if the article could be produced, tests could be made. Because of the lack of firm evidence with which to make a case against Edward Fletcher, Mobsby had decided that Lydia Cunningham's weird confession must be thoroughly investigated. Most cranks were not connected with the crime for which they claimed responsibility, but she was linked with this one through her daughter. That business about the child was odd, too, and should be borne in mind.

'We'd like to see the torch you mentioned,' Mobsby told her. 'And we'd like to take a proper statement.'

'I'll fetch the torch,' Lydia said.

'No, let me,' said Young, and he followed her to the cloakroom where the torch rested, head downwards, on the shelf beside the washbasin, kept there in case of some emergency. Young picked it up gingerly. If she'd really used it as she said, wouldn't she have wiped it clean? He dropped it into a plastic bag and sealed it, while Lydia watched with interest. Betty hadn't been to clean since that evening, or she would have dusted it. What would they find on it?

'What about the clothes you wore that night?' asked Mobsby.

'I burnt them,' Lydia said. 'All except my shoes and raincoat.'

'We'll take those, then,' said the detective inspector.

'They're in the cloakroom,' Lydia said. 'The old beige raincoat and the walking shoes.'

This time, since he knew the way, she allowed Young to fetch them unaccompanied.

Then, sitting in her own armchair, she described what she had done, including how she had watched the house for several nights while waiting for her opportunity. Young wrote it down while she was speaking; she marshalled her narrative so methodically that he took it down verbatim; she waited while he caught up with her. Mobsby sat there with her while she read it though before she signed it, and Young went down the garden.

Lydia worried, while he was absent, lest he peer into the shed. He came back with some more little plastic bags containing fabric fragments he had found on the bonfire pile.

Lydia signed her statement in a small, neat hand. Then she looked up at them.

'Edward Fletcher is exonerated now,' she said. It was a statement, not a question.

'We still want to talk to him,' said Mobsby.

'But you'll be arresting me,' she said.

'We'll be pursuing more inquiries first,' said Mobsby. There was no point in taking the old woman into custody; she would hardly do a flit and there would be a dreadful rumpus if they took her in without sufficient grounds. From what WPC Cotton had said, she was a little odd, maybe paranoiac, but that did not mean she was a murderer. And this was murder; whoever injured Arthur Morrison had not dealt him a lethal blow though the injury was serious; but by setting a fire and leaving the man unconscious in the room, the arsonist had definitely planned a killing.

They left the house without searching it or looking at her car, and they did not go into the kitchen where they might have seen the plate of sandwiches.

Edward had remained silently in his room while they were in the house. He would wait upon the consequences. When they had gone, he came downstairs.

'Do they believe you now?' he said. If they did, wouldn't they have arrested her? Had they cautioned her?

'They took away some things – my raincoat and the torch I used to hit him with,' she said. 'And my shoes.'

'Oh,' he said. They might find something on the shoes: soil from the old man's garden, maybe. Surely she'd cleaned the torch? He didn't ask her because he didn't want to know the answer, either way.

'You'd never stand it,' he said.

'What?'

'Prison.'

'I've been in prison nearly all my adult life,' said Lydia.

He did not understand her.

'You're ill,' he said.

'I'm not. I knew exactly what I was doing,' Lydia said. 'The thing I hadn't thought of was that you would get the blame. That was the unexpected factor.'

'You'll go to Holloway,' he said.

She hadn't thought that far ahead.

'I suppose I will,' she said.

'But it's dreadful there, if you're ill.' It was dreadful anyway, but psychiatric patients needed treatment, not incarceration. She'd end up a gibbering idiot. 'Oh, why did you do it?' he wailed, like a child, and he knuckled his eyes to hold back the tears.

'I told you. It was for Thelma. All her life, everything I've done has been for her,' said Lydia. 'Now, don't grieve, Edward. It won't be for long. I'm quite old, you know.'

'You're not.' People lived to ninety these days. She could face years of horror and he could not bear the thought of it. Miserably, he cast himself against her, and Lydia found herself gently embracing a young male creature in distress. A pleasant, warm sensation filled her thin body as she held him to her, smelled his clean, crisp, curly hair. He was just a little taller than herself – much Arthur's height.

'Dear Eddie,' she said. 'Don't take on so.' She gave him a little hug, then she released him. 'Let's forget it now,' she said. 'They'll come for me when they are ready.'

What should he do? Should he ring Gerald? Edward did not know at all. He wouldn't leave her here alone, however; he must stay with her until the police made their move.

In the end they spent a peaceful time, talking very little. Without discussion, they left the television off for neither wished to see the local news. This would be their last evening together; somehow both knew that. Earlier, Lydia had gone upstairs to make sure her hair was orderly, and while in her room had taken the telephone off the hook. She wanted no incoming calls or further complications now.

That night, while Edward tossed and turned in bed, she slept well. She had tidied up as carefully as always, washing her tights and underwear, putting her skirt away and covering her sweater.

Edward was tormented by visions of her shambling round a prison yard, set upon by other, madder women. When on remand, he'd known the worst himself. Things had been better for him later at a prison set aside for young offenders.

She'd only owned up to save him.

He could still take the rap for her. He could confess. The police would rather believe him guilty than accept her story. She'd told him that they'd taken the torch away; he'd say he'd used it. But she'd stick to her confession; she was stubborn. Now that they had something to look for, they might discover other evidence against her. Those scientists could find a needle in a haystack.

He could still save her from a sentence. There was a way. Which was the worst offence, to let her go to prison or to release her from the possibility? Edward did not know the answer, but he couldn't let her suffer, either way.

At two o'clock in the morning, after racking his brains for a different solution, Edward got out of bed and, carrying his pillow which now was damp with tears and sweat, he tiptoed across the landing and opened Lydia's door. Soft, regular breathing could be heard. He stepped over the carpet to the bed, the pillow raised. Faint light coming from his room across the landing revealed to him that she lay sleeping on her side, knees drawn up, a hand beneath her cheek. Edward pressed the pillow down over her face, but as he did so he could not hold back his sobs. In the same moment, she woke up and, without much difficulty, pushed his attempt at suffocation aside.

She sat up, gasping slightly, and turned on her bedside lamp, not at all frightened but anxious to show no physical signs that might alarm him.

'Eddie, dear, what are you thinking of?' she asked him.

Edward had collapsed backwards, the pillow clasped against his body, near hysteria.

'I couldn't let you go to prison,' he sobbed. 'It would kill you.'

Lydia put a hand to her head. The fine hairnet that she wore in bed was slightly disarranged by Edward's action. She adjusted it, pulling down a fold of hair.

'And have I done it all for nothing?' she demanded. 'You'd be charged with murder. I'll probably get off with manslaughter if Gerald finds a clever counsel. Nonsense, Eddie. It's bad enough as things are. We can't have murder in the village. What would Gerald think? And Julie? They're quite fond of one another. That would all be spoiled.'

It would be anyway. There would be no hope for either of them now, thought Edward. He felt as if a ton of lead was weighing on his heart.

'Go down and put the kettle on,' Lydia instructed. 'We'll have some tea and settle down again. Oh, and don't forget your pillow.'

26

Lydia had foreseen no dreadful consequences of her violent action because she had not expected it to be detected. Would the examination of the torch and of her clothing yield enough evidence to make the police believe her story? What more could she do to convince them? Someone might have seen her car in the side road where she had left it while she reconnoitred. Detective Inspector Mobsby had said he would make inquiries, but one blue Metro looked much like another. In a way, it would be a relief to have the struggle ended. She had a vision of herself in an overall among a lot of other women, queueing for food which would be served in a tin dish. It would be like going back to boarding school but without the opportunity to lift herself above the rest as her success at games had done in youth. There would be smells and noise. There would be rough treatment, even bullying. She might have to share a cell and lose her solitude. If only she could be sent to some retreat: a cool convent with a bare, lonely room where she could leave behind the pain of life.

In saving Thelma, she had unwittingly endangered Edward, and now his rescue would bring shame and disgrace upon Gerald and his children.

When Edward had gone back to bed, Lydia again sat by her bedroom window waiting for the dawn, and again, when it arrived, she left the house, but this time she took Boris with her.

She drove to Worton Bay and parked the car on the headland where she had come with Gerald before the start of all this horror. They had walked together on the beach and talked more frankly than ever in their lives.

One way out, assuming the police were going to accept what she had told them without further testament, would be to drive straight over the edge of the cliff. That might not be interpreted as an accident, however, and if it were not, it would be another cruel legacy. She would have to devise some other means. such as driving round a bend apparently too fast and running into a tree, as Charles had done.

For the first time since his death, it came to Lydia that it might have been suicide. She pushed it from her mind: not that, to add to Thelma's other failures.

Lydia got out of the car and set off with Boris to walk along the headland. Gulls called below, and two cormorants dived for fish, but she took no heed of them, head down, staring at the tussocky grass while Boris rooted on ahead hoping to find a rabbit. They'd go round by the golf course and return along the shore, thus pleasing both of them for Lydia preferred walking on the sand.

The day was damp. Lydia took a scarf from the pocket of her jacket and tied it round her head. Hands in pockets, on she trudged, and after a while a course of action she could follow came into her mind. She would write a careful statement of everything she had already told the police and address it to the Chief Constable. She would describe the things she had noticed at The Shieling – the details of where the matches were, and the taper, the colour of the carpet – things she could not have known if she had not been inside the house. She would mention Henry's position in the county and request the Chief Constable's discretion in settling the case; influence might still count for something and at last, after death, she would make use of Henry. She must trust the man to manage that.

Gerald would never understand, of course: even Edward had found her explanation unacceptable, but the only motive she could offer was the one she had already given the police. They would just have to believe she had been temporarily deranged. She saw now that one could not escape retribution; all those years ago she had sinned against the truth, and the devil, laughing, had caught up with her. Well, she'd beat him in the end.

Gerald would pick the pieces up, put his life together, settle with some woman. Men usually did: it was women who forged on alone, whether from chance or choice.

From ahead came a single sudden bark.

Boris had been snuffling on in front of her, seeking intriguing scents in the hollows and crannies of the headland. Now he had vanished.

Probably he'd found a rabbit hole.

'Boris,' she called, then called again, 'Boris? Boris?'

He did not reappear, but she heard another bark and then a frightened whining. Lydia went to the edge of the cliff and looked over. There, on a ledge below, stood Boris, trembling. Scrabbling at an interesting hollow in the ground, he had disturbed the soft topsoil and caused a tiny avalanche of earth, enough to carry him over.

'Oh, Boris, you silly boy! Look where you've got to,' Lydia cried aloud. She peered down. The ledge was no great distance below her and if she could reach it, she would be able to lift him back to the top. 'Stay there. Stay,' she instructed.

Trustingly, Boris looked up at his mistress, his large

strong tail waving gently. Lydia looked about for a way to climb down to his level. To his side, there were footholds in the cliff face. Ignoring the menace of the rocks below, she took off her jacket so that it would not impede her movements and lay down on her stomach, her head facing inland, easing her long thin legs in their ribbed navy tights over the edge. Some small hard object in her skirt pocket pressed against her skinny hipbone as she moved backwards, feeling about with her feet for a place to rest them. She found a hold for one foot, inched down and reached out for another, her hands on the top. There was no scrubby bush to grab to keep herself secure.

In Worton Bay, an old retired seaman who lived with his daughter and son-in-law in a bungalow where he spent much of his time watching the local life through his binoculars, saw the whole thing. He had noticed the small blue car earlier; at this time of year there were few headland walkers and he had seen this one before. He saw the dog running on ahead and he witnessed the whole rescue, the woman edging her way along the cliff to where her pet was marooned. She successfully lifted him back and the dog was safe when the ledge on which he had been stranded gave way and she fell to the rocks below.

She died before help could arrive.

PENSIONER DIES SAVING PET ran the headline in the *Cheverton Gazette*, with below it the eye-witness account, as told to their reporter, of Lydia's heroism.

A small paragraph on the same page announced that the police investigation into the tragedy at The Shieling in Heronsmouth had been concluded and no charges would be preferred.

'Lucky for her, I reckon,' said Detective Superintendent Sawyer. The police had been forced to accept that her death was an accident, since a witness attested to the whole thing and she had left no suicide note. She was taken to Cheverton Hospital, and her identity was only discovered by means of the tag on Boris's collar: he had stayed at the cliff top, barking continuously, looking down at the recumbent form of his mistress while the ambulance men summoned by the watcher in the bungalow loaded her on to a stretcher. The Cheverton police dealt with the details and it was a little time before their colleagues in Heronsmouth heard what had happened.

A single fragment of a jigsaw puzzle was found in the pocket of her skirt. Later, Edward could fit it into none of those waiting to be completed at the lodge; then he remembered the jungle scene with one piece missing; here it was.

Meanwhile, the forensic pathologist who had carried out the post-mortem examination on Arthur Morrison had concluded that the wound on his skull matched Lydia's torch, on which had been found traces of tissue which, on analysis, had come from the dead man. There were scorch marks on Lydia's old raincoat more likely to have come from tending a bonfire than from the fire at The Shieling, but earth particles found on her shoes were being checked to see if they matched soil from the garden of the house where she claimed to have set the fire. It was too late to seek a footprint, and too much traffic had passed the house for one to be found inside.

'She must have gone right round the twist,' said Mobsby. It tied in with her action when she had abducted a small girl apparently to teach the parents a lesson. 'Didn't like what the daughter might be up to and tried to play God.'

'Something like that,' agreed Detective Superintendent Sawyer, who seldom made moral judgements. He was a just man and had told Edward Fletcher – who had been found at the lodge when

Gerald Cunningham arrived there after his mother's accident – that the case against him had been dropped.

Mud stuck, though; Edward knew that well. His always precarious world, which had briefly seemed secure, had fallen apart again; and he grieved for Lydia.

He found enough courage to ask Sawyer about her confession. The fact that he had been in the house the whole time Mobsby and Young were taking her statement was now known to the police.

'I suppose you didn't believe her,' Edward said.

'We needed proof,' said Sawyer.

'And you've got it now?'

'Enough.' The boy could have used the torch, of course, but he would have had the sense to wipe it clean, or dump it.

'Must you tell her family?' asked Edward.

Sawyer looked at him, weighing him up: a thin-faced ex-con who gazed back at him unswervingly.

'I shan't let on,' Edward said. 'It would shock them something rotten, a lady like her doing such a thing.'

'It won't be my decision,' Sawyer replied. 'But I'll see what I can do.'

It might all die down. No journalist had got hold of the story and unless any member of the force blabbed, the truth might remain locked in the files, though the coroner would have to be told and Morrison's son might need reassuring that there had been no miscarriage of justice.

He could be told that the attack came from an intruder known to the police but who subsequently had died. Time would tell if that would satisfy him.

On a grey day Lydia's ashes were interred in her husband's grave at Milton St Gabriel. She had left no instructions about a funeral and this seemed the best compromise between the various choices.

Gerald still felt stunned by the finality of it, the suddenness of her death. Now he would never win her love or her approval, and he felt as though the core had gone from his life. Julie found him still in the graveyard after the small ceremony which only he had attended. At the crematorium, some days earlier, a respectable number of mourners had put in an appearance out of respect for Henry if for no other reason.

'Come on,' said Julie. 'It's over now,' and she took Gerald's hand to lead him away. They went back to the lodge together and walked down the garden to look at the angry orange roof which had so annoyed his mother.

'Look, there's some moss growing on it,' Julie said. 'See – up there in the gully.'

Gerald followed her gaze and descried a small thread of dark green adhering to a tile.

'That'll improve it,' he said.

'What will you do with the lodge?' Julie asked.

'It's only leased from the developers,' he said. 'That was arranged for her lifetime. They'll pull it down and put up two or three bungalows, I expect.'

'I see.' Julie had thought he might use it for week-ends.

'I never want to come down here again, once everything's settled,' he declared.

'Never's a long time,' said Julie.

'I know.' He turned to face her. 'Will you come to London with me?'

She nodded, trying to control the huge smile of joy which she felt stretching across her face.

'What about Eddie?' she asked.

Gerald laughed at that.

'And her brother came too?' he said.

'He needs a job and he's very sad,' said Julie. 'He loved Mrs Cunningham.'

'I'm going into business on my own,'said Gerald. He had decided to take his money out of the hotel group. 'I don't know what, or where,' he added. 'Maybe the wine trade. I was quite taken with all I saw when I went to visit my son.'

'So you might have a post for a strong young man?' Julie said.

'I daresay,' Gerald answered, smiling. He took her hand and held it against his cheek, then kissed it. No one had ever kissed Julie's hand before and her inside lurched.

'What about Thelma?' She tried to speak in level tones. There was no need to fall on his neck; there was plenty of time.

'Oh – I suppose you haven't heard the latest. She's taken a shine to that old man's son – Nicholas Morrison. A nice bloke, too, as you'd expect. She's off to Leeds, where he lives. Says she doesn't know that part of the world and it's time she had a look around.'

'What'll she do?'

'Find a job if she can, I suppose,' said Gerald. 'She's going to rent a flat for the rest of the winter. Maybe she'll join another dramatic society. But she's chasing him, of course.'

'Isn't he married?'

'Yes, but that won't stop Thelma,' Gerald said.

'Perhaps she won't catch him,' said Julie.

'Perhaps not,' Gerald agreed. 'Who can tell?'

THE SMOOTH FACE OF EVIL

1

The lonely ones were settling down for the night.

In high-rise apartment blocks and thin-walled cell-like bed-sitters; in cottages nestling in dark hamlets and in terraced houses; in bungalows and suburban villas; in mansions and even, perhaps, in a palace or two; in cities, towns and villages, inland and on the coast, the nightly rituals of the solitary were performed.

Some people put out the cat; others gave the dog a last run. Many checked bolts on doors and windows after leaving the milkman's instructions on the step. Some made cups of tea or malted milk; others poured tots of whisky. Some swallowed pills; some read; some listened to music. The lucky ones fell asleep quickly; others fretted restlessly, suffering old wounds again.

Terry Brett, at the moment without a regular source of income, was walking through the quiet streets of Westborough. An occasional car drove past as he paused to look at the lighted display in a radio and television shop whose window was protected by strong metal mesh. Some months before, bricks had been hurled at the plate glass

1

windows of one of Westborough's supermarkets, breaking them; three boys had made off with bottles of liquor, and more had been broken and spilled. The culprits had never been caught.

Such actions were not Terry's style at all. Violence was crude, uncivilized, and unnecessary. He picked things up by other means – articles left in unlocked cars; or cars themselves, locked or unlocked, parked in quiet streets. Over the years he'd built up a useful collection of keys from various sources – garages, scrap merchants, junk shops – and when funds were low could always dispose of a newly acquired car to a workshop where, in a few hours, it would be resprayed, given new number plates and sent on its way to a buyer. Because of his skill in lifting cars he'd been approached, after his jail sentence, by more than one gang planning a robbery to find them a getaway car, but always he had turned such suggestions down. They might carry guns. They'd be ready for violence. He wasn't.

There were so many opportunities for someone alert. Women laid their handbags, often unzipped, on benches beside them in cafés and snack bars, never suspecting the nicely dressed young man who looked like a bank clerk or an insurance salesman, sitting nearby, when later they found their purses had gone. He'd worked as a barman, a waiter, as a door-to-door salesman, as a market researcher and in a department store. Despite his lack of the correct papers – lost, he always explained, in a fire – he was given jobs ahead of other applicants because of his good appearance, his clean fingernails and his respectful manner. His door-to-door selling experience had led to more; he'd bought damaged prints cheap after a warehouse was flooded and had gone round a housing estate with them. In this way, he had met more than one discontented middle-aged housewife and had become her lover. The grateful women paid well for silence when, later, Terry explained that unfortunately he would have to speak to their husbands unless they could help him clear up some outstanding debts.

The women all paid, always with tears and never with anger. Terry was good at selecting them. He was their benefactor, leaving them precious memories to nurture through the ensuing arid years of their dead marriages. He guaranteed satisfaction until the moment was reached, in every affair, when the level of boredom and the cloying devotion became nauseating. Then it was time to present his account and depart. They were so silly, the women: so soft and so greedy. They were as demanding and stupid as kids would be if given the freedom of a sweetshop.

Terry had just ended such a relationship and had five hundred pounds in hand. The silly cow hadn't been able to raise any more cash, but she'd given him her engagement ring and a locket that had belonged to her grandmother. The ring was quite nice; he'd sell it somewhere well away from where she lived. He'd say it was the sad result of a broken engagement. Terry knew that the jeweller

3

would believe him; he'd done it before.

His parents thought Terry worked in computers. He'd had a spell abroad, they told their friends in Woking, where they lived. Terry didn't keep in touch as much as he might, they lamented, but young people were often thoughtless. They had no idea that while they imagined him in Germany, Terry was in prison. Terry's father was a minor civil servant who travelled to London each day, spending a fortune on fares; his mother was a soft, faded woman not unlike those he now exploited. Terry had a married sister who was a librarian, and a brother who had followed their father into the civil service. Terry himself moved about the country taking a room in whatever town he was working. Now and then, if his papers were up to date, he registered for unemployment benefit, even working for a while if a job was offered; it might lead to a crock of gold; you never knew.

He picked male victims sometimes. He found them in bars. They paid exceedingly well, especially the married ones, and he controlled what happened. There were depths to which Terry was not prepared to go.

Now, Terry felt like tackling something new. He had come to Westborough because he had never operated there and he wanted to look around. It was time to leave Swindon while wounds there healed. So far, none of his victims had met one another and he must take care to keep things that way.

Terry walked past the Rigby Arms, a timbered

hotel in the main street of Westborough. He saw a blue Rover 3500 parked outside with a briefcase on the back seat but it was too near the street light to touch. There was a white Porsche, too. He sauntered on, then turned back. It was past closing time, too late to go prospecting in the hotel bar.

A man and a woman came out of the Rigby Arms and went up to the Rover. The man unlocked it and opened the passenger door for the woman to get in: so they weren't married, thought Terry, watching from the shadows. The woman was young, the man much older. Terry made a mental note of the car's number before moving on; he often did things like that; you never knew what information might come in useful.

He walked on through the cold streets, looking at every car, for it was time to go home.

He found an old Marina with the key in the ignition. What fools people were! Terry drove it back to Swindon, leaving it in a street a mile from his digs.

His landlady never heard him enter the house. He was always so quiet and thoughtful; she liked young Mr Terence Brett, who paid his rent regularly and was always polite.

While Terry Brett was prowling the streets of Westborough, six miles away in her granny flat at Harcombe House, Alice Armitage was removing her cosmetic armour of beige foundation, coral lipstick, plenty of eyeshadow and mascara with which, with a touch of Je Reviens, stud earrings, artificial pearls and several bracelets, she daily

5

faced her foes: isolation; ennui; the rudeness of shop assistants. She creamed her papery skin and brushed her thinning hair which was tinted honey-blonde and permed in a frizz round her small head. Before getting into bed she crossed the narrow landing and entered the living-room of her tiny apartment, going to the window and drawing back the curtain to look at the wintry landscape. Because the trees were bare she could see the lodge, where a glow of light showed at the curtained windows. The outside light was on, so Sue wasn't back yet. It was her late week. Sue was a receptionist at the Rigby Arms in Westborough. Jonathan would have gone to fetch her, wouldn't he? For a moment Alice experienced a faint unease. Before now, Sue had been brought home by Alice's son Giles, who had begun to spend too much time in bars. Still, if he happened to be in the Rigby when Sue's shift was over, it was only neighbourly to give her a lift, Alice rationalized.

Thinking thus, she saw the white beam of a car's headlights at the gate, then the bright circles as it turned in. Jonathan in his beige Granada, or Giles in his Rover? Alice waited to see.

The car stopped at the lodge, and a figure got out. Then Giles, in his blue Rover 3500, drove on to the barn which was used as a garage for their four cars – the Rover, the Granada, Alice's Metro and Helen's Volvo. Helen was Giles's wife and it was because of her, and her aspirations, that Alice had thrown in her lot with her family after her husband died. By selling Windlea, her home on the outskirts of Bournemouth, and adding the money to theirs, Alice had enabled her son and his wife to buy Harcombe House, on which Helen had set her heart.

'It's the sensible thing to do, Alice,' her daughter-in-law had said, when Walter had died suddenly after a minor operation. She'd said nothing about wanting to have her with them, Alice had often remembered since.

Harcombe House was a large granite mansion built by a Victorian tycoon. It had barns and outbuildings, and, at the end of the short drive, a small lodge with a high gabled roof. When the Armitages moved in it had been empty for some time, and needed a thorough renovation. Much had been done: the kitchen was modernized; the main rooms papered and painted, but the anti-quated heating system still remained. There were heavy, old-fashioned radiators in Alice's rooms but the warmth never reached that far, and Helen decreed that using electric convector fires was far too extravagant. Besides, the aged wiring might not stand the load.

The parts that showed downstairs had been made pleasant and comfortable, and some of Alice's own furniture had been used in the draw-ing-room. Helen was developing the scope of the interior decorating business she had begun a few years before. Then, she had merely advised on curtains, covers, lampshades and so on; now, she undertook an entire house, including buying the furniture. She wanted to make her own home a

7

shop-window for her skills and she was striving to build up a circle of acquaintances – whom she called friends – who would recommend her because they had seen her taste reflected here at Harcombe. When money was easier, plumbing heating and draught-proofing would be tackled; meanwhile, a swimming-pool had been built in the grounds, and the old hard tennis-court rescued and resurfaced. There were eight acres of land with the house, part meadow, where now Dawn and Amanda, Alice's granddaughters, kept ponies. Giles, helped by a jobbing gardener, was slowly reducing the jungle growth that had swallowed the flower beds.

'She's set her heart on the house,' Giles had said to Alice, explaining that the sale of their house in Pinner would not begin to cover the cost. Even with her contribution the mortgage was vast and terrifying.

'Couldn't Helen's father – ?' Alice had hazarded, when Helen was out of the room helping Alice's Mrs Bennett wash up after the cold meal they'd had when they returned from the crematorium.

'Not again,' said Giles. 'I'm beholden enough as it is.'

Giles worked for his father-in-law in a firm that made plastic casings for other industrial users. It was a sound business, but its profits had dropped in recent years and a takeover bid was in the air; Giles saw no point in telling Alice this. Helen's father had given them their first small house when they married, taking Giles into the firm with a higher salary than he had received as an accountant and promising him a place on the board before long. Giles had his directorship now, but to justify it he laboured long and hard, and at home spent hours poring over sales figures and production statistics.

Alice and Walter had loved their only son and delighted in his modest youthful successes. When he first brought Helen home, they were overjoyed. She was a fair, pretty girl just back from a year abroad. There was no sign, then, of her driving ambition, but Alice and Walter had seen its birth. They had worried together, knowing that Giles lacked whatever was needed to keep her content. What would Walter have advised, Alice had wondered, faced with Helen's scheme?

Before going into hospital, Walter had explained that if anything went wrong Alice would have the house and a good pension, but she had barely listened. Soon he would be home, able to enjoy car outings, bowls with his friends, their weekly theatre trips. Since his retirement they had drawn closer together – a surprise for Alice, who had seen her friends irritated at having their husbands about the place all day, requiring lunch. But Walter had had a heart attack after his operation and died without regaining consciousness; their new joy had been wiped out. That was a week ago, and now here were Giles and Helen offering her a chance to share their home.

Alice hadn't needed a lot of persuading. Windlea was too big for her alone, as Helen had

pointed out. Vague thoughts of a bungalow somewhere near drifted through Alice's mind but she
dismissed the idea. She'd be alone. Of course,
she'd be alone in her flat at Harcombe House, too,
but the family would be in the main part of the
house and she'd make friends in the village.

'Mrs Bennett – ' Alice had said. Mrs Bennett,
who had cleaned and polished Windlea twice a
week for the last twenty years was a friend; she it
was who had dried Alice's tears when she came
back from that last hospital visit and had had to
telephone Giles.

'There'll be someone like her,' Giles had reassured her. 'Helen will need help. There's a lodge.
We'll put a couple in there to work the place.'

But they hadn't. Helen had found Mrs Wood,
who came five days a week from her house in the
village and seldom had time to do any work for
Alice because of all that Helen required her to do.
And the lodge had been let.

When Jonathan and Sue had moved in, the
lodge had been screened from Alice's dormer
window by the huge beech tree that spread wide,
shady boughs over the gravel sweep in front of the
house and the barn, and which, in autumn, cast its
leaves like copper filings on the ground. They
weren't married, but Alice felt sure that they
would be, soon. There was some hitch about a
divorce; Helen had not realized this when she
arranged the lease and was annoyed; she did not
like any sort of messiness. Sue was so friendly;
Alice thought she must be well suited to her hotel

work. Jonathan seemed quiet and calm; he must have been sadly provoked to have left his wife and children, Alice felt. He often looked rather sad. But the two were obviously so much in love that Alice was enchanted with them. She hoped that it would last. Things didn't, always.

Now, Jonathan would be welcoming Sue home from work. Alice imagined them together and felt happier. She watched Giles walk from the barn across the gravel sweep to his own front door. His tread was heavy, odd to think that he was well into middle age. When he had gone, Alice drew the curtains across the window, turned out the light and walked across the landing to her small bedroom which was almost totally filled by the big bed she had shared with Walter. Helen had wanted her to have a small divan which would take up far less space, but Alice had refused to do so. Now she drew the covers around her and tried to pretend that Walter's large, friendly bulk was at her back.

In the night, she woke from a frightening dream. It concerned Giles. She'd been running to warn him of some impending danger, but her legs were slow and heavy, as if stuck in treacle, and she could not move them fast enough. She'd been calling and shouting to him: then she woke.

Alice sat up in bed, hands to her thin chest that was covered by a printed viyella nightgown and a knitted bedjacket.

The dream faded, as dreams so often do when the dreamer wakes. Alice sipped water from the glass at her bedside and lay down again. The room was chilly. It was a long time before she slept.

2

Alice's first weeks at Harcombe had been spent in a haze of misery. It was summer, and the overgrown garden was full of roses, many of them old-fashioned scented varieties. On fine days, bees hummed among the twiggy overgrown lavender, and at weekends, when Giles cut the grass, sitting on a large mower which left huge stripes across the lawn, the sweet smell of the fresh-mown grass reminded Alice of Windlea, where Walter had cut their lawn with a Suffolk Colt and where the scent was the same. Alice, sitting with her library book on the terrace if Helen was out, or round the side of the house out of sight if she were at home, tried not to weep as she mourned the loss of a companion who had never been exciting but who had been gently amiable and always dependable for the greater part of her life, even during the war, for his job with the ministry was a reserved occupation.

Alice had expected to see much more of her grand-daughters after the move, but they were sent to boarding-school, and as soon as term ended in July the family went to Corfu for a fortnight, leaving Alice alone. They'd booked their villa before Walter died, and it was not large enough for her to go too, Helen had stated.

'Couldn't I – ?' Alice began.

'Couldn't you what?' Helen asked sharply.

Alice had been going to suggest that she might stay in a hotel near their villa, but she saw how Helen would respond to that idea and changed direction.

'I might pop back to Bournemouth, just for a few days,' she said. 'See my friends, and so on.'

'I hope you won't,' said Helen. 'Go when we return, by all means, if you must, but I'd been counting on you to keep an eye on things here. With a house this size, if one's away thieves get in, but if someone's about they're discouraged. Besides, the workmen are still around.'

The surround to the swimming-pool hadn't been finished. During her lonely days Alice had liked going out to talk to the men making the pool, which had been done very quickly once the hole was dug and the container dropped into the cavity.

She gave in.

'Well, of course I'll be glad to be useful,' she said.

Alice's sense of isolation, during the fortnight, was almost more than she could endure. She recalled Helen's words and often woke in the night imagining that she heard intruders. She would get up, and with a large torch held before her would patrol the house, which was always empty. When Mrs Wood arrived, Alice would invent reasons for pottering about the main part of the house. She would perch in Helen's own sitting-room, which faced south-west and on fine days was full of sun, when Mrs Wood was busy elsewhere, guiltily enjoying the light airy room which was such a contrast to her own dim, north-facing attic.

'Shame they didn't find you a better part of the house, Mrs Armitage, dear,' Mrs Wood said once, catching her there as she read the paper. 'It's big enough, Lord knows.'

'We all value our privacy,' said Alice repressively. 'It wouldn't do if I were on top of them.' She folded her paper and left the room, giving Mrs Wood the impression that she was, after all, a stuck-up old biddy, which until then she had not appeared to be. After that Mrs Wood made still less effort to clean Alice's rooms, but they didn't need it; Alice was quite able to clean and polish her tiny apartment.

Mrs Wood did not come on Fridays. By Saturday evening Alice had not spoken to a soul for two days, nor seen another human. Sue was on day shift, and Jonathan had gone to see his children. His wife insisted that he took them to his parents' house in Kent; she did not want them meeting Sue.

In desperation, on Sunday, Alice went to church. She had learned from Mrs Wood that there was no vicar in Harcombe; a roving one came twice a month to take services, which were not well attended, and Alice found herself one of a congregation of five, three other women and an old man. She sat at the back, stood, knelt, mouthed hymns and responses and fled from the building without speaking to anyone. Religion had played no great part in her life with Walter; they'd gone to church at Christmas and Easter; that was all.

That evening, when she turned on the television, Alice began to talk to the announcer, just to see if she could still converse.

She'd imagined a populous village, before she came, with the big house at its centre, but Harcombe was only a hamlet, a single road ending at the church, with two or three large cottages – tasteful conversions of former labourers' dwellings – a few smaller ones and some bungalows bordering it. Some council houses had been built after the war, but there was no recent development. The school had been closed; there was no pub; and the single small shop only succeeded because it was also a sub-post office. That was now under threat of closure, and pensioners would have to go to Great Minton to draw their money. Most of Harcombe's residents shopped in Westborough; there was no bus service through the village, but by walking a mile you could catch the bus on the main road. A fish van came every Wednesday afternoon and parked for an hour outside the shop, and a butcher from Great Minton delivered once a week. The village shop sold mass-produced bread.

Alice, when she first arrived, had explored by car. She saw few people about, and no one had come to call. People didn't, these days. One of her duties was to visit the fish van each week for Helen. She would buy herself a small trout, if the fishmonger had one, as a treat. A few faces grew familiar from these excursions; there might be a nod and perhaps a smile, but no one spoke to Alice, though they all knew each other. She was too shy to break in to their talk and introduce herself. Why should they want to bother with her? She took to going further afield in her Metro – to Westborough, where there were several inns and cafés in which by turns she had lunch, and where there were, as in most towns, Boots, two supermarkets, a good dress shop, and, down a side street with plenty of room to park, the public library. Alice joined it, but found that she could not concentrate on the books she brought home; she would turn the pages, her eyes moving over the print, and at the end be unaware of what she had supposedly read. This worried her and she went to the doctor in Great Minton; he thought her predicament natural after bereavement and a removal, prescribing Mogadon but only when really needed. She'd soon settle down, he declared.

Alice, already thin, had lost seven pounds when Giles and his family returned from Corfu, but because make-up hid her pallor, and she looked, as always, elegant, in a long-sleeved cotton dress and her pearls and bracelets, he did not notice.

Giles, Alice thought, looked better after his holiday; a tan was superimposed over his heavy, florid features. They'd all swum a lot, and he and the girls had enjoyed using the boat which went with the house. Helen had made friends with some people in a neighbouring villa and had thus acquired potential clients, since they were moving

17

into an old house in Wiltshire quite soon and were faced with a big renovation programme. He'd had to admire the subtle way in which she had found out all this and made apparent her own ability to lift the burden of selection from her new friends. She had all the ruthlessness he lacked; in his job, she would have reached the top, family firm or not, whereas Giles himself laboured away to earn a salary that was far higher than he merited. He was always tired, and often had a pain in his stomach which he feared was an ulcer, if nothing worse. Sometimes, when he read of men struck down by heart attacks in their prime, Giles wished it could happen to him; it would solve all the problems he could not handle.

Giles had begun calling at the Rigby Arms rather by chance, though he often stopped somewhere for a bracer or two on the way home. The first time he went there after the holiday was the day the girls went back to school. He would miss them. Things were better at home when they were there; there was the illusion of contented family life at meal times, and Amanda's infatuation with her pony, Mr Jinks, was an enchantment. But tonight there would be just Helen. She would have plans to draw, patterns to choose. She worked most evenings now.

He'd forgotten about Sue until he went through the swing doors of the Rigby Arms and saw her in the foyer.

He did not stay long that first time, but soon, when she was on the late shift, he began to stay on for a meal. It seemed only sensible, then, to suggest that he should take her home to save Jonathan turning out. Sometimes, on such nights, alone in his bedroom at the further end of the passage from Helen's, Giles would have sensational dreams.

Alice noticed the poster about the coffee morning when she went to the shop for a tin of soup. In aid of the NSPCC, a cause all must approve, it was to be held at Meadow Cottage.

She would go to it, Alice resolved. She would meet people there, some of the women she saw in the fish queue, no doubt. They were probably pleasant when you became acquainted. She asked the dour woman who ran the shop where Meadow Cottage was, and on the appointed day set forth, inwardly quaking. She'd taken pains with her appearance and wore a fawn woollen two-piece and smart patent shoes.

The poster had advertised the time as ten-thirty; Alice arrived at ten forty-five to find several cars outside Meadow Cottage, and, as she turned off the Metro's engine, she could hear a loud hum of talk coming from the open windows. She almost turned back, but forced herself on.

At the door, a girl in jeans and a loose pink sweater smiled as she accepted Alice's entrance fee.

'Coffee's through there,' she said, pointing to an open door.

Alice's head was swimming slightly as she walked into a sitting-room which seemed filled with women all on the most intimate terms with each other. It was several minutes before someone offered her a cup of coffee and a bourbon biscuit. There was no spare seat, so she took her cup to a corner of the room and shrank against the wall. Her hand shook, the metal spoon chinking in the saucer.

She was far too smartly dressed, she saw, glancing round. The younger women were all in jeans or cotton skirts, the older ones in tweeds. Alice possessed no such clothes. Walter had always liked her to look smart, and she owed it to him, she felt, to keep her standards up.

At last someone spoke directly to her, but only to ask her to buy a raffle ticket. She was a large woman with big bosoms billowing softly beneath a pale cream sweater, and wide hips covered in muted checks.

'Will you be here for the draw?' this woman asked, tearing off Alice's tickets, five for a pound, the least you could decently buy, Alice inferred.

How could she stay? At that moment Alice, her ears buzzing with the unaccustomed high-pitched chatter, thought she might not last out another five minutes.

'No – I have to go,' she said. Her voice sounded harsh even to herself.

'Ah – well, tell me your name,' said the woman, grasping the ballpoint pen which hung on a string round her neck.

'Armitage,' Alice croaked. 'Alice Armitage.'

'Oh – so that's who you are!' the woman

exclaimed, in booming tones, and beamed at her through her spectacles. 'From the house?'

Barbara Duncan knew everything that went on in the village, and almost everyone who lived there. Her cleaning woman brought her a good deal of news, and her early walks with her elderly spaniel took her past most of the houses, so that she kept abreast of change, but though she often passed the gates of Harcombe House, she had not met the Armitages. She knew that the husband worked in Slough, and that the wife ran her own business – wallpapers, went the rumour, not altogether incorrectly although Barbara had pictured a do-it-yourself shop of some kind. The two girls had been briefly descried on their ponies. There was an old lady, people knew, but Alice Armitage, standing here and recognizable as someone occasionally seen at the shop, was not aged; merely fragile, and somewhat over-dressed.

Barbara now took her round the room, briskly introducing her to everyone present. Most of the younger women lived in Great Minton.

'Come to sherry on Sunday,' Barbara instructed. 'At noon. I live at the Old Vicarage, just by the church – you can't miss it.' She swept on, allowing no time for Alice to refuse.

The following Sunday, Alice set off in some agitation. It was raining, so she went by car – she would have, anyway, whatever the weather: she felt safe in her little red box on wheels. She wore the black and white suit she had bought after Walter died. He'd liked to see her in pastels, like the Queen Mother, but she no longer felt like dressing in pink or yellow.

Two cars were parked outside the square brick house. Alice reversed hers neatly in beside them and walked up to the front door which opened as she reached it. Her hostess had seen her arrive and had been impressed with her skilful parking.

Today, Barbara Duncan wore a grey flannel skirt with two sharp box pleats front and back, and a pale blue sweater. Among her pearls rested spectacles on a gilt chain.

Alice was introduced to two elderly couples whose names she didn't take in – one was Colonel something – and two women who had been at the coffee party. After a while, Alice sorted out their names – Violet Hedges and Nancy Wilson. She drank two glasses of medium dry sherry and was talked to kindly by everyone present. The colonel and his wife came from Great Minton, the other couple from another village further away. It seemed obvious that Barbara was a widow, but what a much more capable one than herself, Alice reflected. The colonel poured out the sherry and the other man proffered peanuts and crisps. They all asked Alice how she liked the village and if she was settling in, and Alice replied, 'Very well, thank you,' to both questions, the blackest lies she had uttered in her life.

Harcombe was quiet, they told her, and she agreed. There'd been more going on in Bournemouth, where she'd come from. It was beautiful here, though, she said; the views from the house were lovely, but she missed the sea.

After a while it was time to leave.

She'd forgotten about lunch, and had to scramble an egg. She rarely had lunch with Helen and Giles; Helen had soon killed any idea of that as routine. They often had guests who would bore Alice, she said, making it clear that she really meant Alice would bore the guests.

The following Tuesday evening, Alice's telephone rang.

Giles and Helen must both be out, she thought. There was one line to the house; by day it was switched through to her, and she took messages for Helen, but the rest of the time the caller was connected to the main part of the house.

But the call was for her. It was Barbara Duncan. She and three other women – two of them Violet Hedges and Nancy Wilson, whom Alice had met on Sunday – had tickets for a matinée in London the next day. The fourth woman had severe bronchitis and couldn't go. Would Alice take her place? Barbara would collect her in the morning and drive her to Westborough station in time for the nine-forty train. They liked to shop or go to an exhibition on days when they made these trips, which Alice now learned were regular events.

She answered evasively, taken by surprise.

'What else are you doing tomorrow?' asked Barbara, who in her time had been head girl of her school, a junior commander in the ATS, the wife of a brigadier, and was now chairman of the women's branch of the British Legion and the local

Conservative Association. She was also the mother of three sons and had four grandsons, was unused to female competition and accustomed to getting her own way.

Alice had no plans beyond going to the library. Despite cuts in its budget, there were still periodicals there, and she liked sitting comfortably in the reading area leafing through them.

'Well – ' she admitted. 'Nothing important.'

'Good. Then you'll come,' stated Barbara. 'Could you be at the gate if it isn't raining? I'll be there sharp at nine.' So Alice went to London, and had her first happy day since Walter's death.

There was a routine about these trips, Alice saw, as she sat quietly in the train listening to the other three women's talk. Each had her own theatre ticket, in case they failed to meet for lunch in the coffee shop at the Strand Palace Hotel, which was close to the theatre. All could act freely if detained in any of the various ways they intended to spend the morning.

At Paddington, Barbara Duncan plunged down the stairs to the tube while Violet and Nancy set forth towards the hotel, bound for the ladies' cloakroom.

'Much nicer than the one on the station,' said Nancy, neat in her brown tweed suit and fawn polo sweater.

Alice followed them up a flight of stairs. How should she occupy the morning? She was unused to visiting London: she and Walter had seldom been there, for Bournemouth had so much to offer. She wondered how to fill the time as she patted powder on to her short, already matt nose. Violet and Nancy were going shopping. Alice went into the tube with them but when they got off at Oxford Circus, she stayed on. At Piccadilly she changed trains and returned to Paddington, where she spent the morning in the hotel lounge reading *Homes and Gardens*, which she had bought on the station concourse. She had lunch at the hotel, too; you could get a nice snack, she found. She felt safer doing that than facing the Strand Palace alone, or feeling herself an intruder among the others who had known each other for years. After another visit to the cloakroom she went into the tube again, this time with confidence, and travelled to Charing Cross with ease. She walked from there to the theatre, in her smart black shoes which pinched her toes a little. She was in her seat when the others arrived, Nancy and Violet with carrier bags from Selfridge's and Marks and Spencer, Barbara with two from Harrods. No one commented on Alice's lack of shopping, merely asking if she'd had a nice morning and enjoyed her lunch, which she had.

It was in this way that Alice formed her attachment to Paddington Station and its hotel. She went there often, whenever she was overburdened by her solitude. At first she had hoped that the other women might invite her to join their regular excursions, but then she remembered that she had been a stopgap because of the fourth person's illness.

Four was a good number; four filled the car. She must not expect admission to this group.

Sometimes she had lunch in the hotel restaurant, where, from a small carvery, you could choose your cut of meat or poultry. There was often a great piece of beef such as no family, now, would buy except for a special party. Greedily, Alice would eat her large helping, with roast potatoes, vegetables, and a glass of red wine. Flushed and warm with food and drink, sometimes she went on to a matinée, as on that first occasion, sometimes to a cinema, but as the days shortened she caught an early train home because of the dark drive back through the lanes to the village. The flat would be cold when she got in. To supplement the ineffective radiators, Alice had a fan heater she had bought herself, and a two-bar electric fire which Giles had secretly brought her after Helen had refused, because it would be extravagant, to let her borrow a convector heater. With both of these full on, and wearing her overcoat, she would drink coffee laced with brandy as she waited for the room to warm up.

It was when she was bound for the station one day that she met Terence Brett.

Giles had something important to say to his wife. He must do it today – he'd been putting it off ever since he'd made it necessary, two nights ago, when he last brought Sue home from the Rigby Arms.

Breakfast – always a silent meal in the big kitchen where, expensively and, in Giles's opinion unnecessarily, Helen had had a ceramic floor laid over the stone flags so that now they walked on Italian tiles – was over, and Helen was stacking the crockery in the dishwasher. Guests were expected for drinks, as was usual most Sunday mornings unless the Armitages were going out themselves.

'I've invited Jonathan and Sue round this morning,' he plunged.

'Whatever for?' asked Helen.

'I thought it would be friendly,' said Giles. 'We've let them use the pool but we've never asked them in.'

'They're our tenants, not our friends,' said Helen.

'Why shouldn't they be both?' asked Giles boldly. 'Don't you like them?'

Helen had found them as tenants, after all. She

had met Jonathan Cooper in the estate agent's office where she had gone to put the lodge on the books. Jonathan was there seeking somewhere to rent because he had left his wife and was living with Sue, whom he'd met when he stayed at the Rigby Arms. He was an agent for a firm selling chemicals and called regularly on various factories in a wide area.

'She's such a common little thing,' said Helen. 'I can't think what he sees in her.'

Giles found Helen's remark offensive.

'She's not common,' he snapped. 'Though it's true that she hasn't been to school in Switzerland. She's had a rough time.' Sue had married young, she had told him; she had had a miscarriage, and after that her husband had left her. She'd used money from their settlement to train for her present post.

'Oh, sorry, sorry,' said Helen in a caustic tone. 'I didn't know you had a lech for her. By all means ask her in, if it will give you a kick.'

'I haven't – ' Giles began. But he had. 'I just thought it would be friendly,' he repeated, sulkily, his small burst of rebellion dying.

'She's hardly likely to return your interest,' Helen said. 'Even if she is on the make.'

'Helen, why must you talk like that?' Giles asked. 'I only invited them because they're our neighbours. We've had no one here from the village.'

'There's no one to interest us here,' said Helen.

That might be true of herself, but what about his

mother? Giles knew that they should cultivate local acquaintances for her, although there had been no overtures made towards them from the village. Whose fault was that? Helen bought nothing from the shop. They were all registered with the doctor in Great Minton, but otherwise, apart from Mrs Wood and the gardener, they had no contact with the locals. His mother seemed to go out in her car quite a lot, though from the mileage clocked up, which he glanced at now and then, she never went far. He assumed she found things to do; he must ask her.

'I haven't time to argue now, Giles,' said Helen. 'And since you've asked them, I suppose it can't be helped today, but please don't do it again.'

Why not, Giles fumed, when this is supposed to be my home and my mother has sunk all her capital in it? But he said nothing aloud. He went to see to the drinks. This was always his job, while Helen thawed canapés she bought from a girl who undertook to stock your freezer or cope with your party. With what she bought from her and the cooking done by Mrs Wood, Helen spent very little time in the kitchen herself. Mrs Wood refused to come in on Sundays, but her two schoolgirl daughters were glad to wash up the glasses; they were pleased with the money they earned and found it a bit of a giggle.

This weekend, Alice had done the flowers. Like buying the fish every week, it was one of the tasks Helen often delegated. Giles always recognized his mother's free, light, airy arrangements. Helen arranged flowers well, but she regimented the blooms into stiff, massed displays, often with bold and effective colour combinations that his mother would not attempt. Her style reflected her, Giles thought: she was brilliant in appearance, always dressed in strong colours and made up rather more vividly than seemed current fashion, with a lot of eyeshadow and her hair a brassy gold. He was constantly astonished at finding himself sharing a house with someone who looked like an exotic butterfly and was just as restless. Dawn, their elder daughter, was heading the same way already but Amanda was more like him – slow, cautious, plodding. Giles knew he was dull. He had few thoughts, now, outside his work, for if he let his mind stray he became very depressed. He lived with a stranger, and an unfriendly stranger, at that. Had he ever known her at all? Could she really have changed so much? What had he expected from her, and she from him, when they were young?

He'd wanted a wife, of course; in those days young men got married and young girls wanted husbands and families; people didn't just live together freely, as now. Helen had been pretty and lively. He'd felt lively himself, in her company, and had been proud to be seen with her, heads turning as she passed by. He'd wanted, he thought now, gratification of his lust, all the while telling himself that this was love – as it could have become, if she had been gentle and he less complaisant. She had always run their lives on her terms, chosen the girls' schools, picked their holidays, consulted him about nothing. It was difficult, now, to remember how things had been at first. All Giles could recall with clarity was the pressure he had been under, since joining his father-in-law's firm, to keep up with the demands of his job, which exceeded his capabilities.

There had been moments of joy with the girls when they were small. He'd liked reading to them and playing with them. He still enjoyed their company on the rare occasions when he was with them. He played tennis with them, and romped in the pool, but Dawn, he sensed, had, like her mother, already begun to despise him. Things hadn't changed, with the move. They were simply happening in nicer, more spacious surroundings, at greater expense.

He liked the ponies. They were new. Before, the girls had hired ponies from a riding-school. Now, in the field, there were Trixie and Mr Jinks, whom Giles looked after in term-time. The ponies had soft whiskered muzzles, and whickered to him when he went out with their hay. He'd had nothing at all to do with horses before this, but Helen had known what was required, as she knew what was needed for so much. She'd given him the necessary instructions. He was glad to do it; it was a way to be busy and useful, and he enjoyed it much more than the parties.

How Helen loved entertaining! Vivid in a bright dress, she would circle about, admired by all the men – lusted after, no doubt, Giles thought. If only they knew!

He didn't think about that so much now. It was probably all his fault. He had been inexperienced when they married, and he was inexperienced still. Sometimes it amazed him that they had ever had the girls.

Naively, he now saw, he had expected, when Helen suggested that Alice should throw her lot in with theirs, that his mother would join them for meals, be part of the household, a true member of an extended family. He'd been grateful, at first, for what had seemed a real kindness on Helen's part. Then he'd learned the extent of his mother's welcome.

'It'll save trouble as she gets older. You won't have to keep going to see her. We needn't bother a lot about her – old people value their independence and we must respect her privacy. I'm sure she won't try to intrude upon us. She can live an entirely separate life,' Helen had said.

Giles had dreaded the interview in which he must explain Helen's attitude to his mother, but it never became necessary. Alice seemed to divine the position without explanation. He never knew that Helen had made things clear.

Now, as Giles lit the big fire in the drawing-room and piled it with logs, he found the party preparations bearable, for today would be different: Sue would be there. He hummed under his breath as he took bottles from cartons and set them out. What a lot these things cost: why couldn't Helen pay for them out of her business turnover? They were her guests.

Helen's friends were never punctual. None of them ever came before half-past twelve, though invited for noon, and they rarely left before two. Sunday lunch was always eaten during the afternoon. In the school holidays, Dawn and Amanda staved off starvation with crisps, but Giles thought the whole thing a waste not only of money but also of time. It happened too often.

At last the bell rang. The first arrivals were a computer analyst and his architect wife. Then came a television announcer. Giles had met none of them before. Where did Helen find them? He knew she hoped to win work by showing them her own gracious life style. Giles moved about pouring gin and tonics, vodka, campari, his mind switched off except for a tiny part that was watching for Sue.

She and Jonathan came at ten minutes to one, both flushed and smiling. They'd only got out of bed half an hour before. How happy they looked, Giles thought, handing Sue her vodka and tonic. She glowed, standing there in a scarlet dress, her long dark hair drawn softly back from her face and into a ponytail. She wore it up at work, and it gave her an austere look, but now she seemed, to Giles's fanciful eye, like a foreign princess. How thin her little neck was, he thought: like Mary, Queen of Scots. He pulled his wandering mind together. He must attempt to introduce the two to some of the other guests; Helen wouldn't. The trouble was that Giles could recall none of their names.

But meanwhile Sue was looking around.

'Isn't your mother here, Giles?' she asked.

'No,' said Giles. Some explanation seemed to be required, so he added, 'It would be too noisy for her.'

'Oh – I'd have thought she'd enjoy it,' said Sue. 'She's ever so sweet, Giles. She gives me a lift to work when she sees me at the bus stop.'

'Oh!' Giles was surprised, but why not? It would be natural for his mother to pick up someone she knew.

'I don't see a lot of her,' Sue went on. 'But then I'm not around all that much. I'm either at work or with Jonathan. He likes your mother. He gave her some dahlias, once.'

'Did he? But there are – ' Giles had been about to say that there were plenty of dahlias in the garden. Then he realized that his mother might not want to pick them without Helen's consent and might not want to ask permission. But she should feel free to help herself to anything; the place was as much hers as his and Helen's. Giles vowed to sort this out later, then put it to the back of his mind, where it remained interred.

'I think that Helen's really mean,' said Sue, when she and Jonathan returned to the lodge after the party.

'She's a hard piece,' said Jonathan. 'But why is she mean?'

'The old lady wasn't there. I bet Giles wanted her asked,' said Sue.

'Maybe she doesn't like Helen's parties,' said Jonathan.

'My guess is she hasn't tried one,' said Sue. 'She's quite lively for her age, after all. Nicely dressed and all that – hasn't let herself go.'

'I'm not sure that it's a very good idea to pluck up old ladies and plant them in new areas,' said Jonathan. 'They're like trees – they need established roots.'

'Makes sense, though, doesn't it?' said Sue. 'What if she's ill?'

'Well, there's no one to look after her,' Jonathan said. 'Helen's out all day.'

'She goes out a lot in her car,' Sue said. 'She's been into the Rigby for lunch. I don't think she liked it much. She told me she'd been to lots of places and some weren't nice to be in on your own. I can imagine that, at her age.'

'Poor old thing,' said Jonathan, who thought this a bleak life style for Mrs Armitage to pursue. 'There must be some other old ladies in the village, surely?'

'Maybe, but she may not like to ask them round,' said Sue. 'That flat of hers is tiny, and bitterly cold. I carried up some shopping for her once and I thought she'd ask me to stay, but she didn't – pushed me off as fast as she could before my teeth began to chatter.'

Sue knew a lot about physical deprivation. After her father abandoned her mother, sister and brother, they often had no money for fuel and shivered indoors in threadbare, outgrown coats bought at jumble sales. There was no more violence; no more punch-ups between her parents on Friday and Saturday nights after her father came back from the pub; no more cuts, bruises and black eyes and screaming matches; but there was hunger. Sue had resolved to escape from all that as soon as she could. She had rushed into an early marriage at the first opportunity; then, pregnant, she had seen her new, precarious security threatened: with a baby, money would be short. She had had an abortion. As soon as he discovered what she had done, her husband had left her.

Jonathan knew only Sue's tailored version of this, but hearing her talk about Alice and theorize about her made him uneasy. He knew that her imagination sometimes carried her away into fantasies about wonderful holidays they would have, which there wasn't a chance they would ever afford with the payments he made to his wife. She would talk about what she would buy one day 'When I'm rich' – not 'When we're rich', he'd noticed.

He knew that Sue had had several affairs between the breakup of her marriage and meeting him. He excused her in his mind; she had been young and inexperienced; people had taken advantage of her. With him, she had found the stability she needed; in time, Jonathan thought, she would give up her dreams of the unattainable and settle, as most people had to, for what was possible.

There was no question of marriage for them yet. Jonathan's wife was holding out for all sorts of things before she would divorce him. But Sue was only twenty-three and one experience of marriage had shown her its restrictions. She might not stay with Jonathan, if someone with more to offer her came along. Like Giles. She'd got Jonathan away from his wife; she could do it again.

Sue liked older men. She had met plenty at the hotel, and several times had been to their rooms, though if the manager had ever found out, she'd have lost her job at once. Older men were grateful. Some were so ignorant: it was fun, teaching them things: like Jonathan. Maybe Giles needed that sort of schooling, too. Sue thought Helen was just the sort to short-change him, but he wouldn't know any better.

At that stage, the idea was just a fancy to Sue, an amusing notion to think about when she was bored.

4

Helen loved skiing, and after spending a year at school in Switzerland, was good at it. Every winter, when the works closed for Christmas and remained shut until after New Year's Day, she and Giles and the girls went for a winter holiday to the Alps. Giles, a poor performer on skis, thought the three females would enjoy themselves as much – more, even – without him, but he had no excuse for remaining behind.

Alice had shared their Christmas dinner. Everyone had dressed up, the girls in pretty long dresses, Alice in a sweeping black velvet skirt and silk blouse. She'd worn a wool vest and her mohair stole, for although the heating worked in the downstairs rooms, the house was draughty. Helen, in dark green, had looked magnificent; she also looked austere and remote. The dinner was delicious. Amanda supervised the turkey; the pudding had been made by the caterer Helen often used.

Two days later the family departed and Alice was left alone, feeling very forlorn.

The sky was grey and lowering. If it snowed – Alice didn't think it was cold enough, and the sky wasn't yellow – she would be quite cut off. She took the car out for a spin in case, in the days that followed, the roads grew too icy and she became a prisoner. Helen had given her what was left of the turkey, and returned some of the mince pies which Alice had made as a contribution to the meal, so she decided not to stay out to lunch. In any case, with so many people on holiday, the cafés and pubs would be full and therefore alarming.

Presents were so difficult. She'd given Helen bath oil, done up in a gift box with soap and bath powder, the same as last year.

They'd given her a bottle of port. She and Walter had liked a glass of port after dinner. Amanda had knitted her a pair of gloves. Dawn gave her a box of notelets, sold in aid of a charity.

When Alice came back from her drive, she parked her Metro next to Helen's Volvo. The family had gone to the airport in the Rover. Jonathan's car was out; he and Sue must be off somewhere together, Alice decided, forgetting that Sue would be on duty for part of the day. This was a busy time at the hotel.

Alice had brought a pile of novels back from the library. She was concentrating better now, but only on things that were easy to read. She'd found an M. M. Kaye she had not read, and three family sagas, and after lunch began one of them. It was heavily romantic, and the tender passages brought tears to her eyes so she skipped those bits, paying attention to the background detail, which was about mill workers during the industrial revolution.

Love worried Alice. She had loved Walter – quietly, gratefully, and he had loved her – she had never doubted it. But once, before they met, Alice had loved someone else in a wilder way. He had died of pneumonia, as people did then, before the discovery of antibiotics. Alice still thought of him sometimes, and remembered the very different form of that love. It might not have lasted – might have burnt itself out with their youth. The feeling between her and Walter was more like a fire that glowed – was tended and fed, and burned steadily on. She often wondered about Giles and Helen. She supposed there was love between them. Certainly, when they married, Giles had been infatuated with Helen. It had worried his mother. It had seemed too febrile an emotion to last, and she had seen no answering excitement in Helen. Alice had noticed Helen look at Giles calculatingly, as if weighing up the prospects for their future. Walter had had reservations about her, but he could not say what it was that made him uneasy. She certainly had both looks and brains. Alice hoped it was all right. To think otherwise was too frightening, but she wished her son looked happier, and now there was Sue, on the doorstep, a threat if he were unsettled. But Sue wasn't a danger Alice told herself. Sue and Jonathan were close; otherwise they wouldn't be living together in what used to be called sin. And Giles had most of the things that money could buy and some that it couldn't, such as his daughters. Alice had loved her rare moments in their company when they were small, but she and Walter had seen them only for fleeting visits. She still didn't really know them, she felt sadly. She could discuss few of their interests for she knew nothing about horses and hated pop music. At first the girls had never come to her flat without being asked. Helen had told them not to bother her, Alice discovered. Now, Amanda often came up to watch television when Dawn wanted a different programme on the set in the girls' sitting-room. But often was a relative word; the girls were away at school for most of the year.

Alice decided to go to London the following day. She wouldn't go far. The sales were on so the shops would be crowded, she'd settle for just lunch at the Paddington Hotel, then back again. She'd stick to that plan, unless it snowed. Rain wouldn't put her off, for she'd be back before it was really dark. The day after that she'd go somewhere else. She'd make an excursion every day and soon the fortnight would end. Then she'd ring Audrey, who'd urged her to come back to Bournemouth and stay, asking if she might visit after the family returned.

When she went round drawing the curtains, the lodge was in darkness. Time switches turned lights on in the main house, and Alice always drew the curtains. That was wise. Prowlers would think someone was in, with the lights on and curtains closed.

As she went back to her own apartment, Alice heard the timbers in the house creak, as if it stretched itself in sleep. Sometimes she wondered if the ghost of Mr Goring, the previous owner, who had died there aged nearly ninety, stalked the dark passages.

She made herself keep busy for the next hour, washing out underclothes, sorting what she would wear the next day, ironing a blouse. Then she did her nails, filing them carefully, painting on pale varnish. She polished her smart boots with their low heels, and put out a new pair of stockings. Alice had never taken to tights; though she was thin, she liked the support of her girdle.

There was a film on television which looked as if it might be worth watching; it would certainly pass the evening. Before switching it on, Alice drew the curtain aside at her attic window and looked out at the lodge. She was just in time to see Jonathan return from wherever he had been in his Granada. He drove it into the barn. Alice watched him close the big heavy door, dropping the bar that latched it into position, and then, in the light cast by the exterior lamp which was fixed to the barn wall, walk over to the lodge. As he did so, the porch light there came on. That was good. His princess was inside, waiting for him, Alice thought, smiling as she turned away from the window. She felt happier, thinking of them there together.

In the morning it was raining and Alice's resolution faltered. Propped up in bed with her morning tea, and the electric fire taking the worst of the chill off the room, she wondered about going to London. It would be so much easier to give up –

she could even spend the day in bed. With the fan heater and the fire, the room would soon warm up.

'No, Alice,' she admonished herself aloud. 'You're to go. You're quite well. It's raining, not snowing. If you don't go out and see some human faces, you'll rot.'

The sound of her own voice, speaking so sternly, made her giggle nervously. Was she going potty, talking to herself? She drank her tea, and then got out of bed. Soon she was dressed, and had made up her face ready for the day. She added her bracelets and pearls, and fastened stud earrings in place. Then she put on her boots, her lined raincoat with the fur collar, her brown felt hat with the feather, took up her umbrella, and set out to the barn.

It was always difficult for Alice to open the door. Struggling with the heavy bar, she looked round once, wistfully, at the lodge, hoping that Jonathan might be a witness to her difficulties and help her, but he didn't come. Perhaps he'd gone back to work, she thought. Not everyone ceased until the New Year, and when at last she got the door open, she saw that, indeed, his car had gone.

Alice got into her Metro and turned the key to start it.

Nothing happened. She turned it again, fiddled with it, took the key out and reinserted it, but the car was completely dead. Not a sound came from beneath the bonnet.

She almost wept with frustration. Indeed, she laid her head down on her folded hands which

43

rested on the steering wheel for a few despairing minutes. Then she tried the key again. Nothing.

You could put the car in gear and rock it. Sometimes that worked. Alice engaged first gear, got out, went to the front of the car and pushed as hard as she could, then climbed back into the driver's seat and tried again. Nothing happened.

So she couldn't go to London after all. Now, after her earlier reluctance, the disappointment seemed, paradoxically, hard to bear. She could telephone the garage, but they would be unlikely to get out to Harcombe and fix the car in time for her to reach London for lunch.

Slowly, Alice got out of the Metro. The burden of the day's isolation pressed upon her; even Mrs Wood was absent, still revelling with her family. With the young people at the lodge gone for the day she was all alone. What if she had an accident – burnt herself – had a fall? It would have to be bad to prevent her from reaching the telephone, Alice thought, trying to calm herself down. Meanwhile, the whole house was hers to use: she could light the drawing-room fire, watch Helen's television set which was so much bigger than her own.

Why not take Helen's car?

Alice looked at the blue Volvo parked in the space beside her Metro. Surely she could drive it? During the war she had driven a canteen van; she had regularly driven the Peugeot they'd had until Walter died, when Giles had persuaded her to exchange it for a smaller car which had been wise advice. The Metro was economical and easy to park, and hitherto had whizzed along in lively fashion. She was only going to Westborough station where the car would be safely parked all day; she would make sure to return before dark. Why not? No one would ever know.

Dare she? The idea was rather exciting!

Alice knew she should change her plans. She'd no commitment, no one to meet in London, but she'd made up her mind to escape.

She knew where the Volvo keys were kept – on a hook in the lobby by the kitchen.

She went back to the house, through the back door, her normal entrance. There were the keys. She took them down and went out again, locking the back door once more.

Alice padded back to the barn and got into the Volvo, which wasn't locked. None of them locked their cars in the barn. Helen was tall, and Alice had to pull the seat right forward before she could reach the controls with comfort. She inserted the key, checked that the car was in neutral and made sure she could find all the gears. Then she started the engine. It fired at once, running smoothly. Alice's heart beat fast with excitement as she reversed slowly out of the barn, past her silent Metro, slipping the clutch. She stopped outside the barn, putting on the brake and leaving the engine running while she closed the heavy doors, which she wouldn't have done if she'd taken her own car, though who would query the Volvo's absence she didn't know. Jonathan was out, and wherever he was – at work or with his children – he'd be unlikely to return before she did.

Before moving off, Alice made sure she could find the switches for the indicators and the windscreen wipers. Everything was straightforward. It was exciting, driving away in this larger, lively car. She would go slowly. Even with the delay, she had plenty of time as she always allowed more than was necessary.

Alice set forth down the lane, the windscreen wipers swishing to and fro to clear away the drizzle, elated by her own daring.

5

Terry Brett had been home for Christmas. He'd given his mother a bottle of scent and his father a bottle of whisky, one lifted from a department store and the other from a supermarket. His parents were pleased to see him and his father had given him a cheque for fifty pounds. His mother had given him a sweater which he was wearing under his smart car coat as he drove into Westborough. The previous day he had told his parents he was getting a lift from a friend he'd arranged to meet at a roadhouse half a mile from where they lived. There, he had picked up a Ford Escort parked in the yard with the key in the ignition. He grinned to himself as he drove off, imagining the horror his parents would feel if they could have witnessed his action. They thought it was time he had a car of his own instead of depending on lifts. Surely he could afford one? He'd promised to think about it.

They'd seemed sorry to see him leave, but forty-eight hours was all he could stand of the family scene. His sister and her husband and children were due to call on their way back from spending Christmas with his parents in Leeds. Terry's brother, who had been at home too, had already left for a walking holiday in the Fells, an odd thing to do in winter, in Terry's opinion.

He dumped the Escort on the outskirts of Swindon. It didn't do to borrow a car long unless you changed the plates; the police were pretty quick off the mark if you parked in a prohibited spot or committed any sort of misdemeanour, and with the strict rules about tyres, it might be that the owner hadn't kept things up to scratch and you'd be nicked for a fault of his, which would be very unfair. Terry never borrowed a car that did not display a valid road fund licence on the windscreen.

Next morning, he lifted a pale green Vauxhall from the station. Among his selection of keys was a good variety of Vauxhall keys which he'd got after a chance visit to a dealer one evening when there'd been just a single attendant on the pump. Terry had been able to amble in and help himself while apparently waiting to find out about new models. It was amazing what you could pick up while seeming to be on innocent business if you had nimble wits, quick fingers, sharp eyes and the nerve.

Terry had nerve for most things. In Westborough, which he'd reconnoitred just before Christmas, he intended to call on a woman he'd met soon after he'd grabbed the scent for his mother. He'd knocked into her, apologizing effusively as he helped her collect the packages he had caused her to drop. Then he'd offered to carry

48

them to her car for her. He had stolen nothing from her. His success as an operator depended on knowing when to yield to temptation and when to resist for greater gain in the long term. Virtue was rewarded when he was able to read the address on an envelope which fell from her unfastened handbag. He memorized it. She'd been reasonably nice-looking, about forty or so. He wouldn't mind earning his keep with her for a bit. Her clothes had been expensive and she had a well-kept look, a promising target. He had an excuse for calling on her: he would show her a silver propelling pencil he'd acquired and say he had found it after she'd left the car park that day and wondered if it was hers. She might be alone in the house, though that wasn't likely in this holiday period, but in any case she'd be sure to invite him in, and he'd have a chance to survey the prospects – maybe the husband, too. If she wanted to know how he knew where she lived, he would tell her the truth. She'd be flattered, and might offer him a meal.

Thinking of food reminded Terry that he'd had no breakfast apart from a cup of coffee. He'd forgotten to take some supplies from his parents' larder, and the sliced loaf he'd left in the cupboard had grown mould. He'd have a snack now then wash and brush up before calling upon his prey.

Terry saw a space in the main street of Westborough and slid the Vauxhall close against the kerb. He felt safe with this car; its owner had left it while he went off for the day, for certain, for the bonnet was warm to the touch when Terry took it. He'd return in it to Swindon tonight, and leave it somewhere not far from the station, he planned, with seasonal generosity. Terry whistled under his breath as he walked round to the Coffee Pot, which he had noticed on his earlier visit to the town. There, he had coffee and hot buttered toast. In the cloakroom he ran a comb through his springy curls, and checked his appearance in the mirror. He looked, he decided, like a schoolmaster or an insurance salesman on holiday: reassuringly relaxed. Then he went back to the car, thinking, as he started it, that if the woman was out he would pursue some other plan so as not to waste the day. Something was sure to turn up, he knew, it always did. He was always stimulated by the challenge of fast thinking; people were easily led by the nose and deserved all they got for being so foolish. Still pondering, Terry rested his right foot on the accelerator pedal while slipping the clutch with his left, the car in first gear ready to move. He turned the wheel to the right and edged forward clearing the car in front, then paused to let a stream of traffc pass. The road was busy; you'd think they'd have built a by-pass by now, Terry thought. He took out his comb again and ran it once more through his curls, which had got damp as he walked back to the car through the drizzling rain. While he did this, he watched in the mirror for a chance to slip out. Ah – now there'd be a gap, after this blue Volvo.

Terry revved the engine, eager to thrust the Vauxhall into the road as soon as the Volvo, which was moving slowly, passed.

'Come on, come on,' said Terry.

The bonnet of the Volvo drew level – went by. Terry had time to notice a woman driver, wearing a hat, before his foot, the smooth sole wet from walking on the rain-soaked pavement, slipped on the clutch and the car bounded out from the kerb sooner than he had intended. The Volvo was almost past, but the Vauxhall's bumper caught its rear wing a glancing blow.

Alice felt this as a severe bang on the side of the Volvo. She had been driving very carefully, attending to the rear view mirror, and she knew there was no one close behind her. She stopped almost at once, her legs turned to jelly by the shock of the jolting collision. She'd seen the wing of the other car edged out from the kerb, but she, on the main road, had the right of way so it must wait. Suddenly there was this dreadful crumping noise.

Alice switched off the engine and levered herself out of the car to examine the damage. She was trembling.

Terry was about to pull out and pass, anxious to get away fast before a copper came along and found the Vauxhall didn't belong to him, when Alice, wavering slightly, blocked his way. Had anyone seen what had happened? Was there a policeman in sight? He glanced round. There were a few pedestrians, but now the rain was falling heavily and each was intent on hurrying on to his destination, head down, ignoring what went on around them. Although the sound of the crash had seemed loud to the two participants, in fact it had not made much noise and had attracted no attention. The following traffic was pulling out to pass the Volvo, now seemingly double-parked, not yet causing an obstruction.

The rear wing of the Volvo was badly scraped and slightly dented.

Fright and anger gave Alice the strength to advance towards Terry, who now could not get past her because of the overtaking cars pinning him in. Young fool, she thought, remembering that you must never admit blame in the case of an accident, even if it was your fault, and in this case it most definitely wasn't hers.

'What did you think you were doing, young man?' she demanded, peering in at Terry's window, trying to control her quavering voice and trembling limbs. One part of her was relieved to see that the offender looked conventionally neat, a collar and tie revealed in the vee-neck of the sweater he wore, his curly hair not too long.

Terry got out of the Vauxhall. He'd try to persuade her back into the Volvo and away from the scene quickly, before any nosy bobbies turned up, but if he couldn't manage it, he'd be able to leave the stolen Vauxhall himself, escaping on his feet. He was wearing gloves. He always wore gloves when driving. He never took chances.

'The insurance,' Alice was insisting. 'Your name and address.'

'There's no damage, is there?' asked Terry, with his most winning smile. He walked round to the Volvo. 'Ah yes – I see there is,' he said, thinking quickly. 'Are you hurt?' He saw that she was quite old – older than he'd thought at first. If she was injured he'd take to his heels at once and get away from the district as fast as he could. Too bad, but there it was.

'No, I'm not,' said Alice. 'Just shocked.'

He seemed a nice young man, and he looked concerned.

'Good – then let's move our cars out of the way and talk things over, shall we?' Already he was beginning to see that if he played it right, he might win advantage from what had happened. He glanced down the road and saw a big space by the kerb ahead. Taking a chance, he said, 'I'm very sorry. Look, you put your car down there, and I'll park mine and join you. Can you manage?'

Alice wasn't sure that she could, but she got into the Volvo. His suggestion was sound. The last thing she wanted was for a policeman to come and find she was driving her daughter-in-law's car without permission. Her legs still felt weak, but she managed to drive the car to the end of the line of stationary vehicles and park. Terry, meanwhile, reversed into the space from which he had so recently and so disastrously emerged. He could disown the Vauxhall from this instant, he thought, jingling his collection of keys in his pocket as he walked towards the Volvo.

Having parked, Alice studied the damage again.

It was Helen's car, and look what had happened to it! Tears of fright and shock filled her eyes, and Terry saw them.

'How soon will I be able to get it repaired?' she asked in quavering tones, instead of demanding more personal details from Terry, as he had expected.

'Right away, I should think,' said Terry. 'There's plenty of body repairers about. Depends how busy they are.' He glanced at her warily. 'But if it's an insurance job, you'd have to wait some time, till it's been inspected.'

She was really swaying now, and he saw that beneath the thick layer of make-up she wore she had lost all natural colour. He put his hand on her elbow.

'What about a cup of tea to get over the shock?' he suggested. 'While we decide what to do?' He could still walk out – take her to a café and leave her there – in fact, it might be the best thing to do, then she wouldn't fall down in a faint in the road, which would be sure to cause trouble.

Giving her no time to refuse and still holding her elbow, Terry led Alice along the road to the Coffee Pot, which he'd only just left. He settled her into a corner seat and went over to a waitress, the one who had served him earlier and with whom he'd exchanged some badinage.

'What – back so soon?' she asked, grinning.

'Couldn't keep away,' he said, and then leaned forward confidentially. 'See the old girl in the corner? She felt a bit giddy outside and I brought her in for a cup of tea to settle her nerves. Bring us one each love, and plenty of sugar. Quick as you can.'

'Seeing it's you,' said the girl, 'I might,' and she turned back to the service area with a flourish of her short green overall skirt.

Terry walked back to Alice, who was struggling to regain her self-control. She had removed her gloves and he noticed her ring at once, an emerald surrounded by diamonds on her wedding finger.

'Would you like to take your coat off?' he asked. Pearls, he was thinking; she'd have great fat pearls, real ones, with a diamond clasp. Some of these old girls were well heeled – rich men's widows. That car she was driving was not your run-of-the-mill shopping car, either. There would be ways of ingratiating himself into the favours of an old dame like this one, he was sure; it was a whole new area to explore. He'd almost forgotten, by now, what had brought them together. He wondered how old she was. Seventy? More than that? She had brown spots on the backs of her hands – not a lot of them, just faint ones, like his grandmother who could be touched for a fiver easily whenever they met.

Alice declined to remove her coat, but she undid it and loosened the silk scarf she wore. There was no pearl necklace, but a diamond and pearl brooch was pinned to her sweater.

Their tea came.

'I'll be mother,' said Terry, the adrenalin racing around in his system. 'Milk and sugar?' He poured out dextrously, and passed Alice her cup.

'I must get the car mended as soon as possible,'

said Alice. 'Do you think it could be done in ten days?'

'Oh – certainly,' said Terry. 'But not,' he repeated, 'if you have to wait for the insurance assessor.' He hesitated, leaning forward and gazing at her with what seemed to Alice to be honest brown eyes. 'Why the hurry? Can't you manage without it?'

'It's not mine,' Alice said. She kept enough control of herself not to tell him everything. 'I – er – a friend lent it to me.'

'Oh jeepers,' said Terry. 'And your friend wants it back in ten days?'

'Yes.'

Terry snapped his fingers.

'Hang on,' he said, and he went to the back of the shop to talk to the waitress again. She soon granted his request, which was to borrow the Yellow Pages of the telephone directory.

Terry took it over to the table where Alice waited. She was feeling deathly tired now and had completely forgotten her plan for the day; her one thought was to undo the damage without being discovered.

Terry, meanwhile, was highly delighted with this turn of events. By now he'd lost all sight of his responsibility for what had happened; his immediate aim was to make what he could of the situation.

'Cars, cars, cars,' he muttered, turning the pages. 'Car accessories – car breakdowns – car and coach – ah, car and coach body builders: that's who we want.' He gazed at a double spread of entries, small itemized ones and large boxed advertisements. Alice could read, upside down, car body and paint spraying, car body repairs, the information repeated in various forms.

There was one firm in Westborough.

'Let's go there,' said Terry. 'Let's take the car there right away and see what they say.' Before she regained her cool, he thought, before she began laying the blame on him once more. 'Finish your tea, Mrs – er – ?'

'Armitage,' Alice said quietly. 'Mrs Armitage.'

Things were steadying down. The room had stopped swaying around her. She looked up, through her bifocal spectacles, at the young man.

'Drink your tea,' he repeated, using the coaxing tone that worked well in different circumstances with younger women.

Alice obeyed.

'Let's go,' Terry said, and was about to push the bill towards her when he had a new thought: a tiny investment now, the price of their tea, might yield future dividends.

She made no demur at all as he counted out the appropriate money and even added a tip for the obliging waitress. Then he stood behind Alice to pull out her chair as she rose, waited while she buttoned her coat and put her gloves on again, hiding the ring. He took her arm once more as they returned to the Volvo.

Alice looked at the damage. The scrape, like a graze, covered quite a big patch.

'Doesn't look much,' said Terry cheerfully, but

he'd seen that there was more than one dent. 'Let's get on with it, shall we?'

Alice went round to the driver's side and began fitting the key into the door. Her hand was shaking.

'Do you know where this place is?' Terry asked. 'Norton Road?'

Alice didn't, but Terry did. He'd spent some time learning the geography of Westborough, on his earlier visit. Knowledge of one-way systems, dead ends and escape routes was very useful.

'Shall I drive?' he suggested.

It didn't occur to Alice until much later that she was taking a great risk in allowing someone who had just, through his own carelessness, crashed into the car she was driving, to take the wheel of it within half an hour. She merely felt unable to do it herself.

'Thank you,' she said, and handed him the keys, primping her lips.

Terry settled her into the passenger's seat, tucking her coat in round her thin legs in their expensive boots. He was whistling under his breath as he walked behind the car to the driver's side. He'd never driven a Volvo. He pulled carefully out from the kerb; it wouldn't do to repeat what had just happened.

Part of Alice's mind knew she should be berating this boy – asking him to face up to what he had done, arranging for his insurance company to pay whatever the repair would cost – but most of her thoughts were concentrated on putting right the damage before she could be found out, like a child who has played with some forbidden object and broken it, and now seeks to remove the evidence before discovery. It wouldn't cost such a lot, she was thinking; you had to pay part of most claims, anyway, didn't you? But not if it wasn't your fault. She'd never made one, though Walter had once had a small contretemps with a milk float in Poole.

Terry drove confidently through Westborough to the end of the main street where there were houses among the shops, and roads radiated out into estates and an occasional factory or warehouse. Down here was Norton Road, where there was a joinery and a printing works as well as the body repairer.

He drove straight through the entrance into a hangar-like building with breeze-block walls, a corrugated iron roof and a concrete floor. Several cars were parked about the place, some with parts missing and one in a devastated condition. A man in brown overalls was working on a dark blue Audi. He did not look up as they drove in.

'I'll find someone,' Terry said. 'You wait here, Mrs Armitage.' Always use their names, he'd found: Jeannie – Diane – Sandra – whatever it was, murmur it, use it a lot: the personal touch. And remember it! Never get careless and use the wrong one! In this case, he must defer to age and status: none of your 'loves' or 'dears' for Mrs Armitage.

He walked over to speak to the man working on the Audi. Alice saw them talking. The man gestured, and Terry went off in the direction he had indicated. Alice got slowly out of the car, moving stiffly, like a really old woman. She seldom thought of herself as old: most of the time she felt, though forlorn without Walter and depressed at her new way of life, much as she had for most of her life; it was only her limbs, which would not move as fast as once they did, and her face, with its lines and pouches, that reminded her of the years. And she tired swiftly: that, too.

There was a strong smell of chemicals in the air of the workshop, and a faint haze in the atmosphere. Alice stood hesitantly beside the car, thinking about money. She must pay whatever price was asked to have it repaired before Helen returned. In her head, in slow motion, she ran a film of what had happened: herself proceeding slowly along past the line of parked cars with the windscreen wipers flicking to and fro; the wing of the green car sticking out from among the others and then the sudden, unbelievable jolt as it drove into the Volvo. The boy's carelessness was incredible: there could have been a serious accident.

Meanwhile, Terry was talking to the body-shop manager.

'I was quite stationary,' he was saying. 'I'd nosed forward a little way, waiting for a gap in the traffic, and along comes this Volvo, much too close to the parked cars. The old lady caught the wing against my bumper. Didn't hurt my car, but it's made a bit of a mess of hers.'

'Is it an insurance job?' asked the manager.

'No,' said Terry. 'Least said soonest mended – her family thinks it's time she gave up driving and she wants to get it fixed without them finding out. And after all, why should I make things difficult for her? My car's not damaged.'

'No one hurt?'

'I had a fright, as you might expect. That's all,' answered Terry, looking at him with frank, honest eyes.

Repairing wrecks was the manager's job, not making judgements. Odd that the rear wing had been damaged, not the front, he thought, and forgot about it.

'Let's have a look at it, then,' he said, setting off briskly towards the spot where Alice stood drooping beside the Volvo.

'Don't say too much to the old girl,' Terry warned. 'She's a bit edgy.'

Terry's words had led the manager to expect an aged crone, not the well-dressed, still pretty, elderly woman, no older than his own mother, whom he now saw.

'Mrs Armitage,' Terry introduced.

'Well now, let's have a look at the trouble,' said the manager in the breezy tone of a doctor cheerily assessing a lesion. He looked carefully at the car, peered underneath, inspected the rear and the door, at last giving his diagnosis. 'About two hundred and fifty,' he said.

'So much?' said Alice, dismayed.

'I understand it's not an insurance job,' said the manager.

'No.' What difference did that make, wondered Alice.

'Might work out a little less, then,' said the manager. 'The paint's expensive, and we have to buy a much bigger quantity than we really need. I've none of that colour in stock. It's new, you see – only about six months old.'

It was true that Helen had not had the car long.

'How quickly can you do it?' asked Alice.

'Hm – let's see. Would you mind coming into the office and I'll look at the book,' said the manager.

The office, heated by a paraffin stove, was small and frowsty. A plump woman with jet black curls sat behind an electric typewriter, a cigarette smouldering in an ashtray beside her. Alice wrinkled her nose. No one smoked at Harcombe House. The manager consulted a large engagement diary on the desk, muttering to himself as he did so.

'If you bring it on Monday, you could have it back on Friday,' he said at last.

'Oh dear, can't you do it at once?' asked Alice. She could not drive it back to the village like this. Anyone might notice the damage – Mrs Wood, for instance, and certainly Jonathan, going daily to the barn. 'I can take a taxi home,' she added.

'Well,' said the manager. 'I can't promise to start on it at once, but as it's urgent, I'll see what I can do.' He noticed that Alice was shaking. Not surprisingly, the accident had shocked her. 'The paint needs time to dry,' he explained. 'Before we spray again, that is. That's why it takes so long.'

'I see,' said Alice. 'You will do your best?'

'Yes,' said the manager.

'I'll pay in advance, if it will help,' Alice offered. Her Barclaycard would see her through this emergency. Silently she blessed Walter for his generous pension arrangements.

'That won't be necessary,' said the manager. It was lucky for her that the other party was being so helpful. She might have hit someone who would have made a real nuisance of himself. 'Mrs Hawkins will make a note of your name and address. Shall we telephone you when it's ready, if we can finish it before Friday of next week?'

It was arranged. The Volvo's registration number was noted, together with Alice's address and telephone number. Terry watched as Mrs Hawkins wrote it all down.

'I'll go and fetch my car to drive you home, Mrs Armitage,' he said solicitously. He looked at the manager. 'Mrs Armitage can wait here, can't she? I won't be long.'

'Yes, of course. Have a seat, Mrs Armitage,' said the manager. He indicated a sagging wooden-armed chair in a corner. 'Mrs Hawkins will make you some coffee.'

Before Terry returned, Mrs Hawkins had led Alice right through the paint-hazed workshop to a squalid washroom at its far end, a trip made necessary by her breakfast coffee and the tea after the accident.

'It's not much,' said Mrs Hawkins, referring to the washroom. 'I'm only part-time, so I don't bother a lot. The men need it, of course.'

The pan was stained. A filthy roller towel hung behind the door. Luckily Alice had an All-Fresh cleansing tissue in her handbag.

There were three men working on car bodies as she followed Mrs Hawkins back to the office. The Volvo had been moved to a bay in a corner, which made her feel it was at least on the way to recovery, a patient awaiting treatment.

'Have you worked here long?' Alice asked, for something to say as they entered the offce.

'Twelve years,' said Mrs Hawkins. 'It suits me. I live just down the road, and I'm my own boss.' She smiled, her ugly face with the mole on the chin lightening. 'I expect it gave you a shock, knocking into that young man.'

'Yes,' Alice agreed. But she hadn't hit the young man: he'd hit her car. Mrs Hawkins had got it wrong. 'I saw his car had edged forward,' she began to explain.

'No one's hurt, that's the main thing,' said Mrs Hawkins. 'And there's no need to report it as you've spoken to the other driver.'

The very thought of the police was enough to make Alice shudder. She'd have no hope of concealing what had happened from Helen if they were involved. The enormity of her own misdemeanour now appalled her.

'I shan't make a fuss,' she said quietly. 'It's better just to pay up and get it done quickly.'

Mrs Armitage looked as if she could pay all right, Mrs Hawkins thought, feeding an invoice form into her typewriter while the kettle boiled.

It did not occur to Alice that Terry might not return to collect her.

6

Terry had no intention of abandoning Mrs Armitage. Not with that ring, her brooch, and the address she had given to the woman in the body repair shop.

The rain had stopped as he strode whistling through the town, along the side streets to the main road. The pavements were crowded, now, with shoppers enjoying a post-Christmas splurge, either changing their presents or looking for bargains in the sales. He felt the excitement that usually lit the first weeks of a new job, as he always thought of them. It was work, after all: he put enough into it, for goodness' sake! All that sweet talk, not to mention the rest of it. He certainly gave full value for the money he extracted when the time for that came. This was a whole new scene, this old woman. He'd have to play it by ear as he went along. He might find milking the elderly a profitable line; on the other hand, they wouldn't be so open to blackmail, not that he called it, even to himself, by so harsh a name. Even Mrs Armitage wasn't a target for that sort of attack; she was just afraid of facing her friend with the damaged car. But wait! Depending on the nature of the friend, he could later threaten to reveal what had happened. If she tried to blame him for the accident, it would be her word against his, and who would believe an old woman who shouldn't be driving at all? She ought to be in a home somewhere, like his grandmother.

If a policeman or a traffic warden were anywhere near the Vauxhall, he'd leave it, he resolved. He'd get a taxi – tell the old girl he hadn't been able to start the car and that it must have got damaged in the collision after all; she'd know no different. She'd pay the taxi. She hadn't uttered a murmur when the price of the repair was mentioned. Of course, Harcombe House, where she lived, might be nothing special; people called even bungalows by such names these days; it might even be an old people's home. But he'd soon see.

As he approached the Vauxhall, Terry looked round. There was no policeman in sight. He'd seen a traffic warden up near the market square as he passed. He didn't know how many of them there were in Westborough – more than one, for sure, but none could be seen from where he stood.

He got into the car, extracted it, this time with extreme care, from its position, and drove back to the body repair shop in Norton Road.

Alice told him which way to go from the town. Four miles beyond Westborough, two miles short of Great Minton, she told him to turn off to the right where a signpost pointed to Harcombe.

'Out in the wilds, isn't it?' he commented, as

they made their way along the narrow winding lane. Trimmed stark hedges bordered it, with, beyond, fields given over mainly to sheep, though some were ploughed, showing rich brown soil not yet spiked with young growth. Terry had never lived in the country; it made him uneasy.

'It is quiet,' said Alice. 'Left now.'

They entered the village of Harcombe at a T-junction. On either side stretched the main street with its row of dwellings, all, at first glance, on a modest scale.

But not Harcombe House. Terry hid his surprise as they turned in through wrought-iron gates past a tiny lodge with a steep gabled roof and went up a short drive to a mansion. It might still be an old folks' home, he reminded himself, swinging round on the gravel sweep in front of the house. At one side was a long low barn, with big oak doors latched across by a wooden bar. On one side of the barn door were more doors. Terry wondered what was behind them. He saw that Harcombe House itself was like a much larger edition of its own lodge – gaunt, grey granite, with high steepling roofs and gabled windows on the top floor. All the windows were densely latticed.

'Nice place you've got here,' he said casually, putting on the handbrake and switching the engine off.

'It's my son's house,' said Alice. 'I have a flat in it.' She reached out to open the door. 'Thank you for bringing me home,' she went on, and added, with an effort at reproof, 'You drove back very nicely, you must be more careful in future. Someone could have been badly hurt.'

'Oh, we've forgotten all about that now,' said Terry. 'That's in the past. And I wouldn't have met you, if you hadn't had an accident.'

Alice hadn't had the accident; it had been his. But before she could point this out, he had got out of the car and was coming round to help her alight, ready to tell a tale to the son if he appeared.

Terry was looking past her at the house. It had the blank look of a place that was empty, though it was so large that there could have been dozens of people in it, at the back or in its inner recesses, whose presence would not show at the front.

'Is everyone out?' he asked.

'They're away,' said Alice. 'Skiing.'

Terry couldn't believe his luck.

'It's your son's car,' he said. 'The Volvo.' The old baggage, telling him such a story.

'It belongs to my daughter-in-law,' said Alice. 'I couldn't start mine.'

'What's the matter with it?' asked Terry.

'I don't know,' said Alice. 'It just wouldn't start when I turned the key. Nothing happened.'

'I'll have a look at it for you,' said Terry. 'I know quite a bit about cars.' One way and the other, he did; he'd picked it up here and there, from casual encounters and in prison. It was useful to know how to get into cars without keys and start them, for instance, and before now he'd made some rewarding contacts helping marooned female drivers with punctures or shattered windscreens, or cars that, like Mrs Armitage's, just wouldn't start. Even if he couldn't get them to go – and mostly he could, or could spot the problem – he could send other help and follow up later with enquiries. He'd met one woman like that who, after three months, he'd forced to come up with a grand: not bad.

'Oh, would you?' said Alice, who felt too frail after her adventures to relish the thought of telephoning the garage that serviced her car to persuade them to come out and mend it.

'Show me where it is,' said Terry.

Alice led him to the barn. Terry opened the door. Within, it was vast; there was space for at least eight cars. The Metro sat there alone. Alice took the key from her bag and gave it to him. He got into the driving seat, inserted the key and turned it. Nothing happened.

Probably the starter had jammed, Terry thought. That was the first thing to try, anyway. He opened the bonnet. He'd had nothing to do with Metros – he liked bigger cars, he liked the sense of power you got, seated behind a long bonnet. But the principle was the same, whatever the car.

'I need a spanner,' he said. 'An adjustable one, for choice.' The Metro contained nothing suitable, but Alice knew where Giles kept his tools. Terry followed her through the back door and along a passage to a small room at the rear of the house. This was Giles's study, from which another door led to the kitchen. He was relegated to what had once been the servants' hall and it had not yet been re-decorated; it was not even on Helen's agenda. From the floor to about four feet up, a chocolate-brown dado circled the walls, and above that, the rest was painted a drab, yellowy cream. The carpet, bought with the house, was a threadbare brown haircord. Here, in a big cupboard, were fuses, insulating tape, glue, boxes of screws and nails, and a number of tools.

Terry selected a spanner.

'You wait in the warm,' he said kindly. 'I'll come in when I've done.'

Alice went into the kitchen wondering how to reward the young man for his assistance. She would not offer money; the accident had been his fault, after all, and he wasn't a pauper; he was nicely dressed, well-spoken, and drove a good car himself. But he'd done his best to make amends. Some people in his position would have driven off quickly before they could be faced with the conse-quences. Perhaps a cup of coffee would do. Not sherry – not when he was driving.

In Helen's kitchen, Alice set the kettle to boil on the Aga. She found cups and saucers and put them on the big marble-effect formica-topped table. Then she sat down to wait for Terry's return. Helen was far away, and Mrs Wood was with her family. Alice stretched out, warm, briefly at home.

Terry soon freed the jammed starter. He enjoyed his tinkering and felt tempted to take the Metro out for a spin, but he resisted the impulse. This was not the right time. The cold barn filled with fumes as he ran the engine. He switched it off, grimacing.

You couldn't be too careful about exhaust fumes; he knew they didn't take long to have an effect. Terry closed the barn door and let himself into the house, padding down the passage towards the kitchen soundlessly on his rubber-soled feet. The door was ajar, and through the space he could see Alice sitting at the table. He glanced to right and left. He would dearly love to look round the house, but if she caught him spying her trust in him would be broken. He'd play it straight – get her to show him round. It shouldn't be hard.

Terry entered the kitchen wearing a wide smile.

'There, that's done,' he said.

'Oh, you were quick,' said Alice. 'Thank you.'

'It should be all right now,' said Terry. 'I'll just put the spanner away, shall I? Through there?' and he nodded towards Giles's study.

'Would you? Thank you,' said Alice.

Terry had a quick glance round the study as he replaced the spanner in the tool-box, but he could hardly open the desk or search the cupboards with the old girl next door. The place looked as if it hadn't been touched this century, with its dark paint and junk furniture. It was not Terry's idea of a gentleman's study, which he imagined as a warm room with book-lined shelves and rich carpeting, a flat desk with leather let into the top, and deep leather armchairs. And brandy in crystal goblets.

Alice made him a cup of coffee with Helen's Gold Blend adding sugar from an Italian pottery storage jar that was kept on the dresser.

'You're on your own, then, are you?' Terry

asked. 'While your family is away?'

'Yes,' said Alice. 'Alone in the house, that is. But there's a couple at the lodge – it's rented. They're nice young people. And a woman comes in to clean.' She didn't mention Mrs Wood's prolonged Christmas break. 'And there's a gardener who comes up to feed the ponies with hay and so on.'

She told it all to him, just like that! Terry was amazed. She couldn't know that he wouldn't tell someone else about it, someone less scrupulous than Terry about what he did, someone who would come into the house one dark night and strip it. It would be dead easy, and Terry knew people who'd pay him to tell them about the place. But this was a plum he meant to keep for himself. This was a rich prize for the plucking.

'Oh yes?' he prompted. 'Ponies?'

'They belong to my grand-daughters,' said Alice.

Terry asked about the girls and soon knew their names, ages and interests. Poor old thing, she's lonely, he thought; it was the same as the women on the housing estates. Give her a bit of his time, listen a while, nod and smile, and she'd eat out of his hand just as they did, and without him having all that other bother which sometimes grew tedious.

'It's a great house,' said Terry. 'Will you show me round? I don't think I've ever been in one this size that was lived in.'

Alice hesitated. She knew she had been talking too much – reaction, probably, to the strain of her morning's adventure – but the young man – culpable though he certainly was – had more than made amends by his kindness after the accident.

'I don't see why not,' she said. No one would know.

She led him along the passage into the dining-room, a big, square room with an oak refectory table in the centre. High-backed Jacobean oak chairs with cane seats were arranged along either side, and there was an old oak dresser against one wall. Alice shuddered to think what Helen had paid for this furniture, which she had bought to set off the room and demonstrate to would-be clients how things should be done. Beyond the dining-room another door led to the hall, where several rugs were laid on the stone-flagged floor, and at the rear a wide staircase led to the first floor. More doors led from the hall. Alice opened one, and went ahead of Terry into the drawing-room.

'Well!' For once Terry was at a loss. This was the life, all right! He stood on the deep pile carpet surveying the velvet upholstery, the brocade curtains, the various ornaments. An artificial Christmas tree, tinsel-branched, decorated with gold and silver baubles, stood in a corner.

Without comment, Alice led him on to Helen's own sitting-room, which overlooked the garden. The walls were ice-blue, the carpet a deeper blue. Two armchairs were covered in chintz with a yellow, lime green and blue design; two others were covered in yellow. There was a bureau against one wall. Here, Helen often worked in the evenings. The room was beautiful, but there was something about it that made Terry almost shiver.

Alice noticed.

'You feel it, too,' she said. 'It's a lovely room but it's somehow cold – though the heating works in here.' She laid her hand on the radiator. The boiler was programmed to run through the twenty-four hours in case of severe frost, though the thermostat was set low. 'The house isn't so warm upstairs,' Alice went on. 'The system needs renewing but they've had such a lot of expense. Things have to be done bit by bit.'

'Yes,' said Terry, nodding gravely. He looked out of the window at the garden which rolled away from the house. There was a wide lawn bordered with shrubs and trees including, some distance from the house, an immense cedar with great spreading branches.

'There's a lot of land,' he said.

'Yes,' agreed Alice. 'Most of it's meadow, though, for the ponies. They're over there.' She waved vaguely. 'You can see them from some of the upstairs windows. Not mine – I overlook the lodge.'

'Maybe you get the morning sun,' Terry said.

'Well – no, it faces north,' said Alice.

She showed him the girls' sitting-room with its television and stereo. From its window he could see a paved path leading down the garden towards the west side of the lawn.

'The pool's down there,' said Alice. 'The girls love that.'

Swimming-pool, she meant.

'I'll bet,' said Terry.

He'd have one too, one day.

Alice knew she must send him on his way and retreat to her own quarters, shoulder her isolation again. She led him back through the house.

Following slowly, Terry paused in the hall to look at the long-case clock which stood there. He knew little about such things but thought it was probably worth a bomb. Breaking in here would be a doddle. If he failed to collect from the old girl, he could always sell his information. It could be useful to see her rooms. She'd show him them if he asked, Terry felt sure; after all, hadn't he gone out of his way to help her when she'd got herself into a right old mess? Borrowing her daughter-in-law's car without asking, indeed!

'How do you get to your flat?' he asked at the foot of the main staircase. 'Up here?'

Alice was about to explain that she used the back stairs when both of them heard a voice calling.

'Mrs Armitage – are you there?' came the question, and Sue appeared from the back of the house. 'The door was open so I walked in and then I heard voices. I could see you had a visitor.'

She turned then, and looked at Terry, who was standing on the lowest tread of the staircase. Her first sight of him gave a false impression of height, but she saw, too, the ingenuous expression, the ready smile, the bright curls framing the round head. His eyes were alert and regarded her with as much attention as she was looking at him.

'Hullo,' said Sue.

'Oh, Sue,' said Alice, and the warmth in her voice was apparent to Terry. Who was this pretty dark girl with the long hair? He had seen her before somewhere.

In all the time that they had spent together, Alice had not learned Terry's name. She looked at him blankly.

'I'm Terry Brett,' he said.

'This is Sue Norris,' said Alice. 'She lives at the lodge.'

'Hullo, Sue,' said Terry, and then he placed her; he'd seen her leaving the Rigby Arms one night and going off with some old guy in a blue Rover 3500.

'Hi,' said Sue, and then turned to Alice. 'I just popped up to see if you were all right, Mrs Armitage, as you're on your own,' she explained. 'Though I could see you had a friend visiting, from the car outside.' Her words hung in the air, waiting for an explanation of the nature of this friendship. Sue had never before known Alice to have a visitor, and she had wondered if the caller was bona fide; you heard of such terrible things these days.

'How kind of you, Sue,' said Alice, and was about to add that Terry had mended her car for her when she realized that this could lead to further explanations which must be avoided if what she had done was to remain undetected. Would Jonathan notice the Volvo had gone? Probably, but would he attach importance to it? The idea of inventing an explanation – saying it was at the garage for service – some lie – filled Alice with dread. She went on quickly, 'What time do you have to be at work?'

'Three o'clock,' said Sue, and turned to Terry. 'I'm a receptionist at the Rigby Arms in Westborough. Know it? It's a nice place. I have to catch the bus at the end of the lane.'

'What – no car?' asked Terry, grinning.

'Not of my own. I don't drive,' said Sue, who meant to get Jonathan to teach her. 'Jonathan takes me when I'm on the early shift, and he comes in to collect me at night when I'm late.'

Unless my son brings you home, Alice thought.

'Jonathan's away at the moment, with his children,' said Sue. 'They're staying at his parents' place in Kent. He'll be home tonight.'

'I could give you a lift to Westborough,' said Terry lightly. 'I'm going that way.' He could, easily; Sue was a looker, and besides, she knew what went on here.

'Oh – that'd be great,' said Sue. 'Thanks. When are you leaving?'

'I'm in no hurry,' said Terry slowly, and he held her gaze. 'I've got a few days off, like most people. I've no definite plans.'

Both of the young people had forgotten Alice for a moment. Then, reluctantly turning their eyes away from one another, they glanced at her. She was their link.

'I was going to have a sandwich for lunch,' Sue said. She would have dinner that night at the

Rigby, where meals were part of the perks. She looked from Alice to Terry. 'Why don't you both come over and have a sandwich with me?'

'Yes please,' said Terry promptly.

'I don't think I will, thank you, Sue,' said Mrs Armitage. 'I'm not very hungry.'

'Oh, come on,' said Sue. 'You must eat something. Mustn't she?' she appealed to Terry.

Terry had been looking forward to having Sue's company to himself, but he'd be alone with her, after all, driving into Westborough.

'Indeed she must,' said Terry. 'Must keep up your strength, you know.'

Through Alice's head ran thoughts about whether it would be proper for Sue to entertain Terry in the lodge without Jonathan. People did these things these days and thought nothing of it, but looking at Sue and looking at Terry, seeing the glances they exchanged while she hesitated, Alice was reminded of how her own mother had always said one shouldn't put temptation in the path of others. Her presence would ensure the absence of opportunity, at least. She was shocked at the direction of her own thoughts. Terry and Sue had only just met; he'd be leaving soon and that would be the last they'd see of him. And anyway Jonathan and Sue weren't married, though that didn't mean Sue was free to spread her favours about. Alice decided that her experiences this morning had made her light-headed. Sue was a nice, friendly girl who felt lonely when she was at the lodge on her own. Hadn't she come

looking for Alice just now from purely neighbourly motives?

She'd been watching too many modern plays on
television, Alice reflected – hence, too, her anxiety
about Sue and Giles seeing too much of each other.
In real life people still had standards and considered
how their actions might affect those to whom they
had responsibilities. Suppressing her base fears, she
nevertheless agreed to go over to the lodge.

Inside it was warm and snug. It was Alice's first
visit, and she looked round at the oak-panelled
living-room with interest. It was rather dark, for
the latticed windows were small, but there was a
big log fire, and also, beneath one window, an electric storage heater which Alice noticed with envy.
She was installed in a large armchair and given a
glass of sherry, and a magazine to read, while Terry
and Sue went into the kitchen to make the sandwiches. She heard them laughing as they worked.
It was nice to hear people happy.

When they came back with a plate of cheese
sandwiches made with Kraft slices and white
sliced bread, Sue refilled Alice's glass and asked
how long she and Terry had known one another.

Before Alice could answer, Terry had launched
into his version of the collision.

'Oh – but it wasn't like that!' Alice tried to inter-
rupt.

Terry swept on.

'She'd borrowed her daughter-in-law's car,' he
told Sue. 'Without permission,' and he pretended
to frown at Alice.

'You didn't!' exclaimed Sue. 'Why, you mischief!' there was approving admiration in her tone although she accepted Terry's description of the crash.

'You don't mind Sue knowing, do you, Mrs Armitage?' said Terry. 'She's on your side.' He went on to explain that the car would soon be repaired and no one would be any the wiser. 'You're not going to give her away, are you, Sue?' he asked.

'Of course not,' said Sue.

'And – er – ?' What was he called, the fellow she lived with?

'Oh, Jonathan won't, either,' said Sue. 'Don't worry. Lucky you weren't hurt, either of you.' She noticed that Mrs Armitage was looking very upset. Naturally she wouldn't like people to know that she had boobed. It was lucky for her that Terry was being so easy about it, otherwise she might have been in real trouble, with the police and all that. If Helen found out, she'd be furious. 'Where were you going?' she asked. It must have been important for the old girl to take such a chance.

'Oh – to London,' said Alice. 'I do sometimes.'

'Do you? Good for you,' said Sue warmly. 'Meeting a friend, were you?'

'No – not this time,' said Alice, and thought that she was almost as bad as Terry in letting an implied untruth slip by uncorrected. She met no friends in London.

She was lonely, poor old thing, thought Sue.

'You ought to have a party,' she said. 'This is the time of year for parties.'

'Who would I ask?' said Alice.

'Jonathan and me, for a start,' said Sue. 'And Terry. And haven't you any friends in Harcombe? Haven't you been invited out?'

'I've met a few people,' Alice admitted. She'd finished her second glass of sherry and now Terry filled it again. Alice took a sip. 'I've been to Mrs Duncan's,' she said. 'At the Old Vicarage.'

'Well – there you are. You must ask Mrs Duncan back,' said Sue. 'Have you done that?'

'I can't,' said Alice. 'My room is too small.' And too cold, she thought.

'Why don't we go and have a look at it?' said Terry, whose earlier attempt to inspect it had been foiled by Sue's arrival.

After all that sherry, Alice was unable to protest with any conviction. Sue and Terry took the plates and glasses out to the kitchen and there were more sounds of laughter. Alice, muzzy by now, found herself smiling too. It was a long time since she'd heard laughter like theirs.

Soon they reappeared, ready to escort her back to her flat and examine it before going to Westborough. After Sue had closed the door of the lodge, which locked automatically on the Yale, they walked across to the main house, one on each side of Alice. Terry steadied her as they went up the steps to the back door, which had been unlocked all this time. Alice led the way up the narrow twisting staircase that rose from the back of the house to the attic floor where, years ago, servants had slept.

The top corridor was icy. Alice walked along it to a dingy brown door and opened it to reveal a tiny lobby in which there was not enough room for the three of them to stand together. Doors led to a sitting-room beyond which was a tiny kitchen, to a miniscule bathroom, and to a bedroom almost totally filled by a double bed. Alice, still feeling the effects of the sherry, showed them all round since they seemed so interested.

'Christ, it's cold,' Terry said, in the sitting-room. His breath puffed into a cloud before him.

Sue went to the window and felt the radiator.

'It's stone cold,' she said. 'Isn't the heating on?'

'It doesn't work very well up here,' Alice said. 'I'll get the electric fire from my bedroom.'

'I'll get it.' Sue had noticed a small two-bar fire in the corner.

While she was fetching it, Alice opened a cupboard in the sitting-room and took the fan heater from it, plugging it in. It purred out warmth at once. It was automatic for her, by now, to put it away whenever she went out, in case Helen came snooping and confiscated it, and she did not notice Terry's puzzled expression as he watched what she was doing.

'You need a couple of good convector heaters,' said Terry. 'They'd soon warm you up.'

'Have you only got this one fire?' Sue asked, bringing it in. It had to run from the same plug as the fan heater, using an adaptor, and Terry raised his brows as he noticed this.

'Yes,' said Alice. 'I did think a convector would

be better, but how would I get it upstairs? I don't think I could do it myself.'

'The shop would deliver. The guy would carry it up,' said Terry.

'I know.' How could she possibly explain that Helen would ban it?

She didn't have to: Sue understood.

'You don't want Helen to know,' she said. 'And Mrs Wood might tell her.'

Alice's averted gaze and drooping shoulders were her answer.

'I'll bring you two tomorrow,' said Terry. 'One for in here and one for the bedroom. They'll soon warm you up.'

'Yes, but – ' Alice looked wretched. They'd take up space. Where could she hide them if Helen was about?

'You do need them, Mrs Armitage,' said Sue, and added, 'Doesn't Giles realize how cold it is up here?'

'Er – I don't think he does,' Alice said. He so seldom came up. When had they last had a chat? She couldn't remember. It would be lovely to be warm, she thought. Giles would understand and wouldn't be cross if he caught her; hadn't he brought her the fire? She could hide the bedroom heater in her wardrobe if she went out, and push the other one into a corner with the big chair in front of it, in case Helen came in.

She opened her handbag, took out her notecase, and gave Terry seventy pounds, in ten-pound notes.

'Will that be enough to buy them?' she asked. She thought they would cost at least thirty pounds each.

'Should be,' said Terry, who could probably get them at cost from someone he knew. He put the money in his pocket. He knew the old duck was loaded. Of course, she'd been going to London, to splurge at the sales, no doubt; hence her well-filled notecase. 'I'll bring them tomorrow without fail,' he said.

They left Alice there, alone, with the electric fire and the fan heater both on as she sat in her armchair. Replete with sherry and sandwiches, she dozed off, only waking in panic when it grew dark, for something dreadful had happened.

No, it hadn't. To be sure, there'd been the crash, but it had brought her a new friend. Now she had two, for Sue was her friend already, and they were going to help her. Before they left they'd mentioned the party again, saying that she should hold it in the big drawing-room while the others were still away. What an idea, thought Alice drowsily. It was out of the question.

7

As they drove into Westborough that afternoon, Terry discovered from Sue that she would be working the same shift all the week.

'I'll give you a lift in tomorrow,' he said. 'After I've fixed the heaters for the old girl.'

'You'll get them, then?' said Sue. 'Buy them, I mean.'

'Of course. She's given me the money, hasn't she?' Terry drove on, his gaze intent on the road ahead; he didn't like these narrow twisting lanes, and he didn't want to run into some idiot belting along towards him not looking where he was going.

'I'd have thought you might be tempted,' said Sue.

'Whatever gave you that idea?' said Terry, but without any hint of affront in his voice. 'I wouldn't take advantage of an old lady.'

'Wouldn't you?' Sue's tone was sceptical. She'd noticed a lot about Terry. His clothes were neat – not trendy, but stylish, and he was driving a fairly new car – but his shoes were shabby – worn, and not polished – which didn't tie in with the rest of his appearance. During her time at the Rigby

Arms, Sue had met a lot of people and had learned to interpret certain signs. At first she'd thought Terry was a salesman of some kind. Now she was less certain. There was something about him that excited her, but she wasn't sure what it was. When they met as he stood at the foot of the staircase, she had felt a strange shock – a sense of recognition unlike anything she'd ever experienced before. Here was someone who, underneath the mild surface, was as ruthless as she was; Sue knew it without any doubt.

'What's your job?' she asked him. 'You are working, I suppose?'

'I'm a middle man,' said Terry grandly. 'I supply things that people want. Like convector fires for the old bag,' he added.

'So you will take your cut,' said Sue, turning her head away so that he could not see her smile if he took his eyes from the road. 'I thought there'd be something in it for you.'

'From the dealer, yes,' said Terry. 'All fair and square – cash down.'

'I don't believe you,' said Sue. She snuggled into the seat beside him, a gloriously comfortable sensation stealing over her. In her whole life she never remembered feeling so much at ease with anyone – and she fancied him, too: she liked his eyes and he had a big laughing mouth.

'Why not?' asked Terry. 'Why should I lie?'

'Did Mrs Armitage really drive into you? Your car isn't damaged, is it?' said Sue. 'Surely it would be, if she'd done that?'

'It was just a scrape. She misjudged how close she could go to the line of parked cars,' Terry explained. 'I'd edged forward a little, ready to move out from the kerb.'

Each time Mrs Armitage had given Sue a lift she'd driven in a very capable manner, Sue had thought. She could not drive herself, but she'd been a passenger often enough to be some judge of competence, and she'd been surprised, because until then she'd assessed Mrs Armitage as an ineffectual old woman, someone who was at the mercy of her not-very-thoughtful family, and to be pitied.

'She's a good driver,' said Sue.

'Even good drivers have off moments,' Terry said. 'And she wasn't in her own car. Those Volvos are lively.'

'She'd be being extra careful, driving Helen's car,' said Sue.

'Well, it was raining,' said Terry. 'Maybe she couldn't see properly because of the rain. I don't suppose her eyes are too good, at her age.'

The rain had stopped now, though the sky was still grey and overcast with heavy low clouds.

'Maybe you were in too much of a hurry,' suggested Sue. Her voice was light; she sounded amused, not reproving.

Terry glanced quickly at her. This one was something again, he thought; this was no ordinary sort of girl.

'I wasn't going anywhere special,' he said. 'Why should I be in a hurry?'

'I expect you were looking for the next opportunity,' Sue remarked. Rather as she had been when she met Jonathan. 'Come and have a sandwich tomorrow,' she suggested when he dropped her at the Rigby Arms. 'I won't invite Mrs Armitage to join us.'

Alice woke in the chill dark hours of early morning feeling clammy with fear and shame. Such a terrible thing had happened the previous day. Clutching the bedclothes round her, she remembered what she had done. How could she have been so silly? It was almost wicked, taking Helen's car like that without permission.

Alice reached out to turn on the bedside light, then sat up, the cold striking her through her bedjacket and the warm, high-necked nightdress she wore, with its long sleeves gathered in at the wrists. It was pale pink, printed with tiny, darker pink rosebuds and trimmed with lace frills. At the end of the bed lay her dressing-gown. She put it on, slid her feet into her sheepskin slippers and shuffled into the kitchen to make herself a cup of tea. Then, while the kettle boiled, she went back to her bedroom where she turned on the electric fire and took the now cool rubber hot-water bottle out of her bed to refill it. This was a quite regular routine in the small hours, and so was a feeling of sorrow and loss, but not this panic, the almost heart-stopping terror.

Alice wasn't afraid of burglars breaking in to Harcombe House, or of being coshed while alone there. Harcombe, she thought, was a safe village;

there were no gangs of louts parked astride motor cycles in the street, as she'd seen elsewhere, and no great local unemployment problem. As far as she knew, all residents of working age who wanted them had jobs. Several cars left the village when Giles did, he had said, bound for London or places like Swindon or Slough. What did frighten Alice was people: the lack of them, for company and stimulation, and the perilous path she must tread among those who comprised her family. And now she had committed a great folly which could bring immense and deserved trouble down on her head.

She'd never see that boy again, she felt sure. He'd wriggled out of the consequences of a collision that had been entirely his fault, but she'd been responsible for making what would have been simply a tiresome event, if she had been in her own car, into a catastrophe by her use of Helen's car. To cap all, she'd given the boy a large sum of money to buy her two convector heaters, and she'd never see that again.

She looked out of her window across at the lodge. There it lay, in peaceful darkness, with Jonathan and Sue enjoying their illicit union under its steep grey slate roof. Alice had felt so happy there for that short time, sitting by the fire in a shabby, comfortable chair, not worrying about dropping sandwich crumbs on the worn carpet. Some of the furniture was familiar; it had been at Windlea. There hadn't been space for it in Alice's flat; Helen had used it and her own cast-off pieces to equip the lodge for letting. Alice had thought her surplus things had been sold: she had felt a pang at seeing these old friends again.

Why hadn't they offered her the chance to live in the lodge? Because it could be let for probably quite a large sum, she thought grimly: because the only way Giles could keep Helen content and their marriage together was to gratify her craving to live in this style. Alice moaned to herself, rocking to and fro, keening softly with grief as she recognized that her son was an unhappy failure. If only he'd never met Helen, she thought; if only he'd stayed with his original firm, married a girl with modest tastes, a generous nature and less ambition; avoided putting himself under an obligation to his father-in-law.

What if Helen found out about the car? What would she say? What would she do? Thinking about it, Alice cringed with dread.

The kettle was boiling its head off in the kitchen; something had happened to its ability to switch itself off – another thing she must see to; Walter had been quite clever at simple repairs and would probably have happily bought some part and cured the complaint. Alice made her tea and got back into bed to drink it. The room was warmer now. She left the fire on, a single bar burning, something she never liked to do when she first went to bed, for fear of fire. But now it was nearly morning.

She fell asleep after drinking her tea and did not wake until nine o'clock.

At noon, the back doorbell rang. Both bells were

wired so that they pealed in the corridor outside Alice's flat. Before Christmas she'd plodded downstairs several times, summoned by youths selling prints and cards in aid of various charities and by small boys singing carols. But most itinerant callers gave up waiting when their summons was not answered promptly. Harcombe House, and its lodge, which was usually empty, were not worth visiting.

Now, when Alice opened the door, she saw Terry outside. He was grinning, his mop of curls standing out brightly against the pale winter sky. The air was colder today; there had been a frost in the night.

'I got them,' he said. Beside him were two large cardboard cartons. He patted one. 'They're good ones.'

After parting from Sue the previous day, Terry had been to a discount centre. He'd bought the two heaters for less than the price advertised because he found two discontinued models, one with a slight scratch. He got a further reduction for paying cash. He'd found a sharp salesman to deal with; each had respected the other and struck a bargain, a fiver passing from Terry to the other young man. The account had been doctored. On paper, Alice now owed Terry a further eight pounds. But she had a genuine guarantee, if anything should go wrong with either heater, which was most unlikely. Terry had bought plugs, too, and an extension lead. He had decided to make himself essential to Mrs Armitage. In small ways, costing himself minimum effort, he would bring cheer to her life and thus gain acceptance by the whole family as part of the regular scene. He'd have a reason for being about the place, for seeing Sue.

What a girl! She was exciting! She'd kissed him before leaving the car – a warm, quick pressure of soft lips against his, a breath of scent. What a change from the older, dissatisfied housewives who formed his main experience of women. Terry had never had sex with someone his age, whom he'd picked for her looks. He never thought of that intimacy as making love: love was a con; it didn't exist, not really.

If ever he did fall in love, it would be with someone like Sue.

Whistling, he carried the heaters, one at a time, up the narrow staircase to Alice's flat. Seated in her armchair, he made quick work of fitting the plugs and he demonstrated the extension lead.

'It could be useful,' he said. 'You shouldn't run too many things from one point, you know. This way, you could run the television on it, wheel it into your bedroom – you can get an aerial extension too, if you need one. You can have the fire on and the iron, for instance. What else would help to make you snug? Mind if I look round when I've fixed this?'

At that moment Alice would have agreed to any suggestion he cared to make. How could she have been so mean and suspicious, she was asking herself, as to doubt his honesty? What did it matter if he'd adjusted the facts about yesterday's accident? He'd probably felt too ashamed to face the truth, just as she was ashamed at the enormity of her escapade. He was only young; he'd learn from this mistake.

Terry felt the change in atmosphere, the dissolution of Alice's reservations. He always knew how to play it, he thought complacently, fitting the brown lead to the positive point in the plug on the extension.

Washing his hands in the bathroom, he saw the rubber hot-water bottle in its knitted cover hanging on the back of the door.

'Haven't you got an electric blanket?' he asked her. 'Or a Teasmade machine? You know – it wakes you up with a cup of tea.'

'No.'

Walter hadn't wanted an electric blanket, and when he was alive, Alice had not needed one. A comforting glow – sometimes, in hot weather, almost too much of one – had emanated from his familiar body curled up alongside her. They didn't sleep entwined, but there he was, pleased if she felt like snuggling up against him, always ready to embrace her. It wasn't sex that she missed; that, in Alice's view, was over-rated, given too much emphasis these days, when friendship was so much more important. It was just the contact that she mourned, the warmth of a human touch. They'd never gone to sleep without mending any small difference they'd had; it had been a rule.

'My granny's got one,' Terry told her. He didn't know if she had, in that home she was in, but his mother, in her single bed in Woking, certainly had. 'There's two sorts, one for on top, and one for beneath. The top one's best, you can sleep with it on. They're quite safe.'

'Are they?' Alice looked doubtful.

'Oh yes,' said Terry.

'I sometimes get up in the night to refill my bottle,' Alice confessed.

'Well, even if you'd turned your blanket off, you could turn it on then,' said Terry. 'I expect you wake up because you're cold.' Or to pee, he thought, at her age; but better not say so.

'Perhaps I do,' said Alice.

'Well, you won't be cold any more,' said Terry. 'You could run it off the same socket as the bedside lamp. That would be all right.'

'The cost,' worried Alice.

'I think they're about thirty-five pounds,' said Terry, who had looked at the discount store.

'Oh, I didn't mean the blanket,' said Alice. 'I meant the cost of the electricity.'

'They don't use much,' Terry assured her. 'And as for the convectors, once you've got the place warm, the thermostat switches them on and off so they don't use power all the time. They're cheaper to run than that bar fire.'

'I'll get a blanket,' Alice decided. 'I'll buy one this afternoon.'

'I'll get it for you,' said Terry. 'I'll bring it out, fix the plug, make sure it's working all right.'

'Oh, I can't put you to all that trouble,' said Alice.

'It's no trouble,' said Terry. 'I'd like to see you again.'

And she'd like to see him. He throbbed with vitality. Alice felt better just for looking at his bright curly head, let alone his cheerful smile.

'I'll get the blanket. You come and fix the plug,' she said. She hadn't got a grandson. 'How old are you, Terry?' she asked.

'Twenty-two.'

Giles was forty-five. It could have been. Alice smiled.

'You'll be back at work soon,' she said. 'What's your job?'

'Selling,' said Terry promptly. 'This and that. I make my own timetable.'

'Oh,' said Alice, accepting it. Rather like Jonathan but at a much lower level, she supposed. Or perhaps he was one of those moonlighters the papers kept mentioning; it sounded so romantic.

Later, over at the lodge, Terry told Sue about the electric blanket. Alice had rejected his suggestion of a Teasmade. He thought she might change her mind later. After all, it was quite an outlay all at once, and there'd be the bill for the car, too.

'Fancy her taking it,' Sue marvelled. 'Naughty old thing. Like a kid. I hope that Helen doesn't find out. She's a cow. Hard as nails.'

So are you, Terry thought. The women on the estates weren't; that was part of their problem. What a combination he and Sue would make together, with her iron will and his soft talk. They'd be invincible.

Upstairs in the bed that she shared with Jonathan, he said, 'You know that party we talked about? For the old girl?'

'Mm.' Sue was trying to count his ribs. He was lean, not flabby like Jonathan who took no exercise and drank too much beer.

'Let's fix it for her. It'd be great.'

'Might be a giggle,' said Sue. 'Poor old thing, she doesn't have much of a time. She deserves a treat.'

'In the main house,' Terry pressed. 'In that swank room.' Terry would have a room like that one day, though maybe more modern. And here, beside him, was the partner who would help him secure it. The means were at hand. She'd already got in with that geezer with the blue Rover, the old girl's son.

'What if the people who came to it told Helen?' Sue asked. 'She'd be in trouble then.'

'Would they meet? Does Helen know these people? Surely they're old ladies too? You could find out – chat her up about them.'

'Yes.' Anyway, it was a risk worth taking for the fun of it, Sue thought.

Later, nuzzling her shoulder – she smelled good, an odd sort of scent, it fairly turned him on – Terry had another question.

'What about the son?'

'Giles? What about him?'

'What sort of fellow is he? How well do you know him?'

'Drinks a lot,' said Sue. 'I know him well enough.'

'As well as this?' Terry took her hand, kissed the palm and gently nipped the fat pad beneath her thumb with his sharp white teeth. He'd learned that trick from a widow in Barnet.

'Not yet,' said Sue. 'But I will.'

There was no need to say more. They did not have to explain their ideas to each other, not at this stage. Both knew they were going to fly high together, and the manner and speed of that ascent would be dictated by Giles's response to Sue. Sue was confident. She'd already levered herself upwards by throwing her lot in with Jonathan; she'd do better with Giles.

Neither had mentioned Jonathan as someone to be considered or as an obstacle. Terry, coming down on Sue, making her moan, knew that he would not be where he was now if Jonathan were going to be any problem.

8

'Now, about your party, Mrs Armitage,' said Terry. 'When shall it be?'

He'd returned the next day.

'Oh, that was just your joke, Terry,' said Alice. 'I can't really have a party.'

'Yes, you can! Leave it all to Sue and me – we'll fix everything. Who shall we ask?'

He pulled the second chair forward so that their knees almost met in front of the softly glowing convector heater from which warm thermals arose. The room was cosy at last.

Alice hesitated, looking at the smooth, enthusiastic face so close to hers. He had a small pimple on one cheek, and his eyebrows were curly; when he grew old, they'd be bushy, she thought inconsequentially.

'We can't,' she said. 'It's not possible.'

'You owe people, don't you?' Terry said. 'It's rude if you don't ask them back. Let's write their names down.' He got up to look for a piece of paper and found a small pad by the telephone, kept there so that Alice could make an immediate note of messages for Helen. Terry slowly began to write, in uneven script. 'Sue and Jonathan,' he said. 'And me, of course. Who else? Who's asked you?'

'Well, Mrs Duncan. That's all, really,' said Alice. 'But I know Mrs Hedges and Miss Wilson. I've been to a coffee morning at their cottage. But this is just your teasing, Terry. We can't really do it.'

'No, it's not. It's going to happen,' said Terry. 'There's all this big house, going spare. What's it to be? Gin and tonic?'

In their young days, Alice and Walter had given plenty of parties. She had enjoyed most forms of entertaining, but in the last years they'd settled for about eight friends at a time, offering sherry or wine; spirits were so expensive. She'd taken pride in constructing tempting canapés – varied spreads on crisp pastry, and cheese straws. But not now: not here. That was all over.

'No,' she said. 'We can't do it.'

'What's stopping you?' asked Terry, regarding her gravely, his eyes large and apparently inno-cent. He'd dangled the idea before her again more for his own amusement than anything else, but now the challenge of making her give way to him spurred him on.

'It's not my house,' said Alice.

'Well, you live here. It's your home,' said Terry. 'Surely you can ask a few friends in?'

Alice looked away from that penetrating gaze. What he said should be so, and it was her house – part of it. She was uncertain how much Helen and Giles had paid for the whole estate but eighty thousand pounds had come from the sale of

Windlea. Surely that entitled her to more than this tiny allotment of space under the eaves?

'They'll never know,' he prompted. 'Your family.'

'It's true that I owe Mrs Duncan,' said Alice. 'I'd thought of taking her out to lunch one day – to a pub somewhere.' She hadn't, until this moment, when the notion came to her as inspiration. But hot on its heels came the knowledge that she would find it a huge strain to impose her will over the managing Barbara Duncan, obtain service in the pub, act efficiently as hostess.

'Do that another time,' Terry said. 'When it's your turn again and your family's here.' He drew a line on his piece of paper beneath the names. 'Now, we'll want plenty of drink,' he went on. 'Gin, whisky, vodka.' He wrote them down, one after the other.

'We won't,' said Alice, firmer now. 'If it happens at all, it'll be just sherry.' As she felt herself yielding over the main idea, some instinct warned her not to let Terry have a free hand with spirits. Besides, Barbara Duncan had offered only sherry.

'Sherry, right,' said Terry, crossing out what he had written and printing the word in big letters. 'Tomorrow, then,' he added. 'About six?'

Alice thought of a way of staving it off.

'That's too soon,' she said. 'We must give them some notice. And Sue's on late shift this week. We must have it when she can come.' That would kill the whole idea. By the time Sue was on the early shift, Giles and the family would have come back and the plan would have to be abandoned.

'Next week, then,' said Terry. 'Sue changes shifts then. You're right, we can't have it without her.'

In the following minutes, Alice found herself agreeing to Friday and telephoning the three intended guests, for Terry insisted that she should do it while he was there. She might change her mind, he thought, and he didn't mean to let that happen. By the time the car had been repaired and they'd had the party, he'd have quite a hold over old Mrs Armitage, who wouldn't want her secrets revealed. He didn't know yet, how he would use this power; time would give him the opportunity, just as time would show what use Sue could make of Giles; quite a lot, he thought, remembering her sharp little teeth, her hands on his back, the rest of her, so soft, warm and moist. He'd never known anything like it, and there'd be more today, quite soon, when he'd got the party set up with the old girl and gone over to the lodge.

All the ladies were at home when Alice reluctantly telephoned. They accepted warmly, sounding genuinely pleased, Mrs Hedges speaking for herself and Miss Wilson.

'Like that, is it?' said Terry, learning that they lived together.

'What do you mean?' asked Alice.

'Well –' Terry shrugged. 'You know – two women – ' he raised his eyebrows with a knowing expression on his unlined face.

'Oh, it's not like that at all,' said Alice, who

didn't know whether it was or not. 'People are so unkind,' she went on. 'Why jump to conclusions?'

'Human nature,' said Terry.

'I expect they just want company,' said Alice. 'And it's cheaper for two than separate houses. They're probably old friends. Anyway, what does it matter? It's their business.' She thought it might be rather pleasant to share a cottage with a woman friend: divide the chores and the responsibility: have someone to talk to, to go out with, to take care of you if you were ill. But when you'd been contentedly married for nearly fifty years, you didn't have women friends in quite that way; she'd never felt close to any of the widows among their acquaintance, except Audrey, who, with her husband, had often made up a quartet with Alice and Walter. 'I wish I'd stayed in Bournemouth,' she said suddenly. For she could have drawn closer to some of those women her own age whom she'd known superficially for years. They must be lonely, too. She could have taken up bridge, like some of them, who played three or four times a week and were busy and cheerful.

'That's where you lived?' asked Terry.

'Yes. Then my husband died,' said Alice. 'And my son and his wife asked me to come and live with them. It seemed a good idea at the time.'

'You had a nice place in Bournemouth, did you?'

'Yes. You could see the sea from the garden. Just a bus ride into town if you didn't want to take the car.'

He could see it all. Terry knew what they'd

done, the son and his wife: stripped her of what she'd got for the house to help with this place. He'd have done it himself, but he'd have made the old thing comfortable until she had to go into a home.

'It's nice when the girls are at home,' Alice went on. 'They come up here sometimes, especially Amanda. We play cards and Scrabble. But they're away at school most of the time. Boarding-school, you know,' she added, to make sure he understood.

'Well, you've got me now,' smiled Terry. 'We're friends now, like as if I was your grandson.'

Though she'd thought of the same thing herself, somehow, when he said it, Alice felt chilled. She looked at him doubtfully. Terry was beaming at her. By the time her son and his family came back, he'd be so much a part of the place that they'd easily accept him, he decided. It was all going splendidly. He'd plan as he went along, as he always did. He was excited by the future and the prospects it held. Who knew where it might lead? The daughter-in-law, Helen, for instance, could be a target for him while Sue got to work on the son. They could bleed this family for thousands, the two of them, make anything he'd done in the past seem like peanuts. Paris, Rome, the South of France, here we come, thought Terry, Sue and me together. She was wasted on that slob Jonathan. Terry hadn't met him yet but he was sure he was a slob. The two of them could conquer the world, and without any violence. There had never been any need for it in his operations; an edge of steel in

104

the voice and glares in place of smiles had been all that was required when he met resistance.

'I'll go and fix things with Sue,' said Terry, eager to get away now. 'Little eats and so on.' But Sue didn't like cooking; he already knew that. 'Maybe she could get them from the hotel, cheap,' he suggested brightly.

'No, I'll see to that,' said Alice, determined at least to set the tone of the party. 'We won't need much, not for so few people.'

'All right. It's your baby,' said Terry.

Alice watched from the window to see him emerge from the house. She was in for it now. At Windlea they'd had their routine; the food had been her department and Walter had dealt with the drinks. It had been team-work. Terry could pour the sherry. He and Jonathan would be the only men present. She saw his curly head below as he walked to the lodge past his parked car. There was something wrong about the car. Alice, about to draw back from the window looked at it again. It was the wrong colour. The Vauxhall he'd been driving that first day was pale green; in her mind's eye she could see it now, its wing jutting forward as she went by. The car parked outside the lodge today was brown.

He said he bought and sold things. Perhaps he dealt in cars. That must be the explanation.

She put it out of her mind.

In order to have a base approved of by Hilary, his wife, where he could see his children, Jonathan had spent part of his Christmas holiday at his parents' house in Kent. He'd fetched the children on Boxing Day and they'd stayed several days. Then he'd taken them back to their mother.

He'd regretted leaving Sue, but it couldn't be helped. She was on duty anyway at the Rigby Arms, doing extra hours, for the hotel was full and had arranged special Christmas festivities. Before they moved into the lodge together, their meetings had been spiced with the thrill of complicated arrangements. Jonathan, after his wife had found out about his affair with Sue and thrown him out, had moved into a one-roomed flat in the town, and Sue had lived at the hotel, but gradually she'd moved more and more of her belongings, and finally herself, into his flat, which was far too small for two. Used to life in a tall Victorian semi-detached house with lofty rooms and plenty of space spread over three storeys, Jonathan found the discomfort of these cramped conditions hard to bear. He'd snapped at Sue several times when he couldn't find his own things among the jumble of her clothes – she had few other possessions. She was untidy, and not always very particular about washing. At first he had found this intriguing, for his wife had always run things in an orderly way, never behind with her chores, the washing done on time, his shirts ironed and put away, the children taught to keep their rooms tidy. Sue's disorder, combined with a degree of abandonment in bed which Jonathan had only met in his imagination before, had sparked in him a reaction which, most of the time, made him indulgent about the squalor and irritations of their life, but after some weeks of this his tolerance had been strained when he found a white shirt tinged pink from being washed with a red sweater of Sue's. The fact that it had been he who had taken their things to the launderette and failed to realize the peril posed by Sue's garment among the otherwise fast-dyed articles only made him crosser. Hilary would never let such a mistake occur.

But Hilary was dull, he reminded himself. Hilary was bored in bed and interested only in their children, to whom she was a devoted and exemplary mother.

'It might be your fault, you know,' Sue had said, when he had spoken about their problems. He'd felt disloyal, mentioning the lack of rapture in their intimacies as he lay, hot and sticky, his limbs still tangled with Sue's in her attic room at the Rigby Arms. She liked him coming up there. Until Hilary found out about them and turned him out, they had nowhere else to go, and she'd have got into trouble if they'd been caught, although she wasn't the only one who broke the rules about conduct among the staff. It would be fun to bring a case for wrongful dismissal for such a cause, she'd thought, though she doubted if, in fact, the manager would go so far. He'd turn a blind eye. But Jonathan wanted no notoriety, and he didn't want Sue to lose her job, for a love affair was very expensive. It was more so when he had to find a place of his own while still supporting his family.

He'd been chagrined when Sue had suggested that he might be to blame for Hilary's want of ardour. How could that be so, he'd asked.

'Well, you've not had much experience, have you?' Sue had replied.

He'd been married for eight years, Jonathan had said, and he'd got two children.

'Anyone can do that,' said Sue. 'It's more than a tap, you know, to turn on and off.'

In their weeks together, he'd discovered what she meant, but he soon saw that their relationship would not survive if they went on living in such confined quarters. He'd already taken over the cooking. Sue had her main meal at the hotel and saw no need to take trouble preparing one for him. After a day on the road, with a snatched lunch in some bar, Jonathan needed a good dinner in the evening; he was used to it. He was a competent cook, and it saved trouble all round if he prepared food in the tiny recess which contained the twin burner stove and minuscule sink rather than letting Sue loose in there. But they had a sharp row one morning after he'd found a grey grubby bra and an unwashed pair of nylon briefs among his clean shirts, washed and ironed by himself and airing by the radiator.

After that, he saw that if they were to stay together they must find somewhere better to live, and that had led him to the lodge at Harcombe House. It was small, and because it was in the country the rent was reasonable. Sue contributed to that; her salary was adjusted when she moved out of the hotel.

Jonathan was very subdued when he came back after seeing his children. Sue did not ask about them. He hadn't let her go with him when he went to buy their presents; the subject was dangerous ground for her to tread. He'd helped them carry their presents to the door when he took them back to their mother, and had half hoped Hilary would ask him in, but she didn't. She'd closed the front door upon herself and the small boy and girl before he'd got back into the car.

She had found out about Sue in such an unpleasant way. One of Hilary's female friends, so-called, visiting the Rigby on her way to London and stopping off for a meal, had seen them together leaving the hotel, and had put two and two together. Hilary ought to be told, she'd said.

Would the break have come anyway? Jonathan didn't know. Couldn't he have managed to keep on with Sue and stayed a good father and a dutiful, if not a loving husband? He was torn, now, between the new sexual excitement he had discovered and his longing for his children, and the adjustment to life with Sue was not easy after years living with neat Hilary. He had to remind himself that Sue was having to adjust too. Country life was new for her, and getting to and from work, except when he took her to Westborough on the early shift or collected her at night, meant a long walk to or from the bus stop. But he liked the lodge; he liked the small garden, enjoyed weeding and planting, keeping it tidy. He'd missed all that, after leaving home, and wondered how Hilary coped with it on her own: competently, he had no doubt. She was a capable girl.

He and Sue would work things out, he was sure. All partnerships needed time to develop and had to be nourished with care – marriage in particular, he thought, and would not let himself wonder whether he and Hilary could have tended theirs more, and saved it.

He seemed unable to avoid thoughts that were disloyal to one or other of the women. Jonathan, driving home, switched his mind from Hilary back to Sue. Soon he'd be wrapped in her thin arms, smelling again her strange musky smell, lost to everything else.

9

Terry did not visit Alice over the New Year weekend. He'd perfected the technique of making himself an essential part of someone's life and then playing hard to get for a while. His return after an interval was always greeted with rapture; Alice, he was sure, would be no exception to this.

She'd listened for him on Saturday, but no visiting car drove up to the house. Jonathan and Sue went off in the morning; Alice saw the Granada's boot disappearing through the gateway when she looked out of the window. The day, spent in solitude, pressed down on her. She took the Metro out in the afternoon and had a mock Devonshire tea with clotted cream and scones at Pam's Pantry in Westborough. On Sunday she saw Jonathan busy sweeping up sodden dead leaves that had lain around the lodge all winter. Alice put on her coat and boots. She'd go out for a walk; that would give her a chance to talk to him.

She loitered as she passed the lodge and he leaned on his broom to exchange trivialities with her. He saw that she was killing time, and, remembering Sue's remarks, asked her in for coffee.

Alice fluttered a little. She longed to accept but didn't want to be tiresome.

'I was going for a walk,' she said.

'Come in on your way back, then,' said Jonathan, playing along with her.

Alice walked the whole length of the village street, as far as the church, and back again. She saw a few people: a woman with a dog, two boys on cycles – and a number of cars drove past, but no one spoke to her as she stepped along in her fur-collared coat and smart leather boots, and her hat with the feather.

Jonathan had just finished clearing away the leaves and sweeping all the paths round the lodge when she returned. He led her inside, sat her down by the fire and poured her some sherry. Sue was upstairs, having a bath; it was her weekend off, before she changed shifts.

'I know you and Sue are great friends,' he said. 'She's told me about your lunches together.'

Lunches? There'd been only the one. And she saw very little of Sue – just glimpses from the window, unless she noticed the girl at the bus stop and gave her a lift. What did he mean?

Jonathan had come home several times that week to find the debris from two people's snack lunches piled any old how in the kitchen. He had begun to enjoy the evenings when Sue was working the late shift. He would pour himself a beer, and cook himself a chop, or sausages – usually something he'd bought on the way home, for Sue's housekeeping was unplanned and she often forgot to shop for food. He would tidy up whatever mess she had left behind, sighing over it, recognizing she could not change her ways. When he realized that someone had been in the house, he had jokingly asked her if she had been entertaining, and she had told him that Alice was so lonely that she had taken pity on the old woman.

As Alice drank her sherry, he sat facing her on the small sofa that had been in Walter's den at Windlea. It had grown shabby over the years. A new cover would give it a fresh lease of life, Alice thought, before she turned again to Jonathan, who seemed tired. His face was soft-featured, with an indeterminate nose and a small mouth. He had pale straight brows over brown eyes that looked mildly bewildered. It wasn't a strong face. Alice hoped Sue would soon appear as she sought a topic to discuss with this dull but amiable man. Sue didn't come, however, and at last Alice left.

'See you on Friday, Jonathan,' she said. 'At my party.'

This was the first Jonathan had heard of any party. When Sue came downstairs, smelling of bath oil and scent and unusually clean, he asked her what Alice had meant.

'Oh – didn't I say?' Sue smiled at him, her long dark hair hanging down on each side of her face. 'She's got this sort of nephew – well, more like a grandson, in actual fact. Terry's his name. He had the idea of her having a party while she's got the run of the place. It's on Friday.'

'Seems a good idea,' said Jonathan. 'She's

breaking out, isn't she – borrowing Helen's car and now this? A bit like a child playing pranks.' He had noticed the Volvo's absence and without mentioning Terry, Sue had described the escapade.

'Well I expect she's not far off getting senile,' said Sue carelessly, shocking Jonathan. She came out with these callous remarks at times. 'It's not much of a party, really,' Sue went on. 'Just three old girls from the village she's met. To pay back hospitality, you know.'

'And this Terry? He's coming?'

'Oh – him. Yes, he'll be there,' said Sue.

Jonathan imagined a gangling lad of seventeen or so. When he met Terry, and found him to be a confident young man in his early twenties, he was so happy for Mrs Armitage. How nice for her to have this relative, who was being so attentive to her as they made the room ready for the party. Once, he thought he saw Terry wink at Sue, but decided he must have imagined it.

By the night of the party, the Volvo was safely back in the barn. Mrs Hawkins from the body repair shop had telephoned on Thursday morning to say it was ready, and Alice had ordered a taxi to take her to fetch it. She had examined the shining door and wing. Not a trace of what had happened could be seen. She had paid by cheque with her banker's card and had driven away with the greatest care.

Terry was put out, when later he arrived full of plans to collect it the following day, the day of the party, and found himself forestalled. But he rallied when Alice produced her new electric blanket and asked him to fit its plug. She had bought a new electric kettle, too.

Euphoric at having pulled off the small coup of the safe return of the car and the exclusion of Terry from its recovery, Alice found herself easily whisked into a state of some excitement about the party. The guests from the village all arrived together. Barbara Duncan had brought the other two in her white Allegro. All were anxious to see how the interior of Harcombe House had been altered by its new owners.

The Armitages had bought the house from Mr Goring's executors. During his last years, ill-health had turned him into a recluse, and little maintenance had been done to the house. Rather as Alice now dwelt in an attic area, he had existed in a few of the main rooms attended by a resident nurse and a succession of housekeepers. A desperate niece had the task of supervising this menage; she came once a month, dealt with the prevailing crisis, hiring a new nurse or housekeeper when required from the relevant agencies, and departed hoping that all would stay tranquil until her next visit.

When Mr Goring died, the house remained empty for nearly two years after failing to reach its reserve at an auction held just as the property market slumped. From time to time there were various rumours in the village about possible buyers, and occasionally a man from the estate agent's office handling the sale showed people round, but no one displayed real interest until the Armitages offered a price which the niece, the main legatee, decided to take. The village sighed with relief; there were fears that the executors, anxious to wind up Mr Goring's affairs, might let it go to a developer who would tear down the main house and build an estate, thus putting Harcombe on the map. But in the present economic climate there was not enough demand for that sort of housing in the district. By the time the Armitages' furniture vans were seen edging down the lanes, only minor interest was shown in their arrival. The house was so far out of the village, and had been a lost cause for so long, that no one cared any more. Helen Armitage asked in the shop about help in the house, and Mrs Rogers produced her sister-in-law, Mrs Wood, who was glad of the job and the run of the place to herself. She, in turn, sent along her uncle, just made redundant at a Westborough canning factory, when a gardener was required.

Barbara Duncan had not ignored the new arrivals. She had waited for several weeks after they moved in to give them time to settle and also to appear in church, the pre-war signal that the lady of the house was now ready to receive callers, but no Armitages appeared among the congregation. On the day she went to the house, workmen were papering and painting, but no one else was at home. Mrs Armitage was at her showroom in Newbury, Mr Armitage at his office, and the old lady hadn't yet moved in. Barbara had meant to call again, but one way and another, she hadn't done so. The fact that the younger Armitages were out all day meant they were busy and unlikely to have much in common with her. Their natural friends would be younger people whom they'd meet in due course, though there was little social life in the village since it lacked a community building and rarely set up any fund-raising events of its own. The Armitages would find their friends outside the village, Barbara felt, for their life style was likely to be far in advance of anything anyone else in Harcombe maintained.

There were lights on in the lodge as the three ladies drove by.

'Who's living there now?' asked Nancy Wilson.

'The girl works at the Rigby Arms,' said Barbara, who had learned this from her cleaning woman. 'The young man's a salesman of some kind. They're not married.'

She parked the car beside a blue Ford Escort near the barn and the three got out. It was a fine night, crisp and cold, freezing hard, and Nancy slithered on the icy approach to the front door, above which shone a welcoming light. There was an old-fashioned bell-pull which Barbara tugged, and almost at once a young man with curly hair opened the door to them, beaming.

'Come in, ladies,' he greeted them, ushering them in. 'I'm Terry. Let me take your coats.'

Alice appeared as the three ladies discarded their coats, scarves and gloves, which Terry swept up.

'Oh, Mrs Duncan, how nice that you could come!' Alice was a little flustered. She had had a pre-party glass of sherry, pressed on her by Sue, and so had sustained her mood of excitement. With natural colour glowing in her cheeks beneath her make-up, dressed in a pale grey knitted suit, she looked pretty and elegant. Pity she didn't let her hair go its natural colour, thought Barbara, running a hand over her own iron-grey head in case her set had been disturbed.

While Terry hung the coats in a cupboard, Alice led her guests into the big drawing-room. The tinsel tree – Helen wouldn't have a real fir tree – had gone. Mrs Wood had been detailed to strip it and pack it and the baubles up in their boxes, and this had been done on her only visit since Christmas. But there were chrysanthemums in pottery vases, and the room with its blazing log fire looked warm and inviting. Terry had turned the heating up at the thermostat and the old boiler roared away loudly in the cellar. Terry had gone to look at it and was amazed at its age.

'It's prehistoric,' he'd said.

He could not understand the delay in installing a new heating system. If you lived in a place this size, it meant you had an income that could support it, or limitless credit. Why wait? Why wait for anything, if you could make sure of it now?

'How lovely you've made this room!' exclaimed Nancy Wilson. 'I used to come here to see Mr Goring before he got really ill.'

The old man had admired Nancy and had

mildly courted her for years. They both studied the market and gambled a little, he in large amounts and she in small ones. His sound advice had helped her to increase her modest investment income. She'd enjoyed his company, and before he grew too frail to go out, had dined with him in various restaurants once or twice a month. He had left her two thousand pounds in his will, most of which she had spent on a Greek cruise.

Violet, whose own husband had died during this time, had been surprised that Nancy had refused Mr Goring's proposals of marriage.

'I'd only be an unpaid housekeeper-cum-nurse who could never give notice,' Nancy had said. 'I'm not going to marry anyone just for a meal ticket.' The price would have been too great, and when the old man lingered on for another six years, she was thankful she had kept her head – and, indeed, her personal integrity.

She and Violet had known each other since their school days and when Violet moved into Nancy's cottage they had extended it, building on a big new kitchen and a second bathroom so that each had her separate bedroom and bathroom.

'Have you met Sue and Jonathan?' Alice was introducing. 'From the lodge?' She had decided to present the pair in this way, without their surnames, to play down their unmarried status.

Barbara began talking to Sue while Jonathan asked the other two ladies about their garden, and Terry soon appeared with their glasses of sherry. Everyone discussed how they had spent

Christmas. Barbara had visited her married son in Dorset and told Terry all about it, including the full tale of her drive each way through fog and frost. Terry listened with earnest attention, but all the time he was assessing her. Oldish, but healthy, he decided, and muscular too. She wore two good rings, and her woollen dress, in which she seemed a cylindrical shape, was expensive. You could always tell.

'And what do you do?' she suddenly asked him. 'Where do you live?'

'Oh, I've a place near Swindon,' said Terry, implying a mansion. 'I do various things – buying and selling. I'm starting a new job soon, in actual fact.' He'd picked this expression up from Sue.

'Where?' asked Barbara.

'Locally. I'll be moving to Westborough,' Terry said, and moved smoothly away to top up the glasses before she could ask any more questions. Nosy old thing, he thought; he was incapable of distinguishing genuine – or at least civil – interest from curiosity.

Jonathan was now discussing roses with Violet; and Sue, who was wearing dark red silk trousers and a black velvet top and looking very pretty, helped Alice hand round the tiny patties she had prepared. She had made them in Helen's kitchen, using the Aga. Some were stuffed with prawns, some with chicken, and there were cheese straws, and prunes wrapped in bacon.

'How lovely,' exclaimed Nancy, when these titbits appeared. She'd hoped there'd be something

120

nice to eat, and now she saw that they'd need no supper – perhaps a mug of soup, nothing more. Sometimes this luckily happened when you went out in the evening. She was always cast down at mere peanuts and crisps.

'What relation to you is Terry?' Nancy asked Alice at one point.

'Relation?' Alice was about to deny kinship when Terry himself appeared at her elbow with more prawn patties and broke in.

'How long have you lived in Harcombe, Miss Wilson?' he asked, to learn that it was longer than the extent of his life. Until she retired, Nancy had been an accountant, working for a time in Swindon, and then in Westborough with her own business. By the time they had finished this conversation Nancy had forgotten what she had originally wanted to know, and only remembered later, in bed, thinking about the party.

When the guests had gone, everyone set about clearing up. The women washed up while Terry vacuumed the carpet and Jonathan took the left-over bottles of sherry up to Alice's flat. When these tasks were done, and no trace of the party remained, Alice produced a pie from the Aga's oven, chicken and ham, with potatoes and carrots sliced into it under the crisp crust. There was wine, too – a bottle of burgundy. They sat round the table in Helen's kitchen enjoying this feast, all with good appetites in spite of Alice's cocktail fare. There was fresh pine-apple to follow. By the time all this was disposed of and the kitchen cleared, it was half-past ten.

Terry insisted on escorting Alice up to her flat, carrying what was left of the party food to put in her refrigerator. When he left, he managed to take with him, unseen by Alice, two of the bottles of sherry from the carton which Jonathan had taken upstairs.

He'd taken ten pounds from her unattended handbag – an easy thing to do during the day. He knew she would never miss it.

She'd noticed, however, that he was driving yet another car.

10

'**H**ow have you been, mother?' asked Giles on the evening of the family's return from the Alps. His conscience had troubled him during the fortnight away, for she would be quite alone most of the time, with not even Mrs Wood coming in to clean. He'd asked Sue to keep an eye on her, fearing that she might fall and break a leg, and no one would notice.

At the prospect of seeing Sue again, Giles's spirits had risen as he sat beside Amanda in the plane coming back. Helen and Dawn were across the aisle, seated near new friends they had made on the ski slopes. Dawn had enjoyed a holiday romance and was engloomed at the prospect of parting from her beloved; Amanda, on the other hand, was looking forward to seeing her dear Mr Jinks again.

As soon as the bags were in the house and the car put away, Giles hurried up to his mother's flat.

Alice had been watching for the Rover and had hurried down to greet them. Then she'd run back again, for perhaps Helen would not want to find her in the main part of the house. She was just about to run downstairs for the second time when she heard Giles's tread on the back stairs. They met on the landing and embraced gingerly. He never held her warmly.

'Safely back, then,' said Alice, ignoring his enquiry about her, wise tactics when anyone asked how one was, for no one really wanted to know. 'Have you had a good time? Was the weather good?' She had received two postcards, one from Giles and one from Amanda, two days earlier, and knew that it had snowed a lot. Amanda had mentioned an avalanche.

'Very pleasant,' said Giles heartily. In spite of three days of heavy snowfall when skiing was restricted and tempers grew strained, he had enjoyed it more than other such holidays. Helen had quickly made friends, so they had seen very little of one another. Giles's skiing had progressed and he had been on some runs with Amanda, who waited patiently for him at the bottom of steep stretches of piste. His life could improve if they stayed friends, but she would develop new interests as she grew older and would even, like her sister, have romances, a thought he found hard to bear. 'And you, mother?' he repeated, peering anxiously at her. The light on the landing was dim. 'You're fit?'

'Yes, dear, thank you,' said Alice. She wanted to hear the girls' tales of prowess, vicariously enjoy some of their pleasures. 'I was coming down to welcome you,' she added.

'No need for that,' Giles said, patting her arm.

Helen had said, as they entered the house, 'For

124

God's sake don't let your mother get under my feet now, Giles. I've got a lot to organize.' She wanted, the next day, to go to her shop where some fabric ordered from France should have arrived. The girls were going to a party across the county and would have to be driven. There would be mail to deal with, enquiries and orders. She knew that Alice and Mrs Wood between them would have obeyed her written instructions about thawing a casserole from the freezer and putting it in the oven for their evening meal.

Alice had delayed boiling her cod in butter sauce in its polythene bag, hoping they would ask her to share the casserole while she heard about the holiday, but now she saw it was not to be.

Giles, who had noticed with relief that his mother looked well, saw the droop of her thin shoulders.

'No problems?' he asked, still in hearty voice.

'None,' said Alice, crossing her fingers at the lie and thinking of the Volvo, safely in its usual place.

'I'll pop up later,' said Giles.

Would he? He might not, and then he'd feel guilty. Alice let him off.

'Don't bother, dear,' she said. 'It's late and you've plenty to do if you're to get off on time in the morning. There are so many letters waiting. Come another time.' She smiled at him brightly, too brightly.

Giles took the raft she had floated towards him.

'Soon, then,' he promised, patted her arm again and lumbered away down the stairs. He was getting so heavy, unlike his father who had kept his trim figure all his life. Alice blinked back tears as she returned to her flat.

Amanda came, however, in her dressing-gown, just as Alice, who in the end had had no appetite for the cod, was drinking some Horlicks.

'Oh good, Gran, I thought you'd be having your night-cap,' said Amanda. 'Can I have some?' She loved Horlicks. Helen did not encourage milky drinks; the extra calories, she said were bad for the figures of growing girls.

'Of course you can, darling,' said Alice, brightening at once. 'It's only instant. There's not enough milk for ordinary.'

'That's all right,' said Amanda magnanimously.

Alice cheered up as the kettle boiled and she mixed the drink in the mug with the Smiley face on it which Amanda liked.

'Mince pie?' she asked.

'Mm, please,' said Amanda, who had already eaten two with her meal. 'It's lovely and warm up here tonight, Gran. What have you done?' Then her gaze fell on the new convector heater. 'Oh, you've got a new fire,' she said. 'That's good. About time.'

Alice had forgotten the need for secrecy and had not hidden the fire when she heard the car. Would Amanda mention it to her mother? Alice worried away for a minute or two, wondering whether to ask Amanda not to, then decided that she could not make the child a partner in a conspiracy against her own mother. She would have to risk it, and, if Helen made trouble, have some sort of show-down.

Thus bravely resolved, Alice settled down to hear Amanda's account of the holiday and was soon laughing at the girl's barbed description of her sister's swain.

Terry came striding through the entrance doors of the Rigby Arms into the oak-panelled restored Tudor foyer and walked up to the reception desk. Sounds of typing came from the office beyond, whose door was open, and he rang the bell on the counter.

Almost at once, Sue came through the doorway, her dark hair swept up round her small, neat head into a French pleat, making her look strangely austere. The professionally attentive expression she wore on her face was replaced by a look of surprised delight when she saw Terry.

'What are you doing here?' she asked him.

'I've come to see you, haven't I?' said Terry, grinning.

'I'm on duty. I can't really talk,' said Sue. 'Bruce will be here soon to go through the bookings.' Bruce Troughton was the manager.

'I'll take you back when you finish,' said Terry.

'Great,' said Sue. On this shift they could have more than two hours together before Jonathan came home.

'I thought I'd go over now and see the old lady,' said Terry. 'I might take her out for a spin somewhere.'

'You're not working.' It was a statement, not a question.

'Not just now,' Terry agreed. 'I'm looking around, in actual fact. Anything going here?' He gazed about him at the heavily beamed hall which had an oak settle against one wall and a log-effect electric fire in the hearth. Sporting prints hung on the walls.

'Like what?' asked Sue.

Terry shrugged.

'I can do most things,' he said. 'Bar, maybe?' There would be chances, there, to fiddle the till. 'Or maybe there's a vacancy for a waiter.' He flourished an imaginary table-napkin over his arm and said, in an affected voice, 'I can thoroughly recommend the scampi, madam.'

Sue giggled, then frowned, furrowing the smooth pale skin of her forehead.

'Not at the moment,' she said. 'We're fully staffed.'

'Pity,' said Terry. 'It'd be nice to be here with you.' He wanted to stay in the area while their plans, still not discussed, evolved, and he would have to get a regular job for a while as he needed a car for visiting Harcombe. He couldn't start taking them from Westborough; the town was too small and the police would soon notice and be on the alert. He would buy some clapped-out old heap that would last as long as he needed it.

Sue was leaning towards him over the counter, and he reached across, walking his fingers along her arm in its black cardigan, worn over a plain white blouse. She shivered. He turned her on as no one else had ever done.

'We'll have to see,' she said. 'Something might turn up.'

'See you later,' said Terry, and walked away, his head an aureole of crisp curls against the pale sky as he went through the doorway, not looking back. In that moment it seemed to Sue that if she were never to see him again she would die.

She had never felt like that in her life, never felt such acute desire. The urgency of it forced everything else to the back of her mind. Since leaving school, her one aim had been to protect and promote her own well-being, heedless of any person or object that got in her way, for no one else was likely to do it for her. Jonathan had been the exception; he cared for her, and for a while she had weakened, feeling kindly towards him, but now she was bored. His devotion was cloying; there was no spare money for discos or even the cinema; and since Christmas he had started to talk about Hilary and the children in what seemed to Sue a stupid, soppy way. They had had several rows, with Sue accusing him of wishing he had never left home, and Jonathan retorting that it was all her fault that he had. They had made it up, each time, in the usual way – in bed. But now, in the evenings, Jonathan spent more and more time sitting glumly silent and brooding.

Without thinking too much about the future, Sue knew that it would not last, though she would not leave Jonathan until she had something better lined up. Now Terry had come into her life and she saw in him someone akin to herself, someone quick to seize the moment. When he was around, she felt able to tackle things she'd never dreamed of before.

Like finding him a job at the Rigby. Bar work, he'd said.

There were two on duty in the bar at night: George, the regular barman who lived in the town and had worked at the hotel for years, acting also as cellarman in conjunction with the wine waiter. In the evenings a rota of married women worked with George, who managed alone at midday with occasional help from her or the other receptionist, or sometimes the manager, if he was pressed – say, at weekends or on market day.

Every day, certain duties had to be done in the cellar. The pipes must be cleared after switching off the night before – the stale beer in them emptied. The barrels had to be spiled, the taps cleaned. Fresh supplies had to be taken up to the bar and stacked neatly behind what was already beneath the counter – bottled beer, spirits, mineral waters. New stock had to be checked in when deliveries came. George spent a lot of time down there in the morning, before the bar opened, carrying out these regular tasks. It was his job, too, to turn the beer on every day, and to turn it off at night, and to turn on and off the CO_2 for the keg beer.

Each day he came to the office to fetch the key before going down there. He had already completed his routine work today.

Sue did not plan it consciously. She just let it happen spontaneously when the chance arose the morning after her talk with Terry.

When George came into the office to collect the key, there was no one around. No one waited by the desk for Sue's attention; the guests checking out had already gone and the telephone was silent. Bruce Troughton was conferring with the chef about a forthcoming Rotary dinner.

Sue quietly followed George, hanging back while he unlocked the cellar door and turned on the light, then began to descend the old stone steps. He never heard her behind him, though he felt the sudden hard push she gave him in the small of his back and he gave one faint, gasping cry as he fell. He struck his head on a keg near the foot of the steps and then lay silent.

Sue had not waited. She was back behind the reception desk answering the telephone before he lost consciousness. The manager, passing the open cellar door some time later, was the one who found him.

George was not dead, but he was still unconscious when removed in the ambulance and he had broken one leg and some ribs. It was possible that he had fractured his skull. X-rays would show the extent of his injuries. He was not a young man to sustain such a fall, and his condition was serious.

Sue's intention had simply been to get him out of the way but she felt no remorse when she heard how badly he had been hurt; she was glad. He wouldn't remember what had happened.

Meanwhile, the Rigby Arms urgently needed a barman. Bruce's immediate plan was to enlist the aid of the women who worked there regularly while he sought someone, but Sue told him she knew of an experienced barman who might be free. She was not certain if he understood cellar work, but no doubt that could quickly be learned.

When Bruce saw Terry – young, but not too young, clean, conventionally dressed, he thanked his stars. He accepted Terry's explanation that he was between jobs because he had just returned from abroad, and alas, his references had temporarily got lost. He could supply addresses, if the manager wanted to check, but – and here Terry took a chance, but you had to when the stakes were high – Mrs Armitage senior, at Harcombe House, knew him well, and would vouch for him.

The old lady wouldn't be able to say a word against him. Thanks to him, she was living in far greater comfort than before, and he had proved himself honest over money when buying the heaters.

Bruce took Terry on at once, and gave him a room in the staff quarters where he and Sue made frenzied love during her lunch break before he went off to Swindon by bus to fix himself up with a car and collect his belongings.

Sue did not tell him how George's accident had occurred.

Bruce intended to ring Mrs Armitage up about Terry when he had a moment, but he kept putting it off because there was so much else to do straight away. Terry soon proved his competence, and it seemed pointless, then, to bother.

11

The staff at the Rigby Arms were shocked at George's accident. It was hard to accept that such a thing should happen after so many years of daily descents to the cellar.

'Maybe he had a heart attack,' Sue suggested while she and Bruce Troughton were having lunch at a corner table in the restaurant after most of the guests had finished. She was eating a large rare steak; she felt very hungry, more so than usual, though she always ate well and enjoyed her perk of a first-class meal elegantly served.

'You could be right,' said Bruce. 'He is getting on a bit, after all. It can happen to anyone.' It had happened before now to guests, involving their hasty removal from the public area, which was hard to combine with proper concern for the victim. 'It was lucky your friend Terry Brett happened to be free. At least it will give us time to find someone permanent, if George isn't able to come back.'

'Yes,' agreed Sue demurely, piling *pommes frites* and cauliflower on to her fork and wondering what sweet to choose; the cold trolley held a wide choice but the chef had made steamed syrup pudding today and she rather fancied that.

'I do hope poor George will be all right,' Bruce went on. He had had the sad task of telling George's wife what had happened, considering it part of his duty.

Sue thought it would be so much easier all round if he wasn't. She cut into her steak from which the blood oozed pinkly. George was old; he'd nothing left to live for, she thought, dismissing him.

Giles, postponing his return home that evening with a visit to the Rigby Arms, was surprised to find Sue still there, for her shift should have ended in the afternoon. She was behind the bar with Mavis, one of the regular barmaids, and a new young barman with a mop of crisp brown curls.

She seemed pleased to see him.

'This is Mr Armitage, one of our regulars,' she said to Terry, nudging his leg with her knee so that he paid extra attention. 'He likes a double Scotch with ice and soda. That's right, isn't it?' and she smiled at Giles in such a way that his heart turned over. She looked like a ballet dancer, he thought, so small and slight, with her pale oval face and her smooth dark hair drawn back in its pleat. What would that hair look like spread out on a pillow? It would be like fragrant silk. He dragged his mind back to the present.

'What's yours – both of you?' he invited, taking a ten-pound note from his wallet.

'Oh, thank you very much,' Sue said promptly. 'We'll have it later, if that's all right with you.' She did not have to explain to Terry how this was done, the money stacked and saved for the end of the day; he knew all about that sort of thing. 'Terry's helping out,' she explained to Giles. 'George is in hospital.'

'I'm sorry to hear that,' said Giles, gulping down most of his drink. 'Nothing serious, I hope.'

'He had a fall,' said Terry. 'He broke his leg.'

'Oh dear. That means he'll be off for some time,' said Giles.

'Could be,' said Terry, polishing a glass. He moved away to attend to another customer, not liking to think about George in pain.

'And you're lending a hand too?' Giles said to Sue.

'Just getting Terry started,' said Sue. 'It's a while since he's worked in a bar. He's got to get used to the prices and that.' He was good, though; he had just the right way with the customers. She felt proud, watching him pull beer, getting the head on the glass just right. 'He'll be all right now, with Mavis,' she said, and knew what would follow. It did.

'Like a lift home?' Giles asked.

'Please,' said Sue, with that quick curving smile which lit up her serious face. She had rung Jonathan to say she'd be late because of George's accident and that she'd telephone when she could

136

get away. Jonathan had grumbled a bit. Although they had no money to spare, he had intended to take her out to dinner that evening. He wanted to try to recapture some of the earlier magic.

Sue had wanted to spend all the evening there in the bar with Terry – go back with him to his room, even if only for just a short time since Jonathan would wonder why she wasn't ready at closing time. But it would have been tricky: there were the barrels to close down, the CO_2 to turn off – all the late-night routine work which Bruce would be going through with Terry tonight and for some time until he could do it alone.

Now Giles had come, and that was great. Sue didn't know quite what she hoped for from him; she had never blackmailed anyone for money, and she didn't yet know that this was Terry's main occupation, but Giles was rich and knew important people. Faces familiar on television had been seen at the parties at Harcombe House. Through Giles she, and Terry too, now, might enter that glittering world. Opportunity would come, if she cultivated Giles; besides, it was always a challenge to try to make a man; to Sue it was automatic.

Driving back to Harcombe with Giles, she gave no thought to George, felt no guilt.

George died in the night.

The police came round to the Rigby Arms the next morning. There would have to be an inquest, Detective Sergeant Rivers explained to Bruce, and he must present an account to the coroner of how the accident happened.

'It's shocking,' said Bruce, collecting his jacket from the back of his chair and putting it on. He was never seen in the public part of the hotel dressed other than formally in his dark jacket and pinstriped trousers. People needed to know who was in charge and he did not want to be mistaken for a guest. 'He'd been down those steps hundreds of times – thousands, probably – in his working life, and never once, as far as I know, even stumbled. Now this.' Bruce was very distressed; he had been fond of George, a most reliable man.

He took Detective Sergeant Rivers along to the cellar and unlocked the door with the duplicate key he had in his own set.

'Has anyone been down here since the incident?' asked Rivers, noticing how Bruce turned on the light at the top of the straight stone staircase with its uneven treads.

'Oh yes,' said Bruce. 'There's work done down here every day. I've been doing the routine myself, but I've taken on a temporary barman.' He explained what had to be done. Terry and he together had moved the stock that morning and cleared the pipes. 'George had been going to do these jobs when he fell,' Bruce went on. He remembered Sue's theory. 'Perhaps he had a heart attack?'

'Maybe,' said the sergeant. 'The post-mortem will show what he died of.' That was in progress this morning. The hospital thought that the head wound had been the cause of death, but a heart attack would account for the fall.

'People must have been coming up and down here for centuries,' said Bruce. 'There was an inn here three hundred years ago.'

'Is that so?' Rivers was unimpressed. He had lived in the area all his life and was familiar with its heritage; he had visited many an old tumble-down cottage and many a renovated one, too. 'Dangerous, though,' he commented. 'No rail.' He indicated the sheer drop to the right of the steps. On the left was the painted brick wall.

'I suppose it could be – well, falling down any staircase could be dangerous,' said Bruce. The steps were so narrow that fitting a banister rail would have restricted the freedom of a man carrying boxes of bottles up the stairs. 'I don't think George thought of them as dangerous,' Bruce went on. 'You're always careful carrying bottles.' He wondered about the insurance; the hotel was well covered in case of accident to an employee and such matters were usually settled smoothly, but it would be unfortunate if there were to be any suggestion of negligence.

'He had his own key?' asked Rivers.

'No. He collected it from the office,' said Bruce.

Rivers examined the area. There was a small stain on one of the worn flagstones of the floor, and he looked at it carefully. The dead man had sustained a head wound of great severity and the skin had been broken, though it had not bled severely. Most head wounds bled freely and Rivers had expected to find evidence of this at the scene of the accident, but the keg on which George had struck his head had already been replaced with a fresh one.

The stain had best be examined, Rivers decided, circling it with a piece of chalk, but there had been so much traffic up and down the steps since the accident that any evidence of how it had happened would be covered with more recent traces.

'We have to make sure it was an accident, Mr Troughton,' Rivers explained, and when Bruce looked puzzled, he added, 'I mean, that he wasn't pushed.'

'Pushed? George!' Bruce was appalled. 'What a dreadful idea! Who would want to push poor old George down the stairs?'

'It doesn't seem likely, I agree,' said Rivers. 'But we have to be certain. Now, who would have known that he would be going down there?'

'Everyone,' declared Bruce. 'All the staff, that is. As I say, it was routine.'

'And he went at the same time each day?'

'More or less. He comes – came on at ten. He works – worked late, you see.' He had had time off every afternoon.

Rivers nodded.

'I'd like you to keep people out of here, just for a while, Mr Troughton,' he said. 'We'll want to look around. It won't take too long.'

'The wine waiter may need to come down,' Bruce warned.

'Well, I expect that can be managed,' said Rivers.

140

Traces from him must already be present in the cellar. 'And I'd like to see the staff. Every one of them. Find out who was about that morning and may have seen him.'

'It's quite possible that no one did,' said Bruce. 'Just the duty receptionist when he collected the key. She'd be busy in the office. The domestic staff would be working upstairs – all the public rooms, except the restaurant, which is wanted for breakfast, are cleaned early.'

'Anyone with a grudge against the deceased could slip down, though,' said Rivers.

'Well – yes, I suppose so. But no one had a grudge against him,' said Bruce.

'I expect you're right, Mr Troughton,' said Rivers. 'But it's my job to make sure.'

While he was making the necessary arrangements word came through from the hospital that the post-mortem had shown no sign of a heart attack; for his age, George's heart was in good condition. A thorough enquiry must be made to establish that no foul play had occurred.

Sue was the first of the staff to be interviewed.

She said she had not seen George the morning of the accident, though usually they exchanged a few words when he fetched the key. She might have been in the washroom when he came for it; he would simply have taken it from the desk drawer, which she had unlocked earlier after opening up when she came on duty.

'Did this often happen?' asked Rivers.

'You mean, was I often in the washroom when George fetched the key?' asked Sue, bristling slightly.

'I mean, did he often fetch the key without your knowledge,' said Rivers patiently.

'Sometimes,' said Sue. 'If I was busy with a guest, for instance, I might not notice him.'

'And you didn't notice that he hadn't brought it back?' asked Rivers.

'I never thought about it,' said Sue, truthfully.

It took the police some time to question everyone. No one had specifically seen George go down to the cellar that morning but some of the kitchen staff had spoken to him when he arrived and found him in his normal cheerful frame of mind. Everyone knew his cellar visits were routine.

Detectives inspecting the cellar found nothing suspicious. There were no fingerprints that could not be accounted for and explained as belonging to someone with a reason for being in the cellar.

Sue had touched nothing: not the door, nor the light, nor the wall: only George, and he could not tell.

The inquest was opened and adjourned to allow time for tests on various organs. These would show if the deceased had taken any drugs which might have made him giddy. Bruce Troughton, having found the body, had attended the inquest. The widow was there, dressed in grey, her face pale and drawn, her married daughter beside her.

'Everything can change so suddenly,' the

daughter said to Bruce. 'In minutes – just like that. No warning. That's the hard part.'

'I know. It's dreadful,' said Bruce. 'We'll miss him a lot,' he added, and went on to offer what personal help he could with the funeral arrangements.

'He'd have been retiring in two years,' said the widow, dry-eyed, still in shock. 'We'd so many plans.' She looked bleakly at Bruce.

'I'm very sorry,' said Bruce again.

'They said he wouldn't have known anything about it,' said the daughter. 'He never came round. That's a comfort. But there was no goodbye.' Her soft, pretty face crumpled as she began to weep.

Bruce drove them home and rang the undertaker. The funeral could go ahead now, and was arranged for the following Thursday, the earliest date the crematorium could offer, for January was always a busy month.

Sue learned the result of the inquest when Bruce returned to the hotel. He explained about the adjournment, saying this was usual.

'Upsetting for the family,' he said. 'Means it's all to do again.'

'Can I help at all?' asked Sue. 'We want to have a collection among the staff – for a wreath, you know. I'm arranging it.' It had been the housekeeper's idea.

'Oh, good,' said Bruce, who hadn't got that far in his thoughts. He pulled a ten-pound note from his wallet and gave it to her. 'I should order some nice flowers and give the balance to the family.'

'Some of the bar regulars might like to contribute to that,' Sue suggested. 'Shall I ask Terry to fix up a tin?'

12

Alice was surprised to learn that Terry was working at the Rigby Arms. She did not know he was free to take on a new job.

'Oh, I thought you knew I was looking for a change,' he told her airily.

'What exactly were you doing before?' Alice asked.

'I was an agent,' said Terry. 'I handled various lines. It was a bit up and down. Now I know where I am – regular hours and regular pay.'

'I thought you must be something to do with cars,' said Alice. 'You seemed to have a different one each time you came over, and you do know a lot about them.' She remembered how he had mended her Metro that day.

He hadn't thought that she'd be so observant.

'That was the firm's policy,' he improvised. 'They own a lot of cars and you just take whichever one's handy when you set out for the day.' He rushed on, before she could query this system. 'Of course, now that George has died, they'll be wanting a permanent barman at the Rigby, and I'm not sure about that, but I'm staying for the moment. I'll be able to come and see you often. I get time off in the afternoon because of all the late nights.'

Did she want that? Alice wasn't sure. Sometimes he made her uneasy, though she was grateful to him for making the flat so snug.

Terry's mind had turned towards Giles.

'I've met your son,' he told her. 'In the bar at the Rigby. He's one of the regulars.'

'Is he?' asked Alice, a slow dismay filling her.

'Didn't you know?' smiled Terry. 'Likes his drop, doesn't he? But he can hold it,' he finished, deciding that now he could end his visit. He hadn't seen the old girl for a few days because he'd been busy getting the hang of the job, and he was eager to see Sue; while she was on the early shift their hours restricted their time together.

He had brought Alice a plant in a pot, a small, rather weak cineraria he had bought in the market when the stall-holder had knocked down his prices at the end of the day. Alice sat staring at it while she pictured Giles in the bar, holding his drink.

She hadn't known about that. Oh, a drink or two, yes, like everyone else; but Terry implied that he was a heavy drinker. No wonder he gave Sue lifts so often.

She tried to put it out of her mind in the weeks that followed and went up to London three times, seeing two matinées and a film, though there was little on that appealed to her. She rang up her friend Audrey in Bournemouth several times but could get no reply. She went to supper one evening with Violet Hedges and Nancy Wilson, and then worried for days about how to invite them back, at last telling Terry, who said she must take them to dinner in a restaurant.

How easy it seemed, when he made the suggestion. He was perfectly right, yet she hadn't been able to think of the idea for herself. She'd no one to talk things over with; only Terry, when he came on his brisk visits. Gradually Alice's reservations about him were dispersed. She found herself looking forward to seeing his cheerful face and curly head. How springy those curls must be if you touched them. She supposed he had lots of girlfriends.

'Well, I have had,' he admitted, when she asked him one day, teasingly. 'But now there's just one. Someone rather special.'

'Who?' asked Alice, and then, frowning, added, 'Not Sue, is it?' She knew he saw Sue most afternoons, for the old red VW he drove now was parked outside the lodge every day. He brought her back when she was on the first shift, and took her into the Rigby Arms when she was on the late one, for in each case he, himself, was free until just before opening time after his lunch-time stint.

'No, you silly,' said Terry. 'It's you, isn't it?' and he laughed at her in a kindly way.

It was all just his fun. He was such a joker, thought Alice. He certainly cheered her up.

A verdict of accidental death was returned at the resumed inquest on the dead barman. No trace of any drugs had been found in his body, and there was nothing to show why he had slipped. His shoes had been examined and were sound: no loose edge of sole could have caught anywhere, no slippery substance adhered to them. He might have felt suddenly giddy, though there was no trace of disease. The wound to his head was the cause of death; possibly he had toppled forward as he fell and in this way could have caught it against a keg. It was suggested that a hand rail be fitted to the cellar steps to avoid another such accident.

Sue, by this time, had almost forgotten the part she played in the incident. More important to her, now, was the deterioration in her relationship with Jonathan. Since Christmas he had become increasingly morose. He was often irritable, constantly complaining about her short-comings. When she was on the early shift, why couldn't she have a meal waiting in the evening? Didn't she want to eat too, in spite of the fancy lunch she had every day? And couldn't she at least shop for food when she was on late herself, leave something ready for him to cook? They must pull together, he said; work out a system. Couldn't she do the washing sometimes? He seemed to be always the one who went to the launderette, and no one but him ever used the vacuum cleaner or dusted round.

Often, it ended in argument, with loud, angry shouts from Jonathan who then stormed out of the lodge and went off for a furious walk round the lanes, even at night. Sue sometimes wondered if he would be run over on one of these nocturnal expeditions. But there wasn't much traffic around Harcombe at night.

Jonathan was finding Sue's careless ways increasingly hard to bear. He was tired of collecting her dirty clothes from wherever she let them fall. He was tired of finding no bread in the house when he came back from work, and only cheese in the refrigerator. But he still liked to hold that thin, insatiable body in the crumpled double bed.

One day, returning the children after a weekend spent with them at his parents' home, Jonathan hovered beside the car while he watched them walk up the path to the front door of the house where they had lived for all their short lives. Hilary stood there, waiting for them. On impulse, Jonathan strode up the path to speak to her.

'Hilary,' he said. 'Don't – ' He wanted to stop her from closing the door in his face.

'What is it?' She faced him, the children, inside the house, peering round her at him. Her eyes were hostile in her pale face. She had lost a lot of weight, he noticed.

'Oh – I just wondered if you were all right. Is there anything you want done? Any little jobs in the house?' he asked.

'You've made it very clear that you don't want that sort of responsibility,' said Hilary.

'You hate me, don't you?' said Jonathan.

'Are you surprised?' asked Hilary curtly.

'Couldn't we – couldn't we be a bit more friendly?' he pleaded, and looked down at the children who stared back at him, round-eyed. 'For them?'

'You should have thought of that before,' said Hilary mercilessly. 'Goodbye, Jonathan,' and she shut the door on him.

When he had gone, she burst into tears, quite frightening the two children.

Now, Jonathan was depressed and afraid. He saw no good long-term future with Sue, and if they parted, he would be quite alone.

Perhaps even that would be better than things as they were, he began to acknowledge, when Sue turned away from him in bed. She had never done that before.

Jonathan could not know that Sue had spent an extended session in this very bed with Terry that afternoon, and for the first time in her life was attaching emotion to the experience. Why should she bother with Jonathan, who was now so bad-tempered most of the time and had become such a nag? If she moved back to the Rigby Arms she would see much more of Terry but she would lose the opportunities to be alone in the car with Giles, which she knew Terry wanted her to take; Terry wasn't into the money, and Giles was.

'Would you want to live here, if you could? In the big house, I mean?' he'd asked her.

'Only if I could get away from it often enough,' said Sue, who did not know what she really wanted from life except an improvement on the present.

'To what? Bermuda or somewhere?' Terry quite

fancied spending a few weeks lolling in the sun, though after a while he'd probably want to move on to some fresh excitement.

'Something like that,' said Sue. She had been to Spain and to Greece with various fellows. The hotels, concrete blocks, had been poorly plumbed and their food didn't compare with the Rigby, whose chef was first class. 'I'd like the best,' she declared. 'Only the best for me,' and as she said it she smiled a slow, lazy smile.

'You could get that Giles, you know,' Terry had told her, his hand on her thigh. He had seen how the men watched her at the Rigby, seen how she lapped up their admiration. She fed on it. 'Make him fall for you, I mean. He's halfway there already. Then he'd give Helen the push and you'd have the lot. Old Alice, too – she'd like that. She doesn't go much on Helen, as we know.'

'You mean marry Giles?' Sue asked.

'If you like. In time,' said Terry. He traced a circle round her nipple; funny how they jumped up like that when you turned them on: some of those poor, bored cows on the estates hadn't known about that and were they grateful when they found out! 'Of course, I'd be part of the family too. We'd both be all right then.'

It was said, put into words between them at last.

'You'd have to make him think he couldn't live without you,' said Terry 'Like in bed.' Then, later, she'd have to make him pay for it.

Sue stroked the few pale wispy hairs on Terry's chest.

'I could get him in here easily enough,' she said. 'When Jonathan's off with his kids. I could say I needed strong masculine help for some job. He is the landlord, after all.'

'He's drinking a lot. You'd have to choose a good time,' said Terry. 'When he's able.'

'And before he drinks himself to death,' said Sue. 'He could do that afterwards, couldn't he? When we've got the lot.'

Giles was spending more and more time at the Rigby Arms. Until Sue and Jonathan moved into the lodge, his habit had been to stop at different bars on his way home; now, knowing Sue might be glimpsed behind the reception desk, he forsook his other haunts and went there every evening, though when she was on the early shift he missed her. Terry, however, always greeted him warmly and would talk to him in the intervals of serving other customers before the bar became crowded. Terry was acquiring the smattering of knowledge needed to keep conversation going among lonely men postponing returning home to their wives. He would run his eye down the sporting page of the paper every morning as soon as he opened up, gleaning the latest football, golf, or racing news. There was cricket in distant climes; there were sometimes athletic feats worthy of note. He could turn on the patter with ease.

Giles seemed uninterested in any sport. The state of the pound was more his concern, and Terry, who cared only about the pound in his pocket, not its international value, found that by nodding and making encouraging noises he could coax Giles into almost a monologue, which didn't require much effort. Mrs Armitage was quite a sporty old thing, in Terry's opinion, but her son was a pain. Terry found most of the older men in the bar a boring lot; things cheered up when the younger element came in later.

When Sue was on late, more and more frequently Giles stayed on until closing time and took her home. Sometimes he had something to eat in the restaurant – in the evening the Rigby did not serve meals in the bar. But often, drinking steadily, he forgot about food. Helen never waited for him; her arrangement was that she ate at eight; if he wasn't there, too bad. His meal was put in the Aga. Often it was still there in the morning, dried out but not quite a cinder. Helen never looked; she didn't want to know. It was Mrs Wood who daily investigated and removed the evidence. She had some sympathy with Giles; she thought Helen a hard piece and in her opinion the girls were left to themselves too much in the holidays, though they seemed to keep busy, what with the pool and the ponies, and they both played tennis, though the older girl was too good for her sister and often grew bored with the uneven game. Mrs Wood saw it all, from the separate bedrooms to the empty bottles that went out with the rubbish.

There was no risk of meeting Helen when Giles came home so late to the hostile house that he called home. He knew that some would call it beautiful, though in his eyes it was too grey, too cold, too gaunt with its high gabled roofs. Inside, the elegant decor reflected Helen's taste, and the furniture was right for the setting, but pieces he liked tended to disappear as Helen sold them to clients. She had a contact who bought items at sales, restored them as required, sometimes cutting them down to make them acceptable in smaller houses than those they had been designed to grace, and then passed them to Helen who would place them among her customers. Even her own bedroom, with its oak fourposter draped in cream silk, was not safe from this pillage. Various chaises longues had already moved in and out of it, and three different dressing-tables.

When he brought Sue home, Giles would stop at the lodge to let her out of the Rover, always with a single soft kiss on her warm mouth, and then drive on to the barn to garage the car. He drove carefully at a moderate pace, aware that if he made any error on the way back to Harcombe, or was involved in any one else's driving misdemeanour, he would fail a breathalyser test. For her part, Sue was not nervous with him. The distance was not great and there was seldom much traffic about once they left the town, and, as Terry had told Alice, he could carry his drink. It was the one thing about him, apart from his life style, that she admired. Drink made Giles neither cheerful nor aggressive; it merely dulled his misery.

Walking from the barn to the house after leaving the car, Giles was freed from the need to concentrate. He would gulp great breaths of the night air, and that, combined with the alcohol, would at last make him befuddled so that he often had difficulty unlocking the front door. Sometimes he stumbled in the hall or on the stairs, but in the end he would reach his bedroom, at the opposite end of the landing from Helen's. His bathroom – not yet renovated – was stark: an old-fashioned tub with curly feet; a mahogany-seated lavatory with a wood surround. Here, he would pour himself a glass of water into which, as a nightly routine, he dropped two alka seltzers. Then he would fall into bed, sleeping heavily, snoring. In the morning, three cups of strong black coffee and some aspirin would clear his head enough for the drive to work.

He had got much worse in recent weeks. Helen, glancing at him at breakfast in the kitchen, could see that. He had looked quite fit when they came back from their skiing holiday; now there were threads of veins on his nose and his colour was high.

She had noticed him drinking a lot on their honeymoon, which they spent in Greece. It was very hot, and they had swum and water-skied. Giles was a good swimmer, having grown up near the sea, but his natural balance was poor and he never stayed upright long on the skis. Helen, however, soon became expert. It seemed to him that she excelled at everything she attempted, and he could not believe his luck in capturing this wonderful girl.

He was the failure. Helen lay passive in bed, her

head turned away, enduring with martyred patience Giles's tentative efforts to stir her. He trembled with nerves, humble yet urgent. By the time they returned home he had begun to feel that he was gross and his touch an insult, and he had started to drink in a search for courage.

Once installed in their bright new house, Giles put all his energy into his new job, determined to succeed. It occupied his mind and took up much of his energy, so that he was able to ignore the bitter disappointment he already felt in his domestic life. Helen was still beautiful; she was his wife; and she was pregnant.

She was angry about that. She had not wanted a family yet – not until she had established herself in the best social circle available to them then. Later, because everyone had a pair of children to set them off, so would they. She had not allowed herself to dwell on the cruder aspect of the production process, but now she was made acutely aware of just how fundamental it was. She felt sick; soon her body grew ugly and heavy.

Giles, secretly exultant and proud, showed anxious concern. He hovered about, offering to fill hot-water bottles or make cups of tea. These were the only attentions she permitted for the whole of her pregnancy and for a long time afterwards. It was only when he had built up his nerve with several drinks that he ever dared to approach her intimately, and then his overtures were more often rebuffed than suffered. They had not been to bed together since Amanda's birth.

Giles no longer thought a great deal about this side of his life. He was not an overly sensual man, and because he had never experienced shared physical rapture he was not aware of what had been missed in his marriage. The family joined a country club; he swam, played tennis poorly and squash still worse, and enjoyed the company of his daughters who, when they were small, were very affectionate. He and Helen never quarrelled, but they communicated on an increasingly superficial level. The years went by, and the girls drew apart from him more as their outside interests grew. Sometimes Dawn looked at him, now, with an expression on her face just like her mother's, as if she despised him; but Amanda still twined herself round his neck when she came home from school and allowed him to help her with Mr Jinks. He thought that his life must be little different from that of many men. Others in his place would, he knew, look for a mistress, but he lacked the drive even for that. Whenever he felt unduly depressed, alcohol helped dull his thoughts. He had expected a big improvement after the move to Harcombe, building a fantasy in which, surrounded at last by the setting she craved, Helen would fall in love with him all over again. For surely she must have loved him once, or why had she married him?

Now he knew that this was a delusion. She had never loved him. She wanted a husband because girls of her class, in her generation, expected to marry, and early. He did not know what made her accept him for the role.

Helen had recognized his manageability. The husband she had to acquire must be one whom she would have no problems controlling and guiding into the pattern she ordained.

She had met other suitable men, but all had sheered away before making any commitment. Helen did not know that the appeal of her moneyed background and personal elegance had not been enough to outweigh the apprehensions of these other suitors. She would be hard to live up to; she would expect too much from them; above all, though she was lovely and desirable, she lacked warmth. The more experienced young men sensed that she would be difficult to arouse, and none of them put this theory to the test.

Helen, tireless where she was interested, was absorbed by her work and was often late home. She would notice that the Rover was still out when she parked her Volvo, but there were always patterns to match, plans to inspect, other details to attend to in her own sitting-room. She would have a drink, then help herself to the meal prepared by Mrs Wood and left ready. Sometimes there were dishes to heat through in the Aga; often there was a casserole dish or a pie already in the slow oven and a salad in the refrigerator. Helen ate sparingly, and she never put on weight. She would spend the evening in her sitting-room, working, or watching television. Giles, if he wanted to see some programme, used the girls' set in their sitting-room.

She would get his mother out in the end. That

was her long-term plan. At the moment Alice was useful. She took messages efficiently and dealt with minor matters when Helen was out. The moment she fell really ill or made any mistake, she would be condemned. She could go to some sheltered home or other, Helen thought; local councils ran places for elderly people, with wardens in charge. At some point she must put Alice's name down for somewhere appropriate that would not cost more than the old woman's pension.

The only cloud on Helen's horizon was the fact that her father's business had now been taken over and Giles would never be chairman. He had never had the ability. But he still had his job, which kept him out of the way all day and paid a large salary.

She might have to look into this drinking. She did not want him disgracing himself, making scenes, though that wasn't his style.

13

Sue was not one to waste opportunities. A chance came, and she took it. In just such a way she had, on impulse, enrolled for a short hotel training course when her husband left her with enough money to keep herself for a year. She had known about the course because a girl she was at school with had done it and had secured a job with a big hotel group. Sue saw hotel work as a way to move upwards; she had the tenacity to tackle the course because of the goal; she would meet a lot of people. You never knew who might book in at a good hotel, and what pickings there could be.

Now she turned her mind towards Giles. The idea of trapping him amused her, and she didn't think it would be difficult, but sometimes older men grew sentimental and Sue found that irksome. She thought he might be one of those.

Would she really consider marrying him? Marriage need not be permanent, but it put restraints on liberty. He was certainly rich and the idea of living in Harcombe House had its attractions. The first thing she'd do, if she moved in, was to sort out poor old Alice, give her a suite of rooms on the first floor and treat her properly. That was it, she thought: move in. There was no need to get married. But if Giles were to die, and they weren't married, she might not get the money. There was Helen to be got rid of, too. Perhaps Helen would take off when she knew about Sue. Like that Hilary, throwing Jonathan out. If Giles was thrown out, he and Sue would set up somewhere just as grand, Sue thought. And Terry would be there in the background, waiting.

In idle moments Sue's thoughts wandered along these attractive lines, and in the evenings, because she was on the late shift, Giles took her home. He had been doing this continuously, and at the weekend her shift would change.

In melancholy tones he mentioned this as they drove along.

'It won't be long till I'm on late again, you know,' Sue said lightly.

'It'll seem a long time to me,' mourned Giles. 'I'll be counting the days.' His heart beat fast at his own daring words.

Sue did not reply, but she moved a little in her seat, edging nearer to Giles although their seatbelts and the handbrake kept them apart. His heart was thundering. He peered out at the night as the black road rolled out ahead in the headlights. They turned into the lane, and the big, powerful car, a warm cocoon humming through the darkness, seemed to Giles to be heading for paradise. Tonight he did not stop at the lodge but drove straight into the barn, where he parked the Rover in its usual place and switched off the lights and the engine. Then he sat motionless, breathing heavily. He undid his seatbelt.

'What's this, then?' asked Sue, smiling in the darkness. 'Abducting me, are you?' She groped for the catch on her seatbelt.

'Here, let me,' said Giles. He fumbled about and freed it. Sue pulled it off as he clumsily seized her and began mumbling into her hair. 'How little you are, and how lovely,' she heard and then she felt schoolboy kisses landing all over her face.

She wanted to laugh. He really hadn't the least idea, she thought, turning her open mouth to him.

He hadn't. It was obvious, and Sue spared a moment of pity for Helen, who had been married to him for years. Even Jonathan had been in a more advanced grade than this, she thought, guiding his hand.

They couldn't do it here, in the car. It would be too uncomfortable, and he had drunk so much. In fact, she wondered if maybe he'd drunk too much altogether.

'Oh Giles,' she sighed, her fingers making sparks fly in his mind, as well as his body.

'Come into the house,' he croaked hoarsely. 'Come in with me, Sue. Helen's away.'

She was up in Yorkshire, inspecting work on a house she was decorating there.

'All right,' Sue breathed, and broke free. She got out of the car. A dim light filtered in from the lamp outside the barn enough for her to find her way round to the driver's side and help him extract himself.

Giles's head was swimming as they went together to the house. His arm was around Sue, but she was supporting more than embracing him.

Alice had heard the car return. She had watched from her window as it turned in at the barn without dropping Sue at the lodge, so she thought Giles was alone, but he didn't come out of the barn for some time. Alice began to worry. Was he ill? She stayed there, watching, until at last she saw them both moving together across the gravel sweep to the house, their arms entwined, a large dark blur of two bodies closely linked.

'Oh no!' she whispered aloud. 'Oh no, please!'

She stayed at the window, her mind refusing to accept what she had seen, until after some time she saw Sue return alone and walk down to the lodge, whose porch light still burned. Then the light snapped off.

Alice went to bed, but not to sleep.

Various explanations for what she had seen came into her mind, and each seemed as dreadful as another. The only one she could bear to admit was that Giles had been taken ill and Sue had seen him into the house and up to his room.

She decided to believe that theory. It was the safest.

When Jonathan heard the Rover pass the lodge without stopping, his first feeling was irritation. Now he would have to turn out to fetch Sue. He was sure she had said she would ring if she wanted a lift. Giles had brought her back every night that week, and Jonathan had been grateful. He was increasingly tired these days and it was no fun turning out on a cold night to collect her. This evening he had ironed eight shirts and cleaned the bathroom, which was filthy. Then he'd had a bath, dressed again in his flannels and jacket and gone to the Bull in Great Minton for steak and chips at the bar. He'd stayed quite late.

He went out to the window and looked across at the barn. The doors were still open, but sometimes Giles left them overnight and Jonathan, the first to leave in the mornings, found them so when he went to fetch the Granada. He let the curtain fall back. Giles spent too much time in the bar at the Rigby, but that was none of Jonathan's business. It had not yet crossed his mind to feel jealous; he imagined Giles in the bar, and Sue at reception, simply together in the car for convenience. It was his naiveté that had made Jonathan fall prey to Sue; until now the same innocent outlook had let him ignore the perils of propinquity.

He dialled the number of the Rigby Arms.

The telephone rang for several minutes before it was answered.

'Rigby Arms,' said a male voice.

'Who's that?' asked Jonathan. It might be the manager.

'Terry Brett, the barman,' said Terry. 'Can I help you?'

'Oh – Terry – this is Jonathan Cooper. Is Sue still there? Is she expecting me to collect her?' asked Jonathan.

164

Terry grinned to himself as he sat at the switch-board. It was lucky the call had come through before he switched the line to the manager's flat, as happened at night. Sue hadn't wasted much time. What now, though? He couldn't say Sue was still at the hotel and let Jonathan come over in vain. That would only start a hue and cry. He glanced at his watch. She'd had long enough, he thought; long enough for starters, anyway. The main course could follow another time. He could trust her to play her hand solo.

'Mr Armitage was giving her a lift,' he said. 'Perhaps they broke down?'

'No. His car's back, but Sue hasn't come in,' said Jonathan.

'Well, perhaps they're just having a chat,' said Terry soothingly.

'At this time of night?' said Jonathan. 'What sort of chat would that be?'

'You tell me,' said Terry silkily.

'Goodnight, Terry,' Jonathan snapped, and replaced the receiver. Then he began pacing round the room as scenes from the past came into his mind. He remembered Hilary angrily asking him why he was late, and his answer that he had met a man in a pub and had stayed talking too long. Then Hilary had asked who the girl was he'd been seen lunching with, who'd also been seen in his car. He had replied that she was a business colleague. There had been lies and excuses then on his side, with Hilary the one deceived. Sue had been free to do as she liked, and in a moment of revelation Jonathan saw that she would always want that freedom. The miscarriage that had ended her marriage – she had told him her husband had left her after that – had been the key that opened the door. There had been other men besides him; she had not denied it when he asked her.

'It's only fun, isn't it?' she had said.

Was it happening again, with Giles, who was ten years older than Jonathan, flabby and red-faced, already going to seed?

Was she out there in the car with him, smooching like some adolescent? She'd done it with him, after all.

Jonathan opened the front door, on the point of going to see; then drew back. What would he do if she was? And what if she wasn't – what if neither was there? The implication of that possibility was much more serious.

By the time Sue came back to the house, Jonathan had worked himself into a fit of jealous rage.

'Well, where have you been?' he demanded. 'In bed with Giles Armitage?'

She mustn't break with him yet. It was too soon for Jonathan to flounce out of the lodge. Tonight nothing had happened. Excitement and alcohol had proved too much for Giles and he had passed out as soon as they reached his room. Sue had left him sprawled on the bed. She had removed his shoes and tie, and covered him up, as she would for anyone over the top, and left him to sleep it off.

There would soon be another chance. Jonathan would be off visiting his kids again before long.

'He wasn't feeling well,' she said smoothly. 'I helped him into the house. Helen's away, so I made sure he was all right before leaving him. I gave him some aspirins.'

'Oh yes? And what else?' sneered Jonathan. 'Held his hand, I suppose, and bit more too?'

'What on earth's bugging you?' Sue demanded. 'I told you, he felt ill. He drinks too much,' she added.

'And whose fault is that? Your friend Terry's, I suppose,' said Jonathan, the blood pounding in his head.

'Terry just does his job,' said Sue.

'And what's that?' asked Jonathan. 'Next thing, you'll be fucking him too.' He hadn't meant to say it: the words seemed to rise up from some awful pit of suspicion deep in his brain. He stood glaring at her, his mind seething, and saw her slow smile. Suddenly, crystal clear, he realized what had been happening in the weeks since Christmas. There had been all those times when Terry had come over here, ostensibly visiting Mrs Armitage, the lifts that Terry had given her. 'By Christ, that's it!' he cried. 'It's been Terry in the morning and Giles at night, and I'm the poor sucker in the middle. You bitch!'

He raised his hand and struck her across the face.

It was a determined blow, and though tears of pain filled Sue's eyes, she didn't pause for thought.

167

She had seen her father go for her mother and pull fistfuls of hair from her mother's head; she had seen her mother's eye blacked. No man would ever do that to her. In one quick action, Sue looked round and saw the heavy iron poker in the hearth. She grabbed it and brought the handle down hard against Jonathan's temple.

He stared at her for one instant before his knees sagged and he toppled over.

Sue stood gazing down at him, panting, the poker still in her hand. He lay still.

'You bastard,' she said. 'That'll teach you to try that sort of thing on me.'

Jonathan did not move. Sue replaced the poker. She looked at him. Faking hurt, she thought, wanting her to fall on her knees and say she was sorry. Well, she wasn't. She'd do it again.

She went upstairs and got ready for bed. He'd soon give up his silly trick. But he didn't, and she fell asleep.

Some time later she woke, feeling hungry. She got up and went into the kitchen to find something to eat. There were some chocolate biscuits in a tin and she crunched up six with her sharp white teeth. Then she went into the sitting-room.

Jonathan still lay where he had fallen. He was dead.

Sue would not believe it at first.

'Get up, Jonathan,' she ordered, prodding him with her naked toe. His head was turned to one side, and she went down on her knees beside him, patting his cheek hard. Nothing happened, and she moved his head to face her. It was heavy, and flopped to the other side, the jaw open, the eyes staring. Sue shook him, and one arm that had lain across his body fell back with a thud to lie limply, the hand turned palm upwards, the fingers half curled.

Sue was terrified. She moved backwards, gazing down at him in horror and disgust. She'd only meant to stop him from hitting her again. What did he mean by going and dying? It wasn't fair.

What was she to do? She looked around the room as if something there would give her the answer, and saw the poker. She took it out to the kitchen and washed it thoroughly, wiping it dry before replacing it in the hearth.

The police, she thought: she ought to ring up the police. But they would want to know why she had not telephoned straight away. Leaving Jonathan lying on the floor for hours wouldn't look good. What about saying they'd thought they'd heard someone in the house and Jonathan had gone down to investigate? She could make it look as if someone had broken in. Yes, that was the thing to do. Then she remembered the bruise on her cheek. She could cover it with make-up but there was a mark and a tiny graze where his signet ring had broken the skin. They might notice and be curious. Sue felt a great reluctance to let the police come nosing around here. Suppose they grew interested again in George's accident and began asking about that? She felt concern for neither victim, but a lot for herself.

She sat down on the sofa to think. The room was cold now, and shock hit her; she began to shiver. That wouldn't help; she must keep her head.

Sue got up and crossed to the sideboard, where she poured herself a good tot of whisky from a half-empty bottle, their last. Then she went over to look at the body again. Why had he died? She had struck one single blow, and she could see no blood. Gingerly, she lifted a lock of his dark hair and saw bruising on his temple. There was a tiny abrasion; it had scarcely bled. His eyes stared up. She knew you should close a dead person's eyes, but she had never seen a corpse before and was aware only of revulsion. She went into the kitchen and fetched a white polythene bin liner which she put over Jonathan's head, biting her lip while she did it, concentrating on the task, heaving his heavy head up and rolling the bag over it.

That was better. Now he could not stare at her with those brown unblinking eyes. Next, she rolled him away to the side of the room where he would be out of the way. It was an effort; he was very heavy and his limbs flopped as she edged his torso over, using her knee and leg muscles. She tucked him neatly against the wall beside the storage heater. Then she fetched a spare blanket from upstairs and covered him up.

Terry would know what to do. She came to this decision as she tidied Jonathan away with the same concentration she showed in her work but lacked in domestic matters.

After that she went back to bed. She couldn't get hold of Terry until the morning.

The shuddering began again as she lay there in the darkness. Sue turned on the bedside lamp and sat up hugging her knees, telling herself not to be frightened. She had been afraid as a child and had overcome her fears; she had learned not to let her feelings control her head.

No one had suspected that George's death was not an accident. She had got away with that, and she would do the same now. Terry would know how to deal with things, he would be able to spirit Jonathan away.

She sat up in bed until the sky grew light.

No one saw the glow from the bedside lamp.

14

With the morning, confidence began seeping back. It was no good dithering and wondering what to do: that had never been Sue's way and now she could act.

The body lay where she had left it, a long mound under its blanket.

Sue made herself some strong black coffee and sat drinking it while she waited for the duty receptionist to start the early turn at the Rigby Arms. She wanted to by-pass the manager over this.

At last it was time. Sue asked Anthea to get Terry to ring her back as soon as he could.

'Jonathan's not well,' she added. 'But I'll be in as usual. It's lucky I'm on the late shift.' And after today, she had forty-eight hours free. Terry would think of something, somewhere to take Jonathan and get rid of him. Soon it would all be over.

As she ended the call, the milkman's float stopped in the drive and she heard his brisk step on the path. Sue remained motionless. Often, if she was up when he came, she would open the door and exchange some backchat with him; he was a cheerful middle-aged man who had been doing the village round for years. She heard the bottle clank down on the stone floor of the porch and his retreating tread.

She left the sitting-room curtains drawn, in case anyone looked in, though if they did, they wouldn't be able to see Jonathan who lay close up to the wall to one side. Luckily almost no one called at the lodge apart from Terry. Sue sat in the kitchen drinking more coffee until Terry rang.

'Come over, will you?' she asked. 'Right away. It's serious.'

'Well, I've got to do the cellar,' said Terry. 'It'll have to be quick. Can't you tell me what it's all about?'

'No,' said Sue. 'You must come, Terry.'

He had never heard her speak like that before. Her voice was steady – too steady, the words all uttered in a monotone.

'Jonathan isn't well, I hear,' he said.

'No.' She didn't elaborate.

'I'll be right over,' said Terry.

She was waiting for him, dressed, now, in black slacks and tight sweater, her long hair in a pony tail, no make-up on, and she opened the door as he came up the path.

He saw the mark on her face at once, even before she cast herself against him.

'What is all this?' he asked, holding her away from him and laying a finger against her cheek. 'What's happened, Sue? Where's Jonathan? Is he in bed?'

Sue shook her head.

'He's over there,' she said, and began to tremble

173

as she pointed to the bundle against the wall. 'He's dead.'

Terry stared at her.

'No!' he gasped. 'No!'

'He is,' said Sue.

'Why? How? What happened?' There had been some sort of accident, obviously. Terry let go of Sue and went over to the long blanket-covered heap, drawing back one end of the blanket. He saw the white polythene bag. 'Suicide?' he said, but he knew it wasn't, not with the body tidily placed like this beside the storage heater.

'No. He hit me,' said Sue. 'I didn't think, Terry. I picked up the poker.'

Terry covered the dead man's head again and stood up. He came over to Sue and looked again at her face, inspecting the bruise and the tiny scrape.

'Oh dear,' he said. 'Better tell me what happened.'

'Let's go into the kitchen,' said Sue. 'I don't like him being there.' It was as if Jonathan could hear himself being discussed.

Terry didn't care for it either. They went into the kitchen and sat at the table. Sue told him the story exactly as it had happened.

'Jealous bugger,' said Terry. 'He shouldn't have hit you.'

'No,' said Sue. 'I was scared.' But that wasn't true. She hadn't been scared until later; she had been ragingly angry.

'If you'd called the police, you could have said it was self-defence,' Terry pointed out. 'You could still do that, Sue. You could say you panicked and that's why you didn't do it at once. Did he die straight away?'

'I don't know. I didn't look,' said Sue. 'I thought he was putting it on, for sympathy. I went up to bed.'

Terry gulped.

'You mean you left him there – you didn't – ?' But he knew she had not tried to find out how badly hurt Jonathan was. He swallowed, horrified. How could she just leave him?

'He'd hurt me, Terry,' said Sue. 'He hit me.'

'You'd better ring the police, Sue,' Terry said.

'I can't,' said Sue. 'They'll think I meant to do it.'

'Well, you can prove he hit you. You've got a bruise to show for it,' Terry said.

'It's not just that,' said Sue. 'I can't risk the police, Terry.'

'Why not?' Terry could see it would be tough for her especially if the police realized she hadn't tried to help Jonathan. Perhaps she could say he had died straight away or she thought he had, and had panicked. That made sense.

Wasn't he going to get rid of the body for her? Sue had been so sure that he would.

'You've got to get rid of him, Terry,' she said, on a rising note.

'But- but – ' How could he? Where to? Terry didn't like this sort of thing at all.

She had to persuade him. How far dared she go?

'If we tell the police, they might think I'd had something to do with George's accident,' said Sue.

'Oh no! They wouldn't do that,' said Terry. 'Why should they?'

'They might,' Sue insisted. 'Just because I was around at the time.'

'But you – how?' Terry stared at her, unable to follow her reasoning.

'They might think I'd pushed him,' said Sue, keeping her voice level. 'After all, you got his job because I'd recommended you. They might say I'd done it deliberately to get you in at the Rigby.'

'Oh, but that was just a coincidence,' Terry began, and stopped, for he realized that the police could look at it differently if they took it into their heads to consider the matter again. Sue would have no defence if they set out to build up a case against her, she'd been at work as usual that morning with no witness to say that she had never left the reception area. He saw the danger there could be for both of them if this happened. The police might even accuse him of having conspired with her to remove George, so devious were they, in Terry's opinion. At best, they would investigate what he had been doing recently, and Terry couldn't risk that happening. Some of his deals would not stand up to inspection.

On the whole, the wisest course would be to get rid of all trace of the accident and its victim.

'Let's see,' he said, beginning to plan, and Sue saw that she had won. 'You told Anthea he wasn't well,' Terry went on. 'What about his office? What were his plans for today?'

Sue didn't know. She had never been interested

in how Jonathan earned his living.

'His diary,' said Terry, almost irritably for him, to Sue's surprise. He was never cross. 'Where does he keep it?'

'In his pocket, I suppose,' she said.

'Would he have been making calls or going to the office?'

'I don't know,' said Sue.

'We'd better find out,' said Terry grimly. 'We don't want his boss ringing up wanting to talk to him, do we?'

He was going to help her. He would deal with it. Sue relaxed a little. She followed as Terry returned to the sitting-room and began unfolding the blanket. The body had not yet begun to stiffen, for Jonathan had not been dead so very long. The inter-cranial haemorrhage that had killed him had not taken fatal effect at once.

Terry held his breath as he felt in the dead man's jacket and found Jonathan's slim black leather diary in his inside pocket. His wallet was there, too. Terry left it. He turned the diary pages until he came to today's date. Several names and times were entered, and his office number was listed on the page provided for personal notes.

He gave the diary to Sue.

'Ring up his office. Say he's ill and give them these names. Say you don't know what's wrong exactly but that he's been very depressed lately. That's the thing, depression.' It would make suicide, if somehow this death could be arranged to look like that, understandable.

Terry covered the body again while Sue went to the telephone. Her voice was calm as she made the call.

'Depressed, yes,' she said. 'For some time, really. Since Christmas. Yes, yes. Thank you. I'll tell him.' She hung up and turned to Terry. 'They said he'd better see a doctor if he isn't all right by Monday,' she told him.

'I'll have to go now,' Terry said. 'I'll come back as soon as the bar closes.'

'But we can't leave him here all that time!' Sue exclaimed. 'Suppose someone calls?'

'Who's likely to? Only Alice, and you can tell her Jonathan's ill and you can't let her in. You'll have to sweat it out this morning, Sue. I'll be thinking of something to do meanwhile.'

'What if Helen comes?'

'Does she ever?'

'She might, to see what we're up to.'

'Do the same to her – say Jonathan's ill and sleeping. Ask her to come back another time,' said Terry. 'You can handle that, Sue.'

She could, of course.

'You will come back?' she asked, clinging to him.

'Of course I will,' he said, unwrapping her arms and moving towards the door.

He thought about it, driving away. He could clear out, be gone, leave Sue to cope. Seeing that large, log-like bundle tucked against the wall, feeling in the jacket pocket, had really choked him.

But they would be able to get rid of it – he and

Sue: careful planning would be needed, and he thrived on that. It would be safer for his own skin than lighting out.

Sue went back to bed after Terry left. She could not stay in the sitting-room with that shape beneath its blanket lying there by the wall. She drank some coffee laced with whisky and swallowed four aspirins – she had no sleeping pills; Sue never went near a doctor – and slept for over two hours.

There was still a long time to fill in until Terry came. She dared not go out, not even to see Alice, in case someone came to the house. She had a bath and got dressed, then leafed through some magazines with the radio on. She could not watch television because the set was in the room with the body.

Terry arrived just before three. He always came then, when she was on late shift. They would go to bed and then he would drive her in to work. Alice would not think it odd if she noticed his car outside.

'Have you got a plan?' she asked. 'What are you going to do?'

'Put him in the boot of his own car, to start with,' said Terry. 'Then, when there's more time, fake an accident.' He hadn't worked out the details yet, but they'd come to him. He was rather surprised that a splendid plan had not yet sprung into his mind, for usually his ideas rapidly grew from the needs of the occasion. The trouble was that this wasn't his kind of thing at all; he'd never been mixed up with anything violent. But Jonathan had hit Sue. Terry told himself that without this trigger it wouldn't have happened. 'Who's about the place today?' he asked. 'It's Thursday. There's the cleaning woman, isn't there?' He had seen Mrs Wood on her cycle several times, a doughty soul with headscarf and boots, steadily pedalling.

'She's gone.' Sue had seen her ride past the windows earlier. 'She has her lunch and then goes.'

'What about that gardener fellow?'

'I don't know if he's there. He comes when he feels like it,' said Sue. 'There's Alice.'

'Yes. Well, it won't take very long to wheel – er – him over to the garage in the wheelbarrow,' said Terry. He had developed an aversion to uttering Jonathan's name.

'What if the gardener is using it?'

'Oh!' Terry had not thought of that.

'There's that truck Giles uses for moving the logs,' said Sue. 'It's kept in the barn. It's bigger than a wheelbarrow. A sort of handcart.'

'Ah! Well, I'll use that, then,' said Terry. 'Now, you go and see what the gardener's doing. Check that he'll be busy for about twenty minutes. It won't take longer than that. See if he's digging a big patch – ask him.'

'But I never go and talk to the gardener,' Sue said.

'There's always a first time. Tell him that – er – Jonathan's at home ill and beg a cabbage or something off him. Say you want to cook something special. If he's leaving and packing up we'll have to wait till he's gone.' Terry didn't fancy that. He didn't want to be forced to take Sue in to work and then return and extemporize alone: not over this.

'Why not bring the car out – park outside?' Sue said.

'And have someone see us piling him into it? No. Besides, if he really was ill, he wouldn't be using it. It must stay where it is,' said Terry. 'Things must go on as normally as we can manage. Off you go – chat up the gardener. Be as quick as you can but make a good job of it.'

Sue put on her coat and boots and went off round the side of the house. She was gone nearly ten minutes but it seemed much longer to Terry as he waited alone with the corpse.

Sue came back with a tight green savoy cabbage.

'He's digging a patch for sowing beans,' she said. 'He'll be busy for a bit yet.'

'How do you know?'

'He'd been drinking his tea – he had a flask – when I got out there. It's to last him till he finishes that strip of ground,' said Sue. 'He said so.'

'Right,' said Terry. 'Now you go and visit Alice. Get her to make you some coffee. Keep her there talking. Do a sob-stuff act – tell her – ' he made an effort. 'Tell her that Jonathan's been acting strangely lately. Say he hit you. You can say he's sorry – that he was drunk. That won't be anything new to her, seeing what Giles gets up to. The main thing is to keep her away from the window.'

Sue nodded.

'How will I know when you've finished?' she asked.

'You won't. Stay as long as you can, leaving time for us to get you to the Rigby on the dot. Leave this end to me.'

'You're wonderful, Terry,' said Sue, meaning it. He was so firm and decisive. She moved against him, but he pushed her away.

'No time for that now, Sue,' he said. 'Get going.'

He watched from the window as she walked up to the back door and pressed the bell. Soon the door opened and she went inside. Terry gave them three minutes to get settled. Then he went over to the barn, looked around for the cart and finally saw it at one end, beside the pile of neatly stacked logs. He wheeled it round to the back door of the lodge.

The task of moving Jonathan was almost too much for Terry. He couldn't lift the body but had to drag it by the heels across the floor, bumping into furniture and the doorposts, hauling it into the kitchen. The blanket came unwrapped and he had to bundle it up again, rolling it up like a carpet. The head and shoulders were stiffening. Terry knew nothing about rigor mortis and did not realize that the warmth of the storage heater had delayed the process somewhat as he managed to heave the heavy torso into the cart and roll the legs in after it. Then he went round to the front of the lodge and glanced up and down the drive.

There was no one in sight.

He pushed the cart briskly into the barn, elated

until he realized that he had forgotten to get the keys of the Granada from Sue and he had not brought his own set of keys with him. He ran back to the lodge and was searching for them when the doorbell rang. Looking out of the window, Terry saw a white van outside. For a wild moment he imagined that a policeman stood on the step. He thought about leaving the bell unanswered, but he had not closed the front door when he came in to search for the keys.

A small man with ginger hair and a large book stood on the doorstep: the representative of the electricity board come to read the meter.

Terry didn't know where it was, but the man did; it was in a cupboard under the stairs, reached through the sitting-room. A short time earlier, a dead body had lain, wrapped in a rug, not ten feet from the cupboard door.

Terry smiled pleasantly at the meter man, standing beside him while he noted the figures, showing him out, watching him drive on in his van to the main house. Sue would have a turn when she saw him, he thought.

Those few moments when he had to be calm had steadied Terry. He remembered seeing keys on a hook on the kitchen dresser. They were there.

He'd forgotten his gloves. Terry found a pair of Jonathan's on a shelf in the small lobby and went back again to the barn chiding himself for being so careless.

He opened the boot and steeled himself to lift the body in.

He was sweating when he went back to the house to wait for Sue.

'Oh, my dear!' exclaimed Alice when she saw Sue's face with its pale bruise under the delicate skin, and the small abrasion. 'Oh, how dreadful!'

Sue found it easy to cry in the aftermath of tension. She allowed Alice to pat her arm soothingly and lapped up the expressions of concern which Alice was uttering.

'What shall I do?' wailed Sue. 'Oh, what shall I do?'

'He can't have meant to hurt you,' said Alice.

'He was jealous,' said Sue. 'Jealous because I come home from work so often with Giles. But he should be glad. It saves him from turning out to come for me.'

Alice remembered what she had seen, the intertwined figures crossing from the barn to the house, and Sue's return alone. She hadn't been in the house long. How long was long enough, wondered Alice.

'Perhaps it isn't very discreet,' she said.

'Well, he's lonely, isn't he?' said Sue. 'Giles, I mean. Helen's out such a lot, and so busy.'

'That's true.' Alice sighed. 'It wasn't a good idea, my coming here. I thought if Helen had the sort of house she'd always wanted – ' her voice trailed away

'You should think of yourself, not them,' Sue said, and meant it. 'You aren't at all happy here.'

'Well, it's been better since I got to know you

and Jonathan,' Alice said. 'Are you planning to marry?'

'Not really. His wife won't agree to a divorce. You can easily get one in two years if you agree. If not, it takes much longer. And I'm not sure about anything permanent. He's been acting so strangely lately. We've had several rows, but he's never hit me before.' Sue found it surprisingly easy to give this truthful reply.

'Perhaps you should give up taking lifts from Giles,' Alice suggested. 'If it upsets Jonathan?'

'You don't think – ?' Sue began, and Alice broke in.

'No, of course not.' But however innocent Sue's presence in the house last night, the temptation was there. What had they been doing? She found that she did not want to know the answer.

'You must make it up with Jonathan,' she advised. 'When he comes home tonight.'

'He hasn't gone in to work,' Sue said. 'He's in bed. He won't talk to me. Terry's with him now. I thought if I left them together – ' she wrung her hands and looked at Alice in a genuinely anxious way. How was Terry getting on? Had he done it?

There was Terry, too. She had got them all in her thrall, thought Alice and was astonished at the direction of her thoughts. *La Belle Dame Sans Merci*, that was; Walter had quoted it sometimes when he was doing the crossword. In her own young days, one's reputation was precious; girls guarded it by avoiding conduct that might be misinterpreted. Nowadays, nobody seemed to care about that sort of thing. Alice remembered feeling doubtful about Terry and Sue being alone in the lodge together that very first day.

Sue said she must go. It was nearly time to leave for the Rigby and she had to change and do her hair.

Perhaps she would leave the lodge, Alice thought when she had gone. Perhaps this quarrel would prove to be final. It would be much better for Giles if Sue were to leave.

15

During the night in which Jonathan died alone in the sitting-room at the lodge, Giles had woken to find himself lying on his bed fully dressed, with the eiderdown over him. His shoes lay untidily on the floor a yard apart; his tie was on a chair.

He woke just in time before vomiting.

In the bathroom, he splashed cold water on his face and tried to remember what had happened the previous evening. He'd been in the bar at the Rigby Arms where by now he had friends among the regulars. Two were keen punters and told him of their betting successes, not referring to their failures; Giles took a courteous interest in their fortunes.

He had brought Sue home. Slowly, painfully, Giles dredged up the memory of the night. He had driven straight into the barn and, in the kindly darkness, begun to make love to her.

Love. Even in his fuddled state, Giles knew that what he felt for Sue was not love. But she had been responsive. He'd experienced delicious sensations.

Memory blanked out after they'd got out of the

car. He'd passed out, obviously. And just as obviously, he hadn't been sober enough to get far with Sue.

No doubt he'd made a crass fool of himself.

Giles took off his clothes and crawled into bed, where he tossed and turned for a while before he slept again. In the morning he had a foul taste in his mouth, and his head throbbed. Luckily Helen was away, so he did not have to listen to any breakfast-time comments on his pallor. Before leaving for the office he looked at the engagement pad by the telephone. They were going out to dinner on Saturday and on Sunday there were guests for lunch. It wasn't a weekend when the girls came home so there was nothing to look forward to at all.

He had a meeting that morning, and in the afternoon had to go through some complex figures. He liked that; he was good with figures; you knew where you were with them. In between, there were letters to answer and routine matters to handle. At lunch-time he sent out for sandwiches, surprising his secretary, for usually he took himself off to a nearby pub. He worked on hard through the day, intending to be home in good time that evening, wearing a welcoming expression when Helen came in, if he should be first, or greeting her with a display of pleasure if she were already home from Yorkshire. Should he buy flowers? He thought about it. He never did, except for form's sake on her birthday.

At three o'clock he sent his astonished secretary

out to buy three dozen carnations. He gave her the key of his car and asked her to put them in it. At five o'clock he left for home, and soon after six walked into the house. He knew she was back. Her car was in the barn.

Helen was in her sitting-room writing up some notes about the house in Yorkshire. Giles's footsteps in the passage were muted by the Persian runner that covered the stone flags. He paused. Of course I don't have to knock, he told himself. This wasn't her bedroom. He took a deep breath, opened the door and walked in.

'Ah – Helen – you're back,' he said. 'Did you have a good trip?'

'Very.' Helen pushed her glasses up on to the top of her head and tilted her chair back, drumming impatiently with her fingers on the paper before her. Now what?

'And a good run back? It's nice that you're home early,' he tried, and swallowed. Then he proffered the flowers, which he had been carrying head downwards by his side. 'I thought you'd like these,' he said.

Helen turned to look at him. She saw a flabby man who had once been slim and handsome. His face, now, was florid, but not with the glow of health; there were pouches beneath his eyes and he had a small paunch. At the moment he was looking at her with the apprehensive, eager expression of a small boy who has committed a misdemeanour as yet undetected for which, in advance, he wants to make amends.

Helen interpreted all this perfectly.

'Well!' she said. 'Flowers! And it isn't my birthday! What have you been doing, Giles, while my back was turned?'

'Just going to the office as usual. What else?' asked Giles.

'I don't know. You tell me,' said Helen. She waited, watching him, a cat alert for prey.

'I – er – I've missed you.' Sweat broke out on Giles's forehead, and the flowers, still thrust forward, wavered in his grasp.

'I doubt it,' said Helen. 'Since we seldom meet.' She turned back to her work and settled her glasses back on her nose. 'If you're having an affair, Giles, I don't want to know. Just be discreet. And you needn't think I'll ever divorce you, for I won't. You keep your goings-on away from here – I won't put up with gossip. You can give your flowers to your girlfriend. I don't want them. And grow up, for God's sake. Just look at you – you're drinking so much you're falling apart.' She gave him a last scornful glance. 'I'm surprised that anyone will look at you,' she told him. 'You're a walking disaster.'

Giles turned on his heel and walked out of the room without another word, still holding the flowers, and Helen returned to her work, putting him out of her mind.

Giles went straight out to the car and drove to the Rigby Arms. He'd tried and Helen had snubbed him. She had only herself to blame for what happened next. He'd give the flowers to

Sue, and he'd be sober when they parked in the barn.

But that night she asked to be dropped at the lodge. Jonathan wasn't well, she said, and they were going away the next day for the weekend.

'Some other time, Giles,' she promised, opening her mouth to him, making him gasp.

'He's forgotten to put the outside light on for you,' said Giles.

'Yes. Never mind,' said Sue. 'I can see all right.'

He waited while she went up the path. He saw her use her key to open the door. There were no lights on in the house. Jonathan must have gone to bed, Giles supposed, driving on, putting the car away.

Because of her make-up and the surrounding darkness, he hadn't noticed the bruise on Sue's face.

She'd forgotten the flowers. They were still in the car. Giles took them into the house and flung them into the kitchen waste bin, where Mrs Wood found them the next day. She revived them with plenty of water and took them home, where they bloomed for some days giving her a great deal of pleasure. Her guess as to how they had come to be thrown away was not very far from the truth.

That afternoon, as they drove to Westborough leaving Jonathan's body stowed in the boot of the Granada, Terry had told Sue that he wouldn't take her back after closing time, as she had proposed.

'But you could stay,' she said.

He was shocked.

'I couldn't,' he said. 'He's supposed to be upstairs in bed, remember.'

'But you'll be dumping him somewhere,' said Sue. 'You can take the car out and drive it into a river or something. Make it look as if he's had an accident.'

'Not just like that, I can't,' said Terry. 'There's got to be a proper plan. He wouldn't just drive off.'

'He might,' said Sue. 'He's been going for walks at night.'

'No,' said Terry. 'It's got to be thought about.' And he needed time to get over the revulsion he felt about the whole business to which now, it seemed, he was committed. 'Tomorrow,' he said. 'We'll do it tomorrow. You're off then, aren't you, for the weekend?'

'Yes.'

'I've got it!' Terry felt the sudden lift that came with a good idea. 'You and him – ' he still avoided using the dead man's name. 'You book in at a hotel for a weekend. You've had a row and you're making it up, see?'

'But – '

'No, wait!' Terry liked his plan more as it began to take shape. It was vital to get the dead man away from the district so that any hunt for him, when he was missed, would not be local. The problem would be to fit it in with his own shifts at the bar; he had to keep his routine going. 'Pick somewhere about thirty or forty miles away – not too far. Near the motorway. I'll have to do a lot of travelling around.'

'You will?'

'Well, you can't drive, can you? And someone's got to be at the hotel with you, taking his place.'

'But you don't look like him,' objected Sue.

'No one's going to see me – or only in the distance. You'll check in, saying I'm not well. Or rather, he's not well. It will have to be a motel or somewhere like that, where the rooms are away from the main block and reception area. A place where guests can get out at night without a hall porter.'

'Money,' said Sue promptly. 'It's going to cost.'

'I'll find some,' said Terry. He'd get Sue like this, he saw, bind her for ever, and she in turn would get Giles; it would be an investment. He hardened his heart as he turned his mind towards what had to be done. 'During the night, while you're in the hotel, I'll get rid of him,' he said. 'Somewhere where he'll never be found. Or at least, so that no one will ever find out what happened.' What had? Why had a single blow been fatal? He'd heard of paper-thin skulls; was that the explanation?

'Like setting the car on fire, do you mean?' Sue asked.

'That's a good idea,' said Terry. 'Yes, something like that. It's better if you don't know too much about it. Leave that to me.' He'd work it out as he went along.

'How will you get back to Westborough?' Sue asked. 'By train?'

He'd lift another car, but he couldn't tell Sue that. There were some things it was better for her not to know about him; at the moment he was the one with the upper hand.

'Yes,' he said. 'Or I'll hitch a ride.'

'Had we better go to a hotel in a town, then?' said Sue.

Terry didn't like that idea. There were always people about in a town, busybodies minding other people's business. A car driving off in the night might be noticed, and the fact that the driver had not emerged from the hotel be seen and remembered.

'Somewhere quiet would be better,' he said. 'And you'd go somewhere in the country, wouldn't you, to make it up? Somewhere romantic.'

'There's that place at Twistleton,' said Sue. 'The Court Grange Hotel. It's got an annexe block. We've often booked touring Americans in there and we've just had a couple who'd been there. They liked it a lot.'

'Twistleton?' Terry was trying to place it.

'It's not far from Swindon,' said Sue. 'There'll be something about it in the office.'

She checked when they reached the Rigby. Terry was still off duty and looked Twistleton up on the map. It was only a mile and a half from the motorway.

'Book yourselves in tomorrow for the weekend,' said Terry. 'Two nights. We'll plan later.'

'Two nights?' asked Sue.

'Two nights,' confirmed Terry. 'A weekend, remember. In the annexe.'

How had he got himself into this? It was way outside his normal scene. Terry wished Sue could drive; it would make things so much easier. She could have done it herself, once it was in the car. It was easier to think of Jonathan as it than as him, a person once warm and breathing.

The thing was, if Sue had done the obvious, rung the police when it happened, they would have given her a hard time and she might have found herself going down for manslaughter, and it was an accident, after all. But it would work out all right. All Sue need do was act sad for a while when she came back from that place, the Court Grange Hotel, saying Jonathan had gone off and left her there alone.

Terry had told her that he would hitch a ride back, but he wouldn't. Before he nicked a car, however, he'd have to get clear of the Court Grange. It wouldn't do to lift a car out of their yard. Pity about that: there'd be some good ones there, for sure. What a waste!

Terry told Mavis, the barmaid who was on duty with him on Thursday evening, that his car needed a repair and he knew this bloke who was going to do it cheap over the weekend, but he'd be stuck for getting about. Would she lend him her bike?

Mavis's bike was a small folding one, and she wouldn't be on duty over the weekend.

As she hesitated, Terry smiled at her winningly and explained that there was this bird he wanted to visit who'd be ever so upset if he couldn't get over.

Mavis said she could spare the bike if he'd run her home tonight after work. She sometimes went out cycling on Sundays with her children, but as it happened, this weekend her mother was coming to stay and there wouldn't be time.

'Thanks, Mavis. You're a true pal,' said Terry, and kissed her cheek.

Mavis, a plump forty-year-old with blonde-rinsed hair who worked to earn money for holidays and for music lessons for her daughter, blushed and pulled his ear.

'You'd charm the hide off a monkey, Terry,' she told him.

Had he thought of everything? Terry lay in bed that night going over his plan, only a fragment of which he'd so far told Sue. The timing would be so tight, but he dare not risk asking for any time off in case, later, it was remembered and thought an odd coincidence. He mustn't be seen with Sue so he must leave his own car outside Harcombe where it would not attract attention and where it would be safe until he could go and collect it on Mavis's bike. There was Alice to think of, too. What if she looked out of the window and saw him? In a coat of Jonathan's, at a distance, she might be deceived, but what about Helen? She'd be back from Yorkshire and might take it into her head to go past the lodge just as they set off. Terry lay in bed mulling it over. Should he go to Harcombe now and move the car, in the dark? No.

In the morning Giles would see that it had gone and could question their story later.

He thought of a plan, lying there, that would take care of Helen. For Alice he was going to need inspiration.

The next afternoon, Terry left his car in Great Minton, where twenty houses were being built in what had once been a patch of allotments. He drove down the unmade road past the shells of houses to where the foundations of the last few were laid. Here, a bulldozer and a cement mixer stood on waste ground at the side of the site. There was no sign of activity. At the end of the new estate two cars were parked under a chestnut tree whose buds were sticky, ready to sprout when the warm weather came. Terry turned the car round so that it faced outwards for a quick getaway and took the bike from the back. It unfolded easily and he screwed it into its working position. Then he pedalled quickly back to the main village street. One of the new houses had a sign saying SOLD pasted across its windows. Another was nearly complete, and more were ranged in varying stages of construction. Someone must be there to account for the cars, but he could see no exterior work in progress. Perhaps there were painters and plasterers working inside, Terry thought; or perhaps the developers had run out of money. No one would pay any attention to his old car; they would think it belonged to some worker on the site. It was safer here than in the village itself, where it might be the subject of curiosity.

It was a hard ride to Harcombe on the small bike, taking up precious time. Terry's legs ached as he pedalled the last stretch. He left the bike under a hedge just before he reached the gateway to Harcombe House, and approached the lodge on foot from the back, coming in from the neighbouring field over the garden fence.

He gave Sue a fright. She was expecting him to arrive in the normal way up the drive and she knew that Helen was in, which was worrying her, although it was unlikely that she would be looking out of a north-facing window since all the main rooms faced the garden side.

Terry came in by the back door and went softly through into the sitting-room where Sue was watching by the window. He whistled and she turned, her eyes large in her pale face. The bruise on her cheek stood out now.

'Oh, you scared me!' she gasped, clasping him.

'I came the back way so as not to be seen,' said Terry. 'Mrs Wood's gone by now, hasn't she?' He held her away from him.

'Yes – and the gardener. I watched for them both,' said Sue. 'What took you so long?' She had expected him soon after the bar closed.

Terry explained about the bike.

'I'll tell you the rest as we go,' he said. He was pleased with his plan. 'What about Helen and Alice? Are they in?'

She told him that Helen was, but there had been

some luck about Alice. Sue had gone over, as instructed by Terry, to tell her that she and Jonathan were going away for a honeymoon-type weekend.

'What a good idea!' Alice had said, and the next minute she had decided to go away too. She had telephoned a hotel in Bournemouth not far from where she used to live and booked herself in. She had left before lunch.

'I've packed two cases,' Sue said. 'What he'd need for a couple of nights, and my own.' She indicated the bags by the door.

'Good. And I'll need one of his coats and a hat. I suppose he's got some sort of hat?'

Jonathan sometimes wore a tweed cap in cold weather. Sue had teased him about what she called his 'toff's hat'. It hung in the lobby together with an anorak and raincoat. Terry put on the bulky anorak and the cap, pushing his curls up under the cap, and laid the raincoat over the suitcases.

'How's that?' he said, posturing before her.

'Someone might take you for him on a dark night, at a distance,' said Sue doubtfully. 'But not up close. You're thinner. Oh Terry, someone else might come, like the meter reader yesterday.'

'Even if someone does, it probably wouldn't be anyone who knows him,' said Terry. 'People see what they expect to see. Don't lose your nerve, Sue. I'm going out to get the car now. I'll park by the gate while we put the cases in. You dial Helen's number on the telephone while I'm getting it, and then hang up when she answers. Now, where are the keys?'

He'd left them on the sideboard the day before; they were still there, beside Jonathan's diary. He picked them up and went to the door.

'Now dial,' he told her.

The Granada started first go. Terry backed it out of the barn and drove up to the lodge gate, where he left the engine running. He put the two cases and Jonathan's raincoat on the back seat of the car. When he went into the house again Sue was standing beside the telephone, the handset in place on the rest.

'Dial again, and leave the phone off,' he instructed. 'As soon as it's ringing, leave it and run.'

'The back door!' Sue said. 'It's not locked.'

Terry went quickly through and locked it, then came back. Thank God she'd remembered, but he should have thought of it. He forced himself to concentrate and to ignore the reason for what they were doing, that long silent form in the boot of the car.

'Dial now,' he said.

Helen's voice was clacking into the receiver as they hurried off down the path and into the car. They left the village by the Great Minton road, stopping to pick up the bike from where Terry had left it and covering it up, in the back of the car, with Jonathan's raincoat.

Helen gave up on the telephone when nobody spoke, as she had the first time it rang. In the lodge, the receiver lay on the sideboard beside Jonathan's diary, emitting the whirr of a line that has not been cleared.

16

Terry would not think about what lay in the boot of the Granada as he drove fast towards Twistleton. Every minute was precious if he was to get back to the Rigby Arms by opening time. He outlined his plan as he went along, and Sue became more confident as she saw that unless something went wrong with the journeys he had to make, it would work. He seemed to have thought of everything, even the fact that if the Granada was in the hotel car park on Saturday morning because of some hitch, there was still another night in which it could be disposed of; and he told her how, if that happened, she must get through the day, ordering meals in the room to make it seem as if Jonathan was there with her, feeling unwell.

The hotel stood at the foot of a hill beyond the village of Twistleton. A river wound towards woods in the distance. Picturesque cottages, most of them thatched, bordered the village street which was deserted on this Friday afternoon.

Terry drove through the gates and up to the main entrance. At the side was a row of cottages made from what had been the stable block of the mansion which was now the hotel. There was parking space beyond. There might be a second gate, a tradesmen's entrance, at the further end.

'It looks expensive,' said Terry.

'It is,' said Sue.

'We'll drive on and have a look round,' he said, sliding the car into gear and going on past the cottages. Sure enough, at the far end a gate led into the lane. Terry drove back up the hill and turned off along a narrow road which went to the church. He had noticed the spire from below.

'I forgot the bike,' he told Sue. 'I can't risk taking it out of the car down at the hotel. I'll leave it in the churchyard. That should be safe enough, for Christ's sake.'

Sue waited in the car while he wheeled the bike through the gates leading into the churchyard. He vanished between the graves. In a few minutes he returned, grinning. He had left it by a fence under a yew beyond the church. Then they drove back down the hill to the Court Grange Hotel. Its mellow brick was soft in the last of the day's slanting sunshine. Ancient trees studded the lawn. A gate led into a walled garden where there was now a swimming-pool complete with changing pavilion. What a place, thought Terry, peering from beneath Jonathan's cap as Sue went in to register and collect the key. An elderly couple, arm in arm, walked past as he waited. They took no notice of him.

Sue soon returned with the key, relieved at accomplishing the first task. She had registered herself and Jonathan in their correct names – she didn't want trouble over that later if there were any enquiries – and had remembered to glance at the registration number of the car before approaching the desk, aware from her own job that it would have to appear on the form.

'It's number five,' she said, getting back into the car, nodding towards the annexe.

'Good.' Terry had noticed as they drove past that the lowest numbers were nearest the main building; the further away they were, the better.

He parked outside number five and carried in their cases, hesitating over the raincoat, then took that in too. Afterwards, he parked the car at the furthest end of the parking area, close to the rear gate. He need only slip in through that and drive away. Then he walked quickly back to the annexe where Sue was waiting. He shouldn't be doing this, he thought: he should have gone at once, but he had to seem to be Jonathan, in anorak and cap, in case anyone noticed.

Sue sprang at him as he entered the room, eager and ardent, turned on by the excitement.

'Isn't this great?' she exclaimed, twining her arms round him, effectively blocking his view of the pretty room with its yellow sprigged curtains, pale carpet, and bleached furniture picked out with gold. 'Makes the Rigby seem a dump.'

Terry firmly detached her, holding her away, not letting her press herself against him.

'I've got to be back at that dump, as you call it, by six, remember,' he said. 'And I need all my strength for that bloody bike.'

Sue's expression hardened.

'What am I going to do all the evening?' she said. 'I'll be bored out of my mind.'

'You've got the telly,' said Terry. 'You can look at that. Or read a good book. They're bound to have some here.'

But Sue never read more than magazine gossip about the jet set and the showbiz world, and the fashion news.

'You can go over to the bar later,' said Terry. 'Bring a drink back for – ' he swallowed – 'Jonathan. That will be a natural thing to do. You can order dinner while you're there. Make a bit of a thing about it, apologizing for causing trouble and that. Charm them.'

'All right,' said Sue. She caught him again, fiercely, and pecked little kisses all over his face but once again Terry held her away from him; he felt no desire at all.

'Have a look out of the window,' he instructed. 'See if there's anyone about.'

Sue obeyed.

'There's an old woman with a dog,' she reported. 'She's going down towards the river. I can't see anyone else.'

Terry had kept Jonathan's gloves on all this time. Now he removed them while he took off the anorak and cap. He laid them on the bed and put on the dead man's raincoat. His curls sprang up in their usual manner as he ran his fingers quickly through them. He took the car keys from the anorak pocket and then replaced the gloves.

'I won't see you now until it's all over,' he told Sue.

'What – not tonight? You'll come in then, when you get back, won't you?'

'No. Someone might see me. I'm off now,' he said, and was gone, closing the door quietly behind him.

Sue watched from the window as he left the building and walked quickly away through the rear entrance. He did not glance back. His head was held at a jaunty angle and he looked quite unlike the apparently thickset man in the anorak and cap who had entered earlier.

Sue patted the wad of money he had given her to pay the bill. There was plenty. She had decided not to ask him where he had got it. They were both playing for high stakes now and this was his investment in the future.

Terry, carrying crates of beer and mineral waters up to the bar from the cellar, had taken more exercise lately than for a long time, but his leg muscles ached with protest as he pedalled towards the motorway. Once out of the village the road looked level, but the small bike found and fought every rise.

Terry had passed a few people as he walked to the church to collect the bicycle, and as he pushed it out through the churchyard gate a woman had approached carrying a basket containing brass-cleaning equipment.

Terry held the gate open for her.

'Thank you,' she said, adding, 'Hasn't it been a lovely day?'

Terry agreed. He was hoping it would stay dry until the night was over.

'It won't be long now until spring,' said the woman. She looked curiously at Terry.

'That's right,' agreed Terry. An explanation of why he was there occurred to him, and he gave it. 'I've just been looking for my granny's grave,' he told her.

'Oh – did you find it?' asked the woman.

'Yes, yes,' said Terry, sure that if he said no the woman would offer to help him.

'That's good,' said the woman. 'It's among the old ones, then?'

What could she mean?

'Right,' said Terry. 'I must be off now. Goodbye,' and he mounted the bike to speed away before she could ask more questions.

He put her out of his mind as he pedalled on. Close to the slip road leading to the motorway, he left the bike in a field under a hedge, noting the place carefully as it would be dark when he returned. Once on the motorway, a lorry soon stopped to pick him up. His luck was in for it was going to Swindon. Terry got the driver to drop him close to the town centre. Now he was on familiar ground.

It was weeks since he had lifted a car. He walked into the nearest pay-and-display parking lot and looked around for an unlocked car. He'd brought his sets of keys with him and soon found a Honda

Accord whose passenger door had not been locked. He got in, started up, and drove away whistling. The first part of the plan had gone better than he had hoped, and there was enough petrol in the stolen car to last for the trip to Westborough now and the return late that night.

He left the car in a side road near the Rigby Arms and was in time for a bath before going on duty. If he'd been even five minutes late, Bruce might remember and connect it with the weekend of Jonathan's disappearance, once that was known, and though certain that nothing could ever be proved against him, Terry wanted to run no avoidable risks. He thought that he wouldn't stay at the Rigby much longer; he and Bruce had agreed a three month trial on both sides before deciding on anything permanent, but perhaps he would leave before then. The regular hours were beginning to pall and with Jonathan out of the way there would be no problem about visiting Sue. He would still need money, but he'd find some other project while she worked on Giles. Terry thought about that quite calmly. His attitude to Sue had hardened; he'd got her, now; she could never escape, once this weekend's work was done.

He soaked his aching muscles in hot sudsy water, dreaming of future opulence, and shaved and put on a clean shirt before going on duty.

Terry always liked to be clean and neat.

That afternoon, at Harcombe House, Helen crossly replaced the telephone receiver after finding no one there for the second time. The call that had not come through could have been from an important customer who might be discouraged by failed attempts at dialling. She waited for it to ring again, but in vain, and as she did not need to make a call herself that day, she did not discover that the line had not been cleared.

Giles returned from the office in a subdued frame of mind. He sat in his study drinking until sounds from the kitchen indicated that Helen was dishing up the fish *au gratin* which Mrs Wood had prepared earlier.

'Oh, so you're here tonight, are you?' she said, when he appeared in the doorway.

He did not reply and they ate in silence. When the meal was over they shared the tasks of clearing away and stacking the dishwasher, still not speaking, until Helen reminded him that they were dining out the next night.

'We're alone here all weekend,' she said. 'Sue and Jonathan are away and your mother's gone down to Bournemouth. She left me a note.'

'Oh,' said Giles. 'I didn't know she was going anywhere. Did you?' He meant his mother, but he thought also of Sue.

'No, but neither you nor your mother tell me what you're doing,' said Helen.

Giles stood at the sink drying a cut glass sherry glass which Helen had used and which was too good to go into the machine.

'Do we have to go on like this, Helen?' he asked. 'Can't we at least be civil to one another?'

'Am I being uncivil?' asked Helen. 'Oh, I do beg your pardon, Giles.'

'We should be so grateful to mother,' he said. 'Without her, we wouldn't be living here in this house you wanted so badly.'

'I don't see it like that at all,' said Helen. 'She should be grateful to us for taking her in. Many families wouldn't. But for us, she might be living alone in some nasty little seaside villa or flat.'

Giles did not say that his mother might be much happier doing just that. What was the point? He hung the tea towel carefully in front of the Aga and walked back to his study where he poured himself another tot of whisky. He had tried.

The stolen Honda was still parked where Terry had left it when he went to collect it late that night. After the bar closed and he had turned off the beer and locked up, he had gone to his room and changed from collar and tie into a dark roll-neck sweater. He put on his own car coat and a pair of soft shoes and pocketed his key collections. Tonight there would be no tough cycling; he'd use the bike only to coast down into Twistleton village. It had lights, but if he could see without them, he'd leave them off.

He did not go through Swindon, where the car, by now, had no doubt been reported missing and local police would be watching for it. Terry joined the M4 at the next junction and headed west at a steady seventy miles an hour. There were more cars about than he had expected so late; weekenders, he realized, delaying their departure from London until the main rush was over. He made the journey without any problems and collected the cycle from where he had left it. He would need it again after dumping the Granada. Terry thought in terms of disposing of the car, not what was inside it; he had never found it hard to suppress uncomfortable thoughts.

He abandoned the stolen car on a grass verge above Twistleton village and freewheeled quietly down the hill towards the Court Grange Hotel. He had to use the lamp, for the few street lights in the village were out and there was no moon. Even the hotel was in darkness. Terry folded the cycle and left it a short distance from the gateway. Then he walked quickly back and got into the Granada.

What if it wouldn't start?

But again it fired at the first touch and in minutes Terry had loaded the bike into it and set off up the hill to safety.

Sue heard him go. She had watched television until it closed down, then lain waiting on her bed in the dark. When all the exterior lights at the hotel went out, she had been very relieved, for at the Rigby one burned all night in the car park as some of their guests kept very late hours.

She ran to the window in time to see the Granada's brake lights flash and then disappear.

That was that. That was the end. It was over. Now there was nothing to think of until the next day.

Sue had had her drink in the bar, as Terry had

recommended – vodka and lime – and ordered the meal, confiding that her companion had been unwell for a while and that this was why they had come away for a break, but that now he didn't feel up to dining in the restaurant. She had chosen their dinner carefully – a fish dish for Jonathan who, she said, wasn't very hungry, and steak for herself. Sue liked a good piece of rare steak and often chose it at the Rigby. When the two waiters who brought the dinner over to the annexe came into the room they could hear the sound of water running out of the bath. Sue had watched for them with the bath filled and as they knocked on the bedroom door she had pulled the waste plug and closed the bathroom door.

They had brought the whole meal at once; Sue had particularly chosen cold starters and a cold sweet for herself and cheese and biscuits for Jonathan, to make this possible.

'That will be easier for you and less disturbing for us,' she had said, smiling at the Spanish head waiter.

'I hope the gentleman will be better tomorrow, madam,' the head waiter had said.

As they set out the folding table and arranged the dishes, the main course keeping warm balanced over a flame, the waiters heard Sue call out to Jonathan.

'Dinner's here, darling. Don't be long.'

She gave the waiters a pound each for their trouble. It went against the grain with her, but she knew it was wise insurance.

Sue was very hungry. She had eaten nothing since her sandwich lunch, and she demolished one avocado with prawns, Jonathan's fish dish and her own steak, her cherry *torte* and his cheese and biscuits. She flushed most of the extra vegetables down the lavatory leaving a new potato and some spinach on Jonathan's plate for effect, and she spread his toast with his *pâté de maison* and set it aside for herself later. She poured what was left of the wine into a toothmug. Then she put the table and all the dishes on the landing outside the room and hung the *Please do not disturb* sign on the door.

When the waiter came to remove the table and dishes, he could hear the television on in the room. It drowned any possible sound of voices.

Sue finished the toast and *pâté* and the tumbler of wine when Terry had gone with the car. Then she went straight to sleep and did not wake up until eight o'clock the next morning.

She remembered to muss up Jonathan's bed and crumple his pyjamas as if they had been worn before getting dressed and going over to the main hotel for breakfast.

In the dining-room she expressed surprise at not seeing Jonathan. He had already dressed and gone when she woke, she explained, and she thought he must have decided to go ahead without her. Perhaps he had gone for a walk. She ordered coffee and toast, and ate the whole rackful that was brought, and two warm, crisp rolls.

Then it was time to discover that the Granada

was gone, and to ask at the desk if Jonathan had left her a message.

Needless to say, he had not.

17

Terry knew about the old gravel pits from visits there with various ladies afraid of entertaining him in their own houses too often. In summer, it was pleasant among the leafy undergrowth bordering the pits which had been filled in with water and now formed deep dark lakes. He had only to get Jonathan into the driving seat of the car, turn on the ignition so that if the car was found the key was in the right position, and push the car over the side. The fact that it was out of gear would not matter; the impact might have jolted it free.

It was better to do this than set the car alight. Someone would see the blaze and there would be an investigation. This way, Jonathan's disappearance would, in time, be noticed and even looked into, but unless he was found there could be no full enquiry. Water would do its work on the body. Terry did not like to think about all that, but the longer it lay undiscovered, the better.

It took him less than an hour to reach the place, making speed on the motorway though keeping within the limit. He was not in a stolen car now, but he did not want to be stopped by some nosy copper with nothing better to do than harass the innocent. When he turned into the side roads he went on steadily, the headlight beams piercing the darkness. He met no oncoming lights when he reached the lanes.

What a shame to ditch this good car, he thought, enjoying its power. There were years of life in it, and it was worth a tidy bit.

The old pits lay up a track leading away from a lane a mile from the nearest village. It would be all right if the lights were seen; Jonathan, if it were he who was coming here to commit suicide, would need a light to find his way, but the place was so isolated that the chance of witness was remote. He left the track and drove along the rough ground at the edge of the artificial lake, looking for a place where the bushes thinned out and it would be easy to tip the car into the water. In summer people came here with canoes, but it was too small for a marina, as had been suggested by some people. Children had drowned here, stumbling to their deaths down the steep sheer sides. By night it was eerie, too silent: no creatures squeaked or moved in the darkness and all Terry could hear was the sound of his own breathing and the noise of his movements as he got out of the car and went round to the boot. Now came the hardest part, the part he had not practised in his imagination: the fitting of Jonathan in behind the wheel.

As soon as he opened the boot, the sweet sick smell of putrefaction met him; the smell of death. Terry hadn't thought of that, nor had he any experience of it. He held his breath as he took a grip on the blanket and dragged out the body. Rigor mortis had come and gone and the body sagged as he heaved it out of the boot and on to the ground. Terry pulled the blanket off and the dead man's head lolled over. The bag that covered it must be removed, and Terry pulled it away, casting it from him. Bile rose in his throat as he dragged the body towards the door of the car. The sickness seemed likely to overcome him, so he laid the corpse down and moved away to gulp down cold fresh air. This was terrible. Jonathan had been a decent enough fellow who didn't deserve to die so soon. Still, he had struck Sue, Terry reminded himself; he had hurt her and frightened her. That was why he was here now, a dead man to be disposed of. Terry inhaled new resolution with the pure air and returned to his task, putting his hands under the armpits, lifting Jonathan up, heaving him towards the car.

Why do it this way? Why not just tip Jonathan over the edge of the pit and into the water? Then he could go off with the car. It would be so much easier than putting the body behind the wheel, and without the car it might be lost for ever. There was always the risk of part of the car remaining above the surface or being reflected upwards into someone's vision. And getting away with the car would be a piece of cake; he could simply drive off, and in two hours' time or less be in London, where he knew someone who would pay a good price for a Granada. It would soon be a different colour and have a new number plate, no questions asked and money in Terry's pocket that would keep him for two or three months without needing to work.

The decision was easily made.

Soon Terry was on the road to London, driving hard again but watching the limit. Jonathan's body lay beneath the dark still waters of the gravel pit, the surface restored to the glassy calm that had been broken by one loud, single splash.

Early traffic was entering London as Terry reached Hammersmith. He blended with it, driving down the side streets that led to the inno-cent-seeming workshop which fronted a thriving unofficial used car business. This was a place where someone was on duty all round the clock and Terry soon concluded his deal. He pedalled away on Mavis's bike and reached Paddington station with time for a really good breakfast before catching the train back to Westborough.

The blanket that had covered the body was in the boot of the car.

Sue sat in the hotel lounge after breakfast looking at *Country Life*, which she found dull. It was full of advertisements for houses like Harcombe and bigger. At intervals she rose and went to the door to look out. Twice she walked up to the car park and looked around her as if seeking the Granada.

Major Smythe, the hotel proprietor, noticed the restlessness of his pretty guest as he moved to and fro himself on hotel business. Sue judged her moment and told him that either during the night or early that morning Jonathan had got up, dressed, and driven away without waking her and without leaving a message. The major looked at her warily, hoping there would be no trouble. A conventional man himself, he had opened the hotel with his wife's money on his retirement and he did not like unmarried couples who openly signed the register; a decent concealment of adultery was only good manners, in his opinion. This time, if the fellow didn't turn up, there might be an unpaid bill to chase as well as a missing guest.

He saw the bruise on Sue's cheek, and noticing his gaze Sue touched the place with her own long fingers, their nails newly varnished blood red.

'Odd that he left no note,' the major suggested.

'Yes.' Sue sighed the answer, turning her head so that the light fell more directly on to her face. 'He's been very depressed,' she explained. 'His wife won't divorce him, you see, and we had a quarrel.' She touched her cheek again and the major felt chilled. 'This was to be a sort of honeymoon weekend, to forget.'

'You're not thinking of telling the police?'

'Oh no!' Sue looked directly at the major. She had large, dark, tragic eyes. How could the fellow go off and leave her? 'He'll come back,' she said. 'Won't he?'

'Of course he will,' the major assured her, relieved that she didn't seem panicky, simply sad. 'Perhaps he's just thinking things out,' he suggested. He wanted no scandal at the hotel. It would help no one to have the police here when all that had happened was a domestic dispute.

Major Smythe was on good terms with the Chief Constable and had been grateful for police discretion before now when dealing with pilfering staff. So far, no guests had reported problems more serious than the loss of a few trinkets. A notice warned them to place valuables in the hotel safe and absolved the management from responsibility. You couldn't watch everyone all the time.

With luck the fellow would reappear in time to pay his account and go.

Somehow, Sue got through the day. There was nothing at all to do. She strolled in the grounds and round the village. At twelve she had a drink in the bar and started talking to a middle-aged man who was waiting for his wife. The wife looked daggers at Sue when she found the pair of them in lively conversation. Sue smiled inwardly as she recognized the look. It was so easy. You just had to make them think themselves important, flatter their stupid male egos; then they ate out of your hand, as Giles was doing.

Giles. Her thoughts hardened. She wouldn't wait long: just a decent amount of time while people accepted that Jonathan had left her. Once Giles knew that Jonathan had hit her, he would be Sir Galahad himself, Sue thought.

Lunch was not included in the weekend terms, so she had cold ham and chicken in the bar. The other couple ate there too, but did not ask her to join them. The husband made a small, sad *moue*, shrugging silently as he caught Sue's eye. She sat demurely with a second vodka and lime – the first had been bought by her new friend – and her meal, exchanging glances with him while his wife's attention was fixed on her own plate.

It passed the time.

She had a bath and repainted her nails before dinner, using a different varnish: bright coral. The maid had tidied the room. Jonathan's anorak and cap were both in the wardrobe. Sue lay on the bed watching television before going over to the restaurant.

Major Smythe was in the hall greeting his various guests. He asked Sue if she had had any news, but there was nothing to report.

'Have you tried ringing your home?' asked the major. 'He may be there.' He assumed they lived together.

Sue thought quickly. It was a reasonable suggestion. 'I've tried,' she said. 'There was no reply.'

'You mentioned his wife,' said the major, with some embarrassment. What messy lives people led! 'Might she know where he is? Do you know her address?' This was more tactful than suggesting that Jonathan had returned to her.

'I do, but I couldn't ring her,' said Sue. 'She hates me. She won't let her children meet me.'

'Tch, tch.' The major pondered. 'Should I ring her?' he wondered aloud. 'Just ask for him? If he's there, she'll say so. If he comes to the telephone you can speak to him and ask him his plans.' And I, perhaps, can refer to the account, the major reflected. 'Perhaps a male voice – ?' he added.

Sue turned the idea over in her mind. It could do no harm.

'I'm not sure – ' she began, but the major broke in. 'Surely it's reasonable?' he insisted.

Sue understood the major's problem about the bill, though she would not allude to it; what would Bruce do at the Rigby in such a case? And what would be wisest for herself? Terry had not foreseen this complication.

Sue did not want to offend the major. She gave in and went with him to his offfice while he looked up Hilary's number in the complete set of directories which he kept there. While he dialled and the number rang, Sue sat in a deep leather armchair trying to wear an expression combining the right amount of concern and apprehension; it was not difficult.

'Oh – ' she heard the major say. 'May I speak to Mr Jonathan Cooper, please?'

There was a curt reply. The major glanced across at Sue, shaking his head.

'Not there? I see. Where can I find him, do you know?'

There was a further short squawk from the telephone.

'Yes, I have that address,' said the major suavely.

Sue could hear the interrogative note in the next remark from the telephone. 'My name is Smythe,' she heard the major answer. 'I am the owner of the Court Grange Hotel, Twistleton. Mr Cooper has been our guest and we want to get in touch with him.'

Hilary said something else.

'I quite understand,' said the major calmly. 'I'm sorry to have troubled you. Goodbye,' and he replaced the receiver. 'She hasn't seen him for two weeks, since he last visited the children,' he told Sue. 'I'm sorry.'

Sue turned a tearful face towards him.

'Thank you,' she whispered.

The major himself escorted her to a quiet corner of the restaurant and ordered her a half bottle of the best burgundy with the compliments of the house. He murmured to the head waiter. Sue received assiduous attention throughout the meal, some of it from the two waiters who had served dinner in the room the previous night.

She knew she should peck at her food, but she couldn't hold back.

'Worry always makes me hungry,' she told the waiter, with truth. So did anger and sex.

Everyone disappeared from the residents' lounge as soon as their coffee was finished. Off to fuck, Sue thought. She would not stay there alone, and she did not want to talk to the major again. She went to her room where she took off her black dress, loosened her hair from the tight knot in which she had worn it for dinner, and lay on the bed watching television.

After a while she began to day-dream about the future when Giles would be eating out of her hand, granting her every whim. They would go to Barbados or Nice in the winter, she planned, and with them would be Terry. Perhaps he could become Giles's valet or chauffeur, or maybe his secretary. Giles would age rapidly and they would have plenty of chances to be together. The fact that Giles would need to earn his living was ignored in this scenario.

She wished she could ring Terry, to see how things had gone, but the call would be billed and might be traced. She blessed the day Alice Armitage had crashed her car into Terry's. They would be kind to Alice; she was resolved about that; they would take her about with them when they travelled, and find her some nice flat. They wouldn't want her around all the time.

The one flaw in this bright future was Helen. Would she make trouble? She might use some of the money. She could have an accident, Sue mused, lying there in the warm, comfortable room alone, while in other apartments in the hotel guests soothed old hurts with caresses or tried to recapture youthful illusions. Terry knew a lot about cars; he could fix Helen's in some way. They must be ready to snatch any chance that came for although they were both young, now was the time for the good things in life before you were too old to enjoy them. Look at Giles. What was the good of having all that money and being too miserable to enjoy it?

Restless, she got up from the bed, put on slacks, sweater and jacket and went out of the building into the grounds. Lamps were placed here and there on the paths and walks so that guests could safely ramble after dark. The night was full of sounds. A dog fox barked in the distance, although

Sue did not know that that was what it was. Some silent creature brushed past her face as she wandered along – a bat? Horrified, Sue put her hands to her head, holding her long hair tight against invasion. There were small squeaking sounds in the grass, and a faint singing came from the river. Sue reached a small bridge that spanned it and looked down at the dark water sliding by.

She shivered, standing there, and turned back towards the brightly lit block of the main hotel, an urban product hurrying back to known comfort.

Sue slept badly that night and dreamed of Jonathan wringing his hands and weeping, with blood pouring down his face from a wound above his eye.

18

Sue dropped off into a heavy slumber with the dawn, and did not wake until nine.

She rang for breakfast in her room, thinking to hell with toast and coffee and ordering eggs and bacon. She ate every scrap of food that was brought.

It was nearly eleven o'clock by the time she was ready for the day and went over to the main building. Major Smythe saw her enter the hall and could tell from her expression that she had had no news.

He suggested that she should telephone Harcombe again. By now the wanderer might have returned. Sue saw that he would think it unreasonable if she refused and allowed him to put through the call.

The line was engaged, he told her, coming out of his office all smiles.

'Engaged?' How could it be engaged when no one was there?

'If you ring again soon, you'll be able to speak to him,' said the major.

Sue's heart was thudding. Then she remembered the call she had made to Helen before she and Terry left Harcombe on Friday afternoon. The phone had been left off the hook.

'Yes,' she said, and then, 'No, I don't think I'll do that – I think I'll just get back.' She opened her eyes wide at the major. 'Not to make a fuss, you know.'

The major didn't. He thought the whole thing most regrettable. Sue asked for her bill and the major himself made it up.

'There's no phone call on it,' he said, frowning. 'You said you had telephoned your home.'

'Yes – yes, I did,' said Sue. Drat him! He was out for every penny he could get.

'Our mistake – never mind,' said the major, determined to check the arrangements for billing telephone calls, as if one was missed, others would be and that must be stopped. The major presented Sue with the totalled account, less telephone call.

Sue paid it in cash with some of the money Terry had given her. That would finish the matter as far as the major was concerned. She asked about trains, and the major looked them up. There was one in just over an hour.

Sue doubted if she would be ready in time to catch it as she hadn't yet packed, but the major, although he thought her a taking little thing, wanted this ended. He assured her that there would be plenty of time and ordered a taxi. He had been relieved to see that her wallet was comfortingly full of banknotes.

She was eager to leave, but when the taxi dropped her at the small country station, she saw a blackboard notice on the platform announcing that the train she had come to catch had been cancelled. British Rail regretted any inconvenience.

'You can say that again,' muttered Sue. She left her cases in the ticket office and went into a pub near the station, where she had two vodkas and lime and a ploughman's. It was after four when she reached Westborough and she took a taxi straight to the Rigby.

'Terry about?' Sue asked Anthea, on duty at reception.

'He was. He's gone off,' said Anthea.

He would have, of course, since the bar was closed. Their plan had ended with her taking a taxi back to Harcombe but now she had altered the script. She went down the yard and up to his room.

Terry, exhausted after his night without sleep on Friday and all his physical exertions, had arrears of sleep still to make up and was lost to the world when she tried his door. It was locked, but she rattled it, calling his name, and he woke with a jerk, hurrying over to open it, finger to lip, his expression furious.

'What are you doing here?' He hissed the words at her.

Sue came into the room.

'What do I do now?' she asked.

Terry put a hand over her mouth. One of the waiters slept in the next room and was probably in there now.

'Don't say anything,' he whispered, nodding at the thin dividing wall, and then, more loudly, 'Oh – Sue – did you have a nice weekend?'

Sue stared at him. Then she got the message.

'Well – er – no. Jonathan went off,' she said.

Terry nodded encouragingly.

'Went off? What do you mean?' he said.

'He disappeared on Friday night,' said Sue. 'Took the car and vanished. I don't know where he is. I waited until today, but he hasn't come back.'

'Oh, I expect he'll turn up,' said Terry easily. 'Maybe he'll be at home when you get there.'

'Do you think so?' said Sue.

'Yes, I'm sure of it,' said Terry. 'Better get back, hadn't you, and see?'

She stared at him. Surely he would take her?

'Get a taxi,' Terry said, impatiently. Then, as she still stared at him blankly, he whispered, 'I haven't got the car yet. My car.'

'Oh!' Sue was briefly at a loss, but then she said softly, 'Come with me.'

Terry pondered. He must collect his car as soon as he could. If they went in a taxi to Great Minton, he could fetch it and drop her off at the lodge. It would save him a bus ride or a trip on the small bike – he hadn't decided yet how to go. He grinned.

'All right,' he said.

He would leave Sue at the gates to Harcombe House. She would have to manage the next bit alone; he had done his part for the present.

Alice's weekend visit to Bournemouth had not been a great success. She had felt adventurous setting off on the spur of the moment and making such a long trip, for all her recent journeys had been short ones in the Westborough area. The hotel she had chosen was in a side road not far from the sea and only a mile from Windlea. It was small and quiet; there was a bathroom just along the corridor from her bedroom. Alice unpacked her case and set out her bedroom slippers, pink fluffy mules, ready for use. You soon grew accustomed to having everything near at hand, she thought, feeling strange for a moment. Then she pulled herself together and went down to the hall where there was a pay-phone.

Alice dialled her friend Audrey's number. Perhaps, when Audrey heard how near she was, she would invite Alice round for dinner. Alice waited patiently for an answer as the telephone rang in Audrey's house, but there was no reply. There was nothing for it but to make the best of the evening on her own.

The drive had tired her. She went in to dinner promptly at half-past seven, finding three other elderly ladies ahead of her at the door as two strokes on a gong rang out. A friendly middle-aged waitress showed her to a distant table, smiling pleasantly. Dinner was served at a good speed. Alice enjoyed a glass of the house burgundy with her meal, and took coffee later in the lounge. The other three ladies and a couple all finished eating at much the same time. The couple, after conferring together in low voices, left the room, and the three ladies asked Alice if she played bridge. When she said that she didn't, they looked disappointed.

'We can often make up a four with a weekend visitor,' said one of them.

Alice discovered that they lived in the hotel. In the winter they had excellent rooms, but in the summer they had to move to lesser apartments, leaving the best rooms free for holiday guests. Their weekly payments helped to keep the hotel solvent through the winter. The three began complaining about the meal, which Alice had thought was good. Wearied, she soon said good-night and went up to her room where she whiled away the rest of the evening watching television, just as she did at home.

In the morning she telephoned Audrey and again there was no reply. Alice put on her coat with the fur collar and went for a walk past Windlea. She stood in the road looking up at the house. The room with the bow window on the first floor had been hers and Walter's; there they had lain together in unexciting contentment through most of their long marriage, their roles at home calmly dove-tailed. The years of Walter's retirement had been, in some ways, the best. He had spent happy hours at the bowls club; Alice had joined a flower arranging group. Never great walkers, they often went out for the day in the car to look at country houses and Walter became interested in paintings because they saw so many. At home, he gardened while Alice cooked or read novels from the library. They did not talk a great deal because most of the time they knew each other's wishes and views. Each, now, accepted the other's limitations and strengths. We trusted one another, Alice thought, noticing how the window frames had been painted blue. As she walked on she could see a swing in the garden. It was good to know that other children would enjoy the garden where Giles had bowled to Walter and where they could climb the old apple tree and build a camp fire in the spinney.

Giles should have married some local girl who would have been content with the unambitious security he could offer. He was orbiting around in a world he wasn't equipped to deal with. Amanda and Dawn were growing up; soon they would be leaving home and what would be left for him then? Alice had made a dreadful mistake in letting herself be persuaded to join them, but how could she pull out now? She could never get her capital back – or not without a terrible row involving the sale of the house, and that, she saw, would break up the marriage. She switched off her mind at this thought. Alice belonged to a generation who took its marriage vows seriously.

She came to Audrey's house. It had the blank look of one that was empty. She turned away and went to the end of the road where she caught the bus into town, an easier thing to do than taking the car on a busy Saturday. She spent the rest of the morning strolling round the shops and bought a new pair of bronze patent shoes with ankle straps and slim heels and a fawn fluffy sweater. Then she had lunch in a salad bar which was new since she left, and after that went to the cinema.

She left Bournemouth straight after breakfast on

Sunday without making contact with any of her former acquaintances, and as she drove home the painful tears came into her eyes. She belonged nowhere now.

She put the car in the barn. The Granada was missing; Jonathan and Sue would not be back until later from their weekend away, she supposed. Alice hoped it had been more successful than hers. There were two strange cars parked outside the main house; Helen's guests for lunch, presumably.

Letting herself in, creeping upstairs, afraid of meeting her son's awesome wife, Alice wondered how she could go on living like this for what might be another ten years – maybe more. What would happen then, when she could no longer manage the stairs? Would she be packed off to some home for the ancient, to spend her days propped up in a row amid other old people with no teeth and few wits, waiting for death? It would be better to get there first, to beat the fiend. Helen would not mind at all, she thought bleakly; indeed, she would be relieved. Dawn would scarcely notice, though Amanda, for a while, might miss their Scrabble and Horlicks and her grandmother's interest in Mr Jinks. What about Giles? Would he grieve? Would it lift her from his conscience?

She knew that it wouldn't; she would remain on it for ever if he found her one day with a plastic bag over her face.

Perhaps she could build up some sort of life, if she really tried. Mrs Duncan, for instance, was pleasant and friendly, though forceful and always busy. She was not in the least pretentious. Could Alice ask her round for a glass of sherry, or even supper, here in the flat? Or Mrs Hedges, who was perhaps less alarming? But then she must invite Miss Wilson too, and there wouldn't be space.

Alice thought she would try Mrs Duncan. She spun a brief fantasy in which, instead of accepting Alice's invitation, Mrs Duncan asked her down to the Old Vicarage.

But the telephone was out of order. Alice jiggled and pushed at the receiver rest but could get no dialling tone. At first she thought someone was there, connected and listening silently to her own tense breathing as she held the receiver to her ear. But no one spoke. The line was dead.

Later that afternoon, Alice was asleep with the television set on when Giles came in.

'Oh mother, you're here,' he exclaimed in surprise. 'I didn't think you'd be back yet.'

Alice abruptly woke from a dream in which Helen had turned into an octopus and was slowly strangling Giles with one tentacle after another. Now, she focused on her unstrangled son who stood before her, a middle-aged man with a high complexion and fleshy nose, thinning hair and a harassed expression. How had that pretty little boy, to whom she had read about Winnie the Pooh and Toad, turned into this defeated figure? Where was the long, lean lad who had played cricket on the lawn at Windlea with his father and keenly followed the Test matches?

'Oh – yes, dear,' Alice said, blinking. 'I'm back.'

Giles, in his turn, was for the first time seeing his mother as really old. She was always so elegant and had kept her neat figure, and though her face was lined, he never saw her without her extensive make-up. Now, surprised in sleep, she sat up in the armchair with her hair disordered and her face blotchy. She couldn't have been crying, surely? He peered at her more closely.

'Are you all right?' he asked. 'Didn't you enjoy your weekend?'

'I'm quite all right, thank you, Giles,' said Alice. 'It made a nice break.' There was no point in telling him otherwise. She looked at him questioningly. There must be a reason for this visit – and at a time when he expected her to be out. She was guiltily aware of her illicit heater burning its head off a few feet away.

He was explaining.

'I came to see if your phone was working,' he said, anxious that she should not think either he or Helen might pry round in her absence. Old people's privacy was important. Old people: he reminded himself that his mother was old. 'Ours is on the blink,' he went on. 'I thought perhaps it was just us and that yours was all right.'

In fact, Helen had suggested that Alice might have left hers off the hook, though Giles had pointed out that if she had – and such carelessness was right out of character – the instrument would be buzzing. Now he could see that the receiver was in place. Before Alice could say that she had already discovered her telephone was out of order he had lifted the receiver and pressed the rest. Nothing happened.

'No,' he said. 'It's dead too.'

'Oh dear,' said Alice. 'Do you want to make a call?'

'Helen does,' said Giles. 'No one's called us for a couple of days but we haven't wanted to ring out so we didn't realize something was wrong. Helen wants to speak to a client. It's important. I'll have to report it.'

'They won't mend it today, will they?' asked Alice. 'Not on a Sunday.'

'No, I suppose not,' said Giles. 'Well, I'm glad you're back, mother.' Then he lost his head. 'Come down and have supper with us, will you? I'm sure there's plenty.'

Alice's heart glowed and she smiled at her son, whom she loved. She knew he would regret the words as soon as he realized he would have to tell Helen what he had done, so she saved him in advance.

'Thank you, dear, but I won't, if you don't mind,' she said. 'I'll probably eat early and go to bed. I'm a little tired after the drive.'

Giles's slow-moving mind had caught up with her thoughts in just the manner she had anticipated and he heard her with relief.

'Another time, then,' he said. 'When Helen's out. She's out a lot these days. Just the two of us, eh?'

Alice nodded, eyes bright.

Giles glanced round the room. He had noticed how cosy it was when he entered, and was pleased; she must be quite snug up here. Now he saw the convector warmly glowing. Funny: he hadn't seen it before, but then he so seldom came up here. He thought she had just the fire and the fan he had bought.

Alice followed his glance and again forestalled him.

'I see you've noticed my new heater,' she said briskly. 'I don't leave it on when I'm out, and it was rather cold.'

'No – well – ' Giles hoped Helen wouldn't discover what Alice had done. 'It'll be better next year, when the new heating system's in,' he said lamely.

Alice wept a little more when he had gone. He was trapped. And so was she.

'What an age you've been, Giles,' said Helen when he returned. 'Well?'

'Well, what?'

'What about the telephone, of course? Had she left it off?'

'No. It's dead,' said Giles shortly.

'Well, I must ring my client,' said Helen. 'I'll use the telephone in the lodge and report this out of order at the same time.'

'Jonathan and Sue are away,' said Giles.

'I know that,' said Helen. 'But I've got a key, haven't I? I can go in and use the telephone, for God's sake.'

'Couldn't you go down to the call-box in the village?' said Giles. 'They may not like you wandering round the house while they're out.'

'I shan't be wandering round, as you put it,' said Helen. 'I'll simply be using their telephone, and I'll do it through the operator, ADC, and refund them the cost. Will that satisfy you?'

Giles saw that it was useless to argue. He went off to his study with the *Sunday Times* while Helen, in her tight black pants and padded Indian jacket, took the spare keys of the lodge from her desk and walked off down the drive.

Some ten minutes later the telephone rang. There were three instruments in Harcombe House apart from the one in Alice's attic, and one was in the kitchen. Giles crossed through and lifted the receiver.

'Hullo?' he said.

'Oh – so it is working now,' said Helen's voice. 'How strange. I thought I'd just try it, after I'd made my call. The receiver here was off the hook. How very odd. Ring back, will you, when I've hung up, to make sure it's all right.' She cut the line.

Giles hung up, waited a short time and then dialled the lodge. Helen answered at once.

He worked it out while she was on her way back to the house. Jonathan or Sue must have called on Friday, been somehow distracted and failed to clear the line before going away. Sue had been ringing him, he thought fatuously, forgetting that this must have happened during the afternoon, while he was at work.

'How extraordinary to go away leaving the telephone off the hook,' Helen said, so puzzled that she actually spoke to Giles about it. 'I had two false calls on Friday afternoon – I answered but no one was there. I suppose that was just coincidence.'

She hadn't understood, Giles thought, almost tittering in delight that here was something she wasn't so wonderfully clever about. He didn't tell her. Let her work it out for herself.

It was strange that Sue had rung twice, without speaking either time. Perhaps the first call had been some other misdial, and Sue, hearing Helen, had realized that he would be out and had lost her cool, leaving the receiver off.

The flattering nature of this deduction blinded Giles to its oddness; by the time that dawned, he had learned that Jonathan was missing.

19

Alice was restless when Giles had gone. She fidgeted about, tidying the already tidy sitting-room. Then she washed through stockings and underwear worn in Bournemouth. After that she looked out of the window wondering if Sue and Jonathan were back.

She could see a thread of light between the drawn curtains at the lodge window, and outside, in the rays cast from the exterior light, she recognized Terry's car.

What was he doing there?

Spending the evening with Jonathan and Sue was the obvious, straightforward explanation, but Alice was not certain just how straightforward a person Terry was. Things happened when he was about, and not always for the best.

As she stood at her window, watching and wondering, the lodge door opened and Terry emerged. He walked quickly down the path, got into his car, started the engine, turned on the lights and drove off. A moment later the door opened again and Sue came out. She walked up to the front door of the main house, just out of Alice's line of vision. There was an instant when a panel of light fell on the ground as the front door was opened and then all was dark once more.

Sue had gone for advice.

She and Terry had discussed what to do, what would be natural had things been as they seemed.

'Was it all right? No one saw you?' she had asked him, and he'd reassured her, not giving any details.

'It's not nice, manhandling a dead man,' he told her. 'I don't want to go into it.'

'Well, what now?' Sue had said. 'I can't just go on as if nothing's happened, can I? There's the rent, for a start. It's paid to the end of the month, but I can't manage after that on my own. And there's his work – Jonathan's. Do I get in touch with his boss?'

Terry pondered. What would be best? She was right, she couldn't just do nothing; but if anyone reported Jonathan missing, the police would start nosing around looking for him. They would not find him, of course – nor the car. It would be an unsolved mystery. He did not want Sue to find out what he had done with the car but he was very glad that he'd changed the plan. That money under his mattress was a nice little piece of insurance. Though it went against the grain to do it, he had paid back what he had borrowed from the till. That alone justified selling the car, for if the money had been missed, he would have been the obvious suspect. He would have had to find some cash – and fast – otherwise, and had not looked ahead to that beyond thinking that Mrs Armitage would come up trumps if he pressed her.

Funny that he didn't fancy Sue any more. She hadn't changed. She was still lively and pretty, and Christ, did she want it! But he didn't, now. She was the only girl he'd ever truly fancied for herself, but he'd suddenly gone right off her.

'You're on good terms with Giles,' he said. 'I think you should tell him. Go up to the house and ask their advice – both of them. That would be normal.'

'And then?' asked Sue.

'Do as they say,' said Terry. 'If they think you should ring his boss, do it.'

'What if they think I should tell the police?'

'Oh – stall. Say you'll give it a bit longer in case he just comes walking in, as then you'd feel silly. Besides, he might be angry.'

Sue nodded. She had wanted to go to bed then, but he wouldn't, so when he had gone she went straight up to the house.

Giles opened the door.

'Why, Sue, oh!' His delight at seeing her was plain. All the sagging folds on his face lifted, his mouth curved into a smile of joy, his eyes crinkled. Sue thought he looked quite nice when he was happy. 'Come in, come in,' he said.

Sue stepped over the threshold. She wore a red suede jacket over her slacks, and her long dark hair was loose. She smelled of the scent she always used, plus that indefinable other essence that was always about her and which Giles did not recognize as sheer femininity.

'I don't know what to do, Giles,' she said, standing close to him, looking up at him. The bruise on her face was fading now. He would be furious if he knew that Jonathan had hit her.

'Why, what's wrong?' he asked. He led her into the big drawing-room where they had held Alice's party and where a log fire burned. The air was smoky from the cigars and cigarettes of the lunch-time guests. Though she never smoked herself, Sue liked the smell of tobacco. 'Come and sit down,' said Giles, leading her to a seat by the fire. 'Shall I take your coat?'

She let him, allowing the weight of her hair to brush against his hand. Now was her chance to make a bid for sympathy. She sat at one end of the long sofa, hoping that Giles would think of sitting beside her. He might not; he was so dumb.

But he did, timidly placing himself not at the further end, yet not too close to her. To see her clearly he must either put on his glasses or keep a distance between them.

'Now, what's wrong?' he said.

'Jonathan's gone,' said Sue.

'Gone? What do you mean?' cried Giles. 'You don't mean he's left you?' That couldn't be true.

'I don't know. He just vanished while we were at Twistleton,' said Sue. 'Took off in the car during the night while I was asleep, and never came back.' She told him what had happened at the hotel –

243

how Major Smythe had telephoned Hilary and how in the end she had come home alone.

'You should have rung me,' said Giles. 'I'd have come for you.' He forgot that their telephone had been out of order.

'How could you? You had guests,' said Sue in a gently reproving tone. 'But what shall I do, Giles? If he doesn't come back – ' she did not end the sentence.

'Oh, he will – he'll get in touch, anyway,' said Giles. What a scoundrel the mild-seeming Jonathan must be! 'He'll want his things – his clothes and so on, if he's really left. I'm sure he'll come back, Sue.' How could he not return to this delicious girl? 'Perhaps he's ill. You said he was depressed. It's the only explanation, isn't it? Maybe he had a blackout. Have you rung the hospitals?'

She had not thought of doing that, she told him.

'I'll do it,' said Giles, becoming masterful.

It took him quite a long time, and while he was telephoning, Helen came to speak to Sue.

'Giles told me what's happened. I'm sorry,' she said. 'Beastly for you. Embarrassing.'

'Yes,' said Sue.

'You paid the hotel?'

'Oh yes,' said Sue, surprised that this should be Helen's first question. Giles hadn't thought of that. Money wasn't important to him, but it mattered to his wife, just as it did to her.

'I'll get you a drink,' said Helen. 'I'm sure you need one. How did you get back?'

Sue told her about the train and added that she had gone to the Rigby Arms and Terry had brought her home.

'Oh, of course – he's an old friend of yours, isn't he?' said Helen, who had seen him about the place. 'I suppose you'll move back to Westborough, if Jonathan's gone for good.' I'll need new tenants, she thought. She'd put up the rent.

'I don't know,' said Sue. What if Terry shared the lodge with her? That would be great. He would keep out of the way while she worked on Giles.

'Oh well – time enough to decide when you know what's happened,' said Helen.

She fetched Sue a vodka and lime and a gin and tonic for herself, and began to tell Sue about a house she had been asked to do up near Slough, for a pop star. She had never done that sort of place before and was finding it hard to adapt her ideas to his wish for psychedelic effects. Sue found the conversation fascinating.

'Not your scene, really, is it?' she said.

'No. I thought of turning it down at first,' said Helen. 'But one should seize every opportunity that comes along. You never know where it may lead.'

'That's right,' agreed Sue, who also never passed up a chance.

She had almost forgotten why she had come by the time Giles returned, having drawn blank at all the hospitals he had called.

'The next thing to do is to tell the police,' he said.

'Oh no!' exclaimed Sue. 'Nothing can have

happened to him. If he'd had an accident, the hospitals would know.'

What if he'd been killed, wondered Giles.

'You'd hear, if he'd been in a road accident,' said Helen. 'The police would get in touch with you.'

'Would they?' asked Giles. 'Wouldn't they tell his wife?'

'What address would he have on him?' asked Helen.

Sue didn't know. She said the car belonged to the firm but she did not know if it was registered in their name or his.

'Shall I ring his wife?' Giles suggested. 'It's some time since the hotel rang her, after all, and maybe she's heard from him by now. He's fond of his children, isn't he?'

'If he's lost his memory or something, he'll have forgotten about them,' Sue said, rather wildly. She didn't want anyone ringing Hilary again.

But Helen thought it could do no harm. She poured Sue another drink while Giles made the call. He came back shaking his head.

'Would you like to stay here for the night, Sue?' he offered, and went blithely on, ignoring Helen's frown. 'Perhaps you'd better not be on your own?'

'He might come back in the night,' said Helen bluntly. 'You'd better be there.'

Giles escorted her back to the lodge door. He kissed her chastely on the brow.

'Poor little Sue,' he said. 'Let me know if there's any news – anything I can do.'

'You can take me to work in the morning,' said Sue promptly, and he beamed.

'Of course.' He squeezed her hand. Now he had something to look forward to.

'I'm so glad I've got you to turn to, Giles,' said Sue as a sweetener, and went into the house.

The storage heaters kept the chill off, but the fire was not lit and she had nothing for supper except what might be in the fridge. Sue looked round in distaste. Terry hadn't even taken the cases upstairs: there they were, in the middle of the sitting-room.

Sue left Jonathan's where it was and took her own up to the bedroom where the bed was unmade and her discarded clothes were strewn about. It was all very different from the luxurious room at the Court Grange where she had spent the last two nights. A maid – someone to clear up after her – that's what she needed, Sue thought, opening her case and flinging a few garments about. That pop star Helen was working for had one for sure. Sue couldn't think why Helen had only Mrs Wood from the village. Of course, in a place that size you didn't get into such a mess, she thought; there was space for things to lie about. Sue forgot that things were never left lying about in Helen's tidy house.

How could she get through the evening?

Sue went down to the kitchen. Half a loaf of bread, mouldy now, sat on the kitchen table where she had left it on Friday. There was no fresh milk.

Alice would have some. Alice would offer her something to eat, even if it was only scrambled egg. Sue was starving. She had had only a scratch lunch in the pub near the station and now two vodkas and lime.

She had better ring the old girl.

Sue went to the telephone to dial Alice's number. As she waited for the old woman to answer, she was aware of something not quite as she expected it to be, but it was not until late that night, when she was in bed among the grubby, tumbled sheets, that she remembered she had left the telephone off the hook when she went off with Terry on Friday. Who had replaced it? Terry?

At the big house, Helen, too, forgot about it until after Sue had gone.

'We never asked her what she or Jonathan rang up about on Friday,' she said. 'And why they didn't hang up.'

'It must have been Jonathan,' said Giles. 'Perhaps he put the phone down while he fetched something and then forgot about it. He seems pretty mixed up just now.'

'It's all very unsatisfactory,' said Helen.

Giles thought that Jonathan might be having a breakdown. Things might simply have become too much for him, a state with which Giles himself had some sympathy.

Sue had forgotten that when Giles and Helen were in, telephone calls to Alice had to be put through from the main house and she was disconcerted to hear Giles's voice on the line. He switched her through without comment.

'Can I pop up and see you?' Sue asked, when Alice answered.

'Yes, of course, Sue,' said Alice. 'That will be lovely. I'm all alone.'

Giles was listening, and he felt fresh guilt. The main house was so large. Why couldn't his mother be downstairs now, in the warm drawing-room beside the log fire? Their guests had gone and Helen would be spending the evening in her sitting-room. He sighed. He saw no way out of this toil, but if Jonathan didn't come back, he resolved to offer his mother the lodge, no matter what Helen said. He could see that Sue would not stay there alone; she couldn't afford it, and without a car she would be marooned.

But of course Jonathan would return, though surely his future with Sue must be uncertain now. Had he known of their quarrel, Giles's thoughts might have pursued this line in relation to himself further than he let them tonight.

When Sue told Alice what had happened at the Court Grange, the old woman was appalled. There was so much sorrow about; she hated to think of it. She suggested that Jonathan might have felt remorse about having struck Sue and had gone off to think things over, but it was thoughtless to have left no explanatory note. And leaving her in the hotel without paying the bill and with no means of getting home was irresponsible, to say the least.

'I'd have fetched you, my dear,' she said, just as Giles had done.

'You were away,' said Sue, and asked Alice about

her weekend. She laughed at Alice's description of the permanent guests at the hotel and their complaints. She had worked in a hotel like that before coming to the Rigby.

'Have you had supper, Sue?' Alice asked, and when the girl said no, at once began fussing round looking for something to feed her on. She had intended to have a boiled egg herself.

Sue felt slightly ashamed at having forced Alice's hand over providing the meal, but reminded herself that she was cheering the poor old thing up in her solitude. They had baked beans and poached eggs, with toast, and Alice opened a tin of peaches. They ate with their plates balanced on magazines on their knees watching television, and it was really quite cosy. Sue left when she saw that Alice was having trouble concealing her yawns. She promised to let the old lady know at once if there was news.

'Do you think I should ring his boss in the morning?' asked Sue.

'Oh yes,' Alice said, and Giles agreed when she consulted him on her way into work the next day.

She telephoned from the Rigby. She'd forgotten to bring Jonathan's diary, so she had to look his firm's number up in the directory and she couldn't tell his employer what calls he had arranged for that day. Mr Prentiss sounded rather annoyed, but it wasn't her fault, Sue told him. She explained what had happened.

Mr Prentiss sat fuming in his office after the call. Jonathan Cooper was not the world's most wonderful salesman but he was conscientious, his figures were reliable and he was popular with their customers. He could be replaced without any trouble if he was developing a temperament, but it was to be hoped that this was some brief folly which would soon be over.

At eleven-fifteen a customer whom Jonathan was to have met earlier that day telephoned to enquire where he was. Mr Prentiss soothed him. Then he rang Hilary. She was the man's wife, after all, and if she would not report the man missing, Mr Prentiss most certainly would.

Hilary was on the defensive at once, as soon as she knew who was calling, and why.

'How should I know where he is?' she asked. 'You'd better ask that woman – Mrs whatever-her-name-is.'

Mr Prentiss was not so hard-hearted that he did not recognize the anguish in Hilary's voice, nor was he deceived by her pretence of forgetting the name of her supplanter.

'She doesn't know,' he told her. 'He walked out on her during a weekend break they were having at Twistleton. And she rang last Friday to say that he wasn't well. I'm so sorry to distress you, Mrs Cooper, but I need to know what's happening.'

So did Hilary. This was the third call she had received about Jonathan, and her livelihood and the children's depended on him.

'What do you want me to do?' she asked.

'Report him missing to the police,' said Mr

Prentiss. 'I understand that his landlord telephoned the hospitals last night, with no result, but the police will make a more thorough job of doing that. He may not have rung them all.'

'Oh!' There was a shock in Hilary's voice.

'Or I will, if you prefer,' said Mr Prentiss. 'But in any case I'm sure they will want to ask you about him.' He was thinking that Jonathan was unlikely to have been involved in a motor accident, for in that case his car would have been checked out by the police and his identity discovered.

Hilary was still Jonathan's wife.

'I'll do it,' she said. 'If you really think it's necessary.'

'He may need help,' said Mr Prentiss. The man had such a nice, if rather earnest wife, and the children were sweet. What got into people, wondered Mr Prentiss wearily; what made them fly off in their middle years? The fear of missing something? 'The sooner we know where he is, the better,' he said and added that unless she called him first, he would telephone later to see what the police had said.

Hilary sent the children next door to her neighbour while she made the call. It would not do for them to overhear this sort of conversation. She explained the trouble briefly, in whispers. Her neighbour was kind and helpful and had been a great support in the early days of Jonathan's fall from grace; it was she, when she heard of it from someone else, who had felt bound to tell Hilary about his affair.

Hilary kept her voice steady on the telephone. She explained to the female voice which answered that she wanted to report her husband missing. She was asked to hold on and then connected with a different voice, male and slow-speaking, which asked for her name and address. Hilary's control wavered then, and her words came out jerkily as she related what she knew about Jonathan's disappearance.

She was told that an officer would be with her shortly to take down the details.

Very soon, an area car drew up outside and a woman police officer in uniform came to the door. Hilary showed her into the sitting-room. WPC Grace Ferris took a quick look round to gain an impression of where she was. She saw a beige carpet, sand-coloured curtains at the long windows, books in a recess. There were prints on the wall, a Canaletto over the fireplace and Redouté roses on the other walls. It was a relief to see two toy cars parked on the hearthstone and knitting bundled up on the sofa, for the room looked clinically clean and bare.

'It may all be a fuss about nothing,' said Hilary nervously.

'It's not about nothing, if you're worried,' said the policewoman. 'Tell me why you're anxious.' She smiled encouragingly at the pale young woman much her own age who wore a beige shetland sweater over a brown shirt, and a baggy beige tweed skirt. 'Let's sit down, shall we?'

'Oh yes – sorry,' Hilary put her hand to her

mouth. She was very near tears. 'We haven't been living together for some time,' she said.

'I see.' Patiently, Grace Ferris extracted the facts: how the man from the hotel had telephoned first – Hilary understood, now, the reason for that call, and went off at a tangent to wonder how Jonathan could afford to stay at a place like that with 'that woman'. Eventually Grace Ferris learned when Hilary had last seen her husband, and obtained a description of him as well as details about his work. He had parents living; they were in Tenerife just now.

'He might be at their house, though?' suggested WPC Ferris.

Hilary had not thought of that. They dealt with the possibility at once by telephoning his parents' number. There was no reply. Grace Ferris did not tell Hilary that this was not proof of his absence. He might be there, perhaps dead: the local police would soon find out.

'How did he seem when you last saw him?' the police officer asked.

'Oh – I don't know. As usual,' Hilary said. But he had wanted to talk to her, and she had not let him.

'I see. Well, we'll get busy and be in touch,' said Grace Ferris. 'Have you got a photograph of him?'

Hilary took one from a drawer. It was a holiday snapshot showing the four of them – the two children, herself and Jonathan – on holiday in Cornwall.

'That's two years old,' said Hilary.

'I don't suppose he's changed much,' said Grace Ferris. She admired the children and asked their names and ages, and where they were now. Then she explained that if Jonathan was traced and found safe, the police were not obliged to tell Hilary more than just that. If he did not want his whereabouts known, his confidence would be respected.

'You might tell him to get in touch with his boss,' said Hilary bitterly. 'Or he'll lose his job.'

Grace Ferris said that he would be told.

'Most people turn up quite safely, you know,' she said.

When she had gone, Hilary went back to the sitting-room and indulged in the luxury of tears for a full ten minutes.

How could he behave like this? How could he?

20

While Jonathan's body lay in the ice-cold water of the old quarry, police all over the country went about their routine work. They patrolled the roads; strove to control the unruly; attended accidents; investigated robberies, muggings and cases of arson; enquired into fraud; pursued murderers.

An officer in an area car on normal patrol in the Twistleton area saw a Honda Accord parked on the grass verge above the village. There was no sign of a driver and the car was not locked. He checked it out, and in minutes established through the computer that it had been stolen from a car park in Swindon on Friday. It was soon taken away, to be returned to its owner.

Other officers began the task of trying to find Jonathan Cooper, aged thirty-six, five foot eleven inches tall, dark hair, brown eyes, pale complexion. Police at Westborough were asked to send an officer to the missing man's address in Harcombe to interview Mrs Sue Norris, with whom he had been living.

When PC Graves rang the bell at the lodge there was no reply so he went up to the main house, where Mrs Wood opened the door and in response to his question said that Mrs Norris was probably at work. Annoyed at being interrupted as she turned out the kitchen, a fortnightly task, Mrs Wood said, 'Why don't you ask the old lady?'

'Old lady?'

'Mrs Armitage senior. She lives upstairs. Very friendly she is, with them two,' said Mrs Wood, and then, showing some interest, 'Not in trouble, are they?'

Graves ignored the remark.

'Tell me, Mrs – er – ' he began in his most benign tone.

'Mrs Wood,' supplied that lady.

'Mrs Wood, do you know Mr Jonathan Cooper?'

'By sight, yes,' said Mrs Wood. 'Not to talk to. He's normally out at work when I'm here, but I have seen him when he's had days off, like. It's different with her – that Sue. She's often about – works shifts.'

'Where does she work?' asked Graves.

'At the Rigby Arms in Westborough,' said Mrs Wood.

'Mrs Armitage senior?' Graves pursued.

'It's her son owns this place,' said Mrs Wood, unbending, and added graciously, 'I'll take you up.'

So it was that Alice opened her door to the middle-aged constable with greying hair and a spreading waistline, one who had never sought promotion because he liked the job on the ground.

As soon as Mrs Wood – reluctantly, now – had departed, he asked when she had last seen Jonathan.

Alice was glad to know that proper enquiries were under way. She told Graves about Jonathan's alleged depression, the bruise on Sue's face and the weekend away to mend relations between the pair. She hadn't seen Jonathan for some time, herself; he'd been in bed on Friday when she left for Bournemouth. She told Graves what Sue had said about Jonathan disappearing during the night from the Court Grange Hotel.

'Do you think he's had an accident?' she asked.

Graves said that he was not the victim of any accident so far reported, although the possibility could not be ruled out. It was more likely to be a domestic matter; perhaps he wanted to get away and think things over on his own.

Alice thought this was very possible. She said that Sue would be back from the hotel around five, if she came on the bus; sooner if she got a lift. In either case it wouldn't be long for Graves to wait.

When Sue's shift ended that afternoon she went over to Terry's room at the Rigby, but he wasn't there. He was returning the bike to Mavis, though Sue had no way of knowing that.

Sue felt totally abandoned. She did not want to go back to the empty lodge. There would be no one around except Alice. She thought of hanging about in Westborough until opening time, then going into the bar to see if Giles would come in; he'd take

258

her home. He'd be sorry for her. It would be easy to get him to go into the lodge with her.

It was too soon. She knew it. She'd have to wait – not because of any scruples of her own but because of Giles's. He would want to be sure that Jonathan had really left her; then his pity would drive him to comfort her. Sue smiled, imagining it. Perhaps he'd fix her up with a nice flat somewhere, she mused. Why not? She'd rather that than marry him; she thought Terry's idea of that was going too far, although she supposed from the money point of view it would be best. But she didn't like the idea of any restraint on her freedom. She needed to talk to Terry, work it all out.

At the idea of shifting responsibility for some of her actions on to him, she felt easier. He was so inventive. He'd think of a way of getting her somewhere nice to live quite soon, she was sure. She couldn't stand that place on her own, not for long, but she saw that there was nothing for it now except to return there. She caught the bus which dropped her at the end of the lane and trudged the last mile to the village.

A white police Ford Escort was parked outside the lodge as Sue walked through the gates. She felt a moment of panic. What did it mean? Had they found Jonathan's burnt-out car and discovered who it belonged to? They'd be able to trace it if the number plate hadn't burned.

She was ready to receive this news in an appropriate manner as PC Graves got out of his car and came towards her.

'Mrs Norris? Mrs Sue Norris?' he asked.

Sue nodded. It wasn't hard to look solemn.

'I'd like a word, please, Mrs Norris,' said Graves. He remembered seeing her before, when there had been that unfortunate accident at the Rigby not long after Christmas and the barman had fallen down the cellar steps.

Sue remembered Graves, too, but he had not interviewed her; a sergeant had taken her short statement.

'We've met before, Mrs Norris,' said Graves as Sue took out her key and opened the door.

'Yes,' agreed Sue. 'Why are you here now?'

'I'm making some enquiries about Mr Jonathan Cooper,' said Graves. 'He lives here, I believe?'

'Yes, that's right,' said Sue. 'You'd better come in.' She led Graves into the house, took off her coat and settled herself down on the sofa, indicating that Graves should face her in the armchair.

'He's been reported missing, Mrs Norris,' said Graves. 'When did you last see him?'

Sue switched her line of thinking. Mr Prentiss must have rung the police: it had to be him. She must tell her story calmly. It wasn't the first recital, and her other hearers had accepted it easily.

'On Friday,' she said. 'We went away for the weekend.' She clenched her fists on each side of her thighs and spoke steadily. 'We were staying at the Court Grange Hotel at Twistleton for the weekend.' She swallowed.

'Yes?' prompted Graves.

'He went away in the night,' said Sue. 'Or early on Saturday morning while I was asleep. I woke up and he'd gone.'

'I see.' Graves wrote it down in his pocket book. 'Did he take his things? Pack his case?'

'No.'

'So what would he have been wearing, Mrs Norris?'

They couldn't have found the car. That was obvious. If they had, the man wouldn't be asking all these questions.

'Well, I don't know – what he wore for the trip down, I suppose.' What had Jonathan been wearing that other evening when it happened? Terry hadn't thought of this, in his planning – how she might be questioned in such a way. She frowned, trying to remember. 'Dark flannels – ' She was going to say he'd been wearing a sweater when she remembered Terry feeling inside Jonathan's jacket pocket for his diary. 'A tweed jacket,' she went on with more confidence. 'At least, I didn't pack it to bring it back, and he wore it for the trip.' But Terry, posing as Jonathan, had worn the anorak – well, Jonathan might have put it on over the jacket. Anyway, the anorak was here, in the hall. She'd hung it up herself. Luckily she'd taken Jonathan's case upstairs this morning, though she hadn't unpacked it.

'What colour?' asked Graves.

'Brown tweed,' said Sue. 'And a shirt – brown checks, maybe – I'm not sure. I could look through his things and see what's missing. But even then, I might not be right,' she warned. 'He did his own packing.'

'Shoes?' tried Graves.

She could see his feet in brown lace-up shoes sticking out as she tucked the blanket round them. She described them.

'What do you think has happened?' she asked.

'What's your opinion, Mrs Norris?' countered Graves. 'Weren't you worried?'

'Well, in a way, but you see we'd had a quarrel,' said Sue. 'Just a few days earlier. He'd been very depressed.'

'Why was that?'

'It was after seeing his children,' said Sue. 'He often got low, then.'

'You've no idea where he might have gone?'

'No. We had dinner in our room – he didn't feel like going to the restaurant – watched television for a bit, and then went to sleep. Or anyway, I did,' said Sue, regarding Graves with a steady gaze.

'Had he any friends he might have gone to see?'

'Not that I know of. He'd rather lost touch with the people he saw before we joined up,' said Sue.

'I see.'

'You'll let me know if you find him?' she asked. 'No matter what – ' she did not end the sentence.

'Have you any reason to think he might have wished to take his own life, Mrs Norris?' asked Graves. 'Had he ever threatened to?'

'No – no! It was just that he was so depressed, and then going off without a word,' said Sue.

'I expect he'll turn up, safe and sound,' said

Graves. 'You'll be at the Rigby Arms during working hours,' he established.

'Yes.' Sue explained about her shifts.

Graves got up to go. He glanced round the room. A fine film of dust covered most of the hard surfaces. He saw a slim black diary beside the telephone.

'Is that Mr Cooper's?' he asked.

'Yes,' said Sue.

'I'd like to take it, Mrs Norris,' said Graves. 'It might help us to trace him – addresses and such.'

Sue couldn't object. What harm could it do?

'What if he comes back and wants it?' she asked.

'Then he can collect it straight away from the station,' said Graves, and added, 'We'd like to know if – when – he does return, Mrs Norris. Save us going on with our enquiries, you see.'

'Of course,' said Sue.

Graves faithfully noted their conversation in his report.

It was strange that the car hadn't been found. You'd think it would make a lot of smoke and someone would have seen it. Still, if Terry had found a really remote spot, anyone noticing it from some distance away might think it was just a bonfire.

Sue said as much to Terry when she saw him the next day.

'Yeah – well, I did find a place miles from anywhere, didn't I?' he said. 'I told you I would.'
Sue had waylaid him when he came up from the

cellar carrying a crate of ginger ale bottles. 'Who sent them poking around, did they say?' He hadn't been pleased to hear of the visit from the police.

'Must have been his boss, I suppose,' said Sue. She didn't tell Terry about Giles ringing Hilary and the hospitals. 'I suppose it might stay lost for months – years, even. The car, I mean. Like those planes from the war. They've found some, haven't they, lost in woods?' She'd heard someone talking about it in the hotel, some old guy with a lame leg who'd been in the war. Creepy, it must be, with the bodies still there in their uniform.

'Of course it might,' said Terry. 'I shouldn't think we'll hear another word about it. He'll be one of those missing persons who never turn up.' He glanced round. It was risky to talk like this; someone might hear them. 'Didn't bother about the house, did he? The copper, I mean?' he asked, needing that reassurance.

'No. Just wanted to know what he'd been wearing,' said Sue, and decided not to mention the diary.

Terry thought warmly of the wad of notes under his mattress. He'd fade away while the search went on. In the end the police would give up and by then the body in the water would be unrecognizable. He'd return and present his account to Sue when she'd got things set up nicely with Giles. She wouldn't take long over that; she'd need some sort of anchor man; she couldn't operate on her own, as he could.

Terry was paid weekly. He didn't want to provoke any ill-feeling with Bruce so he thought he would tell some tale about his mother being ill and needing him at home, something to counteract any resentment at not working out the full trial period he and Bruce had agreed at the start. It might be useful to be able to quote Bruce as a referee. Terry knew he had given satisfaction; he always did. He wouldn't need to think about work for some time; he might even go off to Barbados or somewhere like that: there'd be pickings, for sure, in those sort of places.

It was weird how he hadn't been able to get enough of Sue at first, and yet now she didn't turn him on at all. Pity, really; it had been great for a while. He'd always be able to find her, for she wouldn't be moving far from Giles – not unless someone else turned up, some better chance, but he'd take care that she wouldn't know how to find him.

Polishing glasses, pouring out doubles, pulling pints, smiling and jesting with the customers, Terry planned for the future.

Morgues and accident reports were checked. There was no sign of either Jonathan Cooper or his car, but the police did not regard the search for him as urgent. He was no small child that might have been abducted; he was a man in a domestic mess who had probably gone somewhere to think things over.

Graves handed the diary in and made his report. In time, someone would ring round the possible contacts but meanwhile other business had to be dealt with too.

Jonathan's parents' home was visited by the local force. There were no signs that it had been entered while they were away on holiday, and a neighbour produced a key so that the police could make sure Jonathan was not there, either dead or alive.

Hilary Cooper lay sleepless at night, wondering where Jonathan had gone. Why was there no news? Her resentment was greater than any anxiety; how dared he do this on top of everything else?

By day, she presented her usual impassive face to the children, occupying them with Plasticine or paints until she was ready to take them out. At half-term she always planned expeditions of varying kinds, mainly for edification. She wondered about telephoning her parents to tell them what had happened. They lived in Suffolk, where her father, a schoolmaster, was nearing retirement, and she always took the children to visit them in the school holidays. If she rang, what could they do? They wouldn't be able to find Jonathan and it would only add to their already great worry about her and the children. Time enough when he turned up and she knew what was behind his disappearance. Had he had some sort of breakdown? She thought again of his attempt to talk to her. What had he wanted to say? What if she'd let him? Would it have made any difference? The mess they were in was entirely of his creation; she had always done her part – cooking, cleaning the house, caring for him and the children. There were always ironed shirts in the cupboard and a meal ready each evening; she had nothing to reproach herself for in that way. Naturally, with two small, demanding children, she was tired and had lost some of her youthful looks, not that she'd ever been much of a one to bother about her appearance beyond being clean and neat. Life wasn't about that; it was about providing a secure home for your family; teaching your children to develop their skills and the right degree of independence appropriate to their age; ensuring they got the best possible education to take, in their turn, a responsible place in the world. Jonathan had seemed to share these views until that little slut got hold of him.

People did have breakdowns. You'd think, though, that she would be the one to do that, not Jonathan. But Hilary had always kept herself under control.

On Tuesday evening when the children were in bed and asleep, she telephoned the police to ask if there was any news. WPC Ferris was not available but Hilary learned that so far no trace of Jonathan had been discovered.

Most of the schools in the country had their half-term holiday that week. Though cold, the weather was dry and children ranged far and wide during their days of leisure. Some went on trips to museums or cinemas; some went shopping; some visited grandparents. Many tore about on cycles or roller skates.

Some went canoeing.

On Wednesday afternoon, two boys who had spent most of the day paddling about on the dark waters of the old gravel pit to which Terry had driven on Friday night, pulled in to the side to refresh themselves with Mars Bars and crisps. That morning they had set out on their day's voyaging armed with enough picnic food to last the day and with instructions as to taking care ringing in their ears. They'd been Indians travelling along the Mississippi, they'd shot rapids and hunted for elk. Wrapped in warm clothes, with wool caps on their heads and bright orange life jackets as protection, they had had a blissful day.

Soon the light would be gone. They must set off to base camp for the night before the snows came – they were now at the North Pole. Once they reached land, there would be quite a trudge, carrying their canoe, down the main track to their village, where the friendly Eskimos, in the shape of their families, would be cooking whale meat stew for their nourishment.

They made landfall at a slightly different spot from where they had put their canoe into the water that morning, which explained why they had missed it then.

They saw the pale white hand of a dead man,

partially screened by a bush that overhung the black water of the artificial lake, breaking the surface.

21

It seemed straightforward at first: a drowned man, a possible suicide. But in sudden death the possibility of foul play as the cause must always be explored.

The doctor certified life extinct and the body was taken away to the mortuary. Papers on him – his notecase, sodden, containing eighteen pounds in notes, his driving licence and Access card, gave a probable identity. The collator soon married up the sad corpse with the missing Jonathan Cooper.

There was no sign of his car, which was odd. Perhaps it was hidden in the scrub area surrounding the quarry. Darkness had fallen by now; a search for it could begin in the morning.

Hilary was just packing up her knitting ready to go to bed when her doorbell rang. A rather young constable stood on the step, dreading breaking the news.

'You've found him,' said Hilary, one hand at her throat.

'Yes, Mrs Cooper.'

Before he went on to say that it was bad news, Hilary guessed from his sombre tone. She remained totally calm while he told her the little they knew, refusing to let him call a neighbour. She would be all right, she said. She'd been alone for months; this was nothing new.

There was the question of identifying the body, the officer said. Was there someone else who could do it? His parents? A friend?

His parents were still on holiday. She would do it. She was his wife. Must she come now?

It would do in the morning, said the officer. Someone would come and collect her. Could she arrange to leave her children with a neighbour?

Hilary was sure that she could. She saw the officer to the door and then collapsed on the sofa in a storm of exhausted tears, pounding the cushions, her face ugly and distorted.

'How could you?' she sobbed. 'How could you?'

For it must be suicide. And would Jonathan's insurance company pay up if that was the case? She'd heard that they didn't in cases of suicide.

She went to bed at last and drifted into sleep.

When she looked at the white face the next day, it was hard to believe that the dead man was Jonathan, but she saw that it was. There would have to be an inquest, she learned, and a post-mortem.

'But why?'

'To establish the cause of death.'

'But he drowned. He jumped into the water,' Hilary said.

'He could swim?'

'Yes. But even so – '

'The water was cold. The weight of his clothes

would drag him down. Yes, I know. But it's routine,' said WPC Ferris, who had taken her to the mortuary.

'He might have had a heart attack,' said Hilary. 'Been looking at the water – thinking about it, maybe – then fallen?'

'Maybe,' agreed WPC Ferris.

In that case it would be an accident, Hilary thought. The insurance money would be safe. She steeled herself against any other sense of grief or loss, and decided not to get in touch with his parents. They were due back at the weekend in any case. She would not say a word to the children, either. In time they would stop asking about him. It would all pass.

The pathologist had expected a routine case of drowning which would lead to a verdict of misadventure if suicide could not be proved, but there were puzzling anomalies before he began his examination. The dead man's car had so far not been found. There had been no trace of frothing round his mouth.

Whilst he worked, police were at the old gravel pit inspecting the area around where the body was discovered, looking for signs of how it had got into the water. Now it became clear that things were not straightforward. The lungs were not in the water-logged state normal in persons who have met their death by drowning: there were no traces of ingested weed nor signs of water having been swallowed in the struggle to breathe.

Decomposition was well under way, but, carefully the alert pathologist now sought further evidence that the man had been dead before he entered the water. Inconclusive in itself, because the body had been immersed for several days, was the fact that there were no fragments of grass or weed in the hands; in cadaveric spasm a drowning man would clutch, literally, at a straw and any substance would be retained in the grasp. There was nothing under the fingernails, no soil collected while scrabbling for a handhold at the side of the pit.

The doctor had noted a depressed wound on the left temple, and an abrasion which might have been sustained in the fall from the top of the pit, but now he looked into the possibility of injury to the head that could cause death, signs of which might show in the meninges. There were other things to look for: if the body had lain elsewhere before immersion, even after days in the water, hypostasis, the typical collection of blood in what had been the lower part of the body, might be found.

He began the slow, careful search to discover the truth.

Several police divisions were concerned with the disappearance of Jonathan Cooper and the subsequent discovery of his body. Even when he had been officially identified, there was no urgency about telling Sue Norris; she was not his widow and it was not she who had reported him missing. It was simply a matter of courtesy for the

273

investigating officers to give their colleagues in Westborough the news before it arrived automatically as the collator updated details of missing persons, and when they told Sue was their affair. She did not hear at once.

Journalists making their routine calls to police headquarters soon learned of the body's discovery, but did not hear about its identification until too late for Wednesday's papers. When the cautious pathologist had pronounced that the cause of death was a depressed fracture of the skull, and that the man had been dead for several days before immersion, the newspapers were able to state that the police were treating the case as murder.

Laboratory tests would attempt to discover how long the body had been dead before being put in the water, and to pinpoint the time of death. The pathologist had reported that the deceased had probably eaten a meal of steak and chips some hours before he died, and Detective Superintendent Howard asked for an analysis of the stomach and intestinal contents. However urgently required, results would take several days to come through.

PC Graves came to the Rigby Arms to see Sue on Thursday.

It was market day in the town and the police were busy; there were always extra cases of theft, and more parking offences and traffic problems than during the rest of the week. The Rigby Arms had a brisk bar trade and the dining-room was full.

The hotel manager could have done without the visit from Graves. Before seeing Sue, the constable told Bruce why he had come and explained that as next-of-kin Jonathan's widow was the one who counted now, but that it was only right for Sue to be told that the search was over.

'What happened?' asked Bruce. 'Suicide?' He was shocked at the news.

'We don't think so,' said Graves, and added, thankful for the cliché, 'Enquiries are proceeding.'

There was no doubt about Sue's horror. She turned white, gasped, cried, 'Oh no, it can't be true!' but she did not break down. She kept asking about Jonathan's car and Graves had to tell her that so far it had not been found.

Bruce, despite the rush of work, asked her if she would like to go home and was relieved when she said no. She was given a brandy and sent to sit down for a while. It was some time before she had any chance of a word with Terry who, in the bar, was surrounded by farmers and farmers' wives and folk from the surrounding district who had come into the market. Terry had heard the news, though, from Bruce, and was ready when, later, she seized her chance. By then, too, his own first dismay had been replaced by his customary optimism.

'You didn't set fire to the car,' she accused him.

'I couldn't,' said Terry. 'It would have been such a waste. But don't worry. It'll never be found. It'll all die down. You'll see. They'll never find out the truth.'

'You couldn't resist the chance of making some quick money, could you?' said Sue, and he shook his head, grinning at her. 'You know me, Sue,' he said.

'You were a fool,' she said, but some of his optimism brushed off on her when he said there was no way the police could find out what had really happened. He meant that there was no way they could connect him with it.

He drove her back to the lodge when her shift ended. Bruce had asked him to do it, and although Terry did not want to be alone with Sue, facing her recriminations, he could not refuse.

She raised the subject again.

'If only you'd burned the car, as we planned,' she said.

'It wasn't necessary,' said Terry. He could not bring himself to admit that he had been unable to carry out the part of the plan that involved putting the dead man in the driver's seat.

'It might be traced,' she insisted.

'It won't,' said Terry. 'I've sold cars before, Sue. To people who are doing that sort of thing all the time.'

'You mean, changing their numbers?'

'That, yes. Painting them, too.' Terry did not want to go into it. 'Relax. The car will never be found,' he repeated. And it wasn't.

'Won't the police find out that he died before Friday?' said Sue. 'Won't they know he wasn't drowned?'

'No way,' said Terry. 'The water, you see.' He

swallowed, not liking to think of it, even now. 'The water will have changed things – him.'

That was true. Sue felt better.

'Let's go to bed,' she said. She could forget like that: put it out of her mind, be reassured.

But he couldn't. Terry, who had made a career of keeping women quiet and who knew how to perform automatically, was repelled, now, at the mere idea.

'Sorry. Got to rush,' he said. 'Things to do.' He did not even get out of the car.

The news of Jonathan's death was soon all round the town of Westborough, spreading from the hotel staff to the clients and so to the streets and shops. People who had never even heard of the dead man felt briefly involved because he was local. Murder did not happen on your doorstep every day, and murder it was, according to rumour.

The facts reached Harcombe through a number of people who had gone in to the market, among them Barbara Duncan who had met a friend for lunch at the Rigby. They had bought their drinks and their bar meal from Terry, and had heard the story from gossip around them. Barbara, horrified herself at what must have been, the bar pundits theorized, a random attack by some sort of mugger, thought that Alice Armitage would be deeply shocked and upset when she heard. The old woman was on her conscience; Barbara had intended to invite her round to a meal, but one way and the other she hadn't got round to it, putting it off for small reasons which did not stand up to examination.

She telephoned Alice as soon as she returned from Westborough and suggested that, if Alice was doing nothing that afternoon, she should come round to tea.

Alice was surprised and delighted; she accepted at once and was soon sitting in Barbara's drawing-room admiring the bulbs in bowls and the burgeoning forsythia in a jug on the window-sill.

She had not heard about Jonathan. Barbara told her as gently as she could, emphasizing that while she knew he had been found in the waters of an old gravel pit, she did not know how he had got there. Time enough, Barbara thought, for Alice to hear about murder when the police gave more information.

'Oh dear, oh dear,' Alice lamented. 'He was a kind young man. Oh dear! Poor Sue!'

'And his widow and children,' said Barbara, whose sympathy lay more with them than with Sue, though how could an outsider ever judge about marriage? It was like an iceberg, only a fraction revealed on the surface. 'I hadn't met him until that party you had after Christmas. The young man from the bar at the Rigby was there, too, wasn't he? He seems to be a great friend of theirs – of Jonathan's, that is, and Sue.'

'Yes,' agreed Alice, doubtfully.

'He's popular in the bar at the Rigby,' said Barbara. 'Has quite a way with him. Rather a charmer.'

It was true. Terry had beguiled his way into the lodge, just as he had into her flat.

The two ladies talked about the tragedy for a time. Alice revealed that Jonathan had been very depressed recently but did not mention his quarrel with Sue, for, however tenuously, her own son was concerned with that. She drove home thinking uneasily about how she and Terry had first met and how he had turned the truth of that encounter on its head. It distracted her from thinking too much about Jonathan, whose unhappiness had been so great that it had sent him to his death.

And so it had, although not in the way that Alice imagined.

22

In order to discover how Jonathan Cooper had died, the police needed to trace his last movements.

He had stayed at the Court Grange Hotel for the last night of his life, leaving it some time during the hours of darkness in his car, which had now disappeared. Had he been alone? Someone at the hotel might have seen him go.

A detective sergeant and a detective constable went to the hotel to take statements from the staff, and when these were studied in the Incident Room a curious fact emerged.

No one could be found who had actually seen Jonathan Cooper. Detective Sergeant Johnson returned to the hotel to find out more. He learned that Sue Norris had made the registration. The card was produced and the clerk on duty at the time was asked about her. The girl remembered that she had said her companion was unwell but had declined help with the luggage. Dinner on Friday night had been served in the room, and one of the waiters who had taken it over, now in the restaurant laying tables for lunch, was questioned.

The young lady was very nice, he said, remembering Sue's tip. The gentleman was taking a bath and she had called out to him that the meal had arrived.

Had the gentleman answered?

The waiter couldn't remember. In any case, an answer might have been drowned by the sound of the bathwater running out, which he had heard.

His assistant, who was off-duty, was called from his quarters where he had been lying on his bed smoking and reading a girlie magazine. He remembered Sue calling out 'Darling' and had noticed an anorak jacket lying on the bed. The room had been untidy, with ladies' clothes flung here and there and madam herself wearing only a negligée but you often saw more than that when giving room service. The waiter had enjoyed his brief view of Sue's charms.

Detective Sergeant Johnson wondered if there was any record of what the late Mr Cooper had eaten for dinner that night, and the waiter recalled that steak had been ordered.

That fitted with what the pathologist said had been ingested. Johnson asked if the full menu chosen that night could be traced. After only a short delay, Major Smythe was able to tell him just what dishes had been taken across to the hotel annexe that night. These could be compared with the analysis of the dead man's stomach contents, when the lab report came through.

Johnson pursued his efforts to find someone who had met, face to face, the deceased, but there was no one at the hotel who recognized the man in the photograph he displayed.

Major Smythe was anxious that the good name of the place should not be besmirched by this sorry affair, yet the truth must be uncovered. He supplied the names and addresses of other guests resident during Friday night; they would all be interviewed, now, by officers from their local stations. One of them might have heard the Granada drive away. House-to-house enquiries in Twistleton would begin at once. Someone could have seen or heard something unusual during the night.

If the car was found, that would help.

Officially, now, Westborough police station's collator had learned that Jonathan Cooper had died as the result of a blow to the head causing internal haemorrhaging rather in the manner of a fatal stroke.

As routine, Graves's report of his interview with Sue Norris was studied. Addresses contained in the dead man's diary had already been forwarded to the police area covering Twistleton, from which the search for the missing man had been conducted. Now, across two counties, the murder team was told that the victim's diary was in the possession of the Westborough force.

How very distressed Sue must be, Alice thought as she turned into the drive of Harcombe House after tea with Barbara. The lights were on at the lodge, and when she had parked the car in the barn, Alice went there.

Sue opened the door wearing a quilted dressing-gown which had toothpaste stains down the front. She had changed from her working clothes after Terry left, and woven a plan for the evening which would include a visit from a concerned and anxious Giles. Its course could be played by ear, she decided, but her earlier resolve that delay would be proper had been superseded by sexual hunger. Terry had gone without administering the only comfort Sue understood; she would have to seek it elsewhere and use maximum temptation to overcome Giles's scruples.

The girl's long dark hair was loose, hanging down over her shoulders. She showed no sign of tears.

'Oh Sue – I've disturbed you – were you resting?' said Alice. 'I came to say how dreadfully sorry I am to hear about Jonathan.'

Sue did a swift calculation. Giles might go into the Rigby on his way home; if he did, he would certainly hear the news there and come on at once. She could get rid of the old girl if she dealt with her briskly.

'Come in,' she said, opening the door wide to admit Alice.

'What can I say?' Alice followed Sue into the house. 'You must be heartbroken,' she said. Though the girl didn't look it. Perhaps she hadn't taken it in. 'Don't blame yourself,' she urged. 'He must have been more depressed than you thought.'

Sue couldn't think what she meant.

'It must have been suicide,' Alice went on.

So she knew very little. It was just as well, Sue reflected, reluctant to sit swapping theories about murder with the old woman.

She shrugged, standing close to Alice in the sitting-room where now the fire burned brightly. Various odours came from her: scent, and others. Alice looked at her curiously. It was almost as if she were not properly washed.

'You were going to have a bath, Sue, I expect,' she said. 'And perhaps an early night – have you something to eat?' Somehow, now, she did not want to invite the girl up to supper though that had been at the back of her mind earlier.

Sue knew that Alice would be shocked if she said she was hungry.

'I don't feel like eating,' she said. 'I'm all right, really I am. I just feel like being alone.'

'I understand. But come over if you want to,' Alice said. She hesitated. Perhaps Sue was still in a state of shock.

'Would you like a sleeping pill?' she offered, though doubtfully – still, one tablet disbursed from her own bottle could surely do no harm.

'No, thank you. I'm quite all right,' said Sue.

Alice left her, and went over to the main house feeling very confused. What was it about the girl? The word *sensual* came into her mind as she went up the stairs. That's what Sue was: even in her working garb and with her hair drawn back into a severe knot at the back of her head, she exuded some physical quality which Alice found embarrassing to think of; that was why she had been anxious about Giles spending time alone with her, Alice realized. A different sort of girl would simply have been accepting a lift and no more: but Sue seemed to be inviting attention. After all, she had lured Jonathan away from his wife.

Walking upstairs, drawing the curtains, Alice thought about Sue and slowly her mind turned also to Terry. What was the connection between them? She had felt uneasy about it right from the start. Alice remembered the day the two young people had met, straight after her own original encounter with Terry. All three had gone to the lodge and she had seen herself in the old-fashioned role of chaperon. Since then, Sue and he had met almost daily; he was always giving her lifts either in or out of Westborough.

Alice was old. Though protected by Walter, she had seen marriages broken by unscrupulous acts. Because of the love she had known before meeting Walter, she understood, though she had long since ceased experiencing it, passion. Could Jonathan have found out that Sue was having an affair with Terry?

She liked this idea. It was better than thinking that jealousy over Giles had driven him to take his life.

Alice was just in time for the early television news. Afterwards, the local station put out its own bulletin and so she learned that the police were treating the death of Jonathan Cooper as a possible case of murder. Detective Chief Superintendent Howard appealed to anyone who had seen his beige Granada on or after Friday night to get in touch with their local police or the Incident Room from which he was handling the investigation.

Murder!

No!

For minutes Alice's mind refused to accept the idea. Then she remembered that Jonathan had disappeared from the Court Grange Hotel. Some stranger – some thief or vandal – must have attacked him as he wandered about on Friday night. Perhaps someone had seen him standing by the edge of the quarry and tipped him in for the sake of the car.

The idea made sense, but Alice could not stop thinking about Terry. She cast her mind right back to the first meeting when he had turned his own careless act round and made the collision appear to be her fault. He had successfully put over that version of events at the body repairer's and in spite of that he had charmed her. He had shown thoughtful consideration, getting the heaters for her and helping Sue with the party.

More and more, as she remembered, Alice warmed to the idea that Sue and Jonathan had quarrelled about him and not about Giles, but even so, Terry couldn't have killed him. He couldn't have followed them to that hotel and arranged to meet Jonathan, without Sue's knowledge, for some sort of showdown. Or had she known? Was Sue covering up for him?

Alice poured herself out a large glass of sherry and drank it quite fast. She was letting her imagination run away with her. Terry might be untrustworthy, a lying charmer, but that didn't make him a murderer. Sue might be amoral, even a whore – Alice's mind accepted the word and sped on – but that did not mean she was an accessory. Such things didn't happen.

But they did. Alice thought of Crippen and Christie, of wives poisoning their husbands with weedkiller. Harmless-seeming, apparently normal people could carry out appalling acts of horror and violence; the papers were full of them.

Not Terry, though. He was just a flanneller – a smooth talker. Wasn't he?

To Sue's disappointment, Giles did not call at the lodge that evening. He had not yet heard the news, and was maintaining a tactful remoteness.

Unaware of this, Sue mooched about in her dressing-gown, watching television and eating a large meal. She had shopped on the way to the bus, buying sausages and baked beans and the sort of chips you cook in the oven. After eating she felt better, more able to forget her fears about the car. It made sense that Terry would have got rid of it in some safe way, even though it was for cash: he didn't want anyone to trace it back to him.

She did not look at the news on television, so she did not see the brief interview with Detective Superintendent Howard, in charge of the investigation into Jonathan's death.

Giles stopped for her in the morning. He wore a smile which he hoped combined joy at seeing her with sympathy for her plight, and she understood his defection, as it had seemed, of the previous evening. He didn't know.

'Any news?' he asked, as she got into the Rover, and she turned her large eyes towards him.

'You haven't heard,' she said. 'I thought everyone knew.'

'Knew what?' asked Giles, feeling even more stupid than usual. 'Tell me.'

'He's dead. Jonathan's dead,' said Sue tragically.

Giles was truly shocked. He felt as if he had been struck hard in the solar plexus.

'Oh, how dreadful!' he exclaimed. 'What an appalling thing. How did it happen?' He reached out and laid a hand lightly on her thigh, for comfort. 'Oh, poor little Sue.'

Time enough for him to find out later what the police were saying, Sue decided.

'He drowned,' she said. 'He was so depressed. He hadn't been himself for some time.' She played with her black skirt, her finger twisting the fabric where it showed in the gap of her coat.

'You shouldn't be going to work,' said Giles. He wanted to pick her up and carry her off to some eyrie where he could protect her and keep her safe from the cruel world.

'It will take my mind off things,' said Sue, who could not have endured a day at the lodge alone.

'I'll come round this evening to see how things are,' Giles promised. 'You must let me know if there's anything at all I can do to help.'

She smiled, thinking about his offer, as they drove down the lane.

'I will,' she said.

Out of her window, Alice saw Giles collect Sue that morning. With Jonathan no longer there to take her to work on her early days, it was the neighbourly thing to do, but he was playing with fire. The girl was free now, for Jonathan was dead.

She must leave the lodge before Giles lost his head. Alice saw the need for this very clearly, although now she was convinced that it was Terry in whom Sue was interested, not Giles, who was old enough to be her father. But Sue had a warm and friendly nature; she had been kind to Alice and she might extend this kindness to Giles, unthinkingly. There shouldn't be any problem about removing this source of possible temptation: Sue would not want to stay at the lodge alone. Alice determined to move there herself. Then she would make a big effort to make her mark in the village before she became too old and frail. Violet Hedges and Nancy Wilson were not all that much younger than she was, and Barbara Duncan must be well into her sixties. They seemed to lead full, satisfying lives. She would humbly find out how they did it, learn from them. She had let things drift too long. If Giles and Helen really needed the rent, they could let her flat to a schoolteacher. What she had done in coming here had been a kindness to no one, least of all Giles, who was being destroyed before her eyes.

Alice tried not to let her mind turn to Jonathan and the tragedy of his death; it was too terrible to contemplate. His wife, with those two little children, must feel such bitter grief. The waste of a life was so wicked.

She switched on the radio news but there was no mention of the murder enquiry. The newspaper – brought to this remote village by van and delivered by a schoolboy before the school bus bore him off to Westborough Comprehensive – told her no more than she already knew.

As Alice read about Mrs Hilary Cooper, aged thirty-four, and the children, an image of Terry's round, ingenuous face with its frame of curly hair swam into her mind.

He couldn't possibly be involved, could he? And if he were, then Sue would know about it, wouldn't she?

She might not. He was very devious and had this knack of twisting things round to confuse the truth. If he had followed Sue and Jonathan to the Court Grange Hotel, he must somehow have whisked Jonathan away without Sue's knowledge. He might be jealous, but surely he couldn't have set out to kill Jonathan! Such a notion was preposterous.

Eating her toast and marmalade, Alice found that the idea would not go away. Perhaps Terry had simply intended to have a talk with Jonathan and it had got out of hand – they'd fought, perhaps; you read of such quarrels, when people were killed by accident. Things had started to go wrong, really wrong, ever since Terry had entered their lives, and now, because of his own good nature – Alice preferred not to think of Giles as weak – and the presence of a physically provocative unattached young woman with a lax moral code, her own son was at risk. In a way it was her fault: she was the one who had introduced Terry into the household, been there when he met Sue, even though he had arrived without an invitation.

The more she thought about it, the more Alice felt certain that Terry might be connected with Jonathan's death. That being so, she had a duty. The police would soon find out, one way or the other, if she was right, and the sooner they got on with it the better, before Giles was exposed to further risks.

The police had made a number of discoveries in the area around the old gravel pit where Jonathan's body had been discovered. The weather when he disappeared had been dry and very cold. There had been no rain between then and the time he had been found, and tyre marks leading to the edge of the pit had been preserved. They were not very clear; the ground was too hard for that; but in one spot soil, near a spring, was damp, and clear tread marks showed. Casts were made.

The Home Office Laboratory would be able to

tell what sort of tyre had made the prints, and the garage where Jonathan's car was serviced would be able to say if they tallied.

There were small scraping marks on the ground, too; twin tracks that could have been caused by a man's heels as he was dragged to the brink. A white plastic bin liner had been found on a nearby bush and had proved to be not the relic of some picnic, but to contain several strands of human hair. It was being tested for other traces, such as saliva, and the hair would be compared with Jonathan's. Hypostasis had shown that the body had lain on its side for some time after death.

It was a puzzling case, and because no one had been found who had actually seen Jonathan Cooper at the hotel, it was developing a sinister aspect. Detective Superintendent Howard was heading away from his first idea that this was a car theft and mugging carried out by a stranger.

Enquiries went on, methodically, seeking any lead from Twistleton. And as routine, the dead man's widow was asked to account for her movements on Friday night.

Hilary's mind would not accept the fact that the police thought Jonathan had been murdered. Still less could she take in the direction of the questions which WPC Ferris was gently uttering.

She had been at home alone with the children on Friday night, as usual. That morning she had gone to the nursery school where she worked, and where Johnny was a pupil. In the afternoon, she had taken the children to the park. She had no car, and she had not known that Jonathan was staying only thirty miles away at that expensive hotel.

She couldn't have done it; Grace Ferris knew that; but she had to be officially eliminated.

The dead man's diary had arrived at the Incident Room. Well-handled by PC Graves, it held a blurred mass of prints, but it must be tested so that Sue Norris's, Jonathan's own, and those of PC Graves might be eliminated, although since it was not on the body at the time of death, the murderer's were unlikely to be there.

By such random but thorough checking are criminals caught.

When Grace Ferris had gone, Hilary sat stunned, at last taking in the full truth. It was some time before she realized that this meant her insurance money was safe. Later still, when the children had gone to bed, she began to think of her husband as the victim of a brutal attack; then, painfully, agonizingly, she started to weep and to wish she had let Jonathan talk when he had wanted to do so the last time she saw him.

A clean breast of things: that's what you had to make when you'd done wrong. Alice remembered the principles by which she had been reared and which she had tried to instil into her son. The consequences for her would be serious when Helen found out, as now was most likely, that Alice had used her car, but the worst that could happen would be that Helen would turn her out of the house, and that might be a blessing. There might be some legal way in which she could retrieve her capital.

Resolute, Alice set off for Westborough. She knew where the police station was: not far from the body shop that had repaired the Volvo so efficiently. She parked in the forecourt between a van and an area car.

When she told the officer at the desk that she wanted to speak to someone about the death of Jonathan Cooper, he looked at her in surprise. This smart, elderly lady a witness? It seemed unlikely.

'Your name, madam?' he asked, and when she gave her address as Harcombe House, in whose lodge the dead man had lived, he looked at her again. She was the sort of woman whom it had sometimes been his unfortunate lot to question in shoplifting cases. He invited her to sit down and went off to find someone to see her.

'She may be a nut, but she does live at Harcombe, or so she says,' he told Detective Sergeant Rivers, who replied that anyone was welcome, nut or otherwise, who might throw light on the mystery. He came out to greet Alice and took her away to an interview room.

Alice told him the whole story, beginning with apologies if she was wasting his time, saying she could not see how there could be any connection with what she wanted to say and Jonathan's death, but she couldn't get it out of her mind and the police could be the judges. Her tale took a long time to relate. She described how she had borrowed Helen's car and been struck by Terry

Brett, driving a Vauxhall – pale green. He had turned the whole thing round to make it seem her fault and had then become friendly with the young pair at the lodge, calling there most days. Rivers learned how kind he had been, buying the convector heaters and not going off with the money, as Alice had feared he might. He heard about the party arranged by Sue and Terry. Alice told Rivers how Terry had taken the job at the Rigby after the barman's accident; how he had visited Sue daily, it seemed – either bringing her back from work or taking her in, according to her shifts and his bar hours.

'He was working in Swindon when I first met him,' Alice said. 'Or so he told me. He knows a lot about cars,' she added. 'He mended my Metro.'

Rivers thought it was a hare – an old lady, worried and shocked by the violent death of someone she knew, seeking an answer, but the details must be passed on to the murder team. It would be for them to decide whether to follow this tenuous lead.

He got Alice to go through it again as he wrote it all down. They brought her a cup of tea and two biscuits while the statement was typed, and were very kind.

'I hope there won't be trouble about the accident,' she said wistfully. 'With the Volvo, I mean.'

She hadn't broken the law, Rivers assured her. No one was hurt, and both drivers had exchanged names and addresses.

Terry hadn't exactly supplied his address, Alice

recalled, but thought she need not mention that fact.

They asked her to stay, even after she had signed her statement.

23

While the police were waiting for the results of the laboratory tests, they continued the painstaking elimination of irrelevance and the gleaning of facts which would clear the route to the truth.

Door-to-door enquiries in Twistleton had produced a sleepless woman who had heard a car going up the hill out of the village during Friday night – or rather, early the next morning. She was not sure of the exact time: perhaps half-past one? A man with bronchitis, also wakeful, had seen a car's headlights against the bedroom curtains. Confined to his room with his illness, he had noticed that the lights of cars turning out of the yard at the Court Grange Hotel shone on his window. Such traffic was rare in the small hours. He had put the time at one-fifteen a.m.

Another woman had noticed something odd that Friday afternoon. She had been going to the church to polish the brasses when she met a young man wheeling a bicycle out of the churchyard. She had never seen him before, and it was unusual to meet a stranger there at that time of year, although later there were tourists and visitors from the hotel. The young man had said he had been to see his grandmother's grave, and this had puzzled the woman, for the tiny churchyard was full. For the last fourteen years burials had taken place in a plot of consecrated ground across the road. She had asked if he had found his grandmother, and he said that he had. Of course, the grandmother might have died when he was a small boy, in which case his interest was touching. She gave a full description of the young man, who had a mop of bright brown curls that, had he been a girl, must have been permed. Perhaps they were. He was about five foot eight or nine inches tall, and was wearing a fawn raincoat. The bicycle was a small one.

With no more than these strands to catch at, the murder team was impatient for fresh news from the laboratory. When the call from Westborough police station informed them that an elderly woman, Mrs Alice Armitage, whose son was the dead man's landlord, had come in with a long story about a young man who had inveigled his way into becoming part of the scenery at Harcombe and whom she suspected of having designs on Jonathan Cooper's mistress, Detective Superintendent Howard came to the telephone himself.

'Ask her to describe this young fellow,' he requested.

Back came the answer promptly: about twenty-two, crisp brown curls, blue eyes, five foot nine or so. His name was Terence Brett.

'Keep your Mrs Armitage till we can get over,' said Howard. 'And find out where this Brett lives.'

'We know that,' said Sergeant Rivers smugly. 'He's the barman at the Rigby Arms Hotel.'

Howard ran a check on the computer on Terry before going over, himself, to Westborough. It showed a conviction for car theft two years before. So his prints would be on file. But at the moment no murder weapon, no object remotely of use as a clue, had appeared in the case.

Except the diary, and that had not been found on the body.

Alice was told that Detective Sergeant Howard, in charge of the murder enquiry, was coming over to see her.

So they were taking what she said seriously! What had she set in motion? Alice began to tremble. They would arrest Terry, question him.

Well, what if they did? If he was blameless, he had nothing to fear. The police were so clever. They would match things up – fingerprints – bloodstains – that sort of thing: Alice was vague about forensic science.

They brought her some lunch. A young woman officer stayed with her while she ate it and told her about her schoolboy sons and her husband who was also in the force but in a different division. The policewoman was small and slight: Alice thought her brave to take on such a job, and said so. The woman smiled and said it was very rewarding. Even today, the presence of a woman officer at a public house brawl, for instance, sometimes helped to cool it.

Detective Superintendent Howard was a tall, thin man with pepper-and-salt hair and piercing blue eyes. He went through Alice's statement before meeting her, then asked her to tell him her story.

She did so, sprinkling it with apologies and saying it might have been her imagination.

'How you met Terry Brett wasn't imagination,' said Howard. 'You said he took the whole thing over – blamed you and did all the talking at the car repair shop.' That part of the tale could soon be checked.

'You believe me? I might be making it up,' said Alice.

Howard looked at her gravely.

'I don't think so,' he said. 'You don't want to get into trouble with your daughter-in-law, yet you may, now, though I hope not.'

'There are worse things than that,' said Alice.

'Like murder,' said Howard.

'But Terry couldn't have – ' Alice looked pleadingly at the detective. 'Surely not?' she whispered.

'We'll find out, Mrs Armitage,' said Howard.

'If he was having an affair with Sue, I suppose he might have followed them to that hotel and perhaps quarrelled with Jonathan. Something like that. An accident, though.' Alice offered her theory.

'Maybe,' said Howard.

'I'm not sure they were having an affair,' Alice said. 'Young people are so casual these days.'

'Did you enjoy driving your daughter-in-law's car, Mrs Armitage?' Howard asked.

'Yes, I did. It's a very nice car,' Alice said.

'You like driving?'

'I used to, but now there's so much heavy traffic about, and people have no road manners,' said Alice. 'I drove a canteen van during the war – only part-time, I had my small son – but Walter and I had to do what we could. He was in a reserved occupation, but he became an auxiliary fireman.'

Howard agreed with Detective Sergeant Rivers that this elegant old lady was in no sense deranged. Her story, retold to him, was consistent in every detail with her statement. It was possible that Terry Brett was involved with the case though the how and the why would have to be sought. At least, now, while the scientists probed further into what the corpse could tell them, he and his men had a name, an individual, who could, for a start, give an account of his movements during the relevant time.

'Well, thank you, Mrs Armitage,' he said. 'You'll be at home, will you, if we need you again? You're not just off to the West Indies, for instance?' She looked the sort of prosperous widow who might well take herself off in search of the sun.

'No, nothing like that. I can carry on, though, can I, as usual? Shopping? Seeing my friends?' What friends?

'Of course. Just don't leave the area without letting the station here know where you'll be,' said Howard.

'I can go now?'

'Certainly. I'll get someone to run you back.'

'I've got my car. It's parked outside. I suppose it's still there,' said Alice, with the ghost of a grin.

Howard saw her out to it, and stood watching while she belted herself in and drove off. She took extra care. It wouldn't do to crash the gears or make some careless slip while right under the noses of the police. As she drove down the High Street she felt a bit swimmy, so she decided to stop for a cup of tea. She could do with spending a penny, too.

Alice found a parking space and went into the Coffee Pot, where she and Terry had had their coffee the day it all began. The same waitress served her. She wouldn't remember her, thought Alice, but she might remember Terry. He had talked to her – chatted her up, even.

She felt calmer after drinking her tea and visiting the cloakroom. She even called in at the library to see if any of the books she had asked for were in, and collected a fat saga about the Civil War which would be nice for the weekend.

She caught up with Sue in the lane leading from the bus stop to the village and stopped to pick her up. The girl was silent, sitting there, but Alice, guilty about how she had spent the day, chattered on, praising the fine weather and looking forward to spring.

The girl could have no knowledge of it, if Terry were involved, Alice was sure. Perhaps Jonathan had arranged to meet Terry near the quarry, slipping off without telling Sue where he was going.

If not, she was sitting here beside someone who had connived at the killing, and that was unthinkable.

Sue was silent because she was worried.

Before she left the office, she had noticed a man in the lounge reading the paper. It wasn't usual for male guests to be about the place during the day, especially not well-set-up young fellows of about thirty who looked very fit.

She had asked him if there was anything he wanted. This sort of remark often evoked a crude response but he simply shook his head and said 'No, thanks,' returning to his paper.

Sue was sure he was a policeman.

She had intended to go to Terry's room to ask him to take her home, but now she changed her mind. The safest plan was to do as Terry had said and keep away from one another; she should scuttle back to the lodge and lie low. He had been so sure that the car had been safely disposed of, but suppose he was wrong: suppose it had been found?

Even so, she told herself firmly, nothing could be proved. They had only to deny all knowledge of what had happened on Friday night and they would be safe. Terry must be right about the effect of the water making it impossible for the police to find out that Jonathan had died before then. You got washerwoman hands after only a short immersion and he had been submerged for days.

The whole thing was so unfair. All this trouble

and worry. It was all Jonathan's fault for being so jealous.

Alice dropped her at the lodge without inviting her up to the flat, as Sue had expected she might. Never mind. Giles would call in that evening. She went into the lodge feeling restless, wondering how to pass the time until then.

Alice, too, felt restless. The days were beginning to draw out now, and it was not yet dark. There were great drifts of snowdrops blooming under the trees in the orchard. She decided to enjoy the last of the fine day by strolling round the garden looking for signs of spring.

She found primroses out on a sheltered bank exposed to the sun and picked some to take to the flat. Then, strolling back across the lawn, she paused beside the swimming-pool. Its waters, now, were muddied, but it had sparkled clear and blue in the summer while Helen and her friends sunbathed round it. Sue and Jonathan had come sometimes. In her mind's eye, Alice pictured Helen swimming up and down in a graceful crawl. Giles, also, swam strongly. Alice couldn't remember seeing Sue in the water, though she could recollect the slight figure in a minuscule bikini, long hair loose across her back, face down on a sun bed.

She looked round the large, lovely garden. What a perfect place it was, yet no one who lived there was happy. Well, perhaps that wasn't quite true: Amanda and Mr Jinks seemed content.

Now this dreadful thing had happened to

Jonathan. It didn't bear thinking of.

Alice glanced towards the house and saw Sue approaching across the lawn. The girl had changed from her working clothes into black slacks, and she wore a black leather jacket into whose pockets her hands were thrust. Her normal bouncy stride was absent; she looked grim.

Had Terry been arrested already? Was that why she had been so silent in the car?

Alice watched her approach and saw that the girl was too deeply engrossed in her own thoughts to notice her. How black she looked, Alice thought inconsequentially: black clothes, black hair, and, as she came close, black expression.

'Why Sue, what's wrong? You do look low,' Alice said, and then, because she was going to be a coward no longer and the moment must come. 'Is it Terry?'

'Terry? Why? What about him?' asked Sue, stopping abruptly. Her brows drew together and she glared at Alice, looking suddenly – Alice sought for the word in her mind, and with a shock, found it – she looked savage.

'Well, they're bound to question him, aren't they?' said Alice. 'I had to tell them, you see.'

'Tell them what? What could you know?' Sue demanded, and, advancing, seized Alice by her upper arms.

'Let me go, Sue, you're hurting me,' said Alice, moving backwards.

Sue followed her, still grasping her arms.

'What have you been saying, you silly old

woman?' she yelled at Alice, her face flushed now with rage.

Alice was suddenly terrified. The girl was like a virago. She tried to speak calmly, ignoring her thudding heart.

'I had to tell the police about Terry, Sue,' she said. 'You must see that. It was my duty.'

Sue's grip on her arms tightened.

'What have you told them?' she screamed.

'How he got to know us under false pretences. How he's so fond of you,' Alice said, trying to free herself.

Sue, who knew only Terry's version of the original meeting, ignored the first part of what Alice had said, latching on to the last sentence. She started to shake Alice, whose head was whipped back and forth, making her giddy.

'You told them what?' Sue demanded. 'What have you said? Come on! Out with it.'

'Stop shaking me,' Alice wailed, trying still to speak steadily. Her words came in gulps. 'I said it was an accident. If he killed Jonathan, that is,' Alice said. 'Let me go.'

Sue started to yell obscenities.

'What have you done, you interfering old bitch?' she screeched, shaking Alice as if she were a rag doll.

For someone so small and slight she was extremely strong, Alice found, fighting now to keep her foothold on the paving stones beside the pool, where matted leaves had collected in damp, soggy clumps.

They struggled there together, both rendered primitive, the one by rage and the other by the urge for self-preservation. Sue's foot, in its smooth-soled boot, slid on the slimy ground and her balance went, but she still clutched at Alice, who dropped the primroses and caught at the girl to keep herself from falling.

They went into the pool together, at the deep end, but Alice, though she had not done so for years and was at first overcome by the rush of water into her nose and mouth, could swim. She fought, instinctively, to bring herself to the surface of the water and in doing so she thrust off Sue's clutching hands. Gasping, splashing, the weight of her clothing dragging her down, Alice struggled to the side and clung to the rail until she had regained enough strength to pull herself, hand over hand, to the shallow end and up the wide steps to the side.

She was far too shocked to think about Sue, whose floundering struggles and desperate cries had ceased by the time that Alice had pulled herself to safety. Long hair fanned out in the water, limbs extended, Sue lay, a black, spread-eagled figure at the bottom of the pool, with the murky water tranquil above her.

24

After the bar closed, Terry had gone off in the car for a haircut. One of the kitchen staff had recommended a unisex barber on the edge of Westborough. Leaving the barber's, he stopped for one or two things – toothpaste, a magazine about cars, a postcard for his mother whom he hadn't been in touch with since Christmas. Outside a newsagent's, a billboard yelled at him: LOCAL MAN DEAD IN QUARRY FOUL PLAY.

Discussing the crime with his bar customers, Terry had theorized that Jonathan had gone for a late-night drive and been mugged by someone who had stolen his car and dumped him. Most of his hearers thought this was the probable answer. So would the police. Terry was ebulliently confident that the car would never be found and there was nothing else to connect him with the affair. He went back to the Rigby, having delayed long enough for Sue to have given up waiting for him and gone for the bus.

He had a great shock when he drove back into the yard at the Rigby and was greeted by a plain clothes police officer who asked for his driving licence and insurance certificate. Terry produced the licence, but the VW was not insured. He said the certificate was in his room. He'd have to pretend it was lost. The officer escorted him there, large and unfriendly beside him.

Two more officers were already waiting in his room. The insurance offence gave them an excuse to take him into the station while they pieced together evidence of a much more serious matter.

It was the police who found Alice.

They had come for Sue, who had some explaining to do about what had really happened at the Court Grange Hotel, and had found the lodge deserted and the door unlocked. They had gone on to the main house where no one had answered the bell. Next, they had looked in the barn, where Alice's Metro was parked, the bonnet still warm. She had to be somewhere about, and they went into the garden to look for her.

Alice was just beginning to think about dragging herself towards the house when the two officers came over the lawn. It was too late for Sue.

By the time Alice was in hospital, where the police insisted on sending her in an ambulance, and Giles had been told and was on his way home, police officers were guarding the lodge until the arrival of the scenes-of-crime team. Terry had talked, and quite quickly. They didn't believe his version of events, but there could be evidence at the lodge.

By nightfall, the living-room carpet had been removed. Fibres from it might match fragments on the dead man's clothing. Soiled sheets from the unmade bed might disclose the identity – or identities – of the source of their stains.

Alice, in her hospital bed, was well enough to tell the police that Sue had seemed very upset and angry, and had grabbed at her, causing them both to fall into the pool. Scuffed marks on the paving slabs and the scattered primroses confirmed her story.

They did not tell Terry that Sue was dead for some time. When they did, his protests grew hysterical. He had never gone in for violence, he cried; he had only been helping – an accessory, right, but not a killer.

It was useless.

A wad of money was found under Terry's mattress; Jonathan's raincoat hung in his cupboard. The woman he had met outside the church at Twistleton picked him out in an identity parade. His fingerprint was found on a page of Jonathan's diary and that was hard to explain. There was the mysterious telephone call made from the lodge on the Friday, and the fact of the uncleared line. Terry admitted that, and gave the true reason for it, but it made no difference. A witness was found who had seen Terry's VW at the building site in Great Minton during the crucial weekend. Staff at the Rigby Arms were questioned and a perplexed Mavis admitted to lending Terry her bike. It was borne off for testing, and yielded fragments of soil from the tyre treads which were similar to the soil around Twistleton – not proof in itself, but supportive. A Honda Accord stolen from Swindon and found later outside Twistleton was called in for forensic scientists to inspect. Tiny paint chips and more soil particles proved, beyond doubt, that Mavis's bicycle had been transported in it. The case was complete. Terry was charged with murder.

Alice followed the trial in the newspapers. Her part in the unmasking of Terry was never made public, for the trail that led to Sue would have led on to him without her intervention. She knew that, reading the account of each day's events in court, but if she had not done what she thought was her duty, Sue might still be alive.

Alice had been haunted, at first, by her memory of that struggle beside the pool: of the girl's evil expression, her violence. It meant that she knew what Terry had done and perhaps had even helped him afterwards. That was dreadful, but Terry was the chief culprit. It just showed what could happen when you set out on a path to deceive. Terry had twisted the truth and had ended a killer. Sue had died as a consequence. The effects of the murder had radically altered a number of lives; and Harcombe House had been sold.

From her paper, Alice learned that Hilary Cooper and her children were now living in a Suffolk village close to her parents. That was good, Alice thought; she would need support. Would she ever get over the hurt of being abandoned?

Sighing, Alice got up to put the kettle on. She

paused at the window of her modern flat to look out at the sea, blue today, sparkling under the sun. She had moved back to Bournemouth before the sale of Harcombe House was completed, aided by her friend Audrey who had been away during Alice's winter visit. Audrey was helping Alice to pick up the threads of her life and thought it bad for her to brood on the case, now that it was in progress. Today she was coming to coffee. Alice wondered how much longer the trial would last. All along, Terry had protested his innocence, blaming Sue and saying that he had helped her because he was sorry for her. It was so like him to twist facts like that, Alice thought. She hoped it would all be over by Sunday, when Giles was coming to lunch. She looked forward to that. He was so much happier now; that was the best thing that had happened as a result of Jonathan's death. Of course, she reminded herself, he would probably have had to accept voluntary redundancy anyway, but he might not have made the break with Helen. As it was, he had used his severance pay to buy a small printing works in Winchester and a flat on the edge of the city. He would probably see almost as much of his daughters as before, Alice thought, since they were away at school for so much of the year. Alice had not seen him drink anything stronger than bitter lemon since the day Sue died.

Helen had finished renovating Harcombe House, including the installation of an effective heating system, as part of the deal over its sale to a television chat show host, and had moved into a small manor house in the Cotswolds. Her plan now was to keep on the move, doing up run-down houses for profitable re-sale.

While the kettle boiled, Alice picked up the paper again. On oath in the box, Terry had sworn that he had been appalled when Sue had shown him the body of Jonathan Cooper, struck down, in self-defence, by her hand.

'Struck down by your hand,' prosecution counsel had maintained, having already established that Terry, or someone with his blood group, which was not the same as Jonathan's, had enjoyed sexual relations with Sue in the big bed at the lodge.

No one had believed him when he said he had never been violent, apart from his mother, who remembered him salvaging a drowning rat as a child. There was something morbid in that, defence counsel had thought, and suppressed the story, but it had appeared in the popular press. Alice recalled Terry's wide, innocent-seeming grin. Who would have believed that he could be so wicked?

She often grieved for Sue.